For Kevin, Donna, Mary Gail, and all the others who have kept me going on this chronicle.

OTHER BOOKS BY DENIS HUCKABY

The Oedipal Saga

The King

Colonnus

The Sisters

The Chronicles of Los Inocentes

Volume 1: *The Poets and the Pilgrims*

Volume 2: *The Sower and the Seeds*

Volume 3: *All Experience is an Arch*

Volume 4: *Metamorphoses*

It Be Okay

Denis Huckaby

Order this book online at www.trafford.com
or email orders@trafford.com

Most Trafford titles are also available at major online book retailers.

Printed in Victoria, BC, Canada.

ISBN: 978-1-4269-2536-8

Library of Congress Control Number: 2010902195

Our mission is to efficiently provide the world's finest, most comprehensive book publishing service, enabling every author to experience success. To find out how to publish your book, your way, and have it available worldwide, visit us online at www.trafford.com

Trafford rev. 4/1/2010

www.trafford.com

North America & international
toll-free: 1 888 232 4444 (USA & Canada)
phone: 250 383 6864 • fax: 812 355 4082

PRIMARY CHARACTERS

PART ONE: THE MURDER

The Changeling [Chief Kasmali]
Astay [his dog, a Husky]

Jack Cramer [Café owner in Valdez]
Janie Cramer [his wife]
Professor Rodrigo De La Cruz
Bernard (Gus) Boston [bar owner in Valdez]
Charles Murray
Ricky Murray [his little brother]
Billy Cole
Hawk [Skinhead at Folsom Prison]

Charley [Cole's cellmate at Folsom]
Margaret [Dr. Watson's nurse]

PART THREE: THE TRIAL

Miles Holcomb [Jack's lawyer]
Stephen Aiken [the district attorney]
Judge Margaret Stein
Hank Klein [the bailiff]
Dr. Friedman [psychiatrist]
E. Francis Chadwell [running for D.A.]
Dr. Sandeen [chief navy medic]
Henry [Judge Stein's husband]
Friar Gerald [prior at Rivotorto]
Bobby Scribner ["The Prince of Inocentes"]
Dr. Watson [Valdez doctor]
Ralph Eston [Valdez Constable]

ADDITIONAL CHARACTERS

PART TWO: THE EARTHQUAKE

Slim Carter [Town drunk]
"Crash" [Helicopter pilot]
Peter Jones [a nurse]
An Inupiaq Family
Joe Ballard [earthquake survivor]

Table of Contents

Prologue: The Entity

Prowling along a narrow stretch of the shore of the John River just below Alaska's Anaktuvuk Pass, the wolf pack sensed a change in the atmosphere and lifted their heads, perked their ears, and growled as a soft wind blew down the pass, the sky took on a multi-colored glow, and the ground shook under their paws.

But as quickly as it happened, the scene returned to its tranquility; and the pack then returned to their hunt as they trotted around a bend of the river where the lush vegetation and dense forest crept down to a lonely sandbar.

A few moments later, a spherical zephyr floated slowly down the pass, hung above the sandbar for a moment, and slowly began to evolve into an amorphous, shimmering globule that then started to drift along the river.

One of many such strange entities that had visited the Earth over the centuries, it was new to the experience. Like the others, it had a mission; but unlike the others who'd been directed to explore the entire planet, its only assignment was to report on the changes in Alaska, the Yukon, and the northern regions. To accomplish this, it, like the others, had certain abilities, among which was the ability to mutate.

For some time, the globule floated above the river as it flowed closer and closer to a mountain range, stopping occasionally before various animals about which it had been informed: beavers amidst the wooded areas, foxes much like the wolves it had seen earlier, brown and black bears, sheep and moose, and many smaller mammals, When it saw its first caribou, a huge male, it settled down to the earth a few feet from it, hesitated, and then mutated into its twin, which frightened the creature into scampering away.

Shaking its newly gained form, it then trotted after it through the forest toward the Arctic National Park until it found its herd. Cautiously, it blended in by imitating their scraping of the tundra to find food. However, it quickly became aware that though they were content to remain at their feeding, it had to begin its mission. For days it traveled through rolling valleys of wild tundra. One day as it was in a lush valley feeding on grasses, it saw a solitary, tall, brown-skinned human a hundred or so yards away creeping toward it with a pointed stick raised in his arm. Curious, it watched as it came closer. Suddenly, a pack of wolves appeared out of the shrubbery and surrounded the human who looked around, searching for safety. However, the human had left himself exposed, and the beasts began circling him menacingly.

The alien knew that if the wolf pack noticed him as a caribou, they would next attack him, so he trotted slowly into the forest and watched as the beasts suddenly charged the human and began tearing him apart. Then, when the wolf pack had satisfied their hunger, they trotted away, and he came out of the forest. Curious about the condition of the human, it looked down at the mangled body, hesitated, and then knowing from the Mentor that such creatures were the masters of this planet, it slowly mutated into what it had seen as its original form.

Once the transformation was complete, it raised the arms of its new body, stretched, and then stumbled, unaccustomed to being on two legs. Soon, however, he adjusted and awkwardly walked away.

Now as a human, he began striding along a trail leading southwest, often stopping to record the scenes around him. After many days of exploring, he suddenly came upon a group of humans similar to the one he'd become and was surprised when they greeted him as their chief. Sensing that they were not a threat, and using his ability to understand their words, he returned their greetings and quickly assimilated into their tribe, which suited him, for he realized that their keen knowledge of the area could help him accomplish his mission. They called him Kasmali, meaning "The Leader."

Over the next few months, he traveled with the tribe into the Arctic Circle and as far south as Mt. McKinley, and he soon began to understand the reason for his visit: the increasing calving of the icebergs, the unusual migration of the wildlife, the melting of the permafrost, and the gradual decrease in sea and bird life, all of which the tribe blamed on what they called the White Man's lust for gold and oil.

As the months passed, and the caribou, the tribe's primary source of food, clothing, and trade, began to diminish, he and the tribe joined with other tribes into what was called The Naqsragmuit Tribal Council. Reluctant because of his eagerness to continue his mission, he nonetheless attended their first meeting with the White Men and quickly became the tribes' spokesperson. However, during a subsequent meeting, he became disgusted by the arrogance of the Whites as they summarily dismissed his and the other chiefs' calmly stated arguments regarding their fears.

Somewhat later, he led the reluctant tribe to the coast of the Arctic. There they saw the massive drilling for oil and minerals that the tribe claimed would inevitably cause the land to justifiably rebel.

Part One
The Murder

Chapter One: The Voice

For years he led the tribe southwest along the Koyukuk River, over the Snow Mountains, and across the plains to Good Hope Bay on Kotzebue Sound where they settled for the winter. One day as he was out alone exploring a glacier, he stumbled as he heard a strange voice speaking to him in the language of his origin. Looking around, he saw no one. Only the Mentor had telepathically spoken to him before; but this voice was different, weak and almost inaudible. Over and over it whispered, "Jack Cramer, Jack Cramer." Not knowing what else to do, he signified his awareness, and the voice then again whispered, growing weaker, "Jack Cramer… See to his safety… He is a friend…" Then silence.

He was confused not only by the voice but also by its choice of words. "Friend" was not a word or concept known by his species, yet the voice had to be one of his kind, for how else could he have heard it? He also had no understanding of the name "Jack Cramer," for he had never encountered one by name. However, he realized that for such a voice to contact him, it had to be important, so he mentally recorded the message and prepared to find this "Jack Cramer."

Deciding that he had learned enough from the tribe, despite their entreaties he left them to heed the voice by traveling to places he knew he would find humans. One day during his solitary travels south, he noticed a huge canine as large as a caribou that seemed too weak to extract itself from a snow drift. Thinking that because of its size the animal could be of use to him, he burrowed his way up to it, grabbed its shoulders, and pulled it to freedom. He then reached into the sack around his waist, grabbed some dried salmon, and held it out. The canine gobbled it down and licked his hand. He jumped back, asking, "Why did you do that, beast?" and then wiped his hand on his bearskin cape. "Come," he then said and walked away. The canine followed him. From that moment, they were rarely apart. He called it "Astay," which was Inupiaq for "Follower."

During his trek, he never forgot the voice. Then, one day he and the Husky came to a city called Nome where many White Men and Inupiaq and other Alaskan Indians gathered for the end of a sled race they called 'The Iditerod.'

Once there, unused to the proximity of so many White Men and aware of the fear the giant canine provoked, he kept to the edge of the town. However, he soon adapted to the chaos, learned their languages, and ignored those who scattered when they saw the huge beast.

During his tour of the city, he became curious about an obviously distressed red-headed young human who was causing a scene by moving anxiously from group to group asking if they had seen something or someone he called "Snowbird." Then, as he watched, a stern-looking human came up to the young man and asked him to identify himself.

Kasmali wasn't surprised when he heard the man call himself Jack Cramer, for he understood that for some reason the strange voice was directing him. He listened as the young man asked the stern-looking man if anyone would be returning to the start of the race in a place he called Anchorage. The stern man shook his head and said he doubted it. Kasmali then approached the young man and told him he was about to make the trip and would be willing to take him along. The man hesitated, eyeing the massive Husky, but then accepted his offer.

Having noticed the humans' use of sleds and canine teams, Kasmali explained he would procure his own sled and team and return. Quickly he searched the area until he saw an intoxicated Indian by himself leaning against a shed, a team of canines lying scattered around him. He put his hand on the man's shoulder, causing him to lose consciousness. Then, speaking to the canines in a strange tongue, he led them and the sled back to Jack Cramer.

During the trip back along the route of the race, Kasmali easily adapted to driving the sled with Astay at its lead, though he was curious why this obviously troubled young human begged him to stop repeatedly so that he could inquire about something called a snowbird, who Kasmali soon learned was a female. He understood curiosity and the urge to explore, but he was confused why the young human was so obsessed about this particular female. There were, after all, many other females wherever they stopped.

On the first of their overnight stops, he patiently listened as the man spoke of the woman's beauty and her prowess as a sledder; but then, when the man became tiresome, Kasmali began to tell him stories he'd learned from the Inupiaq, hoping they would inspire him to think of other things besides this "Snowbird."

Eventually they reached Anchorage and parted, Cramer grief-stricken that he hadn't found the woman. Kasmali let him go, thinking he was emotionally unstable but in no real danger despite the words of the voice.

For the next few years, deciding he'd had enough of the White Man, Kasmali and Astay again roamed the Arctic; and as they traveled along the coast of the Beaufort Sea, he recorded the increased influx of oil platforms and derricks and the effects of the warming as well as the growing frequency of the rumblings of the earth. Then, one morning as he and the dog were heading southwest, once again the voice whispered, "Jack Cramer... Protect him."

However, he had no idea where this human now was and had already done as much as he could for him, so he dismissed the voice and continuing wandering southwest around large and small rivers and over huge mountains.

One day while recording the erosion of the glaciers near the Arctic Circle, he saw a huge cylindrical pipe that snaked southward. Curious, he placed his hand on it and felt movement of what he thought must be some type of liquid. He decided to follow it to see where it ended. For weeks he and Astay traveled, Kasmali wondering what was inside. Eventually as they hiked along beside it through a pass, they saw below them the end going into a complex of buildings on the outskirts of a town.

Content that he had satisfied his curiosity, he began to lead Astay away but then suddenly stopped. "Though the White Men will think us strange," he said to the dog, "I should obey the voice by mingling with them in that cluster of shelters, though they disgust me."

Kasmali, re-accustomed to the silence of the Yukon, was stunned by the noise as he and Astay approached the town – the buzzing, the puka-puka-puka of weird machines on the outskirts, the clatter and chatter of voices – but he was most disturbed by the sky that had changed from clear blue to yellowish gray.

As he and Astay walked along the main street, people scattered; but eventually they came upon a group of men speaking of something they called a café and using the name Jack Cramer. He stepped forward and asked if the men knew where he could find this man. Looking nervously at him, one of the men pointed right, down the street. Another muttered, "The Mexican café."

He quickly found it on the edge of the town, told Astay to stay by the door, entered, took a seat at one of the tables, and looked at the people around him, many of whom were gawking at him apprehensively. A female came out of the back, hesitated, and walked over to him. "Welcome, Stranger," she said kindly. "Can I get you a menu?"

He had no idea, of course, what a menu was, so he simply answered, "Jack Cramer?"

She smiled. "You know my husband? Are you a friend of his?" she asked.

That word again, 'friend,' he thought. He nodded. Again she smiled and surprised him by walking away into a back room. The people around him returned to their meals, and a few minutes later the red-headed human with a red beard he'd met in Nome walked up to him. "I'm Jack Cramer," he said, sitting in a chair opposite him. "Do I know you, friend?"

Unused to small talk, Kasmali simply answered, "We sledded together from Nome to Anchorage. I am Chief Kasmali, and it seems I have been sent to watch over you."

Cramer reared back and laughed. "Now I remember you! The story-teller," he finally said. "That was a rough time for me. It's been years! Things are better now, but tell me. You're going to watch over me? Why?"

Kasmali shook his head, realizing he didn't know the answer; but because of the voice, he sensed he had to make this man believe him. "I do not know why," he answered, "but perhaps I should reveal myself.

Perhaps that way together we can discover why I am here. Come with me."

Jack Cramer was a curious sort, so he followed Kasmali out the front door and saw him nod to a huge Husky that began trotting by his side. He hesitated, frightened by the size of the dog, but then followed him behind the café where Kasmali looked around and then suddenly raised his arms high into the air and began to melt. Jack stood transfixed as he watched him slowly mutate into a twin of the giant dog.

He fainted. When he came to, Kasmali was on his knees beside him. He jumped up, rubbed his eyes, and muttered, "Sam?"

Kasmali again shook his head as he too stood up. "My mission is to investigate the recent occurrences in your northern regions. I know of none named Sam. However, I have come because twice in my wanderings I have heard a voice asking me to help you."

Jack suddenly laughed. "So it's true, you guys *do* exist!" he finally said. "Frankly I had my doubts! I'll be damned! It's all true!"

"I don't understand," Kasmali said.

"Sam!" Jack said excitedly. "Way back, at least five years ago! He was a changeling just like you. Before he left, he promised a friend of mine he'd see to it that we – him, his wife, his son, and I guess my wife and I – would be watched over by one of his species! You must be the one!"

"This Sam you mentioned, you say he could change forms? Where did this occur?" Kasmali asked. "And this Sam, he had a relationship with humans?"

Puzzled, Jack answered, "He sure did! I never met him, but he was a true friend to a lot of people. Most of the time – supposedly over two-hundred years – he wandered all over the Earth; but toward the end he stayed with the son of that friend of mine in a village down south in Southern California.."

Kasmali shook his head. "Illogical," he said. "This person you call Sam could not have been one of my species. Though I appear human to you, in my essence, I and the others do not have the ability to relate emotionally. You say he left? Did he say where he was going?"

"No," Jack answered, "he refused to talk about that. But with all due respect, Chief, I think you're wrong about him. There's all sorts of people who saw him mutate."

Kasmali gazed at him for a moment. "Many of my species have investigated your planet and then returned to have our memories erased. I have told you about the voice. It may be that this Sam spoke to me, but I do not understand how that could be."

"Well, Chief Kasmali, all I can say is that I'm happy you're here," Jack said, still smiling. "I can use all the help I can get. You have to meet my wife!"

Kasmali shook his head. "Perhaps later, Jack Cramer. Now that I have made contact with you and have seen you are in no need of my help, I will continue on my mission. However, I have a sense that I will return. I ask one thing of you, however. My animal is too wild to be part of a sled team. May I leave him with you?"

Intimidated by what he had seen, Jack nodded and then watched as Kasmali walked around the corner of the café and was soon out of sight. Looking down at the huge animal, he cringed and muttered, "How in God's name am I going to explain you to Janie?"

Kasmali was satisfied as he walked out of town, for he felt that although this human called Jack Cramer seemed to be in no danger, at least Astay would be there if anything happened to him.

Chapter Two: The Warning

Standing on a crest above Prudhoe Bay, Chief Kasmali was satisfied that he'd acquired enough data about the conditions in the north and that now it was the time for the next part of his mission – to make the humans aware of the pending disaster. He stared down at the bay two miles in the distance, struck by the contrast of a huge black platform to the white permafrost surrounding it. His fur-lined moccasins were planted firmly in the snow.

The trek with the team across the mountains and around the rivers from Valdez had taken him more than a month, but he felt strong and impervious to the freezing temperature, even though he was covered only in thin clothes and a long fur-lined cape. Suddenly he looked up into the sky and murmured, "I will begin to complete my mission, but I see no hope. The humans I have met do not listen nor do they heed the signs."

He flexed his shoulders, turned, and walked slowly back to the team burrowed behind him in the snow. "It is time," he said gently. "Rest easily. I must leave you now, but I will return."

Breathing deeply, he filled his lungs with the icy air and braced his legs against the sled, stretched, and suddenly thought back to his encounter with Jack Cramer. "These humans are strange," he said aloud to the dogs. "You and the other creatures on this planet seem more rational." He shook his head as he remembered Cramer's frenzied attempts to find the 'Snowbird' woman during their trip from Nome. "And how quickly he has mated with a different female!"

He looked down at his torso. "It is good I took this form, but now I must mutate so I can travel to speak to the humans by the ice. I am commanded to try," he muttered to an Alaskan Malamud, the leader of the team. "Keep the others safe."

He walked to the cliff and gazed into the sky. Within minutes, he saw two large birds, concentrated on them for a moment, and then stripped off his clothes, raised his hands into the air, and began to dissolve into an eagle. The dogs yipped and burrowed into the snow as the eagle fluttered its wings and flew east.

Kasmali had been instructed in the history of Alaska. He knew, for example, that some years before, Valdez had been struck by a devastating earthquake that triggered an underwater landslide which produced tidal waves that washed away the entire waterfront and drowned many of the residents. He also knew that the recent tremors, often light and sporadic, had become commonplace and therefore considered harmless by the humans. And he had noticed the massive cruise ships in the port ignoring the danger.

What he didn't know was that the ship captains were aware of the incremental increase in the calving and had informed the ship owners; but these giants of the industry had ignored their warnings, seeing only the potential loss of revenue if they changed their route.

He had witnessed in the north along the Arctic Sea how the oil drilling continued, and he envisioned Valdez once again being swept under by a tidal wave.

A few weeks before, six scientists, concerned about the effects of the drilling as well as the increased global warming, had volunteered to set up a laboratory at an abandoned station in Camp Fistclutch near Thule at the edge of the Greenland Ice Cap. Of the six, four were veterans of the Yukon; but two, much younger, were new to the posting and therefore were shocked by the severity of the environment and by their isolation.

One afternoon, while out checking their instruments in the ice, these two young scientists saw a solitary figure slowly walking toward them out of the mist. At first, they thought they were seeing things; but as the figure came closer, they were stunned to see a huge, totally naked Indian. Dumbstruck, they stood gawking in their fur-lined parkas as the Indian came up to them and said loudly, "I AM CHIEF KASMALI OF THE INUPIAQ. I HAVE COME TO SPEAK WITH YOU!"

One of the men came out of his daze; and staring at the tall, naked man standing before him, he shouted back, "JESUS, YOU MUST BE FREEZING!" He then beckoned wildly for Kasmali to follow him. Kasmali nodded and obeyed. The other two scientists eventually came out of their shock, shook their heads, and walked after him.

The four older men at the station jerked up their heads as the first youngster yanked open the steel door and yelled, "YOU WON'T BELIEVE THIS, BUT THERE'S A TOTALLY NAKED INDIAN BEHIND ME!"

Just then Kasmali entered. "SHIT!" one of the older men cried, turning to his colleagues. "GET THE MAN A BLANKET!"

Kasmali stood wordlessly as one of the men threw the blanket over his shoulders and stared at him. Finally he spoke. "I have come to you because in this remote camp you have undoubtedly noticed the changes in the environment and may be open to reason."

The oldest of the six, presumably their leader, looked at him curiously and then asked, "Who are you?"

Ignoring his question, Kasmali continued. "With your rudimentary instruments, you have probably measured the increasing tremors; but I, in my explorations north, have seen more than your technology can tell you. I have seen the frenzied migration of the caribou; I have seen the absence of birds; I have seen the glaciers falling into the sea; I have seen tundra where the permafrost has always been; I have seen all this and more; and I have come to tell you it is not just the global warming nor your over-population of this vast, beautiful land that will eventually destroy you. The disaster will be prompted by your ruinous excavations for coal and other minerals and oil. How long do you think your Earth can endure this?"

The six scientists stood transfixed, unable to reply. Kasmali continued. "I have come to you in the hope that as learned men you will heed my warning and consult with those who are your superiors. I chose you, as Americans rather than the Russians or the Canadians, simply because I know people living on the coast who will probably not survive if something is not done."

"Why should we believe you, whoever or whatever you are?" one of the younger men asked rudely. "Out on the ice you just said you were a chief of the Inupiaq."

Kasmali smiled. "Look again at me and my nakedness," he answered. "Surely you must wonder. Also, I have had what you would call a vision."

The younger man smiled. "A vision, huh?" he asked sarcastically. "Listen, Chief, if that's who you are, we're scientists who deal in facts, not fantasies. We've no time for any crazy visions." He turned, intending to return to his desk, but he suddenly stopped when he saw Kasmali shake off the blanket, raise his arms to the roof, and begin to grow taller and taller.

"SHIT!" he yelled as he tumbled into his chair. The other men staggered back, their mouths open.

Kasmali spoke again, this time his voice echoing around the small enclosure. "I SAW THE CARIBOU AND THE SNOW BEARS SINK OUT OF SIGHT INTO THE ICE. I SAW THE WALRUSES AND THE SEALS BEGIN TO FLY. I HEARD THE MOUNTAINS CRY OUT AS IF IN PAIN WITH A GREAT ROAR THAT SPLIT THEIR SIDES INTO HUGE SLABS THAT FELL INTO THE SEA WITH GREAT EXPLOSIONS THAT CREATED WAVES THAT GREW AS HIGH AS THE MOUNTAINS. I FELT THE LAND SPLIT UNDER MY FEET AND THE MOUNTAINS CRUMBLE. I SAW ALL OF THIS AND KNEW IT WAS AN OMEN OF THINGS TO COME!"

He lowered his arms and began to shrink into the man he'd been. "So, my learned scientists," he said calmly. "Believe what I say. Heed my warning and leave this encampment. Tell your superiors what I have related."

He turned and walked out the door, leaving the six men in a daze. Eventually, the young man stood up, his knees shaking, and said, "We've been out on the ice too long. We're beginning to see and hear things."

The other five men continued to stare at the door. Finally, one of them asked, "What'll we do?"

Walking quickly to the radio set, the older man said nervously, "I don't know about you, but I'm going to call the base."

The young man grabbed his arm. "Hold it, George! They'll think we're crazy. Think for a minute!"

The older man hesitated and then sat in the desk chair in front of the radio set. The others collapsed in their bunks. "There are six of us. We all saw him. That's all the evidence we need," the older man muttered.

"Remember Cecil?" one of the others said.

"Crazy Cecil," the young man answered. "That's what I've been trying to tell you. If we tell them what we saw, they'll remember how he went crazy living out here and think we've gone bonkers too!"

Over the next few weeks, they tried to forget the tall Inupiaq as they nervously continued to check their instruments.

Kasmali, once again an eagle, flew over the Arctic Sea back to the dog team, sensing he'd failed. When he finally reached the mountain above Prudhoe Bay, he was surprised to see nothing but snow – no dogs, no sled, nothing but snow moguls. Setting down softly on the crest, he raised his arms and mutated back into the Inupiaq and then searched in the snow until he found his clothes and his boots. He put them on and then began looking for the team. For the next few minutes, he paced the area until suddenly he stumbled, falling into a drift. The Malamud leapt out of the snow, yipped, and violently shook its head. Hearing their leader, the other dogs, also buried, soon appeared.

Lying in the drift, Kasmali shook his head. "The flight must have addled me," he said. "I have been one of you, and, like you, I have burrowed in the snow for warmth."

He rose and began to search for the sled that he soon found buried. He dug it out, grabbed a leather sack from its bed, and reached in. "Here, my friends," he said. "You must be hungry." He threw a portion of salted salmon to each of them, which they attacked ravenously. "Eat your fill," he said, watching them. "We have a long journey across mountains and rivers ahead of us."

While they ate, he worked on the sled, making sure it was swept clear of the snow and its lines unfrozen. Just as he finished, the dogs, led by the Malamud, trotted up. He attached each to the lines, the Malamud at their lead, attached booties to each of the dogs' feet; and, a few minutes later led them and the sled southwest down the mountain back to Valdez where he hoped he could find humans who would listen.

Chapter Three: Jack and Janie Cramer

The coastal town of Valdez, often called "The Switzerland of Alaska," rests on the north shore of Prince William Sound along the Inside Passage with the majestic Columbia Glacier less than 25 miles east and the Thompson Pass leading through the Chugach Mountains immediately to the north. During the winter months, with up to 300 inches of snow annually, it has become a Mecca for skiers and other snow enthusiasts. In the summer, the Valdez Port is filled with kayaks and fishermen and a favorite stop for the cruise ships on their way to Glacier Bay. Being ice-free, it is the most important port in the northern hemisphere and the main terminal for the Trans-Alaska Pipeline that brings crude oil 800 miles south from Prudhoe Bay.

Originally the area was inhabited by the Chugach and Ahtna natives; but with the arrival of the White Man, the subsequent discovery of oil in the ANWR Coastal Plain and the construction of the pipeline, the natives have been replaced by oil workers, shop owners, and migrants. Though it does not rival the big Alaskan cities like Nome or Juneau or Fairbanks or Anchorage in population, it is more cosmopolitan than it looks, with its city hall, community college, museum, convention center, airport, clinic, and even its locally famous Mexican café.

Early one June morning, Jack Cramer, a tall man sporting a scrubby red beard with a woolen cap pulled down over his forehead, baggy jeans tucked into his boots, and a red plaid shirt covering his torso, a huge, pure-white Alaskan Husky beside him, stood languidly on the boardwalk in front of the café staring past the fishing boats moored in the berths in the small boat harbor into Prince William Sound where the massive cruise ships were just coming alive and a Navy Cruiser had just sailed in.

When no one was around, he often talked to the dog. "I'll bet Rodrigo's on that cruiser, Astay," he muttered. "Being a famous scientist has its perks."

He hadn't seen Dr. Rodrigo De La Cruz for at least five years, not since their friend Luke Scribner died and Janie and he had moved to Valdez. Back then, the young Spaniard had just achieved his doctorate and had begun his research and writing career. They'd kept in touch, though, through letters mainly.

He frowned, wondering how he could welcome him affably. In all his letters he'd boasted of how great he and Janie were doing, but it was becoming less and less true. Not that the café wasn't thriving, it was just him. Inside, he realized he should be one of the happiest men alive, considering Janie and their relatively successful café; but lately the boring routine of keeping the café running and the stifling isolation of Valdez had begun to wear on him.

"Jesus! There was a time I was more than this!" he cried. "Hell, Astay, I traveled all over the U.S. and even over to Ireland! Shit, when I was a kid, I even hitch-hiked all the way up here from California!"

Trying to get in a better mood, he struggled to remember when he first met Janie. "It was in the ruins of that Chumash village under Mount Pinos down in California, Astay," he muttered. "We were quite a team."

The memories came flooding back: Cleo killed, Janie's patience at his anger, their love-making in the ancient Chumash village, Billy Cole, Sam who turned into a giant seagull who saved them, the golden statue, Bobby, Nuevo Inocentes, their marriage , and then her suggestion they get away from it all and start fresh in Alaska. "That sure as hell wasn't my idea, dog," he muttered again.

He frowned as he remembered how it had reached this point. "All I was trying to do was impress her. We were sitting on a bench on the strand looking out at the Santa Barbara harbor, and I just blabbered on about when I was a kid working the pipe line. And it worked!" he spat out angrily. "She got all excited about this god-forsaken place. For Christ's sake, I just figured she'd get over it!"

Looking again out at the harbor, he frowned as he remembered how the first time she saw that Valdez had only two tiny diners she'd come up with the idea of starting their own café that would offer a decent meal. Then, disregarding his objection that she was naive, how she'd insisted they could make it work by using her years of experience keeping her parents' diner afloat.

"What could I say?" he asked the dog. "She said she'd use her own money from the sale of her diner! Before I knew it, she barreled right over me and bought that derelict shop and the house behind it! But, damn it, I didn't think it would lead to this! Jesus, it was even me who came up with the idea of making it a Mexican restaurant and calling it 'Roberto's Mexican Café,' after Bobby down in Nuevo Inocentes! Now, here we are, working our butts off trying to keep the damn place going."

Lately, he was rarely seen without the Husky that both intimidated and attracted the tourists. Between it and him with his scraggly beard and rustic outfit, the two had taken on the look of the untamed Yukon. It also helped his image that he was sometimes seen with the tall Inupiaq chief who'd appeared one day with Astay.

That, of course, was months ago. Now the Inupiaq was off on an expedition north, leaving the dog with him, saying it was too independent to be part of his sled team. What he couldn't know, however, was that the chief had actually asked Astay to stay with him because of the voice.

He focused on the cruise ships. Over the years he'd learned to identify every one of them. "Yeah, Janie'll be happy, dog," he muttered sarcastically. "Before long, she'll be nagging me to get off my butt. Right now, I'll bet she's having a hissy-fit."

But Astay wasn't listening. Its tail wagging furiously, it was staring at a man jogging up the walkway. Suddenly it leapt up, trotted toward him, and knocked him back as it jumped on him. He seemed to say something to it, and with that he and the dog walked up to Jack. "You've kept Astay well," he said as they reached him.

Jack grabbed his hand. "Glad to see you back, Chief. Your damn mutt's a pain, but at least he's been a distraction. How was the trip?"

"A boat with guns?" Kasmali asked, returning his handshake and pointing out at the Navy cruiser.

Jack grinned. "You've got great eyes, Chief. The Navy sent it to check on the latest conditions up here," he answered. "I'm hoping an old friend of mine is on it. Tell me about your trip."

Kasmali shrugged. "The dogs," he answered. "As soon as I got into the pass, they became frightened. Animals can sense things, you know. The Ice Cap's melting, Jack. It's only a matter of time."

"For what?" Jack asked anxiously.

"A massive earthquake and perhaps worse. The land is telling me something. The land, the dogs, and my visions."

"I've heard it all before, Chief. Come on, let's go in the cafe. I want you to meet my wife. She's heard a lot about you."

"You told her?"

Jack shrugged. "Of course, we've no secrets." he muttered. "I warn you, though, she thinks I'm crazy. Come on, she's been up for hours getting the menu together. I'll ask her to whip up something for you. You must be hungry."

Though it was not yet noon, the café already had a few customers sitting patiently in the dining room. As they gaped at Kasmali and Astay, Jack greeted them with a western drawl and led the Inupiaq and the huge dog through the tables and into the kitchen where Janie was at the eight- burner range stirring large pots. Behind her, the huge griddle was beginning to sizzle. She was frowning as they walked up.

"Hello, Mrs. Cramer," Kasmali said, holding out his hand.

She stopped her stirring, turned, jumped back, but eventually took his hand. "I'm sorry," she answered. "You surprised me. Welcome back."

"I am called Chief Kasmali," he answered.

"I remember," she said. "We might as well get things straight. Jack claims you're an alien, some kind of changeling." She took a breath. "Frankly, I find that hard to believe, Mr. Kasmali." She turned to Jack. "Damn it, Jack," she snarled. "I told you not to bring that beast into the café! Take it outside!"

Kasmali nodded to the dog. Without waiting for Jack, it trotted to the backdoor. Jack let it out into the backyard.

"I'm sorry about being so rude, Mr. Kasmali," she continued. "It's unsanitary for the dog to be in here, but tell me the truth. You're not really some creature from outer space, are you?"

Kasmali hesitated. Then, speaking softly, he answered, "I am but a visitor who is concerned about this planet and about you and your husband, Mrs. Cramer. I have a sense that a great catastrophe will soon occur in this region, and I have been asked to help you avoid it. However, I do not want to upset you. To you, may I simply be Chief Kasmali?"

She smiled, deciding this strange man was just another of odd natives whom Jack befriended. "Whatever," she answered. "I guess any friend of Jack is welcome here, regardless of his origin."

But Jack wasn't satisfied. "I can't believe you're still so stubborn, Janie," he said. "Especially since Sam saved us those times!"

Janie sighed. "Back to that again?" She looked back at Kasmali. "What he's talking about, Mr. Kasmali, is that a large, confused seagull just happened to do some crazy things that helped us out a few times when we were in a mess down in California, that's all. Then Jack started claiming it was a changeling from another world! He's was a novelist with a wild imagination."

Kasmali just nodded. "A huge seagull?" he asked Jack.

Jack bristled, turning to Kasmali. "It wasn't just that, though it should have been enough for her! There was also the dog Alfred who could understand you when you talked to him and lots of other things; but it's hopeless trying to convince her."

She raised her arms in frustration. "I'm sorry, Mr. Kasmali, our bickering is probably making you uncomfortable." She turned back to Jack. "By the way, isn't it time you shaved and got cleaned up?"

Jack wasn't surprised at her shift in mood, so, feigning indignation, he said, "The tourists expect me to look rugged, Janie. Kasmali and the dog and I help to lure customers in."

"Or scare them away. Are you ready to help now?"

Jack snarled, "Yes'm, just as soon as I whip up a fish tostada for the chief here." He moved around the counter. "Maybe after he eats, he can tell us about his trip."

He asked the chief to sit at a small table at the rear of the kitchen. "How many tostadas you want, Chief?" he asked.

"What are they?" Kasmali answered.

"You'll see," Jack said as he walked over to the large refrigerator and began working. Janie looked over his shoulder, nodded, and went into the dining room.

"Okay, Chief, Janie's famous fish tostada!" he said as he carried the plate over to Kasmali. Ignoring the fact that the tostada was still hot, the chief took a small bite. "It pleases me," he said.

Jack chuckled and went back to the griddle where he began to fry the rest of the tortillas just as Janie came back in. "We're got a crowd out there, Jack," she said. "You'd better get at it. Did you check the ovens?"

"Lighten up, woman," he answered, trying to be patient. "As usual, you've got everything under control." He pointed to the baking pans on the counter behind him. "Enchiladas, chili relenos, Mexican pizza; all ready to go."

She nodded and handed him the orders. "You know what to do. I'll make the fish tacos and tostatas."

Kasmali took a final bite and slowly walked over. "I have never been in such a place," he said enigmatically and then watched as Jack finished his chores.

Later, when the last of the patrons had left, Jack and Janie sat in the dining room with Kasmali. Janie wasted no time. "Come on, tell us about your trip, Chief. So, what did you find out?" she asked.

Kasmali frowned. "The tremors are increasing, causing more calving; the Ice Cap and the permafrost are melting; and the animals and birds are migrating east instead of south. It will come soon. You and Jack should leave Valdez."

She gazed at him and then slowly shook her head. "It's not that I don't respect you, Mr. Kasmali, but you can't be serious about our leaving. This is our busiest season of the year. Maybe we'll have time for a vacation when the cruise ships stop coming, just as we always do."

"By then it may be too late," Kasmali answered emotionless.

Trying hard to be patient, Jack reached over and took Janie's hand. "Janie, listen to him. He knows things. A few years back I was as skeptical as you about changelings like Kasmali here, but maybe I should tell you something I've kept from you." He looked at Kasmali, who nodded, and then took a deep breath. "When the chief first came to Valdez, right in front of me he mutated into a copy of his dog."

Janie looked at him scornfully. "Get a grip, Jack," she said through her teeth. "This changeling's bull is getting out of hand."

He wrenched his hand away and looked at Kasmali. "It's useless, Chief," he said. "She'll never listen."

"Damn it, Jack!" Janie snapped. "Will you get real?" She snapped her head around at Kasmali. "Close up now? Now, in our biggest season? Damn it, Jack. Your fantasies are making me sick! We can't just close up shop on some whim! Get over it! We'll stay where we are!"

Kasmali sat stoically as Jack got up. "I need some air," he said. "I'm gonna take a walk. You wanna come, Chief?"

Kasmali shook his head "No, I must see to Astay."

Jack nodded and left, slamming the kitchen door, seething at Janie's utter dismissal of him, and headed for Gus' bar. Janie, however, didn't have the luxury of running away. She had a café to run so, fuming, she returned to her cooking.

She known for a while he felt trapped. She'd read his books and understood his wanderlust, but lately his mood changes and now his weird idea the Inupiaq is an alien were getting to her, but originally she'd been understanding. Back before their second winter she'd even suggested a vacation south, and, not too surprisingly, he jumped at the idea and even suggested a trip to the village in the Santa Ynez Valley he called Nuevo Inocentes. She knew he had old friends there, so she'd readily agreed. And, as it turned out, everything he'd told her about the village turned out to be true. They had a wonderful time there, and Jack's good-nature was reborn. They stayed for a month helping out with Bobby Scribner and the other disadvantaged men and boys the friars called 'Radiants.' However, after a month, she was ready to go home, but he wasn't. After six weeks, though, she put her foot down.

The next winter, he suggested they return to Nuevo Inocentes; but thinking a little variety would be better, she persuaded him to visit San Francisco instead. However, no sooner had they arrived than he mentioned that Bobby had once had a great time there with his mother and that it'd be fun to have him with them. Janie could hardly object, for not only did she enjoy Bobby, she also realized an outing would be good for him. So they traveled south to pick him up; and predictably they spend most of their vacation at the village, though during the last week they did make it to San Francisco.

During the spring of the following winter, she was determined the two of them needed time alone, so for months she saved money for a cruise to Mexico. Then, when the weather turned cold and the last of the cruise ships were about to leave, she told him of her plan, knowing quite well that he would object by saying it was too expensive. When he did, she proudly announced that she'd already saved their fare and had booked their passage. She saw the disappointment in his eyes and knew why. He'd assumed they would return to the village.

She had a wonderful time tanning herself, enjoying the gourmet food, gambling in the casino, watching the shows, and relaxing; but Jack was like a fish out of water. His redheaded complexion forced him to avoid the sun; he had no taste for gourmet food; he was too frugal to gamble; he thought the shows were inane; and he was incapable of relaxing. So, by the time they arrived back at Valdez, he was even more depressed, and she was totally disgusted.

During the following year, their spats began in earnest.

Gus Boston and his bar had been fixtures in Valdez way before Jack and Janie arrived; and Jack, like almost everyone else, had originally bought into Gus' act about his adventures in Alaska before the pipeline, probably because he looked the part. Not that he was especially brawny, as one might expect from an old miner. It was just that he seemed so true to the image. His face was craggy, what you could see of it through his massive gray beard that flowed down to his chest and his black hair that covered his ears and hung down past his shoulders. Besides, he talked like a guy who'd been through it all – gruff, impatient, and even vulgar when the ladies weren't around. None were in the pub when Jack came in.

"JACK, YOU SON OF AN INUPIAQ WHORE!" he shouted when he saw him. "YOU'D BETTER'VE BROUGHT SOME OF YOUR WIFE'S TOSTADAS!"

As usual, the bar was crowded, and most of the men scattered around looked up to see who Gus was cursing; but, recognizing Jack, they went back to their beer. Jack took a stool. Gus came over, but before he could continue his invective, Jack leaned forward and whispered, "Get your tostadas for yourself, you old fart. And if you don't stop cussing me, I'll tell everybody what a miserable fake you are."

Gus chuckled. "Me a fake? Christ, look at your getup! I've got news for you. No matter what you do or how you dress, to any real Alaskans you'll never be anything more than a California hippy!" He waved to a small man behind the bar. "Take over for me, Scottie, you little shit. I'm gonna take a break with my lousy friend here." He pointed to a small table in the rear of the room.

Once they were seated, he leaned over. "I never should've told about before, Jack; and if you ever tell anybody my real name is Bernard and that I used to be a college prof, I'll stab you with a swizzle stick."

Jack laughed. "My lips are sealed, Bernie," he said. "Not that anyone would believe me. You're a legend."

"I should have done this years ago," Bernie or Gus answered. "Twenty-five years spouting off about Wordsworth, Coleridge, Shelley, Keats, and the rest almost killed me. Trying to explain how 'Hail to thee, blithe spirit' was great poetry was enough to make me puke."

"I've heard it all before, Bernie. Anyway, now you're Gus and you can forget about Shelley."

"Ten years. Can you believe it? A couple of years before the oil spill."

"Well, you chose a perfect time, from what I've heard. All those reporters scouting around for some non-existent news story, and then they started writing about you. What a hoot!"

"Yeah, that was fun, but it wasn't easy, you know. It took a lot of research to come up with my stories."

"Give me a break, Gus, but tell me something. Don't you ever wish you could have an intelligent conversation with someone?"

Gus smiled. "That's where you some in, my friend. As long as you're around, I've got the best of both worlds."

Jack shrugged. "Whatever," he answered. "Hey, Kasmali's back. Remember, the Inupiaq chief? I told you about him taking off to check up north."

"Was it as bad as I've heard?"

"Worse, according to him. He even suggested Janie and I close down the café for a while."

"You gonna do it?"

"Are you kidding? You know Janie. She won't have it. You know, a few years back I would've laughed Kasmali's warnings off; but now with all the warming and tremors, I'm getting worried."

Gus laughed and got up. "There's always been doomsayers, Jack," he said. "I'd better get back to work or Scottie'll start sampling. Stick around. The crowd will soon leave."

Jack nodded and followed him to the bar. Gus drew him a stein of Guinness.

At that moment, two men were standing braced against a railing on the Navy cruiser, gazing at the village. The taller of the two, neatly outfitted in a strikingly white uniform, his captain's hat securely on his head, broke the silence. "I wonder if they're worried?" he asked the man beside him dressed in khakis.

"I doubt it, Captain," the man answered. "But they'll figure it out if the cruise ships stop coming. That is, if the owners start listening."

Rodrigo De Al Cruz, Ph.D. in anthropology and seismology and the history of North American Indians, pointed to the café. "I hope Jack and Janie have a crowd," he said. "Five years getting the place going and now…"

"They must've felt the tremors."

"They're hard to ignore," Rodrigo answered. "I imagine all the Yukon has felt them."

"What about this Inupiaq chief he wrote you about, the one your friend Jack said was taking a look at the Ice Cap? You said you wanted to talk to him."

"That's right, Captain. After spending years being tutored by a Chumash Shaman when I was a kid down south, I've learned there are things science can't explain."

The captain shook his head. "You know best, I guess. The tragedy is that no one ever listens." He shrugged. "Well, maybe this time things will be different. We'll get you ashore as soon as we can. You only have a week or so to find out how bad it really is."

"I hope the Inupiaq's there. Jack wrote me he might be back by the time we got here."

The captain nodded and then walked up a ladder to the bridge. Rodrigo remained standing at the railing looking sadly out at Valdez.

Chapter Four: Charles and Ricky Murray

Sadly, it was an old story, dating back to the Gold Rush days. Out of lust or perhaps loneliness, a man would take a wife but quickly ignore her and the inevitable children by leaving them alone while he searched for gold or trapped or, in this case, worked the pipeline. Sometimes the wife was strong enough to provide a decent home for her children, but not one Mrs. Murray who was neither strong nor maternal and who blamed her two boys, Charles and Ricky, for the way her life had turned out. They thus became her victims when her husband was gone, which was most of the time.

On the rare occasions he returned, she and then the boys became the outlet for his frustrations. To make it worse, she was a whiner, which aggravated his anger; but it was Charles, three-years older than Ricky, who eventually bore the greatest abuse, for, unlike her or Ricky, he often fought back.

They lived in filth and clutter in a house provided by the refinery on the outskirts of Valdez; and Charles gradually learned to survive by using Ricky, who amazingly remained blissfully naive, to beg neighbors for food. When their father finally deserted them for good when Charles was eight and Ricky five, Charles, of course, was glad; but soon after, he and Ricky were left alone when their mother deserted them by leaving with a man she called their uncle. They never saw her again.

Through all this, Charles reluctantly became both a protector of his little brother and a defiant time-bomb waiting to explode. Ricky, on the other hand, remained oblivious to the chaos around him. Eventually, after numerous complaints from the townspeople about their mother's absence and Charles' anti-social behavior, they became wards of the State.

Over the next five years, they were placed separately in foster homes in and around Valdez. Fortunately, Ricky quickly found a kind family; but Charles, because of his explosive temper, was rejected by them and other foster families until finally a naïve man and woman took them in, not knowing what they were getting into. Charles was then thirteen and Ricky ten.

Tall for his age and invariably in thrift-shop clothes too small for him, Charles might have elicited compassion from the man and woman but for his perpetual sneer and his vulgar mouth. On the other hand, they developed a great affection for Ricky, so woebegone and small, looking a little like a character out of one of Dickens' novels, which sometimes galled Charles. Ricky, however, idolized his brother and tagged along behind him wherever he went, even to the point of eventually joining him when he took to vandalizing and thievery.

Inevitably they were caught, but because they were so young they were put on probation and sent back to the man and woman. Charles, however, had had enough of foster homes and took to hanging around the oil refinery; but Ricky returned to them and began to go to school. Because of his lack of literacy, he was put in the third grade.

At the same time, Janie Cramer had volunteered as an aide at the school, thinking she should become a more active member of the community. Though she was completely inexperienced in teaching, nonetheless the jaded principle eagerly welcomed her, though, truth be told, he would have hired almost anyone who was naïve enough to take on the hodgepodge of students under his charge.

The school, Hermon Hutchens Elementary, was located on the west side of Mineral Creek, but a fifteen-mile drive from the café in good weather so it was not difficult for her to take time off, though during the weekdays she had to prepare the luncheon menu in advance. However, on her first day when she was confronted by four boys who'd been segregated from the other students for being incorrigible or illiterate, she quickly discovered she was out of her element.

Having been raised and educated in the semi-cloistered, all-white community of Valencia over the mountains from the San Fernando Valley, and having spent her later years even further away from reality in Gorman up the Tejon Pass, she felt as if she were among aliens.

During her first week, she completely lost control, of course; and the lead teacher, Mrs. McCarthy, a widow from the 1964 earthquake, being as dispirited as the principal, was of no help because she didn't want to hear any more about the boys, one of whom happened to be Ricky Murray.

However, Janie Murray wasn't one who gave up easily. Over the first few days, she tried everything she could to motivate the boys, from prizes to treats and even dollar bills, but nothing worked. Day after day, three of the four sneered or looked through her. The fourth, Ricky, on the other hand, just sat at his desk with his head down. She asked them to join in various group activities; but though they knew they had to go along with her, they rarely if ever finished their assignments. Being an over-achiever throughout her academic career, she was stumped.

One day, after deciding it was hopeless, she ignored the curriculum, sat at the front of the room, and just began reading aloud from one of the Soulful Sam fables she'd found in the bookcase. Immediately three of the boys mocked the childish poems; but Ricky surprised her by raising his head to listen.

Perhaps understandingly, as the days went by, she assigned the other boys busy work that they ignored and devoted more time to Ricky. She read every volume of the fables she could find to him; and when they finished the last one, *Soulful Sam's Homecoming*, she suggested he write one of his own, complete with illustrations. At the beginning, he reluctantly went along with her; but eventually he became enthusiastic about their project. But then, just as they were getting into it, he became truant.

Perhaps she was naïve thinking she'd made some inroads with Ricky, but she didn't want to give up on him, so she decided to check his record and found that he was a foundling, that he had an older brother named Charles, and that they both lived in a foster home outside of town.

Two days later, when Ricky still hadn't come to class, she told Mrs. McCarthy she had an emergency and went to visit the foster home.

There she was told that he and Charles had been arrested for breaking and entering derelict houses.

She rushed to the constable's office where she was told the boys' arraignment was scheduled for later that day all the way up at Anchorage. Somehow feeling she had to be there, she hurried back to the café to tell Jack.

She was surprised he understood. "You've obviously taken a liking to this Ricky kid, Janie," he said. "It's okay. Go and see what you can do. I'll hold down the fort."

Deciding the bus would take too long to negotiate the 300 miles to Anchorage, she decided to take the ferry to Whittier and then the train. When she finally arrived in the big city, she was able to get directions to the courthouse; and once there she was told by a receptionist that the boys' arraignment was assigned for later that afternoon. Having nowhere else to go, she sat on a bench outside the courtroom, unwilling to believe that Ricky, who had just begun to come alive, would now have his future dashed.

Finally the doors opened and she rushed in and took a seat near the front. When the two boys were led in, she almost cried when she saw Ricky looking so lost, but didn't because she was shocked by the filthy appearance of his brother. Ricky saw her and immediately averted his eyes.

The arraignment went quickly. Since both boys were minors, the judge assigned their case to the Juvenile Court and scheduled it for the next Monday.

When Janie got back to the café later that afternoon, Jack was in the kitchen surrounded by pots and pans, sweat rolling off his face. Seeing her, he cried, "Thank God you're back! I don't know how you do it!"

She grinned, grabbed an apron, began cleaning up, and then took over the cooking. A crowd of people began coming in the dining room. "HEY, JANIE!" one shouted. "WE'RE STARVING!"

"I'll tell you what happened to the boys later, Jack," she said calmly. "Right now, we better get at it. You set the tables, okay?"

Two hours later, they finally had a chance to sit. She told him the whole story. "I don't know what to do, Jack," she concluded. "Ricky's whole life could be lost. He's only eight!"

This time, however, perhaps out of frustration, Jack was in no mood to be sympathetic. "Don't be so melodramatic, Janie," he answered. "He'll spend some time in juvenile hall, that's all. It'll probably do him good. Besides, there's nothing you can do about it."

"I know," she said. "It's just that he told me how he and his brother have had such rough lives, right from the beginning. What do people expect?"

"We are what we are," he answered as he got up. "Right now, I'm pooped."

She nodded and went into the kitchen to get things ready for the next day.

Over the next week, she tried her best not to think of Ricky; but it was no good, so the next Sunday night she spent hours preparing the meals for the next day. When Monday morning came, she informed Jack that everything was ready for the lunchtime crowd and that she was going to take the day off to go back to Anchorage. He was angry, of course; but he knew that when she made up her mind there was little he could do about it.

She sat for hours in a small room in the courthouse, this time alone. Finally the judge, a kindly looking old man, came in and waited as the boys were led in by the constable. When Ricky saw her, he broke out into a smile but then again turned his head.

The judge heard the charges presented by the constable and shook his head. "They're at it again, huh, Ralph?" he said to the constable, looked at some notes he had in front of him. "I see you two are on probation," he said, and then focused on Ricky. "I notice here that you're doing well at school, Ricky," he asked. Ricky shrugged.

He then turned his attention to Charles. "But you, Charles, this report from your foster family says they haven't seen you. What have you been doing except breaking into houses?" he asked. Charles also shrugged. The judge cringed. "When was the last time you bathed, son?" he asked.

Again Charles shrugged, his head down. "Well, anyway," the judge continued. "It says here that you, Ricky, were doing well with the family. Why the devil would you break the law with your brother?"

Ricky shook his head, but Charles just sneered. "Well," the judge continued, "it's out of my hands now."

Though it was completely unlike her, Janie stood up and found herself saying, "Ricky's a good boy, Judge. I'm one of his teachers. He's one of my best students!"

The judge smiled. "You're Mrs. Cramer, aren't you, Ma'am? You run that Mexican café in Valdez. Great tostadas. You also a teacher?"

Embarrassed, she sat back down and nodded. "Just an aide," she managed to mutter, "but I've been working with Ricky. He and his brother have had some bad luck. No one seems to care about them."

The judge pointed to Charles. "It's no wonder," he said. "Look at him standing there sneering at us!"

"I'm sure Charles has as much good in him as Ricky, Judge," she said, now becoming bolder. "They're just children! I imagine if given a chance, they'd turn out to be fine young men."

The judge attempted to hold back a smile. "Well, Mrs. Cramer," he finally said. "You may be right, but there's not much I can do. After all, they committed a crime and they have to bear the consequences."

At the time, she didn't know why she reacted as she did, but without considering Jack, without thinking about the obvious problems, she blurted out, "I can help them, Judge! What if you release them to me? Instead of putting them in juvenile hall, they could work at my cafe. That way I could keep an eye on them. My husband Jack will help."

Janie was lucky, for the judge was a compassionate man. After he consulted with the skeptical constable, it eventually was settled. The two boys were released into her hands.

On their way back on the train and then the ferry to Valdez, the two boys sat quietly beside her as she struggled to overcome her revulsion to the rancid odors emitting from Charles. She attempted conversation by describing the café, but neither he nor Ricky showed any interest, nor did they speak a word, even when she mentioned to Ricky how he'd be able to work with her on his fable, which caused Charles to snicker.

She wasn't worried too much about Jack's reaction to this obvious change in their lives because she knew, despite his recent malaise, that down deep he liked kids. After all, it was obvious he idolized Bobby Scribner when they visited the little village in the San Ynez Valley.

However, when she came in the door with the two boys shuffling behind her, he exploded. "WHAT HAVE YOU DONE NOW?" he yelled. Before she could explain, he turned toward the brothers and brusquely asked them to wait outside.

"What are *they* doing here?" he then asked caustically.

Janie tried to explain, but he just kept shaking his head. "So you brought them here, did you? Who's gonna take care of them?" he finally said. "You from that homogenized hamlet called Valencia, from that hole-in-the-wall town called Gorman? Jesus, woman! What were you thinking of? They'll steal us blind, or worse!"

"I really don't know why I did it, Jack," she answered, looking sadly at him. "I told you about them, especially Ricky, but when the judge said they had to be punished, it just came out of me. They're just kids, and you can control them. Besides, we can use some help around here."

He was seething. "You said I'd be involved?" he said between his teeth. "You brought me into it?"

She nodded. "I guess I thought you'd have a little empathy for them, but I see now I was wrong. What do you want me to do? Take them back?"

She sat with her head down. He sat looking at her for a moment. "How long?" he finally asked.

She brightened. "Just a trial period of a couple of weeks," she answered. "Then the constable wants a progress report."

Jack decided he'd better change the subject. "Damn it!" he snarled, "Have you seen my favorite shirt? I can't find it."

"It's probably in the hamper. I'll look for it," she answered, hoping he'd come around. "What about the boys?"

He shrugged and yelled for them to come back in. They did with him hovering over them. He leapt back. "Jesus, kid!" he snorted. "You smell like a sewer!"

Charles looked up and smiled. Jack shook his head and looked at Janie who was wringing her hands. "Okay, Guys, you caught a break, but the first thing you have to do, kid, is get clean!" he said calmly to Charles. "My wife seems to like you, but let's get things straight. First, we're not about to run a prison here, so you'll be paid for your work. Secondly, I expect you to show us and our customers respect. No smart talk. You'll be here every weekday before the dinner crowd and on the weekends for lunch and dinner. I'll leave the rest up to her." He then stomped off into the kitchen, leaving Janie to handle the more difficult details.

After thanking him, she drove the boys to their foster home and informed the woman there of her plan, commenting that she and her husband would still get their stipends because the boys would continue to sleep there. She knew Jack would never go along with the boys staying with them. She then left, asking the woman to see that Charles clean himself up. On the way back, she decided they'd help out at night and on weekends, and that both boys would go back to school.

The next day being a Saturday, she drove them from the foster home, led them into the kitchen, and gave them aprons. Jack looked up, sniffed, and said, "Thank God the kid bathed!" He then took charge. "Okay, you hoodlums, let's see if you can do some work." He showed them around and then directed them how to set each of the tables in the dining room. Ricky was smiling as he worked, but Charles continued to be morose.

The weekend went smoothly enough. Janie kept them out of Jack's way by assigning them chores, and she even found time to work with Ricky on his fable. However, when Jack had to work with them, Charles' laziness began to get to him. The next week, Jack started yelling at him, which brought back memories of other men who'd tried to dominate him so he began to rebel. Assuaged by Janie, Jack took it for a few days; but one evening, after he'd ordered Charles to wash the cookware, the boy calmly said, "Fuck you, old man! Do it yourself."

That did it. Hearing the shouting, Janie and Ricky came running in from the dining room and saw Charles writhing on the floor. She yelled, "WHAT HAPPENED?" and sat down beside the boy and touched his arm, but he jerked away, jumped up, and yelled, "I'LL GET EVEN WITH YOU, YOU FUCKER!" and ran out the back door, grabbing a shirt he saw lying in the corner.

Janie was stunned. Ricky took a step toward the back door but hesitated, anguish on his face. "Don't do it, Ricky," Jack said calmly. "You're not like him. Let him go." He then turned to Janie. "I've had enough," he said. "The little shit told me to ... he cursed at me, and I lost my temper."

Janie felt like crying as she lowered herself on to a stool and leaned toward Ricky. "Mr. Cramer's right, Ricky," she finally said almost pleadingly. "Stay with us, please." Ricky hesitated, looked sadly at the door, but then nodded and went back into the kitchen, totally conflicted. He had learned to like Mrs. Cramer a lot; but Charles, after all, was his brother. That evening, she drove him to his foster home, hoping Charles wouldn't be there. She prayed she'd see Ricky again.

The next day, Janie came early to school, anxious to see if Ricky would be at his desk. When he came in the door and saw him, she was tempted to hug him; but she didn't, of course.

Later, after driving him to the café, she went to Ralph Eston, the constable, to explain what had happened.

"Jack hit him?" Eston asked.

Janie nodded, expecting the worst, but Eston just laughed. "Good for him," he said. "That kid could use a little smack or two. So he just took off, huh?"

Janie nodded again, and Eston patted her on the shoulder. "Don't feel guilty, Mrs. Cramer, it was bound to happen. Charles is a bad apple. What about his brother Ricky?"

She answered quickly. "He's concerned about his brother, but he *did* come back to school. He said Charles never showed up at their foster home last night, though."

Eston shrugged. "Probably gone for good, but I guess I have to keep an eye out for him. This means he's broken his probation. In the meantime, what do you want to do about Ricky?"

"He's a good little boy, Ralph," she answered. "He just needs a little structure. Will you give me some more time with him?"

For the first time in a long time, she felt happy as she and Jack and Ricky finished clearing up from the dinner crowd.

That day, Charles wandered the back streets of Valdez gradually becoming more and more furious. Finally he again hid under the main pier and fumed at the fact that Ricky, whom he'd protected all his life, hadn't followed him out of the café.

He struggled to understand why. He knew Ricky was stupid, but why he would stay with people who were just using him was a mystery to him. He was Ricky's big brother, after all, and they were almost strangers. Finally he decided the woman had somehow seduced Ricky. "That was it, the bitch!" he muttered. "I'll get him back!"

Perhaps down deep, he realized he needed Ricky more than Ricky needed him, but he'd never admit it, even to himself.

Chapter Five: Rodrigo De La Cruz

Early the next morning, Jack stood at the end of the pedestrian pier in a denim jacket that covered a new shirt and watched a launch from the cruiser out in the bay slowly maneuver through the fishing boats toward him. Huddled under the same pier, Charles was just waking up.

When the launch finally docked, a Hispanic young man jumped out, smiled at Jack, and then walked past. Jack chuckled and yelled to his back, "HOLA, SENOR! COMO ES NUEVO INOCENTES? COMO ES BOBBY?"

The man turned and stared at him. "Jack?" he asked. "Is that you?"

Charles, hearing Cramer's name, jumped up and edged out from under the pier to listen, still furious about his treatment of him.

"Yup," he heard Cramer chuckle. "You haven't changed a bit, Rod. You still look like the skinny kid telling Chumash stories to the Radiants."

Rodrigo laughed. "Maybe I haven't, but my God, you sure have! I wouldn't have recognized you except for your lousy Spanish. What's with the beard and the outfit?"

"Part of my image," Jack answered. "Forget about that. How's Bobby?"

Rodrigo hugged him and said, "He's fine, but he misses you."

"I've gotta get back there," Jack said, embarrassed. "It's been too long. Maybe this time I can get Janie to agree when we shut down for the winter."

Rodrigo pulled off his jacket. "It's warmer here than I thought it would be. Is it always like this in summer? It's beautiful! How's Janie? How's your café doing?"

Jack shook his head. "We're going through a heat spell. Enjoy it while you can. Janie's fine, I guess, and Roberto's Mexican Café's thriving. How was it on the cruiser?"

"Long and cramped," Rodrigo answered, curious about Jack's seeming indifference toward Janie. "You call your place Roberto's? You name it after Bobby Scribner?"

"Yeah, it helps me remember him and the village," Jack answered, smiling. "Jeez, it's good to see you!"

Rodrigo, concerned, stood back, looked at him, and said, "Good to see you too, Jack, but everything's all right, isn't it? You seem down."

Jack laughed. "Everything's fine, Rod," he answered. "Why wouldn't they be? I've got it all."

Outraged, Charles crept back into the shadows, no longer willing to hear how good Cramer had it.

Standing together on the pier now out of his hearing, Rodrigo ignored Jack's sarcasm. "I hope so, my friend. You and Janie deserve it." He put his hand on Jack's shoulder. "When can I meet this Inupiaq chief you wrote me about?"

Jack grinned and pointed at the café. "Come on," he said. "You're in luck. Kasmali just came back from a trip up to the Arctic, but I've gotta tell you something first. You remember Sam?"

Rodrigo chuckled. "I remember *of* him, of course. I spent months asking people about him for Luke's book. You know that. Why do you ask?"

"You remember what he said to Luke just before he left?"

"He said a lot of things," Rodrigo answered.

"Yeah, but do you remember when he told Luke he'd ask others of his kind to look over us?"

"Yeah, at the end of the book."

"Well, steady yourself. Kasmali's one of them!"

Rodrigo staggered. "Get hold of yourself, Jack," he said, again worried about his friend. "You're trying to tell me this Inupiaq is a changeling? Give me a break."

Jack became flustered. "It's true, Rodrigo. He proved it to me! He muted into a giant Siberian Husky right in front of me!"

Rodrigo was stunned. "You're serious, aren't you?"

"Sure as hell!" Jack spouted. "Jesus, Rodrigo, you should be the last to doubt changelings. You *know* they're among us! Why couldn't Kasmali be one of them?"

Rodrigo stared at him and then said hesitantly, "I guess I just thought that when Sam left that was the end of it. You say you saw him mutate?"

Jack nodded. "Yeah," he answered, "and he said he'd heard a voice telling him to protect us. Then he left for his trip and just came back."

Rodrigo began to laugh. "Son-of-a-gun! Damn, if he's an alien, he probably has a way of knowing more than anyone about the conditions up here. For God's sake, Jack, let's go see him!"

Realizing that Rodrigo now believed him, Jack quickly answered, "He's probably at the café right now having a tostada. He loves them. Come on, my friend, I'll introduce you. Jesus, it's good to see you! It's like the good old days!"

"Welcome to Roberto's," Jack said as he unlocked the door of the café and led Rodrigo into the empty dining room. "JANIE, GUESS WHO I FOUND WANDERING AROUND THE DOCKS?" he yelled.

Wiping her hands on her apron, Janie came out of the kitchen, saw Rodrigo, laughed, and said, "Goodness, it's you, Rodrigo! It's been a long time. Jack told me you'd be coming. It's wonderful to see you again. You hungry?"

He struggled not to betray his shock at seeing the change in the beautiful, blond-haired, blue-eyed, statuesque, lively woman he'd known. Though still attractive, to him she seemed listless, though she was trying her best not to show it. Her eyes, for one thing, had lost their luster. He grabbed her hand and said with as much sincerity as he could muster, "You haven't changed a bit, Janie. You look great. Of course I'm hungry. I've heard a lot about your fish tostadas from the crew of the ship. I can't wait to try them."

She shrugged. "Yes, some sailors have been in. Come on into the kitchen. I'll make you one. Maybe then you tell us what you've been up to and why you're here." She nodded toward the boy at the range with his back to them. "Meet Ricky, my right hand man. I couldn't survive without him. Ricky, this is Rodrigo De La Cruz, a famous writer, archeologist, and historian."

Ricky turned and muttered, "Hi."

Rodrigo walked over to him and shook his hand. "I'm glad to meet you, Ricky, but ignore Mrs. Cramer. I'm just a guy who used to know Mr. and Mrs. Cramer a long time ago."

Ricky nodded and went back to his work. Rodrigo smiled and sat on a nearby stool. "Ricky doesn't talk much," Janie said quickly, "But he's a hard-worker." She nodded toward Jack. "He's had to be what with Jack here sloughing off so often. Give me a minute. I'll make your tostada."

Trying to ignore her criticism of Jack, Rodrigo turned to him and whispered, "Well, where's this changeling?" Jack shrugged, glaring at Janie. Rodrigo turned back to Janie who was at the range and grinned. "The Navy asked me to come here to check on the geological conditions, to answer your question. For some reason, they think I can tell them more about something they already know. The seismic signs are troubling, Janie."

"You too?" Janie snorted. "We've gone through tremors ever since Jack and I first got here." She finished the tostada and handed it to him. "For goodness sake, Rodrigo, just like the Inupiaq, your alleged changeling! I heard you whispering to Jack. When are you and he gonna wake up? I would think that being a scientist, you'd be more rational."

Rodrigo nodded and bit into the tostada. "This *is* good. They were right," he said. He chewed for a moment. "I don't understand your skepticism, Janie, especially after what you and Jack went through at the ruins of the Chumash village."

She bristled. "Oh no, not that again," she snorted. "It was just a poor seagull, a huge, lost, probably hurt seagull! Jack and I have gone over that!"

Rodrigo shook his head. "I guess there's no convincing you."

Janie shook her head. "Let's not talk about it now. Tell me more about yourself."

Rodrigo chuckled. "Nothing to tell, just teaching, writing, and consulting."

Janie nodded and went to the refrigerator. "By the way, Jack, that weird Inupiaq said he'd see you later," she said sarcastically. "He's out back with his huge monster." She turned back to Rodrigo. "There's not much to do in Valdez, Rodrigo, but maybe you can look around. After Jack and Ricky and I finish with the lunch time mob, I'll make up a room for you in the house."

"You don't have to do that," Rodrigo objected. "I can get a hotel room."

"Don't be silly," she answered, pulling bowls out of the refrigerator.

He looked at Jack who just shrugged. "Don't try to argue with her, Professor. It never works."

"All right," Rodrigo answered, smiling. "I just don't want to be in the way. Right now, though, I think I'll go see the Inupiaq." He motioned Jack to the back door, leaned toward him, and whispered, "Everything okay with Janie?"

"Yeah," Jack whispered back. "She's just in one of her moods."

Rodrigo nodded and walked out into the back yard and hesitated when he saw the Inupiaq talking to a giant dog just like the one Jack had described. He didn't want to embarrass the Indian, so he waited. "I can't save them all, Astay," Kasmali was saying. "Maybe not even the Cramers and the boy." The dog nodded. "You've been a good companion. You'll continue to watch over them, won't you?"

Rodrigo cleared his throat. "Sam used to talk to his dog, too," he said, smiling. "Does your dog answer?"

Kasmali looked at him for a moment. "Again this Sam," he answered. "Jack Cramer claims he was a changeling, but that is irrational. Do you believe there are such beings on your planet?"

Rodrigo smiled. "As a matter of fact I do. Not that I've seen any, but I've heard Sam's voice as he recorded his stories about his time here. Jack claims you're one too."

"You're Dr. Rodrigo De La Cruz," Kasmali said, ignoring Rodrigo's comment. "Jack Cramer said you wanted to talk to me. I'm called Chief Kasmali."

"You're something else too, according to Jack," Rodrigo said. "But maybe he's imagining things. But then again, I was bred by the Chumash not to shut my mind to the unusual. Are you really a changeling?"

Kasmali shrugged. "Do I have to prove it?" he asked.

"Not really," Rodrigo answered. "I believe Sam was a changeling, and I'm willing to concede that you're one too. I also believe you know about some disaster that's coming." Again he hesitated. "I once knew a shaman who sensed things. Have you?"

"I see things," Kasmali answered. "And I've told others about them, including six of your scientists recently. I know rather than sense that a great earthquake is coming."

Rodrigo was intrigued. "You're certain?" he asked.

Kasmali nodded. "I see you have doubts. Perhaps I really must prove myself to you. Come with me." He led him behind the house, the dog following. Once they were there, he stared at Astay and then slowly began to dissolve. The Husky bolted. The next thing Rodrigo saw was a twin of the dog shaking its fur in front of him.

Rodrigo staggered against the house, shutting his eyes and feeling faint. When he finally forced open his eyes, Kasmali was beside him. "I had better find Astay," he said calmly. "He might be on his way to the Arctic Sea."

Rodrigo stood transfixed as Kasmali walked away. After a moment, he came back with the dog. "He was hiding under the porch," he explained. "I've talked to him. He'll be fine now."

Rodrigo, unable to speak, just nodded.

"You asked me how I know," Kasmali said. "Now do you understand?"

Rodrigo just stood, dazed. Finally, though, he stammered, "You *are* a… changeling!"

Kasmali cocked his head. "Why are you so shocked?"

Rodrigo rallied. "Damn it, Chief, if that's who you are! It's one thing to read about you guys, but it's something else to actually see you mutate!" He shook his head. "So you're one of them Sam asked to look over Luke and the rest. If that's true, you're here for Jack and Janie, right?"

Kasmali shrugged. "Again, I know no one called Sam," he answered. "It was but a voice in my head that asked me to protect him. However, for the time being it has been proven to be unnecessary because Jack Cramer and his wife are fine at the moment. I have remained with them instead of returning to my mission, however, because I fear they might be lost in the earthquake." He reached down and scratched the dog's ears. "Astay has been a good companion."

Rodrigo suddenly thought of something. "Were you that doctor who was with Luke when he died?" he asked.

Kasmali again cocked his head. "What doctor? Who is Luke?" he asked.

"Never mind," Rodrigo said, realizing he had the wrong changeling. "This catastrophic earthquake, when will it happen?"

"I cannot see into your future, Rodrigo De La Cruz," he answered. "I only know from the signs that it will be soon."

Rodrigo was getting frustrated. "Can you tell me if there's anything we can do about it? You know, to avoid it?"

Kasmali nodded. "The global warming, as you humans call it, will take years to correct even if you start cleaning up your planet today. What I can tell you is that the earthquake will be the result of the incessant drilling in the Arctic. However, if the drilling stops, the earth may settle." He gazed at Rodrigo. "I'm thinking of taking another trip to Prudhoe Bay to see if it has. Perhaps you should go with me."

"Sure, Chief," Rodrigo said, eagerly grabbing his arm. "The Navy's authorized me to check things out. I've got a week or so. When can we leave?"

Kasmali stared at him. "I've just returned," he finally said. "Besides, *two* men and all the equipment may be a problem. On second thought, it might be better if I just mutate into a bird of some kind and fly there. However, if you really want to go with me, we'll need more dogs. Before I only had six, and it was hard enough keeping them going."

Rodrigo smiled. "No problem," he said. "I'm funded by the U.S. Navy. I'll get your dogs!"

Kasmali sighed. "All right, young man," he said. "If you can do that, which I think will be more difficult than you realize, I'll take you to

Prudhoe Bay. In the meantime, though, you must tell no one who or what I am. Not every human is as open-minded as you."

Rodrigo nodded, grabbed his hand, shook it, and walked back to the café, wondering what he'd gotten himself into.

Jack and Janie were outraged when Rodrigo told them of his plans to go north with Kasmali. "For God's sake, Rodrigo," Janie snorted. "If you two have to go to Prudhoe Bay, why don't you rent a helicopter?"

"A helicopter would get us there fine, Janie," Rodrigo answered. "But I have to see firsthand any damage. It's my job. That's why they sent me here."

"I'll go with you then," Jack said, suddenly thinking it would be a good way to get away from Janie and the cafe.

Rodrigo smiled. "You can't, Jack, though I appreciate it. Kasmali says it'll be tough enough with two men and all the gear. Besides, you and Janie have your café to run. In the meantime, I hope you'll put up with me for a while longer. The chief says I'm going to have trouble finding the extra dogs we'll need."

"At least I can help you with that," Jack answered. "After ten years in this god-forsaken place, I know people."

A week later, early one morning, Rodrigo triumphantly walked into the café hoping to find Kasmali, but the place was empty except for Jack working in the kitchen. After greeting him, Rodrigo asked if he knew where Kasmali was, but Jack shook his head and answered, "No, but sometimes in the mornings he goes to what he calls his asuskwa, some hidden place in a forest. I got the idea it was somewhere outside the town, up in Mineral Creek Heights. It shouldn't be too hard to find. There's not much left up there that's secluded."

Rodrigo thanked him, left the cafe, and started north up Hazelet Avenue until he'd left the town behind. After struggling through the tundra, he saw a decimated row of trees on his left and headed toward them. Breathing heavily because of the climb, he eventually saw Kasmali in a small meadow surrounded by young pines. He seemed to be in a trance.

He didn't know what to do. If Kasmali was praying, he certainly didn't want to interrupt him, so he just sat with his back against one of the trees and waited. Soon he was dozing. He awoke when Kasmali kicked his feet. "You have a habit of taking naps in the middle of the day?" he asked as Rodrigo struggled to his feet.

"I was waiting for you," Rodrigo mumbled, rubbing his eyes. "You were just sitting there."

"Kneeling actually," the chief answered. "I was thinking. You have news for me?"

"I have the dogs," Rodrigo said proudly. "Jack knew a guy outside of town."

Kasmali nodded. "Are they strong?" he asked, sitting down.

"I guess so," Rodrigo answered. "At least Jack thinks so. They sure looked big enough."

"Where are they now, these dogs?"

"In a pen behind Jack's house," Rodrigo answered. "Come on, I'll show you."

As they walked back to town, Kasmali gradually began to dull Jack's enthusiasm. "Even if your dogs are strong enough, they still must be trained as a team. Were they sled dogs?"

"Their owner said they were," Rodrigo answered.

"And Jack said they were capable?"

"Yeah, and he knows where we're going."

Kasmali shrugged. "We'll see," he said. "We've still got a lot to do, and we don't have much time. If we do make the trip, it will have to be before darkness shrouds the Arctic. We only have three months at the outside."

"THREE MONTHS?" Rodrigo cried. "Three months? The captain on the ship told me I only had a week or so before they leave!"

"That's your problem," Kasmali said. "But if you *do* go with me, you'll need at least part of that time to build up your strength. I heard you huffing and puffing when you came up. You'll never make it in the condition you're in now."

As they continued walking, Rodrigo was insulted and determined to show Kasmali up, so as soon as they got to the café he showed Kasmali the dogs and then called the ship to request a launch. It pulled up at the pier an hour later.

Once on the ship, he explained the situation to the captain and was told the cruiser would leave on schedule but could return by winter. An hour later, Rodrigo returned to the pier with a treadmill he'd borrowed from the ship's gym.

The sailors who'd motored the launch then helped him carry the device to the guest room in the Cramers' house. When he had it all set up in the guest room, he stripped down, changed into a sweatsuit, and began warming up. Knowing he had to start slowly, he began jumping jacks but tired quickly. Then, eyeing the treadmill, he hesitated and decided instead to take a brisk walk around the town to get his wind up.

The weather was warm as he wandered up Eagan Drive past the museum, the souvenir shops, and the post office, and then up Fairbanks Road past the library and the civic center. He continued up West Eagan Drive all the way to Mineral Creek and then doubled back, feeling so proud of himself he stopped off at Gus's Bar to have a beer. Surprisingly, Kasmali was there.

"How the dogs doing?" Rodrigo said as he sat on a stool beside him.

Kasmali turned and looked at his outfit. "Just the beginning," he answered and pushed away his beer. He pointed at Gus who was chuckling. "This talkative man just introduced me to what he calls Guinness Stout. I don't like it. It's bitter and it thickens my mind. The dogs? They need training. I'm about to take them out for the first time. You ready?"

"Ready for what?" Rodrigo answered, motioning for Gus to bring him a beer.

Kasmali nodded toward his sweatsuit. "Have you been exercising?" he asked.

"Just started. It's only been a day," Rodrigo answered, feeling a little guilty.

"Do you good," the chief said. "Forget your drink. Let's take a ride. It's a beautiful day." Before Rodrigo could object, Kasmali was out the door. Rodrigo reluctantly got down from the stool and followed him, his muscles aching.

Less than an hour later, they were out on the trail, Kasmali suggesting Rodrigo trot alongside the sled. At first their pace was slow, with the chief training the dogs to work together by yanking the reins from one side to the other. Rodrigo was tiring quickly. Then suddenly Kasmali shouted MUSH!" and the team jumped forward, gathering speed. Rodrigo stopped in horror, but he knew he couldn't show weakness to the chief, so he began jogging after them. It was no good. In seconds, the team was out of sight, though he could hear the chief in the distance shouting, "GEE," "HAW," "LINE OUT," "WHOA," and "MUSH!"

Gasping for air, he gave up and started walking slowly back to town. However, before he reached Mineral Creek, Kasmali and the sled careened up. "WHOA!" the chief yelled as he pulled up a few feet in front of him. Jack stopped and hung his head in embarrassment. "You're going nowhere with me," Kasmali said calmly. "Use one of your fancy flying things."

Rodrigo got angry. "Listen, Chief," he said between his teeth. "You said we've got three months. I called the ship, and they said they'd be back before winter! You just get the dogs trained. I'll be ready!" He stomped away and then began running down Eagan Drive determined to make the arrogant Inupiaq eat his words. When he finally reached the house, he doubled over in pain but gradually pulled himself up and struggled through the door. Gasping, he crawled into the guest room and laid his head on the base of the treadmill. Then, gritting his teeth, he grabbed the base, pulled himself up until he could grab the handle bars, turned the machine on, and first slowly than more rapidly began matching its pace.

Chapter Six: Billy Cole, a Victim

Later that day, a small bi-plane bounced to a stop on the runway of the airport outside of Valdez. Five people got off -- two couples, obviously tourists judging from their brand new parkas and shiny boots, and a pale, thin, middle-aged man who stepped aside from the others to gaze at the snow-packed, glaciered mountains on the horizon. Hearing the couples laughing as they walked briskly to the terminal, he too laughed, muttered, "God's is good," and followed them into the terminal where he found an information booth, picked up a city guide, and walked to the shuttle. When it reached the harbor, he limped off.

Billy Cole had been released from Folsom Prison in California, a few weeks before, after serving six years of a ten-year sentence for manslaughter and kidnapping. But on this day, as he looked out at the harbor, he reveled at his redemption, for in his final months in prison he'd been rehabilitated by finding The Lord.

Looking up in the sky, he silently thanked his god for allowing him his time at Folsom. During most of his first year there, Though he didn't know it at the time, The Lord had made it possible for him to avoid the Mexican, Black, and Aryan gangs by prompting him to stay in his cell with an equally terrified inmate, by sitting with his head down over his plate in the mess hall, and by hugging the walls, his eyes down, when he was forced to go into the exercise yard. But in his God-inspired isolation, nonetheless he began obsessing on Jack Cramer whom he blamed for his imprisonment. Now, however, as he stood on the boardwalk he realized Cramer had only testified to what he'd seen, though it was only half the story. Sure he'd shot the woman, but it only happened because he panicked, seeing the Mexican drug dealers around her. And the kidnapping. He didn't know she was in the car.

Inevitably, however, his anonymity couldn't last. Somehow during his second year – he never found out how – word got out that he was in for killing an Indian woman (which she was). With that, one day the leader of the Aryan Brotherhood came up to him while he was standing against the wall of the exercise yard with his head down. After clapping him on the back and calling him one of their own, the man suggested he was one of them, but he had to undergo an initiation.

The next day, he again came up to him and said they a perfect way to let him prove he could be part of the brotherhood. He could kill a Mexican with whom they'd been having trouble.

Now, even though he'd been jailed for manslaughter, Cole was hardly a killer. He tried to tell them what he'd done was an accident, but they just laughed, thinking he was trying to say he was innocent like the rest of them, So there was little he could do about the situation because he knew to survive he had to live up to their misguided image of him.

Knowing how innocuous he'd been, their leader figured Cole could easily get close to the Mexican in the exercise yard without the guy noticing. Then, just to make sure the Mexican gang wouldn't intervene, he planned a mock fight close by, figuring that would give Cole his chance. It was set up for the next day.

The night before, he shivered uncontrollably, hoping the guy above him didn't notice. He'd never used a knife to hurt anybody and dreaded the idea of sticking it into a body. Even worse, he didn't even know where to stab, though he figured he should try the chest. The whole idea made him want to cry, but he couldn't even do that because his cellmate was probably listening. He couldn't sleep either; and when morning arrived, and he and the others were led into the dining area, he was exhausted and couldn't eat.

A few hours later, the horn blared announcing it was time for his cell block to go to the exercise yard. At first, he thought he could play sick; but when his cell mate said they had to go, he got up, feigned self-confidence, and followed him out of their cell.

Hawk, the leader of the skinheads, watched him walk into the yard and then nodded toward a skinhead standing against the wall under the guard tower. Cole took a deep breath and then slowly began shuffling, his head down, to the wall a few yards away from the Mexican who was standing with his back toward him on the edge of his gang. As usual, no one paid any attention to him except Hawk.

Cole closed his eyes, inched closer, his back scraping against the wall, until he was within arm's reach of the Mexican. Then, pretending he was scratching himself, he fumbled in his underpants and pulled out the shank. Seeing this, Hawk signaled to the skinhead who said something to the Mexican as he brushed past. Within seconds, the brawl began. Knowing he only had a second, Cole lurched toward the Mexican and stabbed at him, but the Mexican was moving so all he did was nick his shirt.

The guy didn't even notice as all hell broke loose when he and his gang fought the skinheads. Quickly the guards moved in and saw Cole shaking as he remained standing against the wall still holding the shank. One grabbed him from behind and wrestled him to the ground, and before he knew it he found himself in solitary on the cold concrete and in total darkness.

For the first few days in solitary, he realized that although the confinement was bad enough, when he got out his troubles would get even worse. He knew the Brotherhood didn't tolerate failures. So he endured his isolation patiently, amazing the guards who clapped him on the back when he was finally released. What they couldn't know was that not only was he reluctant to leave the safety of solitary, he used his time by concentrating on a way to get revenge against Jack Cramer.

Once back in his cell, he waited anxiously for the inescapable retribution by Hawk and the Brotherhood. However, over the next few days, to his surprise they seemed to ignore him as he lay in his bunk in his cell or ate alone in the dining hall or stood motionless against the wall in the exercise yard. Finally, one day he figured he had to find out why they were leaving him alone, so he got up his nerve and approached Hawk who was on his back in the yard working on bar bells. Waiting for an opening, he said, almost in a whisper, "The Mexican moved too fast."

"Doesn't matter," Hawk grunted, setting the bar bells on the stand. "We got him. I guess you didn't know bein' in the hole."

Cole was shocked. "How?" he muttered.

Hawk laughed and pulled him away from those who might hear. "In the fight," he whispered. "I guess he didn't know you tried to stab him, so when he and the greasers rushed us, I cut him and threw the shiv with all the others."

Still standing on the boardwalk looking up at the sky, Cole grinned and whispered, "And then The Lord took my hand." He began thinking of Charley, his cell mate who turned out to be a 'born again' and not the fink he'd thought he was. As time went by, Hawk became his protector, the Brotherhood made certain he had what he needed, and Charley, in for selling drugs, became his friend.

Though years before on the family farm in Oklahoma, Cole had scoffed at his parents' religious fundamentalism; but now, more out of boredom than anything else, he began listening to Charley read aloud from his Bible. And, even though he was barely literate himself, he was amused at Charley's struggle with every big word, so he began taking over some of the reading and found himself enjoying the stories, especially the Old Testament tale of Joshua and the battle of Jericho. The idea of walls tumbling down amused him.

The night before Charley was released, they had their final prayer session; and, with the final "Amen," Charley tearfully presented Cole with his greatest treasure, a small metal cross he'd fashioned from the handles of two spoons bound together by string. From that moment on, Cole became known by the guards, the skinheads, and the other prisoners as "Reverend," and was soon assigned to the prison library where he gave counsel to the other prisoners and read The New Testament. There he discovered Jesus Christ and his message of forgiveness and knew The Lord was on his side.

By the time his parole session was scheduled, he was a new man. When the day finally came, the staid old men on the board, having been told of his conversion, were impressed. On his release, wearing the cross around his neck, he was determined to repudiate his past sins, which included his anger toward Jack Cramer, and was determined that the first step was to find Cramer to ask him for forgiveness.

However, as he stood on the boardwalk, he struggled to think of where to find him. Suddenly he remembered there was another guy who testified at his trial that he'd written about what happened that day in a book. Surprising himself, he remembered his name, Luke Scribner.

Cole couldn't remember the title, but he knew it had something to do with the Chumash Indians, so as soon as he got to Sacramento he sought out a bookstore and, using some of the $521.00 he'd earned at Folsom, he asked a clerk for the section on Native Americans. It took him a while, but then he found a series of books written by Scribner. He sat and leafed through them until he found the one he was looking for. He quickly bought it and took it to a local park. Sitting and marveling at God's gifts in the scenery around him, he skimmed through it frowning at the description of his behavior at the ruins. "I was a different man then," he muttered. Finally he came to the end where Cramer was quoted as saying he was going to move to Alaska.

However, he realized Alaska was a big place, so that didn't help too much. He walked back to the bus station intending to read the book more carefully but was eventually told by a security guard that loitering was not permitted. He went to an information booth and asked for the location of a motel. Then, reluctantly, he used more of his earnings to get a room at the cheapest one he could find.

By now he was starving, so he sought out a fast food restaurant, used more of his earnings to buy a cheeseburger combo, and took it back to the motel. He was feeling great as he sat at a table in a comfortable room, the combo set out in front of him, the book on the bed. "God is good," he muttered as he took his first bite and began slowly reading.

He almost choked on his final bite. There, in the middle of the book, he found what he was looking for. Reading closely, he discovered that as a kid Cramer had worked in the oil fields around Valdez. "That's a start," he murmured.

The next day he went to the airport; and, using more of his earnings, he bought a ticket to Anchorage. Hours later, he found a small plane that had Valdez on its route. He felt as if God was beside him as he buckled himself in.

As Cole looked out at the port of Valdez, his wonder at The Lord's benevolence was reinforced. Though he'd spent some time in Southern California, even on the coast in Santa Barbara, he hadn't bothered noticing the sea. Back then, he had other things on his mind. But now in his 'born again' state, he marveled at the scene, the huge ships oblivious to the waves, and the sky above him that manifested The Lord. He began walking down the street trying to take in all the wonders around him until he saw a bar that looked inviting. He went in, intending to ask if anyone knew Jack Cramer.

Smiling, he pushed his way through the crowd until he found an empty stool at the very end of the bar. Continuing to smile vacuously, he patiently waited for the bartender, a crusty, long-bearded man, to come over. And as he sat he looked at the crowd and felt at home. Many, you see, reminded him of the oil workers from his home in Oklahoma in their dark soiled outfits and oil stained boots. The bartender finally came up to him. "What's your pleasure, stranger," he asked.

Cole was feeling good. "I'm full of The Lord, my friend," he answered, giving the man a toothless smile. "I think I'll have whiskey, Jack Daniels."

"Full of The Lord are you?" the bartender growled. "You one of those 'born agins'?"

Cole continued to smile. "Yup," he answered. "And the world is a wonderful place."

"Shit!" the bartender barked. "You're either drunk or crazy. What the hell are you smiling about? Do you think I'm funny?"

"No, no, not at all," Cole answered, continuing to smile. "I'm just feeling the spirit."

"You got that right, you asshole, full of spirits like cheap wine. I've had trouble with your kind before with your god-damned proselytizing! Get out of here before I throw you out!"

Cole's smile wilted. "I'll go," he said. "I don't want any trouble, but could you just tell me if you know a Jack Cramer? He's a friend of mine."

"I doubt that, but he runs the Mexican café down the way," Gus growled. "Now get out of here!"

Cole pushed his way through the crowd and out the swinging doors, his hopes gone for a drink to bolster his courage. He fingered the cross around his neck, said, "Thank the Lord!" and headed for the café. However, as he stood outside it, he realized he didn't know how to approach Cramer. Finally he decided just to go in and get something to eat, but he remembered he'd already used up almost all the money he'd brought with him from Folsom. He walked away, disgusted.

One thing he'd noticed about this town – it had plenty of liquor stores. Before long, he was sitting under the pier looking at the rocks still stained by the oil spillage from some years before, sipping from a bottle of cheap wine wrapped in a paper bag, and occasionally looking out at the ships in the harbor. Then, wondering how much money he had left, he checked his wallet and discovered he was down to less than $10.00. "I've gotta start to save," he muttered; and decided he'd slept in worse places than under a pier. It had been a long day, and the sunset soon lulled him asleep.

Billy Cole had spent his life being a victim. Later that night, Charles Murray was walking under the pier looking for things the tourists might have lost. When he saw Cole, at first he assumed he was just another drunk sleeping it off, so he sneered and began to walk past him. But, deciding the guy might have some cash on him, he reached down and began to go through his pockets.

Dazed, Cole woke up; and thinking he was back in Folsom, he grabbed Charles by the leg, knocking him over, and pulled out a shank Hawk had given him the night before he left Folsom. "You'll need this on the outside," he'd said, but Cole just smiled and answered that he had The Lord as his protector. He'd kept it, though, as a souvenir of his days with the Brotherhood.

Still in a drunken stupor, he struggled to get up and saw that his attacker, slipping on the oily rocks, was only a kid. Still holding the shank, he mumbled, "Sorry, Kid. I didn't mean to hurt you," and leaned toward him to help him up.

Charles, perhaps reminded of the abuse he'd taken from other men like this, or perhaps still enraged by Cramer hitting him, leapt forward, screamed, knocked Cole back, and began hitting him as hard as he could, all the time wondering why the guy wasn't fighting back. Finally, panting and using his right hand to balance himself on Cole's chest, he rolled off him and crawled away. It was then that he felt the clammy goo on his hand and shirt. Confused, he turned and looked at the guy. He wasn't moving. Slowly, Charles got on his feet, walked over, looked down in the darkness, and growled, "Get up, Asshole. I didn't hit you that hard."

He didn't move, and Charles grinned. "You'll know better than to mess with me," he said and then kicked him again. Still the guy didn't move, and Charles began to get worried. He reached down to shake the guy and his hand slipped against his chest. He felt something hard. Recoiling, he muttered, "Jesus, he had a knife!"

Wondering if anyone had heard their struggle, he looked into the darkness, listened, and then looked at his hand. "Blood!" he yelped and wiped it on his shirt. Stumbling, he ran from under the pier.

When he almost made it to the boardwalk, suddenly remembering how the fight started, he shuddered, looked around, and started back. When he reached the lifeless body, he closed his eyes and searched again through Cole's pockets, found his wallet, took out the ten dollars, and, noticing something shining on his neck, without really knowing why, ripped it from his neck, and threw the wallet on Cole's chest. He then again staggered out from under the pier.

This time he made it to the boardwalk, snuck by the front of the café, and saw Ricky through the window clearing tables. He became furious.

Eventually he made it to an abandoned house, climbed in a window, threw himself on a mattress, and muttered, "Fuck! I killed him!"

Somehow oblivious to the fact that it was an accident or self-defense, he became convinced he'd be blamed. Whimpering, he huddled in the corner and began thinking of how all his life he'd been hated, beaten, and abused. He thought of his brother. "Why him?" he whined. "Here I am in this crummy shack and he's there! That bitch and her bastard husband stole him away from me!"

Cowering and shaking, he then thought of the body. "Shit!" he whined, "What the shit am I gonna do now?" Again he started blubbering. But, true to his nature, he sat up angrily and began to blame others. "THAT ASSHOLE CRAMER!" he yelled. "IF HE HADN'T THROWN ME OUT, I WOULDN'T HAVE EVEN BEEN THERE!"

Writhing on the mattress, he became convinced it was all Cramer's fault until finally he sat up, determined to get even. He leapt off the mattress, started pacing, but then smiled as he looked down at his bloody shirt. Giggling, he ran over to the corner, reached down into a backpack, and pulled out a butcher knife. "Cramer's," he laughed. He then ran to the window, but stopped, frightened, because he knew to make his plan work he'd have to go back to the body to pull out the knife and then stab it again. After a moment, he got up his courage and wriggled out.

No one was around when he got back to the body, so, shutting his eyes, he felt around on the chest, found the shank, pulled it out, and threw it as far as he could into the bay. Gagging while fingering the bloody wound, he stabbed the body with the butcher knife in the same spot in the chest, ripped a sleeve from his shirt to wipe his fingerprints from the knife, and threw it next to the body. He then stuffed the sleeve between Cole's fingers."Cramer's shirt," he giggled. He ran back to the abandoned house, feeling better about himself. "At least that'll make the bastard squirm," he muttered as he lay shivering on the mattress stroking the cross. Then, feeling the blood still wet on the shirt, he sat up, ripped it off, threw it in the corner, and lay back down, smiling.

Chapter Seven: The Investigation

Later that night, Jack was steaming as he headed for Gus' bar. Janie had begun nagging him again, so when he burst into the bar he was ready for a drink but in no mood for Gus and his chatter. He brusquely asked for a beer and shrugged him off, which surprised Gus enough to growl and go about his business. Much later, he staggered home and was glad to find Janie asleep.

The next day, as he was walking back from wishing Rodrigo and Kasmali off at the edge of town, Ralph Eston, the constable, came up. "Hear about the murder?" he asked as they walked together down the boardwalk.

Jack shook his head. "No," he answered. "We haven't had one in a while. One of the men working the line?"

"A stranger ... at least to most of us. Slim Carter discovered it this morning. At first I thought the old drunk made it up, but he took me to the body. Then, when I went through the guy's papers and saw his name, I remembered something. Did I ever tell you I read that crazy book about some changeling? Good read. It has you in it. But you know that."

"Yeah," Jack answered puzzled by the constable's non-sequitur. "So?"

"There was a guy in that book who caused you a lot of trouble, right? You and Janie?"

"Billy Cole? He got convicted of kidnapping and manslaughter. I think he's in prison in California. What's he got to do with anything?"

Eston shrugged. "I guess he was paroled. He was the guy I found dead this morning under the pier. You know anything about that?"

Jack was stunned. "Shit, Ralph," he said. "I didn't even know he was out. What was he doing up here? I can't say I'm sorry, though. You know who killed him?"

"I'm working on it," the constable answered. "Mind if we talk later? I've gotta do a little asking around."

"Anything I can do to help. You know where to find me," Jack answered, still stunned. Ralph nodded and started walking toward Gus' bar.

Jack headed for the café, found Janie in the kitchen, and told her about Cole's murder. She dropped the pot she'd been holding. "Good Lord, Jack," she exclaimed. "You don't think he was after you, do you?"

"I don't know," he answered, plopping into a chair. "Makes sense though. He was found under the pier. I guess someone tried to rob him." He smiled at her. "Not that I'm sorry, though. He sure had it coming."

She looked daggers at him. "Nobody has that coming, Jack," she said. "Where'd you hear about it?"

"Ralph, the constable. He was asking about that time I had trouble with Cole at the ruins."

Janie staggered back. "He doesn't think you had anything to do with it, does he?" she asked, turning pale.

Jack was surprised. "No, of course not! How could he? I'm no killer," he answered as he got up.

She couldn't help herself. The memory of Jack standing over Cole brandishing a burning log came back to her. "How did Ralph know you knew Cole?" she asked anxiously.

Jack sat back down "He read the book, I guess. At least that's what he said."

"My God, Jack!" she blared. "Then he knows you tried to kill Cole when you found out he'd shot that Marston woman!"

Jack was shocked. "Jesus, I guess that's why he wants to talk with me later. He *does* suspect me!" He jumped up. "I've gotta clear this up, Janie. Ralph's on his way to talk to Gus!" He was out the door before Janie could object.

Jogging all the way, he burst through the swinging doors and saw the place empty except for Gus, who was sweeping the floor. "Hey, Gus," he said. "You seen Ralph?"

Gus stopped his sweeping. "For the love of Christ, can't a man get some work done? First Ralph, then you!" He put his broom down and came over. "What's going on, Jack? Ralph told me about the dead guy."

They sat down. "Yeah, stabbed to death under the pier," Jack answered. "It seems I knew him."

Gus nodded. "So that's why Ralph was asking about you."

"Why me? What'd he want to know?"

"Just if I saw you last night. I said I did. Ralph said you knew the guy. Is that true?"

"Yeah," Jack said abruptly. "But it's just a mixup. I've gotta get back to the café. If you see Ralph again, tell him I want to talk to him." He walked out of the bar leaving Gus shaking his head.

Now, Valdez has its usual gossips; and Gus, being a bartender, was one of the best. Before long, almost everyone knew about the killing and that the constable had talked to Jack about it. Sitting on the periphery of a group of oil workers hoping they'd share their lunch with him, Charles overheard them and chuckled. Then, when they mentioned that they heard Cramer had known the guy, he couldn't believe it. "Shit!" he muttered. "What a break! Now they have to think he did it!" When the men heard him giggling, they just shrugged, thinking he was just being weird again.

Jack and Janie were trying their best to get the food together for their lunch time crowd when Ralph came in the kitchen. Jack twitched when he saw him. "Thank God you're here, Ralph. I've been trying to talk to you. You hungry?"

Janie came over to him. "Hello, Ralph," she said gently. "Have you heard anything about that man who was killed? Jack here thinks you suspect him."

"Too early for anything like that, Mrs. Cramer," he said, taking a chair. "I'm just a retired detective from L.A., but I know better than to jump to conclusions." He looked at Jack. "Relax, Jack," he said, noticing

Jack's nervousness. "From what I know of you, you're no killer. We just have to sort out a few things."

"Like what?" Jack asked quickly. "I'm as eager as you are to get to the bottom of it, Ralph."

"Well," Ralph began. "Doesn't mean much that you knew the victim or, as I read in the book, you had trouble with him. Could simply be coincidence."

"That's exactly what it is," Janie said, interrupting him.

The constable shrugged. "Probably, but then there's Gus. He told me you were at his bar late last night. That so?"

Jack was getting worried. "Yeah," he said. "I went there for a drink after we closed the café."

Ralph nodded. "Okay, but there's also the sleeve of a shirt I found in the victim's hand. Seems people sometimes saw you wearing a shirt like that."

"Lots of people wear that kind of shirt. Besides, mine is around here somewhere," Jack almost shouted.

Again Ralph nodded. "Good, maybe you can find it to show it has both sleeves. But then there's the murder weapon I found next to the body. You missing any knives?"

"I don't think so, Ralph," Jack said quickly. "But we've got a lot of knives around here. Why would you think it's one of ours?"

Ralph shrugged once again. "I don't, necessarily. It's just that it's a butcher knife, that's all. One that people don't usually carry around, one that's mostly used by cooks." He nodded toward the counter beside the refrigerators. "I see one's missing from that butcher block, but you've probably been using it. Right, Janie?"

"Of course," Janie answered, smiling. "We do a lot of chopping. It's around here someplace. I'll find it for you if you want."

"Nah," Ralph said as he got up. "You've got work to do. If you find it, just bring it to the office." He groaned as he stretched his back. "Getting old," he explained. "Now don't you worry, we'll sort this out. Right now, I have to walk around town to see if anyone knows anything. I hope my back holds up."

As soon as she was certain Ralph had left, Janie started shaking. "That knife's been missing for a month, Jack," she managed to say. "It's not here! You didn't take it to do some work in the house, did you?"

He was getting angry. "Jesus, Janie, give me a break! I wouldn't use one of your good knives for something like that." He looked at her. "You don't think Ricky took it, do you?"

She bristled. "Of course not, Jack. What would he do with a butcher knife? Even if he needed a knife, why would he want one so unwieldy? There are other smaller ones around here I would have given him!"

"Do we have any more butcher knives?" Jack asked suddenly.

Janie was close to weeping. "I don't think so, Jack. When I first noticed the knife was missing, I looked. What about the shirt? I haven't seen it on you lately. You know where it is?"

He thought for a moment. "I think the last time I wore it was a few days ago when I got grease on it. I took it off and threw it by the back door. Did you pick it up to wash it?"

"Maybe," Janie answered. "I'll check the hamper. In the meantime, what are we gonna do? Ralph expects us to come up with it and the knife. You didn't do anything stupid, did you, Jack?"

He was staggered. "Jesus, Janie, you don't believe I had anything to do with it, do you? My God, you're my wife, you know me! At least I thought you did."

Weeping now, she placed her hands on his face. "I'm sorry, Jack," she cried. "I know you didn't. It's just that I saw you that time ready to hit Cole with a burning log."

He reached across and took her hand. "That was before, Janie. You've changed me, you know that. Don't cry. We'll sort this mess out. I'll find the knife."

Chapter Eight: Jack, the Prime Suspect

Still lying on a filthy mattress in the abandoned house, his hand fondling the cross in his pocket, Charles remembered every detail of stabbing the bum. "Beat the shit out of him, too" he chuckled. He felt different, older and more confident. "Even if Cramer wiggles his way out of it," he giggled, "there's no way anyone can pin it on me."

Suddenly he sat up, remembering Ricky in the cafe. "Nah, he couldn't have seen me; and even if he did, he won't say anything. He knows better," he muttered. He got up and started pacing, his hatred of Jack Cramer beginning to fester. "The son-of-a-bitch'll get away with it," he muttered. "They love him, and then they'll start asking around about me! Fuck!"

Suddenly he stopped his pacing and smiled. "I've gotta put him there," he chuckled. "What if I tell the cop in town I saw him that night?" Laughing, he jumped out the window and sauntered into town.

Luck was with him. Almost as soon as he came around the corner, he saw the constable talking to a shop owner. He waited patiently until he was noticed and then said politely, "Excuse me, sir. I heard about the murder down by the pier and thought maybe I should talk to you."

Ralph Eston was hardly naive. He'd been through the wars down in South Los Angeles, so he doubted that this skinny pain-in-the-ass kid could tell him anything; but he was one who always did his job, so, deciding he'd better listen, he answered, "Yeah, kid, you know something?"

"Maybe," Charles answered shyly. "It's just that that night I was trying to sleep in the alley over there." He pointed to a space between the shops. "I didn't want to go back to the foster home where I live, you know, and I didn't think anybody would mind. Anyway, I saw a guy run right past me. I didn't think a thing about it until this morning when I heard about the killing."

Eston looked at him for a moment and laughed. "You've got brass, kid. You think I forgot you? You're Charles Murray, and I just took you and your brother up to Anchorage and now I hear the Cramers kicked you out. Jesus, kid, you're on probation so now I have to waste my time by taking you back in!"

This wasn't going at all how Charles had planned. He'd thought he'd just tell his story, name Cramer, and be done with it, but the cop seemed more concerned about him. "I hope not, sir," he said plaintively. "Yeah, Mr. Cramer did tell me to leave and I guess I deserved it by mouthing off. I don't blame him, but now I'm working at the refinery, and as soon as I make enough money, me and my brother are gonna get out of this town."

Ralph nodded, thinking Valdez would probably be a better place without Charles Murray. "Okay, anyway, what did you see?"

"Not much," Charles answered, looking at his feet. "It was dark, you know. Just a big guy running that way." He pointed down the street. "I couldn't see his face. As I said, I didn't think too much about it. I just thought somebody was hurrying to get home."

Ralph nodded again as he looked down the street at the café. "Okay, kid. Juvie'll probably just make you worse, so I'll give you a break. I'll check it out. Just keep your nose clean and stay away from the Cramers."

Charles nodded and walked away, disappointed he hadn't mentioned that the man he saw was Cramer.

Ralph watched him for a moment, shook his head, and went back to his office where he sat at his desk and began to think of the evidence piling up against Jack. "Hard to believe," he muttered. "Why would he do it? It doesn't make sense! Sure, he'd tried to beat Cole over the head before, but that was years ago. Now he has Janie and the café!" He began considering other possibilities. Maybe Cole was just at the wrong place at the wrong time, he began thinking. It could have been a random crime. There's been murders like that before in these frontier towns. Besides, from what he'd read in that book, if Jack did it, Cole had it coming to him. Maybe it was self-defense. He shook his head. "I can't just let it go," he muttered. "If Jack did do it, why didn't he just tell me?" With that, he knew he'd have to bring Jack in for more questioning.

Somehow, Jack and Janie had been able to open the café for the lunch time crowd, though they both had trouble keeping up their usual banter. Ricky, working alongside them, had heard the rumors about Mr. Cramer and noticed he and Mrs. Cramer weren't themselves; but he said nothing and just went about his chores.

When the customers were gone and he was clearing the tables, he saw the constable come in and motion Mr. Cramer over to the side. He couldn't hear what they were saying, but Mr. Cramer suddenly yelled for Mrs. Cramer who came running out of the kitchen. The next thing he knew, the constable led Mr. Cramer out of the café. Mrs. Cramer suddenly burst out of the dining room, heading, he thought, for the house. He wanted to go to her, but he didn't. He just continued cleaning up.

Ralph walked Jack to his office as inconspicuously as he could. Once there, he asked him to sit and then went behind his desk, also sat, and pulled out a large pad from the top drawer. "We've got a mess on our hands, Jack," he said.

"I didn't do it! You know that!" Jack said angrily.

"I want to believe you, Jack, but let me tell you what I know. First of all, have you found your butcher knife or your shirt?"

"You won't believe this, Ralph," Jack answered quickly. "We've looked everywhere, but we can't find them! The only thing we can think of is that a bum stole the shirt from the back porch and that the knife somehow got thrown away."

Ralph looked at him for a moment, shrugged, and then said, "Maybe they'll show up, but what about you knowing the victim and once even tried to kill him? That is, if the book isn't just fiction."

Jack leaned forward. "I wouldn't have killed him that time, Ralph. I just lost my temper when Cole told me he killed a friend of mine."

Ralph nodded. "Gus said that last night you were in the bar in a nasty mood. What was that all about?"

"Janie and I had a fight, that's all. Ask her. She'll tell you."

"So I take it you went right home after that? Did Janie see you come in?"

"I don't think so. She was asleep. Long day, you know. MY GOD!" he yelled. "YOU REALLY THINK I DID IT!"

Ralph reached across and patted him on the shoulder. "Calm down, Jack," he said. "These things are all circumstantial. Just one more thing, I've got an eye-witness who said he saw a guy about your size running toward the café late last night. What do you think?"

"What do *I* think?" Jack answered angrily. "I think it's all bullshit! I didn't even know Cole was in town, for God's sake, and all the rest I've explained!"

"Relax, Jack. I'm just trying to put things together." He put his notes in his desk. "Get back to Janie. She might be worried."

As Jack walked back to the café, he noticed the shopkeepers with whom he had often gossiped staring at him. He lowered his head and quickened his step.

Meanwhile, Janie suddenly thought of Ricky being left alone to clean up, so she braced herself and went back into the café. Her heart went out to the boy when she saw him at the sink, dishes and pots and pans all around him. "I'm sorry for leaving you with such a mess, Ricky," she said as she came up to him. "You're such a good boy, I don't know what I'd do without you."

He nodded and began filling the tub with soapy water. "Here," she said, gently pushing him away from the sink. "I'll wash and you dry."

For the next few minutes, they worked silently; but when all the dishes and pots were washed, wiped, and put away, he suddenly said, leaning toward her, "I hope Mr. Cramer's okay."

She smiled. "It's just a misunderstanding, Ricky. Jack'll sort it out," she answered, wanting to hug him. "Hey, I'll tell you what. We have some time. How about working on your story?"

Without answering, he walked over to a cabinet at the rear of the kitchen, took out his notepad, and brought it to her. "Wonderful," she said. "Let's work in the dining room." They walked in and sat next to each other. He opened the pad to where he'd left off, and she leaned over, her shoulder touching his. He smiled.

Jack came in, sat opposite to them, looked at the boy, and gestured toward the kitchen to Janie. "It's all right, Jack, Ricky's one of the family. Tell me what happened," Janie said quietly.

Knitting his brow, Jack hesitated and then shrugged. "Okay, if you say so. It seems I'm the prime suspect, Janie."

Janie jumped up, knocking Ricky a few feet away. "NO!" she screamed. "WHY?"

Jack, seeing her looming over him, shook his head dejectedly. "I don't think Ralph is convinced, though; but I'll tell you this: if anyone else saw the evidence against me, they'd lock me up without a thought."

Janie sat back down, putting her arm around Ricky. "The big thing is a butcher knife, Ricky," she said softly. "The man was killed by one, and we can't find ours. Have you seen it?"

Ricky quickly shook his head, but his heart was racing as he thought of Charles. However, before he could say anything, Mr. Cramer started listing off the evidence against him. "It's not just the knife, Janie. Ralph said he had a sleeve of a shirt Cole was clutching and that people had seen me wearing one like it! Then Gus told him I was at the bar that night. You remember? We had a fight, and when I got home you were asleep, so I have no proof I was here after that."

He paused, his head in his hands. Ricky thought he knew him, but now he wasn't sure. "Everybody wears shirts, Mr. Cramer," he said, trying to see what was so important about it.

"We can't find mine, Ricky," he muttered and then looked up. "You haven't seen it, have you? It was that old red-plaid shirt I used to wear."

Ricky's head swam as he remembered Charles in a shirt just like the one Mr. Cramer was describing. Janie, noticing him shiver under her arm, said, "What's the matter, Ricky? You remember something?"

Unwilling to get his brother into more trouble, Ricky muttered, "No, I just feel cold. I've seen that kind of shirt lots of times."

Janie nodded and turned to Jack. "I'm so sorry, Jack. That night I was exhausted from the argument and the tough day. You want me to lie about seeing you come home?"

"NO!" he yelled. "The truth will come out without that. There's one more thing. Supposedly someone saw a man who looked like me running down the street late that night."

Janie became excited. "The killer!" she blared. "Then Ralph knows there was someone else!"

"Or me," Jack answered, lowering his head. "You forget that Ralph read the book and knows I almost killed Cole that time. It's ironic. I remember Cole's trial when the prosecutor went on and on about how he had the means, the motive, and the opportunity to kill Cleo Marston and kidnap you. Ironic, huh? Here I'm in the same boat."

Ricky felt ready to cry as Mrs. Cramer rose and hugged Mr. Cramer from behind. He knew he should say something about how Charles hated Mr. Cramer and his suspicion about the knife and the shirt, but he couldn't. Charles, after all, was his brother; and besides, although he could be mean, he couldn't be bad enough not to tell them he had the knife. So he got up, put his tablet away, walked out the door, and then jumped when he saw the constable walking down the street toward him. Hoping he hadn't noticed him, Ricky ran behind the café and went to find Charles.

Chapter Nine: Prudhoe Bay

Skeptical about Rodrigo's stamina, Chief Kasmali chose to take the Richardson Highway out of Valdez to Fairbanks where they could pick up the Dalton Highway north, though it took them away from the coast where he knew most of the damage was being done due to the global warming. His goal again was Prudhoe Bay, 800 miles away on Alaska's North Slope where he could check the latest effects of the oil drilling; and the Dalton Highway was the straightest route and easiest for the Spaniard, though it was narrow with soft shoulders, high embankments, and steep hills.

Although on his previous trips Kasmali had not needed to sleep and was able to subsist on jerky, he allowed Rodrigo to load the sled with blankets, a heavy sleeping bag, a tarpaulin, and dried foods. When Rodrigo was done, however, it became clear to him that he wouldn't be able to ride part of the way in the sled, which made him wonder again if he had bitten off more than he could chew.

Once they made it to the Dalton Highway, Kasmali realized that the huge trucks traveling to or from Prudhoe Bay were a hazard, so they traveled far enough away from the highway to avoid the loose gravel spat from their tires. Since it was early July, the weather was warm.

Kasmali figured it would take them no more than a week or so to make the trip; but he hadn't counted on Rodrigo constantly stopping to view the moose, the caribou, the muskoxen, or the incredible vistas: the Yukon River, Finger Mountain, the Brooks Range, and the glaciers. He even convinced Kasmali to camp overnight at places like Coldfoot, one of the original gold rush towns. Amused but impatient, at night Kasmali lay next to the sled with a single blanket and watched as Rodrigo arranged the tarp over their heads, spread his sleeping bag over blankets on the ground, and then wriggled in. But Rodrigo couldn't sleep, so he decided to satisfy his curiosity about Kasmali. "Does your species ever die?" he asked, hoping Kasmali would for once be forthcoming.

"I am not allowed to speak of my origin. I have told you that," Kasmali muttered. "However, your question seems innocent enough. Your word 'die' has no meaning to my species. Eventually we simply mutate into another form."

"Reincarnation," Rodrigo said, smiling to himself. "Some humans believe that happens to us too. I hope so. I think I'd want to be an eagle."

Kasmali smiled. "Good choice," he muttered again. "They can take care of themselves, but you'd have to avoid the humans who'd either want to trap you or shoot you down."

Rodrigo thought about that for a while, but then asked, "Do you procreate?"

Sitting up, Kasmali looked at him. "Like you and animals?" he answered. "Hardly. For one thing, there is no need. I told you we mutate. As such, we are constantly reborn."

At that point, Rodrigo realized he was out of his depth. He turned over and tried to sleep.

After a few more stops, they eventually made it to Deadhorse, the industrial camp that supports the Prudhoe Bay oilfield. It was the end of the highway so they headed back country to the North Slope. As they progressed, Kasmali became increasingly impressed by Rodrigo's perseverance.

During most of their trip, the sky was clear and the temperature mild; but as they neared the Brooks Range, it became colder so they put on their cold weather gear.

One morning they discovered that four of their twelve dogs had disappeared overnight; and as they traveled further north, the remaining eight became more and more fractious, sniffing the air and pricking their ears at every sound. Rodrigo, feeling guilty because he'd provided most of the dogs, apologized to the chief; but Kasmali simply nodded and frightened him by saying that the dogs sensed what was coming. From that point on, at night they tied the remaining dogs to the sled.

At one point, as they traveled across a valley, they had to stop because of a massive migration of caribou. Rodrigo grabbed his camera and began taking pictures. "They're moving east," Kasmali commented. "They also sense the changes. They normally head west this time of year. Have you noticed the absence of birds?"

After camping one night along the foothills, the next morning they discovered that two more dogs had broken loose and disappeared, which was more than enough for Rodrigo. "We can't make it with only six dogs," he complained.

Kasmali frowned. "We will," he answered. "It's not far now to the bay."

Rodrigo, now convinced he would never see civilization again, knew he had no choice but to rely on Kasmali, so together they helped the six dogs pull the sled up and over the mountains. When they finally made it to the last one and reached the top, Rodrigo, exhausted, fell to his knees, crawled to the crest, looked over, and saw in the distance a huge, ugly black slab in a bay surrounded by permafrost. He rose, excited, and limped to the sled, pulled out his binoculars, and struggled back to the crest. "THAT'S ANWR!" he yelled to Kasmali as he focused on the site.

Kasmali shrugged and answered, "I know not what you humans call it, but that and the other constructions on this coast are the reason your Earth is rebelling."

Rodrigo just nodded as he continued to examine the slab but then frowned as he focused on the massive blue derrick in its center, several small and large buildings around it, a large crane, oil storage tanks everywhere, and trucks scattered on the periphery. A huge pipe led southeast. He eventually set down his binoculars, grabbed his camera, and began to take photographs.

Kasmali shook his head as he too looked down.

"It's a major source of oil for the lower forty-eight states," Rodrigo muttered as he snapped away. "But you may be right. Anyway, it's certainly grotesque."

Kasmali shrugged. "I have attempted to warn your scientists of its danger to the environment. Now I think it is up to you. Come, I want to go down into the bay to see if there is any change since I was last here."

"I'm ready," Rodrigo answered, now also curious about the effect the site may have had on the bay. He walked back to the sled and the dogs that were lying in the snow, and slowly he and Kasmali began pulling them and the sled along the crest. Suddenly the sled wobbled as it came to a patch of black ice. "IT'S SLIPPING!" Rodrigo yelled as the sled began to pick up speed. Fortunately he and Kasmali managed to stop it.

The mountain then began to shudder. Terrified, the dogs bolted down the slope, knocking Rodrigo into the snow. Kasmali, his hand caught in the lead line, was dragged behind the dogs down over the snow and rocks. Horrified, Rodrigo watched as the chief finally broke free from the lines and rolled to the edge of the bay looking as if he were dead. The dogs, still attached to the sled, struggled to get their footing and then stopped on the permafrost about twenty feet away.

Rodrigo tumbled down the mountain, thinking Kasmali had to be injured if not dead; but as he finally reached him, he heard him mutter, "I enjoyed that."

Rodrigo, bruised and battered, stood speechless. Kasmali then noticed the team on the ice. "GET THE DOGS!" he yelled.

Rodrigo stared at him but then began walking cautiously out on the permafrost toward the six dogs and the battered sled. When he got to them, he grabbed the lead lines and began slowly pulling them and the sled back to the base of the mountain where Kasmali was sitting massaging his ankle and looking confused. "I'll be fine," he said. "How are the dogs?"

"Docile," Rodrigo replied, looking anxiously at him. "They seem frightened, which makes sense. That was more than a tremor. Let me help you into what's left of the sled. Let's hope the dogs and I can pull you back up the mountain. We gotta get out of here."

Seeing the condition of the sled, Kasmali shook his head. "Not yet," he answered. "It would be impossible for you and the frightened dogs, especially since I cannot help. We are better off staying where we are until I either heal myself or mutate. We should be safe here."

Rodrigo collapsed, totally exhausted. The dogs lay beside him. A few minutes later, he got up to check on Kasmali; but just as he got to him, he heard a roar and felt the ground shake again. He gasped and grabbed his camera, tried to focus on the oil drilling platform, and began to snap repeatedly. "My GOD!" he yelled. "THE PLATORM MOVED!"

Kasmali hobbled up, trying to balance himself against the trembling ground, and grabbed the binoculars from his neck. "It's only the beginning," he muttered. Rodrigo stared at the huge, four-hundred yard square platform half a mile away. Suddenly, he gasped and fell backward.

"WHAT?" Kasmali shouted. Without answering, Rodrigo jumped up and again began furiously snapping picture after picture. "THE TRUCKS!" he yelled. "THERE ON THE SIDE OF THE PLATFORM! THEY DISAPPEARED! LOOK!"

"It has lost a piece," Kasmali answered as he braced himself and scanned the permafrost. "The trucks must have fallen through."

Rodrigo shuddered. "I have to see," he said as he continued to snap pictures of men running from buildings toward the split in the ice. He shouted "STOP!" as loudly as he could, but of course they couldn't hear. Then a second roar sounded and another tremor knocked him and Kasmali down. The dogs scattered with the sled. When he was able to regain his feet, he canned the platform with the binoculars that he'd grabbed from Kasmali. "THE MEN!" he screamed, "THEY'RE GONE TOO!"

Kasmali grabbed back the binoculars back. Rodrigo, holding on to the ground, cried, "WHAT'LL WE DO, CHIEF?"

At first, Kasmali didn't answer as he looked at the platform. "Another slab broke off," he finally said. "It must have taken the men with it." He looked at Rodrigo. "There is nothing we can do," he said. "Let's wait to see if the rest goes."

For the rest of the day they took turns scanning the mountain waiting for an avalanche and the platform that had lost its eastern section, but all was eerily quiet. "Thank God I was able to photograph it," Rodrigo finally said. "Now maybe people will start to believe us. God, I wish we had a radio!"

Kasmali shrugged. "We have to find a safer place," he answered. "We are right under the mountain. Take one of the dogs and do some scouting."

Rodrigo looked at him, wondering if he was serious; but the chief just pointed west. Reluctantly, he made his way to the trembling dogs, grabbed the lead attached to one of them, and began hiking away.

Watching him struggle around a bend, Kasmali was tempted to mutate into an animal strong enough to pull them up the mountain, but he knew his mission was to witness the changes in the North and that the most effective way to do it was as a human who would feel the changes. So, keeping his eyes on where he last saw Rodrigo, he crawled to the bed of the sled, rested against it, and waited.

Hours later, Rodrigo returned. He was frowning. "Damn," he said as he came up, "I found a pass we could probably handle, but it was cut out of the mountainside for the pipeline that's now shattered. Oil is everywhere!"

"The oil, is it still coming out?" Kasmali asked.

Rodrigo shook his head. "No, thank God. I guess they had the sense to turn it off, but the damage is done. The bay will be polluted for years. Besides, there's no way we can get up that pass with all that slop, and it's the only one I could find. What are you doing?"

"Thinking," Kasmali answered. "Give me a moment." He looked up into the sky, hesitated, and then said, "You are right. No land animal would be able to move in a substance like oil, but a creature from the sky could fly above it." He pointed up.

Looking to where he was pointing, Rodrigo saw a bird. "Are you talking about that eagle?" he asked, incredulous. "No way it could pull me, you, the sled, and the dogs up that pass!"

"How far up did the oil spread?"

"I don't know, about half way, I guess."

"I hope you and the dogs can manage to pull the sled to this pass," Kasmali said as he struggled to get up. "How far away is it?"

Rodrigo shrugged, wondering what Kasmali had in mind. "About a mile, I guess," he muttered.

Pacing to test his ankle, Kasmali said, "I don't understand this weakness. It shouldn't happen. I imagine it means I must forego my mission for a while, but at least I can get you back to your town."

Rodrigo looked at him and answered, "How, for God's sake? You can hardly walk!"

Kasmali attempted to smile. "You've forgotten who I am," he said. "Remember the eagle?"

"The eagle?" Rodrigo snorted. "If you're thinking of mutating into an eagle, forget it."

Kasmali just smiled. "Get the sled and the dogs," he said.

Rodrigo was skeptical, but he did as Kasmali asked. Soon he began helping the dogs pull the sled down the shore, Kasmali limping beside it.

"It is good," Kasmali said as they reached the pass. Rodrigo wondered what he could possibly be feeling glad about. All he saw was oil.

"Now you can see what I was talking about," he said. "How the hell can an eagle pull us halfway up that pass through all that gunk?"

"The gunk as you call it is still slick," Kasmali answered, still looking up. "Besides, I'm not envisioning an ordinary eagle."

Before Rodrigo could reply, Kasmali raised his arms into the air, began to melt, and then grew larger and larger. Rodrigo gawked as he suddenly saw a huge bird pacing in front of him. It then stood motionless for a moment and then pecked at its claws.

Rodrigo, coming out of his stupor, suddenly understood. He rushed to the sled, grabbed the lines, and tied them to the huge eagle's legs. He then yelled for the dogs to get in the broken sled.

After looking back at them, the eagle then spread its wings that seemed to have a wingspan that spread from one side of the pass to the other, and began to lift the sled from the ground. Rodrigo jumped in.

At first they moved slowly. The eagle then swept into the sky, sliding the sled and its occupants easily over the oil slick. Within minutes, they were up the pass and on to the crest. The eagle then landed and waited. Again Rodrigo understood. He untied the traces and this time turned his back. After a few moments, he felt a hand on his shoulder.

"Are you all right?" Kasmali asked. "I see we still have the dogs."

"I'm fine," Rodrigo answered, shaking his head. "But I'll never get used to you changing like that."

Kasmali again was surprised when he heard himself chuckling. "Well," he said, "Now I'm only an old, crippled Inupiaq chief again, and we have a long way to go to get you home."

Rodrigo looked down the mountain. "The dogs can pull you now," he said. "It should be easy for them through the snow."

"And you?" Kasmali asked.

Rodrigo smiled. "For once maybe I can be useful because by now I think I can guide the team. Get in what's left of the sled."

Kasmali grinned and did as he was told. Rodrigo then took the lines and began to lead the team off the crest. Inevitably, however, as the slope became steeper, he lost control. The team slipped, tore the lines from his hands, and began chaotically pulling the broken sled wildly down the mountain, with Kasmali bouncing inside.

Rodrigo began charging after them, but the slope was too steep. Within a few strides, he fell and began to roll, careening over snow and rocks. Kasmali, turning and seeing his young friend in trouble behind him, began shouting, "WHOA! WHOA!" but the dogs were too much in a panic to heed him. He finally was able to grab one of the lines, tug violently, and forced them to stop on a plateau.

He could no longer see Rodrigo. Knowing he had to go back to help him, his first thought was to mutate into one of the dogs; but he realized that if he did, he would be of no good to Rodrigo, so he struggled out of the blankets Rodrigo had thrown around him, looked for a patch of snow, threw himself from the sled, and began slowly crawling back up the mountain. With each movement, he marveled at the frailty he was experiencing as a human.

Eventually, he found Rodrigo alive but moaning in a snow drift. "Rodrigo, are you all right? Can you walk?" he asked as he lay next to him.

Rodrigo grimaced. "My leg," he answered. "I think it's broken. What are we going to do now?"

Kasmali looked down the mountain at the dogs pulling the broken sled further and further away. "Not again," he said.

Looking across at Kasmali beside him in the snow, the sled gone, Rodrigo seemed to understand. "A horse would be great," he muttered.

Kasmali struggled to his feet. "A horse would be useless in this environment," he answered. "Be calm. You've forgotten the eagle. I can mutate back into it and fly us back, though as I soar higher the cold may be a problem for you."

"Just do it," Rodrigo groaned.

"First, wrap your parka tightly around your torso and tie your hood. The parka and your insulated clothing should cushion my talons. I only hope you'll be warm enough. When you're ready, lie with your feet forward and hold on to my legs after I retract them."

Rodrigo nodded, did as he was told, and waited, lying in the snow. Within moments, he felt himself lifted into the air.

Mile after mile, over mountains and rivers, they flew. After an hour or so, Rodrigo lost consciousness.

Chapter Ten: The Constable

Six years before arriving in Valdez, Ralph Eston had been one of L. A.'s finest as a detective in "The City of the Angels," a characterization of the city he and his partner had found ludicrous. He was tough but fair, so they said, and especially knowledgeable when it came to the Hispanic gangs. He was well on his way to becoming a lieutenant when it happened.

It was nothing more than a routine hit-and-run; but when he and his partner chased the car and finally rammed it, a guy jumped out and reached into his pocket. Eston shot him. Later, when the Internal Affairs questioned him, Ralph said he was certain the guy had a gun. Unfortunately they never found it.

Eventually, after a lengthy and contentious investigation, he was exonerated but demoted and put on desk duty. He never was the same after that; and having been divorced some years before and having lost any connection with his one daughter, he decided to leave Los Angeles behind and find somewhere to start over. He immediately considered Alaska, the most remote place he could think of. So, without a second thought, he moved to Valdez and luckily discovered the town was in need of what they called a constable.

During his six years as the only police presence in Valdez, he'd investigated a few murders; but they'd been cut and dry, mainly drunken oil workers killing each other or their wives. However, this one bothered him mainly because it seemed so unlike the Cramer he knew.

Sitting at his desk, he again considered the facts. Cramer certainly had a motive, he thought, but why the hell was Cole here in the first place? Then there was the butcher knife. More and more, it looked like it came from his café, especially since neither Jack nor Janie had come up with theirs.

He stared out his front window at the sun just rising and tried to concentrate. Cramer's no idiot. Why would he leave the murder weapon behind? He could've easily thrown it in the bay. Yeah, the scrap of shirt's a problem, but Cramer's right.

Lots of guys wore that kind of shirt. Could be anyone, but what about Jack being upset that night, as Gus said? If Jack is to be believed, he was mad at Janie. Most husbands get mad at their wives sometimes.

He got up and began muttering. "But who was the guy the kid saw? Maybe Cramer, but who knows?" He stood by the window and tried to think of other possibilities. "Robbery, some stranger who came upon Cole and tried to rob him?" He shook his head. "Maybe." Suddenly he remembered the book.

He walked into the back of his office to his living quarters, began searching through the book shelves, and found it next to his Dirk Pitt novels. Then, sitting on his bed, he skimmed through the stuff irrelevant to him and concentrated on Jack's obsession with the woman named Cleo Marston. He kept reading and eventually came to the chapter that dealt with Jack and Janie and Cole at the ruins of an ancient village. "I'll be damned," he muttered, putting the book down. "So he met Janie by keeping her from being mauled by some firefighter!"

He began to talk aloud, trying to understand. "So when Cole confessed to killing the Marston woman, Jack flipped out; but he could've just been trying to scare him."

He began considering the problems of Jack wanting to kill Cole now. He'd obviously gotten over the death of the Marston dame. Shit, he and Janie may have their squabbles, but they seem to be happy. Why would he kill Cole years later? He got up, grabbed the book, and headed back to his office, hoping he was right in thinking maybe Jack was being set up.

He'd just settled into his chair behind his desk when Charles Murray walked in, his head down. "What can I do for you now?" he asked, angry that the kid was bothering him again.

"I'm sorry to interrupt you, Sir," Charles answered, again meekly. "It's just that I remembered something. You know, in finding out who killed that guy."

Ralph sat up. "What now?" he asked impatiently.

"I don't want to get anybody in trouble," Charles answered, fingering the cross in his pocket. "It's just that I feel guilty not telling you before. I just remembered it this morning."

Ralph was getting angry. "Remembered what?" he barked.

Charles was looking down at his feet. "The dog," he answered.

"What dog?"

"The big white dog the guy had with him when he ran past me," Charles blurted out. "The guy had a big dog."

Suddenly Ralph became curious. "Why didn't you tell me this before?" he asked.

"I told you, I forgot. I didn't think of it until this morning, I'm only trying to help, Sir."

Ralph nodded. "That's good, kid," he said, calming down. "It's good you told me. Thanks, and stick around, will you? I may need you later."

It would have never occurred to Ralph that Charles, who after all was just a kid, could harbor such hatred toward someone who'd only hit him once, nor could he have known that in his muddled mind, Charles pictured Jack Cramer as another of a series of men who'd beaten and abused him in the foster homes. To Charles, getting back at Cramer was something he deserved. So as he left the constable, Charles was glad he'd finally got even. Moreover, killing Cole under the pier made him feel fearless.

He'd done what he wanted, and the cop took the bait, so he giggled as he headed for the refinery where he hoped he could pick up some small jobs. He heard footsteps behind him. Turning anxiously, he saw Ricky running toward him.

"CHARLES!" Ricky yelled. "I'VE BEEN LOOKING ALL OVER FOR YOU!" Charles sneered as his brother ran up to him.

"Calm down, Ricky," he said. "I'm right here. How you been?"

"Okay," Ricky answered, breathing heavily. "But I haven't seen you at all. Where you been?"

Charles shrugged. "Around," he answered. "Don't worry about me. Worry about yourself, working for those fucking Cramers." He started walking away.

"Wait," Ricky said. "I want to ask you something."

Angrily, Charles grabbed him. "You always get so excited, kid," he said. "I've always been there for you. What you want? You finally wanna get away from that bastard and the conniving bitch?"

Ricky broke away. "Nah, nothin' like that. I know he hit you, but they're really not so bad, and I think Mr. Cramer's in trouble. I think the constable thinks he's a murderer!"

Charles pretended to be surprised. "Why does he think that?" he asked, lifting his eye brows.

"I don't know," Ricky answered. "But he keeps asking about a butcher knife he says the bad guy used. He thinks it came from the café. Do you remember how you played a lot with their knife a lot before Mr. Cramer got mad at you? Do you know where it is now? The Cramers have to find it to show it wasn't their knife that killed the guy!"

"Why do you care about them, Ricky?" Charles snarled. "You gotta know you're just their slave. What do you care if Cramer is put in the slammer?"

Ricky was about to cry. "I know he hit you, Charles, but you did call him a bad name. Will you help him? Do you know where the butcher knife is?"

"How the hell should I know anything about some fucking knife?" Charles snapped. "I haven't been in that lousy café for days!"

Watching Charles begin to walk away, Ricky remembered seeing Charles wearing a red-plaid shirt just like Mr. Cramer's and was also about to ask him about it, but he didn't because Charles was in one of his moods and would probably have yelled at him again.

Ralph, still in his office, was becoming skeptical about Charles, a kid who'd been nothing but trouble all his life. "Why the hell would that little shit suddenly turn into such a good citizen?" he muttered. He began considering what he'd said. His story made sense at least because he'd sometimes seen him wandering around town late at night, he thought. He could have seen someone, but it didn't necessarily mean it was Cramer. The dog? Maybe. The problem was, if there's a trial, the kid would be a lousy witness. Everybody knew he was a loser.

He decided to phone Folsom Prison to see what they could tell him about the victim, Billy Cole. After going through channels, he eventually got hold of the warden who told him, among other things, that Cole had been a model prisoner in his last year there, that he'd become a 'born-again,' and that when he left, he even had a Bible and a cross around his neck. He added that he'd been given early parole due to good behavior. When Ralph mentioned that Cole had been murdered in Valdez, though, the warden was surprised. "Stupid move on his part, Constable. He knew the terms of his parole, one being that he wasn't to leave California. What the hell was he doing in Alaska?"

Ralph said he didn't know and later hung up. Remembering what he'd read in the book, next he called the police department at Fort Bragg to find out what they remembered about the murder of the Marston woman. After being on a holding line for what seemed like an hour, he was told that at first they thought Jack Cramer had something to do with it but weren't that surprised when Cole was convicted because of his suspicious behavior and the testimonies of Cramer, his girlfriend, and the guy who later wrote the book.

He then called the prosecuting attorney's office in Bakersfield to ask about the trial and was told Cole had confessed and was found guilty in one of their speediest trials. When Ralph asked if Cole had done or said anything to threaten Jack Cramer, the attorney just laughed. "You had to know Billy Cole," he said. "He isn't the type to threaten anyone."

When Ralph told him Cole had been murdered, the attorney said he wasn't surprised. "The guy was a patsy, Constable," he said. "He was a sitting duck for anybody. As I hear it, the only way he got through his time in prison was by acting as a punching bag for the skinheads, if you know what I mean." He started laughing. "I did hear he became really religious, though. Probably an act."

Why the hell did he come to Valdez? Ralph wondered after hanging up. If it wasn't an act and he'd become a 'born-again,' why would he ever want to remind himself of his crime by seeing Cramer again?

Suddenly it occurred to him. Maybe being a 'born again,' he wanted to make amends. The warden said he had a Bible with him and a cross around his neck when he was released! Maybe he wanted Cramer to forgive him. It was far-fetched, but possible. He shrugged and began to think of what Charles had said. "Damn!" he yelled. "Who else has a big white dog?"

He shook his head. Why would the kid lie? he wondered. I know he had trouble with Cramer, but to accuse him of killing someone? For Christ's sake, he's just a kid! Then he thought of the gangs in L.A. "Hell!" he muttered. "Most of them were kids too!" He shook his head. "A different world, though." Suddenly he remembered Charles' brother, Ricky. "Maybe he knows something," he muttered as he got up and left the office, heading for the café.

Jack, busy serving a few customers from one of the cruise ships, frowned when he saw Ralph walk in. "Where's your usual crowd?" Ralph whispered as he came next to him.

Jack set the plate of food in front of an older, dapperly dressed man sitting with his wife. "Word gets around," he answered. The man looked at his plate and interrupted. "Hey, Buddy," he complained. "I ordered a fish enchilada. I don't know what this is, but it isn't what I asked for!"

Jack apologized and then yelled, "Who ordered a fish tostada?" A woman at the next table raised her hand, and Jack took the plate to her and then walked back to Ralph. "What can I do for you, Ralph?" he asked apprehensively.

"Ricky in the back?" Ralph asked.

Relieved, Jack told him he'd given the boy the day off. Ralph smiled, hoping it would make him relax. "I just wanted to talk to him about his brother," he said. "Do you know where I can find him?"

Jack shook his head just as the boy walked in the front door. "Speak of the devil," Ralph said as he watched Ricky dash by him and go in the kitchen. He followed him. He found him putting on his apron. Janie was at the range. "Hi, Mrs. Cramer," he said smiling. "I just wanted to talk to Ricky here for a minute. Is it okay?"

Janie, her back to him, turned toward him, dropping her spatula. "Hello," Ralph," she said edgily. "Of course." She turned to Ricky. "You don't have to be here, Ricky, but when you finish talking to the constable here, maybe you and I can work on your fable." She turned back to Ralph. "You want some privacy, Ralph? You can go in the dining room. There's certainly room in there, thanks to you and all the rumors about Jack." Turning her back on him, she went back to her cooking.

"Just doin' my job," Ralph said. "We'll get out of your way." He motioned for Ricky to follow him. They found a table near the window. Jack went into the kitchen. "I wonder what he wants from Ricky?" he asked Janie as he came up to her.

"Probably more dirt on you," she answered sarcastically. .

Jack hesitated. "It'll be okay, Janie," he murmured; but inside he wasn't so confident.

Ricky was scared to death as he sat facing Ralph who didn't say anything for a few moments. Then, smiling, he asked, "How's your brother? Charles, right?"

"Fine, I guess," Ricky muttered. "I haven't seen him for a while."

Ralph nodded. "Mrs. Cramer's a nice lady, isn't she?" he asked. "If I remember right, she got you two guys out of a mess, didn't she?"

His head down, Ricky nodded.

"Yeah, I think that's right," Ralph went on. "Instead of you two being put in some juvie camp, she took you in and let you both work here. Right?"

Again Ricky nodded.

Ralph continued to smile. "Yeah, nice lady, and Mr. Cramer too." He leaned forward and used his hand to raise Ricky's head. "But you still help them out even though Mr. Cramer kicked your brother out, and even on your day off. Why's that?"

Ricky shook his head. "I just like to help them," he answered.

"That's great," Ralph said, still smiling. "Can I ask you something?" Ricky nodded. "Why'd Mr. Cramer hit your brother?"

Ricky again shook his head. "I don't know. Charles said something, I guess, and that was when Mr. Cramer hit him."

"What did he say?"

Ricky shrugged. "I don't know," he lied. "I didn't hear."

Ralph leaned back in his chair and for a moment they didn't speak. Finally, he leaned forward and asked, "Where's your brother now, Ricky?"

"I told you, I haven't seen him," he lied, getting nervous again.

Ralph nodded, knowing he couldn't get any more out of the boy. "Okay, Son," he said. "Stay here for a while. I wanna talk to the Cramers." He got up, leaving Ricky in a panic. Then, seeing the constable walk into the kitchen, he bolted out the front door, knocking over his chair.

Hearing the noise, Ralph was tempted to go back to check on Ricky, but he just shrugged and greeted Jack and Janie who were at the sink washing the dishes. "I've got a couple of questions about Charles and Ricky," he said as he sat on a stool behind them. "It won't take long."

They turned around. Jack wiped his hands and said sarcastically, "Take all the time you need, Ralph. You made sure we don't have much to do."

Ralph grimaced. "As I told your wife, Jack, I'm just doing my job. What I wanted to know is if there's more to what I've heard about when Charles took off that day."

Janie exploded. "I'LL TELL YOU WHAT HAPPENED!" she yelled. 'THE UNGRATEFUL BRAT USED THE F WORD ON JACK!"

Jack grabbed her hand. "Calm down, Janie," he said gently. "That's in the past." He turned to Ralph. "It was no big deal, Ralph," he said, grinning. "I asked the kid to do something, and he told me to shove it. Actually, he did use the F word, as Janie calls it, and then I lost my temper and hit him. Then he ran out, saying wild things about getting revenge, and we haven't seen him since."

"So you did hit him?" Ralph asked.

Jack shrugged. "Yeah, and I'm not proud of it. It's just that I didn't like him using that word in front of Janie. I can't even say it now."

Ralph nodded. "So you were provoked, right? Where was Ricky when all this was going on?" he asked.

"Right here," Janie answered. "And Jack barely hit Charles. Sure he was provoked. Why are you asking about Ricky? He's a good boy."

Ralph nodded again. "So did he hear?"

"He had to," Jack said. "Charles screamed it. Our customers that day probably heard it too."

"Okay," Ralph said, getting off the stool. "That's about it." He started for the door but then turned around. "Oh, by the way, Jack," he said calmly. "There may be more to this mess than I originally thought."

Janie screeched, "THANK GOD! I KNEW YOU CAN'T BELIEVE JACK WOULD DO SUCH A THING!"

Jack, however, sensed it wasn't over. "You said there may be, Ralph," he said nervously. "So now do you believe I had nothing to do with it?"

Ralph raised his hand. "Let's face it, Jack," he answered. "All the facts point to you – motive, means, opportunity – and then there's the butcher knife and the shirt and the fact that you lose your temper when you're provoked. Just don't go anywhere, okay?"

Jack nodded and sat on a stool, watching him go. Janie, seeing his dejection, knelt down below him. "Ralph will figure it out, Jack," she whispered. "It'll be fine."

Walking back to his office, Ralph felt miserable, knowing that despite his doubts about Jack being the killer, it would be almost impossible to clear him if he couldn't find another suspect. He sensed the only thing he could do next was find Charles to see what he really knew about it. To do that, he decided, I have to find Ricky first, who, despite what he said, probably knows where Charles is.

He started to ask people on the street if they'd seen Ricky, and one woman directed him to the northern end of the village. Heading that way, he began to feel it was hopeless; but, not knowing what else to do, he began walking up the hill toward Mineral Creek and suddenly saw Ricky coming out of an abandoned house no more than a hundred yards away.

He quickly hid behind a tree and watched as the boy ran past him, crying. Waiting until he was out of sight, he walked slowly to the house, waited again, and then knocked on the door. Within a minute or so, it opened and he saw Charles who, startled, said, "I thought you was somebody else, Constable. What do you want?"

"Can I come in?" Ralph said calmly. "I just want to talk to you for a minute."

"Sure," Charles answered, now smiling. "I saw this empty house and thought nobody'd mind if I stayed in it a few days. The people at the foster home don't seem to like me."

I believe it, Ralph thought as he walked in. The place was filthy. "I just have a few things to ask you, Son," he said. "I really don't care if you've broken into this house. Can we just talk?"

Charles shrugged, sat on a mattress, and put his hand in his pocket. "Sure, Constable, but I think I've already told you everything I know."

Ralph nodded and took a step forward. "Well, for one thing, there seems to be some confusion about what happened when you left the Cramers. I talked to Ricky who said you called Mr. Cramer a name. Is that what happened?"

"Yeah," Charles answered, feeling uneasy. "That's about it. He was bossing me around and it just came out. I didn't really mean anything by it."

"What was that word you used, Charles? Your brother said he didn't hear it."

Charles shrugged. "To be honest with you, Constable, I don't remember. All I know is that he lost it and slugged me."

"I heard you said 'fuck' right in front of Mrs. Cramer and that you told Mr. Cramer you'd get even with him for hitting you. Is that right?"

"Maybe I said something like that, but I told you I don't remember. Maybe I lost my temper. What's the big deal?"

Ralph stood over him, glowering. "The big deal, as you call it, Charles, is that I suspect you're making things up. I've been talking to people about you, you know, and, among other things, some of them said they saw you sometimes wearing the same kind of shirt Cramer used to wear. I notice you're not wearing it now. You got it around?"

Suddenly Charles remembered the shirt in the corner right behind them and began walking toward the door. "The people at the foster home give me and Ricky lots of shirts, Constable," he said nervously. "I just throw them away when they get too dirty."

Ralph was getting frustrated. "I'll say this for you, Charles," he said, his voice rising. "You've learned to pretend you're just a poor, abused orphan pretty well; but we know better, don't we?"

"I don't know what you're talking about, Constable," Charles answered and turned away from him. Ralph angrily grabbed his shoulder. Charles turned and swung his fist at him, but Ralph avoided the blow and smothered him in a choke hold. "That was stupid, kid. Now you've attacked a police officer. You've got quite a temper, haven't you?" He freed him. Charles glowered at him, hatred in his eyes.

Ralph grinned. "You thinking of getting revenge, kid? Just like Cramer?" he asked.

Charles's face softened. "What're you talking about, Constable?" he asked compliantly. "I just didn't like you grabbing me. I'm sorry."

Ralph continued to grin. "You're sorry, huh?" he said, knowing he'd gone as far as he could. He stepped back. "Okay, kid," he said. "I don't know why you're lying, but believe me I'll find out!" He turned and left.

Seeing him out the door, Charles sneered. "Sure, copper," he muttered. "Before you find a thing, I'll be out of here." He waited a few minutes and then grabbed the shirt. "I've gotta get rid of it," he muttered. He looked around but suddenly began laughing so hard he bent over. "Shit!" he was finally able to say, "Why didn't I think of that before?"

Stuffing the bloody shirt inside his jacket, he climbed out the window and headed for the café, hoping he'd have a chance to sneak inside.

Sitting at his desk in his office, Ralph realized it was a gamble; but he couldn't think of anything else to do. He had to arrest Jack and then arrange a speedy trial and hope a good defense attorney could break Charles when he testified to his lies. There was no other way. He was now convinced Charles was somehow involved, but he couldn't figure out why. A few minutes later, he went back to the café to arrest Jack and take him to Anchorage.

Chapter Eleven: Kasmali and Rodrigo Return

Knowing the townspeople would be curious at the sight of an unusually large eagle, Kasmali landed near his asuskwa outside of Valdez, thinking he would carry Rodrigo the rest of the way. However, when he mutated back into the Inupiaq chief, he was surprised to feel his ankle still aching. "That is strange," he muttered. Nonetheless, he picked up the unconscious Spaniard, put him over his shoulders, and started limping toward the town. Many painful minutes later, he staggered into the clinic, causing a woman sitting behind a counter to scream.

"This man needs help," he managed to say. "Is there someone here who can tend to him?"

Without answering, the woman jumped up and ran into a back room. Soon a man came running out. "My God!" he said. "Is he alive?"

Kasmali nodded. "I can feel his heart," he answered. "But he has been exposed to the cold. May I set him down?"

"For God's sake, bring him into my examination room, Chief!" the man ordered, unaware of Kasmali's injury.

Once Kasmali laid him on a metallic table, the man began examining him. "Jesus," he said. "He's got a raging temperature! Bring me blankets and some cold compresses, Margaret!"

They wrapped the blankets around Rodrigo and began to swab his face and massage his torso and then began stripping him. "Christ!" the doctor said. "His leg is broken in three places! How long has he been like this, Chief?"

"You know me?"

"Everyone knows you, Chief. Tell me what happened."

Suddenly, Rodrigo moaned, "Earthquake … the dogs."

The doctor turned to look at Kasmali. "What earthquake? Another tremor?"

Kasmali didn't hesitate. "He's a scientist, doctor. We just returned from Prudhoe Bay where the ice shattered and tore a huge slab off the oil platform."

"My God!" the doctor muttered. "Any casualties?"

"Many of the workers," Kasmali answered. "My friend here will want to alert the ship he came here on."

Coming out of his shock, the doctor said, "Not for a while. He's not lucid. Right now I have to check for frostbite and get his temperature down. Then we'll deal with his leg. He's in no shape to alert anyone."

Rodrigo moaned again and tried to sit up. The doctor put his hand on his chest. "Good, you're awake," he said soothingly. "Just lie back. You're in good hands here."

"Where am I?" Rodrigo moaned,

"In my clinic in Valdez," the doctor answered as he probed his legs. "What's your name, son?"

"Rodrigo De La Cruz," Rodrigo mumbled.

The doctor continued to probe the leg. "I'm Doctor Watson – yup, just like Sherlock Holmes's friend. I'm checking your leg." The woman came in. "Good, Margaret," he said, noticing her. "Give me a hand." While they worked on Rodrigo's injuries, the doctor questioned Kasmali. "You said Prudhoe Bay. Surely you didn't carry him all the way?"

Kasmali answered quickly, "No, we lost our sled and team just out of town."

"Well, Chief, you don't look too well yourself. I'd better check you out after I see to your friend."

"I'm fine, doctor," Kasmali said quickly "Just concentrate on my friend."

Overhearing, Rodrigo stammered, "Go talk… to Jack."

The doctor looked up sharply. "Does he mean Jack Cramer?" he asked abruptly. "You won't find him here. The constable just arrested him and took him to the county court in Anchorage. I've heard his trial's coming up soon."

Shocked, Rodrigo struggled up painfully and yelled, "HIS TRIAL? FOR WHAT?"

"You do that again and you'll worsen your injuries," the doctor said calmly. "Your friend is accused of murder."

Kasmali, as shocked as Rodrigo, said nothing.

"Jack?" Rodrigo moaned. "Why?"

"Margaret, would you prepare some antibiotics?" Doctor Watson asked the woman. He then told them about the crime and the evidence against Jack. When he concluded, Rodrigo struggled to get up, saying, "I have to see Janie."

The doctor pushed him back down. "You're going nowhere," he said. "Not for a while anyway. You're in bad shape, Son."

"I will go," Kasmali announced as he took Rodrigo's hand. "I will be back."

As he limped down the walkway to the café, Kasmali was confused why he was so affected by the young Spaniard's injuries so, though he knew he should be checking on Janie, he sat on a bench in front of a shop to rest his ankle and try to figure things out.

The shop owner came out, saw him, and sat beside him. "Haven't seen you for a while, Chief," he said. "You been away?"

Kasmali continued to stare out at the bay. After a moment, the man muttered, "Have you heard about Cramer? It's weird that you think you know a guy and he turns out to be a murderer. But then again, I always thought there was something weird about him."

Kasmali looked over at him and said quietly, "You should leave this town. An earthquake's coming."

The man grinned, got up, and began walking back to his store, muttering, "Crazy drunk Indian."

Kasmali also rose and limped the rest of the way to the café. When he reached it, he peered in the bay window and saw it was dark, so he hobbled behind it to the house to find Astay. The dog, lying on the porch, lifted its head and whined as he came up. "Left alone, Astay?" he said as he sat beside it. "The woman left too?"

He stroked the dog's head. "She must have gone to Anchorage to be with Jack Cramer. Come, let's get you something to eat, and then we'll try to find a small sled and have a nice trip west."

Somewhat surprised that the back door was unlocked, Kasmali led the dog into the kitchen, opened the refrigerator, took out a piece of broiled cod fish, and put it on the floor in front of the dog. A few minutes later, they left and began scouting the periphery of the town. After a while, they found a small sled complete with lead lines propped against an empty house. Easily positioning the sled on the ground, he hitched up the dog, followed the sled back behind the café, and said, "The owner will have to understand, my friend. Rest a little longer. When I return, we'll take a trip; but first, I have to see how our young friend is doing."

With his newly discovered feelings still disorienting him, he began to walk more easily, but then he staggered as he heard the voice again. "Leave this place," it whispered. Shaking his head, he continued to the clinic. The woman was back at her desk behind the counter. She greeted him and then called the doctor who came out of the back room.

"Doctor," she said when he entered. "This man's in pain."

"Sit down," the doctor demanded. Kasmali stepped backward, found a chair, and watched as the doctor knelt on the floor in front of him. "Lift your leg," he asked and then began to feel up and down, finishing at his foot. "A bad sprain," he muttered. "Wriggle your ankle for me, will you, Chief?"

Kasmali did so. "Must have been strained from carrying the young man," the doctor said, looking up. "Here, let me massage it. Margaret, will you get me some liniment and bandages?"

As the doctor kneaded his foot and his leg, Kasmali smiled, wondering why he hadn't remembered his ability to reconstruct himself. The doctor got up. "You're lucky," he said. "All that strain could have caused a great deal if damage. "I'll wrap it up, and you should be fine. However, you'd better keep off of it for a while. And try to wrap it in ice."

Kasmali nodded. Then doctor continued. "You probably want to know about your friend. I put a splint on his leg, but I'm still concerned about the infection. I'd like him to stay with us for a day or so. Just to make sure."

Kasmali asked to see him. The doctor nodded and Kasmali followed him, striding into the examination room. Rodrigo was in a bed, his leg propped up with pillows. "Hello," Kasmali said, the doctor hovering behind him. "Do you feel better?"

Rodrigo smiled. "Thanks, Chief," he said. "Yeah, but hazy. We had a long trip, huh?"

"Longer than you think, my friend," Kasmali answered. "You slept most of the way." He took Rodrigo's hand. "Janie's not at the café," he said. "She's probably in Anchorage with Jack. If you don't need me, I'll take a trip up there to see how bad it is. Are you going to call the people on that ship?"

Rodrigo nodded. "I already did while you were gone. They're going to notify the science group about the tremors and the ice melting, and they were stunned when I told them about the breaking up of the oil platform. They want to take me onboard to their infirmary, but I told them I was fine right here and that I had to do some more investigating. Incidentally, I asked the doctor if he'd noticed any tremors, and he said they happened all the time lately and that they'd gotten used to them. Hurry back, will you? I have to find out what's going on with Jack!"

"I have Astay and a sled," Kasmali answered. "Get well, my young friend."

"You're sledding? Just you and Astay? Why not take the ferry?"

"It only takes you to Whittier and then you have to wait for the train which takes too long," Kasmali answered. "I'll be back as soon as I can, and then we can deal with his situation."

He felt foolish as the huge Husky pulled him in the sled, but the dog didn't seem to notice the extra weight. Occasionally they would stop and Kasmali would pack his ankle with snow. By the time they reached Anchorage, a little over a week later, the swelling in his ankle had decreased and he was able to walk without pain.

Being that it was a well populated city, Kasmali had to hide the sled and hope no one stole it. He also had no idea where the courthouse was; but he soon found a man who was helpful, especially when he saw Astay. He directed Kasmali to it and rushed away.

On the way, Kasmali stole a newspaper and leafed through it, expecting to find an article that dealt with the trial; and sure enough, it was on the front page. Walking hastily, he read through it. When he came to the courthouse, he saw a woman who looked official; and after ordering Astay to heel, he apologized for bothering her and asked if she knew anything about Jack Cramer.

"Jack Cramer?" she answered, looking fearfully at Astay. "The man on trial for murder?"

"Yes," he answered. "He's a friend of mine. He couldn't kill anybody."

She raised her eyebrows. "Well, sir, from what I've heard, they've got a good case against him. You might check inside. I think his trial begins tomorrow." She too rushed away.

Knowing that somehow he had to get in to see Jack, he thanked her and then, figuring his chances would be better if he were less threatening, he walked around the city until he found a store with western wear in its window. He told Astay to stay outside and went in to look around. A man came up to him, hesitated, and asked, "Can I help you?"Kasmali told him he was in need of White Man's clothes.

"Just the thing for you," the man said and led him to a side room. Kasmali was pleased. On the counter were jeans, parkas, shirts, and leather boots. He selected and outfit, thanked the man, and started to walk out.

"WAIT A MINUTE!" the man shouted. "YOU HAVE TO PAY FOR THAT STUFF!"

He smiled at the man and looked deeply into his eyes. Soon the man was smiling back vacantly. Kasmali then gently picked him up, carried him to a chair, and sat him down. The man continued to smile. He walked to the door, found the latch, locked it, and then stood with his arms raised and mutated slowly into a duplicate of the man. Finding the outfit where he'd left it, he dressed, rubbed the man's eyes, unlocked the door, and walked out. The man remembered nothing as he stretched and went back behind his counter.

Gathering Astay, who by this time had become used to Kasmali's transformations, they headed back to where he had left the sled. "Guard the sled, my friend," he said to the dog and then left to go back to the courthouse.

Once there, he asked a man at an information desk it if he could tell him where to find Jack Cramer and was told all suspects awaiting trial were being held at a police station across town. He was given directions and then headed through the city.

When he finally reached the station, he was stunned by all the chaos, the crowd, the yelling, and the line of people waiting to speak to a man standing behind an elevated counter. He too stood in line and waited until he reached the man who sneered at him. "All right, buddy, what do you want?" the man snorted.

Kasmali thought quickly. "Thank Goodness," he answered. "I want to see a friend," he said. "I mean no harm."

"Who?" the man asked.

"Jack Cramer," Kasmali answered quickly.

The man began to search through some papers. "Here it is, Cramer, Jack." He looked down at Kasmali. "He's up for murder. He probably needs a friend."

Sounding as weak as he felt, Kasmali smiled and stared into the man's eyes. "How can I see my friend?" he asked calmly despite the noise around them. The man smiled, gave him a pass, and pointed to a doorway to their right. Kasmali took the pass and then touched the man's hand and whispered, "Thank you." The man respectfully nodded and called the next person.

Kasmali walked through the door, handed a policeman the pass, and was led him down a long hallway of cells and then stopped. "Here you go," the policeman said. "You can talk to your friend through the bars. Don't take long."

After the man left, Kasmali looked into the cell and saw Jack sitting on a cot, his head in his hands. A man was asleep in a cot opposite him. "Jack Cramer?" Kasmali whispered. "I am here."

Jack leapt from the cot and grabbed the bars. "Who are you?" he asked.

"I am Chief Kasmali," Kasmali answered, "Now tell me why you're here."

Jack laughed. "I'll be damned," he chuckled. "What's next?"

"I've come to discover what happened to cause you to be confined," Kasmali said. "Rodrigo and I just returned from Prudhoe Bay."

"It's hard to believe," Jack muttered and then told him the whole story. "It looks bad, Chief," he concluded. "But at least the constable was able to get me a good lawyer."

"What does this lawyer say?"

"The constable's convinced I'm innocent, and I guess the lawyer's one of the best. Anyway, he told me their case against me was mainly circumstantial – a butcher knife, a piece of a shirt, my lack of an alibi, and somebody who's gonna say he saw me running from the scene. He claimed the biggest things we have to worry about are my alleged motive – the fact that in a book it describes how I once tried to kill Cole -- and the eye-witness. His plan is to show how I've changed."

Kasmali nodded. "Sounds reasonable, but wouldn't it be easier if the real murderer were found?"

Jack managed to smile. "Sure," he said, "but I don't think Ralph has come up with any other suspects, except for Charles Murray, a kid who hates me for hitting him and kicking him out of the café."

Kasmali leaned back and thought for a moment. "Ricky's brother?" he asked. "Maybe I can talk to him." Just then the guard came up and said, "Sorry, Buddy, time's up."

Kasmali nodded as the guard yanked his arm. "Have faith, Jack. We'll work this out," he said and started to follow the guard out. Suddenly he stopped, pulling the guard toward him, and asked Jack, "How's Janie?"

The guard waited. "She's staying at a hotel with Ricky," Jack answered sadly. "I've only seen her twice, once at the arraignment where she was ready to post my bail by putting the café up as collateral. Thank God the judge denied it. The trial shouldn't last long, and then she can go back to serving her fish tostadas. Then later on when she visited me, she got so angry at a guard who said she had to go, she hit him. They haven't let her back since. I guess I'll see her at the trial tomorrow."

Kasmali followed the guard out. Jack sat back on his cot.

Knowing it might confuse Astay if he came back to him looking like the shop owner, Kasmali found an abandoned building, went in, and mutated back into the Inupiaq chief. Unfortunately, he was naked.

When he came to the dog still beside the sled, he patted its massive head and said, "Good dog, Astay. Now we have to get back to Valdez, my friend." Kasmali said. "But first I have to find clothes. Come with me. We'll see if I can find something."

After an hour or so of creeping behind the houses on the outskirts of the city, he saw what he needed hanging on a clothesline. Trying to be stealthy, he crept up and grabbed a shirt, a pair of pants, and a heavy jacket. He then ran as fast as his legs would allow back to the sled. Once there, he lowered the sled, stripped, and on the clothes. He then led Astay back to the sled, hitched him, and wrapped some blankets around him that he'd found in the bed of the sled. Soon they were on their way back to Valdez.

Chapter Twelve: Ominous Signs

To Dr. Watson's relief, Rodrigo's fever had returned to normal, and his leg, now encased in a cast, seemed to be strong enough for him to begin practicing with crutches. Then, after a week, the doctor was satisfied Rodrigo would be able to recuperate at the Cramers' house where he'd been a guest, and that he would tell his friend Chief Kasmali he could be found there if he came looking for him.

Feeling relatively confident with the crutches, Rodrigo began struggling down the boardwalk and was almost to the café when a sharp shock hit, knocking him sprawling into the street. "That was no tremor," he moaned, struggling to get to his feet. "I've gotta get the people out of here!"

Unfortunately, his crutches were still on the sidewalk a good ten feet away, so he had to crawl to get them as the tremors slowly abated and then stopped. By using the curb, he was able to lift himself up onto the boardwalk, grab the crutches and, using them for balance, pull himself up and look around. The sidewalk was buckled, and a stiff wind was blowing dirt and dust everywhere; but he was able to see the shops ahead of him and people screaming and scrambling into the street. Windows were shattered, but that seemed to be the extent of the physical damage.

Chuckling, a bearded old man came out of a shop in front of him and cackled, "Well, glad that's over. Now we can get back to business, huh?"

Rodrigo was stunned. "You think that was it?" he asked.

The old man looked at him suspiciously. "You drunk, youngster?" he answered. "Sure," he continued, sarcastically, "that was the terrible earthquake we've been warned about. Some earthquake!"

Disgusted, Rodrigo said, "That was just a minor tremor, you fool. You've got to get out of here before the big one comes."

The old man began cackling. "A tremor?" he managed to say. "A tremor? Hell, it was big enough for me. Get out of town, you say? Jesus, what an asshole!" Still cackling, he walked into the street toward the frightened people still standing there.

Rodrigo knew he had to get hold of the scientists again, so he hobbled his way to Jack and Janie's house, found the back door open, and went to use the radio-phone he'd left there. Within a minute, he was talking to a colleague who told him the tremor measured 5.4 on their instruments. He then repeated the information he'd gathered with Kasmali from Prudhoe Bay and suggested that the entire coast be evacuated. He was told they'd call back but that it might be advisable for him to return to the ship.

He declined, saying he had more to investigate, though his main concern was to remain in Valdez until Kasmali returned with news about Jack and about how much damage had been done at Anchorage.

That done, he left the house to check out more of Valdez. When he reached the main drag, he was amazed to see how few people were still there and how calm the scene was. Confused, he walked into the first store he came to and saw a crowd at the counter. They were laughing. "Gallows humor," he muttered as he came up to them.

"Hi, stranger," one of the men said, smiling. "Feel the big one?" All Rodrigo could do was nod. "We were just talking about the crazy scientists who've been nagging us about a terrible catastrophe." He chuckled. "I told them I've been through worse down in California."

Rodrigo had had enough. "You don't have melting ice and cracking glaciers in California," he barked. "That tremor measured only 5.4! It's only a hint of what's coming!"

The man laughed, causing those around him to giggle nervously. "You must be one of those doomsday people," he finally said. "Well, I'm an optimist, and I say you and your kind are full of shit." He turned his back to Rodrigo and again chuckled with the crowd.

Seeing the disdain on their faces, Rodrigo was tempted to go back to the house to call the ship to pick him up; but he didn't. Instead, he headed clumsily to Gus' Bar where he thought he'd find Gus whom he knew was reasonable. When he came in through the swinging doors, he was engulfed by men and women who seemed to be joined in an orgy of drinking.

"WHAT'S GOING ON?" he shouted to Gus when he managed to make it to the bar.

"CELEBRATION, I GUESS," Gus shouted back. "MAYBE SOME TYPE OF SURVIVAL CRAZINESSS AFTER THE EARTHQUAKE!" He nodded to his helper and then motioned to a vacant table in the corner.

Rodrigo followed him. "Any damage?" he asked when they got there.

"Glasses, bottles, broken chairs," Gus answered. "But when the crowd came in, they cleaned it all up. Thank God my liquor supply in the back room is okay. What do you know about Cramer?"

Rodrigo shrugged. "Nothing. Chief Kasmali went up to Anchorage to see what's going on. I guess Janie's there too. What can you tell me? All I know is that he's been accused of murdering somebody."

"Yeah, as incredible as it sounds," Gus answered. "That's right, you've been gone on one of your expeditions." He leaned forward. "It doesn't look good for Jack, Rodrigo," he said frowning. "He knew the guy, for one thing, and then there's the murder weapon just like one they use at the café and a strip of a shirt they found in the guy's hand just like one Jack wore sometimes. He's got no alibi, from what I've heard, and the worst thing is that there seems to be a witness who said he saw Jack running away from the scene."

"JESUS!" Rodrigo screeched. "HE DIDN'T DO IT, DID HE?"

Gus shrugged. "Of course not, though some of the people around here think he did; but I was talking to Ralph the other day – you know, the constable. Anyway, he gave me the feeling there was more to it, that someone was setting Jack up."

"Well, they sure seem to be doing a good job of it," Rodrigo said. "What's Ralph going to do about it?"

"Damn if I know," Gus answered. "But a few of us – Jack's friends – are trying to figure out who might have done it if Jack didn't. We finally decided it had to be someone who hated him, but we couldn't come up with anyone except maybe the guy who told Ralph he saw him. Thinking he's lying, you know."

"Who is he?" Rodrigo demanded.

Again Gus shrugged. "Nobody knows, and Ralph isn't talking. Some of us think Ralph's waiting for the trial, hoping the guy will recant."

Rodrigo sighed, "Jesus, what a mess. Maybe when the chief comes back, he'll give us some good news." Gus nodded and went back to the bar. Rodrigo, using his crutches, forced his way out to the street.

Knowing there was little he could do either about Jack or the earthquake, he hobbled back to the house. Once there, he went into the kitchen, poured a glass of water, and then swallowed some pain pills. He then went back into the front room and collapsed on a sofa.

Late the next night, Kasmali sledded up to the house. "Whoa," he said quietly to Astay and then began unloosening him from the lines. "You can rest now," he said. "You've earned it." Astay, exhausted, collapsed in the dirt.

Entering the house, he looked around and finally found Rodrigo sleeping in the guest room, his leg propped up on two pillows. He smiled and sat on the floor against the wall. For the next hour or so, he tried to think of ways he could help Jack out of his situation. Finally he knew what he had to do, and with that he made himself fall asleep.

When he awoke, he noticed Rodrigo was not in the bed. Hearing something, he walked into the kitchen and saw him staring out the window, a pair of crutches propped at his left. "Thank God you're back," Rodrigo muttered, noticing him. "Why are you dressed like that?"

"I couldn't find anything else," Kasmali answered, sitting down in a chair at the table. "When I was in that city, I had to mutate in order to see Jack."

"Is he all right?" Rodrigo asked. "I heard about the murder. Jack can't be a killer, can he?"

"I wouldn't think so, but you humans constantly surprise me."

Rodrigo pointed to a shirt on the sink. "I found that when I went into the café's storeroom to get something to eat."

Kasmali rose, walked to the sink, and picked up the shirt. "So?" he asked. "Feel the bottom," Rodrigo said, still looking out the window.

Kasmali did so. "It's crusted," he said. "It's just a filthy shirt."

Rodrigo turned around. His face was ashen. "It's Jack's. I've seen him wearing it. And that crust, as you called it, is blood!"

Kasmali was confused. "So he got blood on it," he said patiently. What are you getting at?"

"Gus, the owner of the bar, told me they found a piece of a shirt in the murdered guy's hand. Look at the sleeve."

When Kasmali did, he sat back down as he noticed part of it was ripped off. "There has to be an answer to this," he said. "For one thing, from what I know of Jack, he wouldn't just leave his shirt stained with blood where anyone could find it. Besides, that could be his blood, as I said."

"Whatever," Rodrigo muttered. "The point is, what do we do with it? If we take it to the constable, it sure as hell will add to what he already has against Jack. And if we hide it, we'll be accused of withholding evidence. They could put us in jail! Christ, if Jack did kill the guy, he would've told me!"

"Perhaps. What are you going to do?" Kasmali asked, leaning forward.

Rodrigo frowned. "I should burn the damn thing, but I guess I should give it to the constable and then hope they can tell if the blood is Jack's!"

Kasmali lowered his head on the table, concerned for his young friend. "I see you're better," he said, trying to change the subject. "The fever must be gone, and I imagine you use those sticks for your legs. Do you want me to tell you about Anchorage? Jack Cramer is frightened, and there were some tremors. Was it bad here?"

Rodrigo frowned. "You know, Chief, I'm beginning to think it's useless trying to warn people. All it did was shake up a few buildings, and when I told them – again – that it was only the beginning, they laughed at me. They think the tremors were the catastrophe I predicted before." He winced. "I hate those damn crutches! Tell me about Jack and Janie," he asked.

Kasmali began quickly, "Jack's in what you people call a jail, and he's worried. I didn't see Janie." He hesitated. "Assuming Jack is not the killer, perhaps I can find a way to help him get beyond his newest problem, though I do not know how."

Rodrigo shrugged. "After our trip to Prudhoe Bay, I believe you can do anything. What do you have in mind?"

"I told you. I don't know yet," Kasmali answered.

Rodrigo shook his head and changed the subject. "You know, Chief, seismologists a whole lot more expert than I have trouble predicting earthquakes. Maybe we're wrong about a big one coming. Maybe that was it up at Prudhoe Bay."

Kasmali stared at him. "We're not wrong," he answered. "One much worse is coming, and soon. That's why we have to keep Jack and you and Mrs. Cramer away from the coast."

Part Two
The Earthquake

Chapter Thirteen: Ricky's Predicament

Giggling, Charles crawled through the open window of the abandoned house, threw himself on the filthy mattress, reached into his pocket for the metal cross, fondled it, and shouted, "HAH! LET'S SEE THE SON-OF-A-BITCH GET OUT OF THAT!"

In his fixation on Jack Cramer, he felt exhilarated as he thought of how clever he'd been to think of shoving the shirt on a shelf in the cafe's storeroom. He continued to giggle. To make things even better, while walking back he'd heard people yapping about Cramer being arrested. "The cop'll probably find it; and if he does, Cramer'll be dead meat. I'm a god-damned genius!"

He suddenly frowned, thinking maybe he'd gone too far; but then he shook his head and muttered, "No, he deserves it, him and all the other assholes who slapped me around." He smiled. "Besides," he muttered. "It's him or me, and you can bet your ass it won't be me."

Indeed, having informed the authorities in Anchorage a day earlier of his details of the death of Billy Cole, Ralph Eston had told that they'd send state troopers to arrest Jack and bring him there for arraignment, though Ralph had thought they were acting precipitously. And naturally, when he arrived at the café to inform the Cramers what was going to happen, Jack became belligerent. Janie, however, surprised Ralph by her naiveté in telling Jack it was nothing more than a mistake and that he should go to with the troopers to clear it up and that she'd run the café and wait to hear what happened.

Ralph knew, of course, that it was a little more serious than she thought and that it would be helpful if he and she follow the troopers to the city; but she seemed more concerned about the café and even Ricky, whom she said she couldn't leave alone.

When the troopers came a few days later, however, she saw Jack so downcast and reluctantly agreed to close the café temporarily and go with Ralph.

Though there were quicker ways to get from Valdez to Anchorage, Ralph decided they'd take the ferry to Valdez and then the train to the city, thinking it might give Janie time to come to grips with the situation. Ricky saw them off and quickly made everything worse when he hugged Janie's waist and wept uncontrollably.

At first, Janie tried to maintain her composure, but eventually she wilted and also began weeping. Embarrassed, Ralph could do nothing but watch and wait. Finally she broke loose and whispered, "I'll be back soon, Ricky. You keep an eye on the café, okay?"

Still sobbing, Ricky nodded and then watched as the ferry began chugging slowly out into the bay. For a long time, he just stood crying, wondering what would become of him. He wanted to believe Mrs. Cramer when she said she'd be back, but he'd been disappointed too many times before by other adults. Even worse, he felt guilty. He'd wanted to tell her about Charles and the knife, but he just couldn't because, despite Charles' recent cruelty, he just believed his brother wouldn't be mean enough to do anything really bad.

He then thought maybe he should just go to school, but he was too miserable, so instead he wandered back to the Cramers' house behind the café and sat on their porch beside Astay. He stayed there until it was dark and then slowly walked to the foster home. When he reached it, he was somehow relieved to see that Charles wasn't there.

The next morning, lonely and depressed, he did go to school. When the dismissal bell finally rang, he wandered along the shore and around the town and eventually sat in front of the café and watched the people come up, read the sign that said it was closed temporarily, and walk away disappointed. No one seemed to notice him. Sometimes, he took a book from his pocket and read about Soulful Sam, the boy in the fable, or recited one of the poems Mrs. Cramer had taught him. Once, when he saw Charles wandering down the boardwalk, he hid in the shadows and waited until he was gone.

The next night, instead of going back to the foster home, he slept under the Cramers' porch beside Astay, even though Mrs. Cramer had said he could stay in the house. He just couldn't. Early the next morning, cold and stiff, he couldn't bring himself to go back to school and decided that being with his mean brother was better than sleeping under a porch, so he walked slowly to the abandoned house and knocked softly on the back window.

For a long time there was no answer, and he thought he'd missed him; but eventually Charles peaked out, saw him, and growled, "Whadaya want, kid?"

Ricky began to cry. "I'm all alone, Charles," he answered haltingly. "Can I come in?"

Leaning out the window, Charles just sneered and said, "What about your new mommy? She throw you out like they did me?"

Ricky reached up. "Mrs. Cramer's gone," he whimpered. "She and Mr. Cramer went to Anchorage. The constable took him to jail."

Charles smiled. Finally, Ricky gathered together his courage and said, "I know he hit you, Charles, but he's not a bad man. I don't think he could kill anybody."

Suddenly Charles reached down, grabbed his arms, and pulled him roughly through the window, causing him to crash on his head on the floor. Stunned, he struggled to his feet and saw Charles looking menacingly at him. "You don't think?" he snarled. "You don't think? She got to you, didn't she, you little shit? All those years I took care of you, and now all you want is to be with her? Well, you can have her. She'll probably just use you even more now that her son-of-a-bitch husband's not around!"

Confused by what Charles was saying, Ricky ran for the window; but Charles grabbed him by the arm and threw him back on the floor. "We're family," he said, suddenly calm. "Stick around."

Too scared to move, Ricky stared at him as he hovered over him -- his face acne spotted and filthy, his body reeking in dirty, ripped jeans and a shirt too big for him, his hair slick and tangled, his lips curled -- and saw a different person. Trying not to move, he looked around. He'd been in the abandoned house before, but now it seemed even more like a hovel. Obviously in the middle of being remodeled, one wall partially torn down, its remnants scattered all around them. Dust was everywhere; and against the wall under the window was the old, stained mattress on which Charles had obviously just been lying. "You can stay here, kid," Charles snarled, looking down at him. "But you're gotta sleep on the floor. There's only this one mattress, and I need all of it."

Hoping he was just in one of his moods, Ricky whimpered, "Okay, Charles. "I won't be in the way."

Charles shrugged. "Whatever, kid, but right now I've gotta drain the noodle." Grunting, he walked over to a wall and began to urinate. When he came back, not bothering to button his filthy jeans, he smiled. "You know, kid," he said as he sat on the mattress, "Maybe you can go with me. I'm getting out of this shitty town as soon as I can get some cash together. It'll be just like old times, just you and me against the world."

"Where'll we go, Charles?" Ricky asked anxiously.

Charles just grinned. "Leave that up to me, kid. Anyway, you gotta be tired of being a slave for that bitch, right?"

Ricky started to object, but he didn't have the nerve because of the way Charles was acting. Instead, he just nodded.

"Right now, I gotta get some cash," Charles continued, yawning. "You got any left over from what the bitch pays you? I'm starving."

Deciding that Charles might be nicer if he gave him what money he had from the Cramers, Ricky quickly pulled two dollars out of his pocket. "Yeah, I've still got some. See?"

Charles grabbed the bills. "Good, kid," he said, stuffing them into his pocket. "You stay here. I'll go get us something to eat from the hamburger joint." He was gone before Ricky could react, so he sat on the mattress hoping that now Charles would take care of him as he'd done so often before. However, after an hour had passed and Charles still hadn't returned, he began to worry, so he got up and went to look for him.

In the meantime, Charles, sitting in the diner eating a hamburger, had changed his mind about Ricky. The kid'll just slow me down, he thought as he got up, paid for his burger, and left, thinking that he'd head for the bus station. He'd wanted to see Cramer get what was coming to him, but now he figured it would be smarter for him to get out of town as fast as he could. But just as he started up the boardwalk,

Ricky bumped into him. Disgusted, he grabbed him by the arm. "I thought I told you to wait in the house!" he snarled, pulling him into the space between the diner and an adjacent building.

"I was worried about you, Charles," Ricky whined, trying to get loose.

Charles suddenly slapped him, knocking him to the dirt. "You were worried about me, you little shit? You ought to know by now I can take care of myself!"

Ricky was terrified. "I'm sorry, Charles," he said, beginning to cry again.

"Oh, quit your sniffling," Charles said, now calmer, "Go back to the house. I've got some things to do. I'll be back to get you."

Ricky got up slowly. "Sure, Charles," he answered, "but what about us getting something to eat?"

Charles smiled sarcastically. "Don't worry about it, kid. We'll get some stuff when I get back."

Confused, Ricky just nodded as Charles finally let loose of his arm and walked away. Automatically he began to follow him but then hesitated. Seeing Charles heading out of town, he stumbled the opposite way behind the shops and began running. Before he knew it, and not really knowing why, he came to the Cramers' house and crawled under their porch, wrapped himself into a ball, looked around, and saw Astay in the shadows not two feet away. The huge dog leaned its head over and licked his face. He wrapped his arms around its leg.

Sitting at the bus station, Charles started to worry about Ricky. "The little shit might tell somebody about the knife," he muttered. He jumped up, ran back to the abandoned house, climbed in the window, looked around, and saw Ricky wasn't there. Furious, he climbed back out the window, determined to find him to beat the crap out of him.

The next morning, shivering under the porch, Ricky was suddenly awakened by Astay's huge body crushing him as it leapt over him. Startled, he peaked through the slats and saw Mrs. Cramer hugging it as it stood with its paws on her shoulders. "Good boy," she was saying, patting its head. "You miss me? I've only been gone a day."

Excited and yet embarrassed, Ricky crept out and stood smiling below her. When she saw him, she laughed and said, "Ricky, is that you? Why are you down there? Why aren't you in the house?"

"I didn't want to dirty it," he mumbled, thinking quickly. "Me and Astay were guarding it."

She smiled, opened the door, entered, and called back, "Come on in. It'll be all right. Bring Astay with you."

She took off her coat, put her purse on the table, and then noticed Ricky still standing by the door. "I came back to get more clothes and to check on the cafe," she said. "It appears we'll be away longer than I thought. Is there something wrong? Come on in."

He couldn't move. Soon he began crying. "I'm scared, Mrs. Cramer," he finally said.

She rushed down to him and grabbed his hands. "Of what, Ricky? What's frightening you?"

"I don't like being alone any more, Mrs. Cramer," he sobbed.

Never having liked being alone herself, she looked at Ricky standing so forlorn, and began thinking how her time in Anchorage would be less boring if she had company. At least he'd be somebody to talk to, she thought, and besides, whenever she could, they could work on his fable. She'd taken money from her savings and certainly had enough to get him a small room in the hotel. Suddenly, however, she thought of his brother. "What about Charles?" she asked. "You've got him."

Overwhelmed by her kindness, Ricky fell into her arms. "Oh, Ricky, my dear boy," she whispered, shocked and in tears herself. "Tell me."

"Charles scares me," he mumbled, his face against her shoulder.

She gently raised his head. "Why?" she whispered.

His shame so overwhelming him, but his loyalty to Charles so deep inside him, he was incapable of explaining. "He just does, Mrs. Cramer. I want to … be with you."

Maternal instinct washed over her. "We'll see about that, Ricky," she answered. "We will, but right now they tell me I have to be with Mr. Cramer. You understand that, don't you?"

He nodded. "But I can't stay here," he whimpered. "Charles'll find me."

Continuing to look into his eyes, she made her decision. "I'll tell you what," she said. "Tomorrow, would you like to go to Anchorage with me? I could get you a room at the hotel where I'm staying. How's that sound?" Ricky's smile brought tears to her eyes.

That night he slept in the guest room; and the next morning they both were up early, Ricky feeling as if he'd died and gone to heaven as he watched her adoringly making their breakfast and repacking her luggage. Later, when she said it was time for them to go, he couldn't stop beaming. However, when she commented that first she'd have to tell his foster-family of their plans, his heart sunk. "You can't!" he cried. "Charles'll find out!"

Frustrated, she answered, "But, Ricky, I can't take you without telling them. They're responsible for you. Besides, you'll have to get your clothes."

He lowered his head, embarrassed. "I don't have any other clothes," he said. "And they don't care about me. All they care about is the money they get for saying I live there. Nobody'll miss me. They won't even know I'm gone."

Perhaps not too surprisingly, Janie was more concerned by the fact he didn't have a change of clothes than she was by his comments about the foster-family. She hesitated, and then, perhaps against her better judgment, she decided that since her life was falling apart anyway, she might as well try to do something about his.

"All right," she said, "The ferry will be leaving soon. We'll get you what you'll need when we get to Anchorage."

That same morning, Charles still hadn't found Ricky, and he was becoming more and more convinced the little shit was blabbing to somebody. Fingering Cole's cross, he racked his brain trying to figure out who it could be. He knew from Ricky that the Cramers were on their way to Anchorage, so it couldn't be them. Neither could it be the foster family because Ricky had lost connection with them. The cop? He was gone, too. Finally, deciding the kid probably wasn't really a threat, he got up and climbed out the window.

Once outside, realizing he had to get some money somewhere, he thought of the empty café. "They've gotta have some cash there," he muttered. "Anyway, I'm hungry!"

Sneaking behind the shops, he reached the cafe's back door; and, finding the key under a gnome on the porch, he began to unlock the door when he heard Mrs. Cramer inside the house yelling, "COME ON, RICKY! WE HAVE TO HURRY!"

Hoping she hadn't seen him, he leapt around the corner of the café and sprawled in the dirt. A minute or so later, he saw her come out of the house, Ricky and the huge dog behind her. "ASTAY WILL BE ALL RIGHT UNDER THE PORCH!" she yelled again. Ricky led the dog to the space, patted it, and ran after her.

When they were out of sight, Charles slowly got up, eyed the darkness under the porch, watching for the huge dog. He was now convinced that Ricky had ratted on him to the Cramer woman about the butcher knife. "Fuck!" he muttered. "They're probably going to tell the cop. I've gotta get out of here!"

Suddenly he thought of the shirt. "Jesus, I wonder if it's still there!" Deciding he'd better find out, he slowly slid against the wall to the back door, unlocked it, closed the door softly behind him, and went into the storeroom to see if the shirt was still there. It wasn't. "Fuck!" he cursed. "The bitch probably has it, and she sure as shit won't tell anybody!" His stomach growled. Eyeing the refrigerators, he opened the first one and pulled out the first big bowl he saw. But he was too excited, and the bowl crashed to the floor, scattering shredded cheese all over.

"SHIT!" he yelled; and standing in the mess, he heard scratching at the door. He realized it was the mammoth dog and that if it got in, it'd tear him to pieces. He hastily grabbed another bowl, saw it was nothing more than chopped up lettuce, and angrily threw it on the floor. Finally, grabbing a third bowl, he discovered cooked fish filets; and using both hands, he stuffed them one at a time into his mouth. He no longer heard the dog. He opened the second refrigerator, grabbed a bottle of beer, and began gulping it down.

Suddenly he heard the front door open and saw Ricky and the dog come in. He jumped behind a counter as Ricky struggled to hold the dog by its collar. Knowing he was trapped and terrified of the dog, he curled into a ball, hoping they hadn't seen him. However, he hadn't counted on Astay's keen sense of smell as it broke loose from Ricky's grip, trotted over, and stood growling over him.

Scared to death, he jumped up, threw the bottle at it, and screamed, "JESUS! GET THAT BEAST AWAY FROM ME!" Ricky ran up and, looking questioningly at Charles, put his arms around Astay's head, and said, "What are you doing here, Charles?" He then saw the mess and added, "Boy, Mrs. Cramer's gonna be mad."

Feeling more confident as he fingered the cross in his pocket, Charles sneered, "Hello, kid. Who cares about the bitch? You get away from her?"

Ricky, holding Astay, whimpered, "Mrs. Cramer's no bitch. She's nice. She sent me back to get … something. I'm going to Anchorage with her. She said she'd get me a room in her hotel."

"Isn't that nice," Charles mocked. "You decided to rat on me? You tell her anything about me and the butcher knife?"

Ricky violently shook his head. "No," he answered. "I'm only going with her because I had nowhere else to go!"

Charles studied him for a moment. "She find anything in the storeroom?" he asked calmly.

"Here, in the café?" Ricky answered, confused.

"Yeah, kid, here." He pointed to his left. "She take anything with her?"

Ricky was trembling. "We didn't come in here, Charles," he whimpered. "I told you, she only asked me to come back to get something for her. In the house, you know."

Charles decided he was probably telling the truth. "And what did she want?" he asked.

Ricky tried to think of something that would keep him from knowing the real reason, but he drew a blank.

"Let's see," Charles said, smiling cruelly. "It might be clothes, I guess, but I'm glad you're here. I need some money, and I'll bet you know where they keep their petty cash." Ricky began crying.

"So you do," Charles said; and deciding Ricky had the dog under control, he moved toward them. "Well, you'll help your big brother find it, won't you?" He grabbed Ricky by the arm. "Show me!"

Holding tightly to the neck of the dog that was straining to get to Charles, Ricky just wanted to get back to Mrs. Cramer, so he pulled Astay to a shelf of cookbooks and pointed to one titled *Mexican Menus.* Charles pulled it from the shelf, found the cash box behind it, and saw it was locked. Letting go of Ricky, he ran to get a knife. Ricky didn't hesitate. He released his grip on Astay and ran out the front door.

"SHIT!" Charles yelled as he heard the door slam. In a panic, he went to the sink to wash his face, and then, grabbing a loaf of bread and the cash box, he started out the back door; but Astay was in his way. Scared senseless, he turned and raced it to the front door, which he was able to open before the dog reached him. He then ran for the house and suddenly bumped into Gus, who was on his way to check out the café.

"What's your hurry, boy?" he asked, stumbling backward.

Charles, also staggering, shrugged, held the cash box behind his back, and snarled, "Get outa my way, old man, I'm late for work!"

Gus laughed. "You have regular hours now, kid?" he asked. "I thought you only did pickup work."

Charles felt like hitting the old fool; but he held back, grinned, and said, "Gotta make money somehow," and began to walk away.

"Hold it a minute," Gus said suddenly. "You're the little bastard Jack kicked out of his café, right?"

In the mood he was in, Charles had no time for this asshole, so he sneered, "Yeah, that's me, but he didn't kick me out. I left after the son-of-a-bitch hit me. Nobody hits me! Now get out of my way!"

"Wait, kid," Gus said, grabbing his arm. Charles turned, cocking his right fist.

Gus leapt back. "Jesus, you've got a temper!" he yelped. "Calm down, kid. I just wanted to talk to you."

Trying to relax, Charles chewed the bread. "Leave me alone," he snarled.

"Sure, kid, whatever," Gus said, eyeing him suspiciously.

Picking up his pace, Charles scurried past the pier and saw Ricky with Mrs. Cramer. Cursing, he turned and headed back to the abandoned house. Once there, he climbed in the window, still holding the loaf of bread and the cashbox. He took out his knife and pried the box open. "HOLY SHIT!" he yelled when he saw the neatly sorted bills. "THERE MUST BE MORE THAN A HUNDRED BUCKS HERE!" Giggling, he stuffed the money into his pocket with the cross and climbed back out the window.

Ricky, running as fast as he could to get back to Mrs. Cramer, stumbled and fell heavily on the edge of the pier and lay weeping. The next thing he knew, she was on her knees beside him. "Ricky! Ricky! Are you all right?" she cried.

Still weeping, he sat up and felt her warmth as she hugged him. "What's wrong, my dear little boy?" she asked. "Couldn't you find the extra money? It's all right. We'll make do."

"Charles…" he blubbered. "He was in the café."

Pulling him away, she looked into his terrified eyes. "Did he hurt you?" she whispered.

Trying to control his weeping, Ricky told her what had happened. "He took the money box, Mrs. Cramer, and he threw things all over your kitchen! He's changed. He's not nice, Mrs. Cramer. I think he stole that butcher knife when we were helping you at the cafe."

Janie felt a surge of joy and hugged him again. "Where is he now, baby?" she asked, hoping that once the constable heard this, the stupid mess would be cleared up and they'd get things back to normal.

Ricky's heart stopped. "I don't know, Mrs. Cramer," he lied.

Janie nodded. "Well," she said, smiling. "At least he won't bother you any more, right?" Ricky wasn't sure, but he nodded back. She took his arm. "I'll tell you what. When we get to Anchorage, we'll talk to the constable. You can then tell him what you told me about the missing butcher knife. Okay?"

Ricky's eyes again began to fill with tears. "But he's my brother, Mrs. Cramer," he whimpered.

Janie again was touched. "I know, Ricky," she whispered. "But you have to tell him about the knife and about Charles stealing the money."

Ricky suddenly knew she was right. Charles *had* taken Mrs. Cramer's money, so he slowly nodded. She smiled, took his hand, and they boarded the ferry that had just docked. With oddly blue eyes, a feral cat watched them from the shadows.

Chapter Fourteen: The Big One

At the same time, unaware that Janie had returned and then left, Rodrigo sat in the shadows at a back table in Gus' bar, staring at the phone on the wall, tortured by the idea that his friend might be a murderer. His backpack with the shirt inside lay on the seat next to him. He knew in his heart that he had to call the constable to tell him about it, but he continued to hesitate. "I'm the only one who knows about it," he muttered. "Maybe I should burn it."

He started to question how well he really knew Jack. Sure, he thought, I've read about him in the books and been with him with Luke Scribner, but we've never been that close, and he *does* have a temper. He's changed, too, no longer the happy-go-lucky guy I saw down at the village. For one thing, his attitude toward Janie. He shook his head and muttered, "Heck, the blood could just be from him cutting himself."

Just as he got up to go to the phone, Gus came up, wiping his hands on a bar rag, and asked, "You're worried about Jack, aren't you, Professor?" He sat down opposite him. "I've been watching you."

Rodrigo slid his backpack closer and answered quickly. "I was just wondering how well I know him."

Gus stared at him and then said, "Jack's no killer. It'll blow over."

"I suppose," Rodrigo answered. "Can I use your phone?"

"Help yourself," Gus answered, getting up. "It's right over there."

Rodrigo dialed information, was given the number of the courthouse in Anchorage, dialed again, got hold of a receptionist, and said he wanted to speak to Ralph Eston, the constable from Valdez. The man said he'd page him. Rodrigo then gave him the phone number of the Cramer house and asked that he tell the constable to call him there.

Nodding to Gus, he left the bar and began hobbling slowly down the boardwalk. When he finally made it to the house, he sat in a chair with his head in his hands and moaned, "You're one hell of a friend, Professor."

The phone rang four times before he was able to pick it up. "Rodrigo?" he heard the constable asked. "What's up?"

Swallowing not only to clear his throat but also to get enough courage to answer, Rodrigo blurted out that he'd found a bloody shirt in the café.

Eston surprised him. "Doesn't make sense," he said. "Why would it be there now? I know Jack and Janie searched the café and the house for it! You sure it's bloody?"

Rodrigo gulped. "It's dried now, but I'm sure it's blood. It's also got a sleeve missing," he answered.

For a moment, there was silence, but then Eston angrily snapped, "Someone's trying to set Jack up, and I've got an idea who. Hang onto it, but don't tell anybody. When are you coming to Anchorage?"

Rodrigo told him of his broken leg and said he had to contact the cruiser first. "They'll want to debrief me on what Kasmali and I saw up at Prudhoe Bay. Then maybe I can hop a ride on a helicopter and get up there. Who would want to frame Jack?"

"I'm not sure yet," Eston answered. "Right now, I'll have to tell Jack's lawyer about the shirt. Then he can figure out what to do about it. Let me know when you get here."

After hanging up, Rodrigo called the cruiser.

Standing in the darkness under the pier, Kasmali, still the feral cat, had been watching as Jack, Janie, and the constable left on the ferry, and Ricky stumbled off. He'd been tempted to follow him, but it was Charles he was interested in. So he waited and considered where he should look.

A few minutes later, he saw Charles running furiously down the walkway toward the pier, yelling toward the ferry that was just pulling away. Kasmali (the cat) leapt up on the pier but stopped when Charles reached the barrier at the end of the pier, began waving angrily, and then turn and stomp back toward him. Knowing he probably wouldn't notice a stray cat, Kasmali moved aside as he cursed his way toward town. He trotted behind him, watching him sneak his way behind the shops until he finally reached the back corner of the café and peak around the corner. Creeping into the shadows, Kasmali saw Astay lying by the door.

So did Charles, who muttered "Shit!" under his breath and crawled away. Kasmali followed him again until they came to the abandoned house where Charles climbed in the window. Kasmali lay in the shadow of the house and waited.

An hour later, Kasmali watched as Charles wedged himself out the window and headed back to the pier. Kasmali followed him closely, wondering what he was up to. After all, he thought, the ferry only goes to Whittier. Keeping to the shadows by the barrier, as close to Charles as he dared, it all suddenly came clear when he heard Charles mutter, "I'll get that little shit!"

The ferry docked and Charles jumped aboard. Kasmali, trotting as fast as his little cat legs would allow, also leapt on unnoticed. Charles lowered himself against a railing, breathing heavily. Kasmali crept between two cars; and, making sure no one was around, he mutated from the cat into a duplicate of Ricky.

Though he was uncertain how he would explain Ricky's presence on the ferry, he then ran up to Charles, shouting in Ricky's voice, "CHARLES, CHARLES! IT'S ME, RICKY!"

Charles leapt up, jerked his head around, his mouth open, and cried, "Shit, Kid! Where'd you come from?" Just then a man came up and asked for their tickets. Charles grabbed Ricky by the arm and pulled him against the railing. Scowling, Charles turned his back, reached into his pocket, pulled out a few bills along with the cross, handed the man what he thought was their fare, and waited for his change.

When the man left, Kasmali giggled, imitating Ricky. "I always knew you were a good person, Charles. I saw a cross."

"Forget it, kid," Charles snarled. "It's just something I found. How did you find me?"

Kasmali, Ricky, giggled again, "I got away, Charles. When we got to Whittier, they weren't watching, so I ran and hid. I had to get back here because I remembered what you said about us going away together, so I took the ferry back. I was scared I wouldn't find you!"

Charles couldn't believe his luck in having the one person who could incriminate him right beside him. "That's great, Ricky," he said smiling. "But don't call me Charles, okay? I decided on a new name. Call me ... Rocky." He grinned.

Ricky smiled back. "Okay, Rocky," he answered. "Now that you've got money, where we going?"

Charles wasn't listening. Instead, he was thinking how things were coming together for him. He had money, his little brother couldn't do any more damage to him, and Cramer was about to be thrown in the slammer. He started laughing.

"Come on, Rocky, where we going?" Ricky, Kasmali, repeated.

"I figured you left with the Cramer bitch," Charles answered. "I was gonna try to find you before you got on the train to Anchorage to save you from her. Anyway, it's time we got out of that shitty town. Now when we get to Whittier, we can see the world. It's good to see you. Just like the old days."

Ricky smiled shyly. "Yeah, Rocky," he whispered. "You're my brother. Mrs. Cramer's just somebody who gave me a job. I feel sorry, though, for her and Mr. Cramer. He's in real trouble."

Charles laughed. "Good," he scoffed. "The son-of-a-bitch deserves it. You remember how he hit me, don't you?"

Kasmali sensed he was getting somewhere. "Yeah," Ricky answered. "He shouldn't have done that, but I don't think he could ever kill anybody."

Charles' smile turned into a sneer. "How do you know, you little shit? Anything could have happened. Maybe he just lost it. You saw his temper when he hit me." He sat back, fingered the cross, and looked at the churning of the backwash as the ferry pulled away from the pier. "Forget about him. I sure have."

Kasmali thought he was getting nowhere, so he sat silently for a few minutes. Finally, hoping Charles hadn't shut down completely, he, Ricky, said, "I guess you're right, Rocky. He probably lost his temper and killed the guy. Besides, I even heard somebody saw him running away that night."

Charles couldn't help himself. He laughed. "You got that right, kid. Somebody *did* see him. Me!"

Now we're getting somewhere, Kasmali thought. Maintaining his innocent pose as Ricky, he said, again shyly, "You saw him, Char... Rocky? But I heard the guy who saw him was going to tell about it at his trial. Will you?"

Charles was beginning to feel uncomfortable. For the longest time, he fingered the cross and just looked out to sea. Finally, though, perhaps remembering Ricky was no longer a threat to him, he leaned over and whispered, "It's time you grew up, kid. The truth is I made it all up because I hate the bastard. We've got to leave because the cop's bugging me." He smiled and put his hand on Ricky's shoulder.

Ricky giggled. "That's weird, Rocky," he said. "Why would he bother you? You couldn't have had anything to do with the murder. You're my brother. I know you."

"Oh, yeah?" Charles answered, sneering again. "You know me? You think I'm too much of a pussy to kill somebody? You think I don't have the balls? You've got no clue what I could do."

Kasmali was stunned. Here, all he'd wanted to find out was what Charles knew about the killing, and now he'd almost confessed. He sat back and tried to think.

"What's the matter, kid?" Charles asked, laughing. "So I knifed a guy. Think about it. Now you know I can protect you."

Kasmali figured he had to do something, but he just nodded. Charles went back to viewing the coast now on the horizon, his fingers continuing to knead the cross in his pocket. Kasmali knew he had to get him back to Valdez, but no matter how he tried, he couldn't come up with a plan.

They spoke little after that as Kasmali, Ricky, watched Charles leaning over the railing violently vomiting. He was puzzled by his sudden sickness and began thinking he would die without confessing. Kasmali stood beside him, hoping he'd say more about the murder.

But just as they reached the entrance of the bay, a loud explosion boomed out of the southeast; and within minutes the ferry began rocking and then listed violently to the port side, throwing Charles into the water. Kasmali, still Ricky, had been able to steady himself on the deck. As soon as he could, he struggled to his feet and jumped over the railing into the water now strangely calm. Once he'd gained the surface, he began treading water, searching desperately for Charles, his frail arms growing weak.

Just as he thought he'd have to mutate into an aquatic creature, he saw him struggling to hang on to a seat cushion luckily floating near him. He swam up next to him and saw he was alive.

Realizing that an earthquake had struck and that if its epicenter was in the ocean not far from them, a tidal wave would probably soon be upon them, he held Charles by one hand, looked into the sky, and noticed a single eagle soaring above fighting against the gusting wind. He nodded, raised his free arm as high as he could, and slowly mutated into the eagle's twin.

Now fluttering in the water, he used his talons to grab Charles by his belt, spread his wings, and slowly rose into the sky rapidly filling with dust and sediment. He then looked out on the horizon and saw a huge wave just beginning to form. The wind was becoming more and more violent as he flew toward Valdez. Looking back, he saw the wave growing bigger, now no more than a few hundred yards behind him, heading like him for the coast. Redoubling his efforts, he soared higher out of the dust and caught a strong current that swept them to the coast. He spread his large wings and let the wind push him.

Even with the strength of a massive eagle, he was having difficulty and suspected he'd have to drop the boy. But at perhaps the last minute, he looked down and saw he'd flown beyond the wave and that dry land was now below him. He flew down, trying to find a spot where he could land, but the earth was convulsing too wildly. Now close to the ground, he found he could ride the wind. Soon he was proceeding more easily and his strength was returning. Desolation was everywhere.

After a while, he saw the tangled cars of a train knocked off its tracks shaking violently with large gashes all around it. With Charles hanging limply and heavily in his talons, he knew he couldn't land there, so he continued to float with the wind. Soon he saw ice huts that he hoped marked a native village. Fighting the wind, he landed softly on the still shaking ground, trying to avoid hurting Charles, and mutated quickly into his original form as Chief Kasmali. He carried Charles to the first igloo.

Struggling inside, he saw an Indian family, a man, his wife, and three small children, sitting calmly. The man was telling stories despite the rumbling and shaking. When they saw Kasmali burst in carrying a body, the children leapt up and screamed, but the man just smiled and said in clear English, "Welcome, Chief. How did you get here?"

Unwilling to lie, Kasmali laid Charles down, shrugged, and answered, "It was difficult. You are correct. I am an Inupiaq chief. My name is Kasmali. This boy needs help. May I leave him with you until I can find somewhere to take him where he can get medical attention?"

The man nodded and said, "Of course, but all we can do is watch over him. What happened? How bad is he?"

"I think he's just unconscious, but it might be worse," Kasmali replied. "We were caught in the wave. I'm sorry about this, but if I'm going to find help, I can't carry him with me."

The man nodded. Behind him, though, the woman was scowling. "You may leave him here," he said, "but the only aid stations are probably way up in Anchorage. By the time you get there and back, the boy may get worse. There's little we can do for him except watch over him."

Kasmali took the man's hand. "Thank you, friend, that's all I ask of you." He turned to leave but then stopped and said, "I'm amazed at your calm. Aren't you concerned by the earthquake?"

The man shrugged and answered, "We have been through them before and survived very nicely, thank you. You're old enough to remember the big one in '64. I'll bet the tidal wave's already hit the coast. In '64, that's what caused the most damage; and I imagine we're not through with the tremors yet."

"You're sure you and your family are safe here?"

The man looked at him quizzically. "This is the best place. You should know that," he answered. "It's far enough away from the coast, and the ice blocks will shift with the tremors. If they fall, we'll just move out into the open and make another. You say you're Inupiaq?"

"Yes," Kamali answered quickly. "But in my travels to get here, I've seen what the earthquake has done."

The man shrugged. "Don't worry about us or the boy. We'll try to keep him safe until you return. Go."

Kasmali nodded and left. Once he was out of the igloo, he struggled along the trembling ground to a group of fallen trees, stood behind them, and mutated again into the huge eagle. His initial idea was to fly west to Anchorage as the man had suggested, but he suddenly remembered the toppled train that was closer and might have someone who could help.

He flew and he flew, trying to recall where he'd seen it, but below him was nothing but floodwater and trembling desolation. Then suddenly below him he saw a figure sitting lifelessly in a kayak, his head down, his arms dangling down its side, floating south in the receding flood. Knowing he couldn't ignore him, he fluttered down and landed on the remains of a nearby wobbling roof and looked at him. Satisfied that the man was in no condition to notice him, he slowly mutated back into his human form and shouted, "DO YOU NEED HELP?"

The man slowly raised his head, saw the tall Indian, and began weeping uncontrollably. Kasmali reached over, pulled the man's kayak next to the roof, and waited. "Sweet Jesus," the man finally was able to mutter, "Sweet Jesus, someone's alive! For hours I've been floating looking for people."

Kasmali again thought of the train, but he didn't want to just leave the man. He waited for him to compose himself. Finally, he put his hand on his shoulder. "Tell me, friend," he said. "I have been in the north. Tell me what happened. How did you survive the wave?"

Floating alongside Kasmali on the floodwater that was now rapidly ebbing toward the sea, the man wiped his eyes and stared ahead. "You felt the earthquake, didn't you?" he asked. Kasmali nodded. "Well, it hit like a bomb; and when the ground began to buckle and crumble beneath me, I figured the big one had finally come. I was at the ferry waiting to go west to meet some friends for a kayak trip, but I missed it. Then the pier began to wobble, and I was just able to grab my kayak, jump in the water, and begin paddling as if my life depended on it. Which it did, of course."

Kasmali interrupted, amazed. "You rode the wave in your kayak?"

"Yeah," the man answered. "Unbelievable, I know. Anyway, all of a sudden I saw a wall of water behind me, so I put my head down and held on to the sides of my kayak. It hit me so hard I flew at least a half a mile, I guess. Then, thinking I was a goner, I felt the wave throw me down and then up on its crest. It was like I was on a roller-coaster. Luckily, though, the kayak was sturdy so I was able to ride the wave as it surged north. Then, just when I thought I'd made it – the water had slowed down, you see – the current suddenly backed up and I was swept back. At that point, I gave up and waited to drown. Then you yelled." He began weeping again.

Kasmali waited, incredulous. Finally, the man looked up and shouted, "WHAT'RE WE GONNA DO?" He pointed ahead of them. "JUST DRIFT OUT TO SEA AND DIE?"

Kasmali pondered the possibilities. He could mutate into a large fish and nose the man north to land, but he sensed that would probably make him even more hysterical. Or he could stay as he was and pull the kayak, but that didn't seem too inviting. He could, of course, just leave him, but that was against his nature. Finally, he decided his second option was best. However, he knew that first he'd somehow have to calm him.

He stood up on the unsteady roof and stared at him. Eventually the man stared back, a questioning look on his face. Kasmali maintained his gaze until the man's eyes became glassy. He then stripped off his clothes, leapt into the water, and began pushing the kayak against the current in an attempt to reach land.

Though it was difficult even for Kasmali, after an hour or more they reached the furthest surge of the wave, and he nudged the kayak onto the shore. The man was still in a stupor when Kasmali awoke him by shouting, "WAKE UP, FRIEND! WE'VE REACHED LAND!"

Shaking his head, the man looked around. "How'd we get here?" he asked, confused.

"I pulled you," Kasmali answered. "If you're all right, maybe you can tell me more about that ferry you missed."

"Where are we? Holy St. Francis, you're naked!" the man said, staring at him.

"Just northeast of Anchorage, I think. I lost my clothes in the water," Kasmali answered. "Are you all right?"

The man nodded and struggled to get out of the kayak. Once out, he reached back in and pulled out a leather bag. "Thank God it's still there," he sighed and then looked at Kasmali. "How the hell did you pull me?" he asked; and then, not waiting for Kasmali to answer, he said, "I've gotta get there. I'm a nurse. People probably need my help."

Amazed by his luck, Kasmali helped him onto the shore and said, "I have a boy who needs help. He's with an Indian family not far away. Would you have a look at him first?"

Now on land and stretching, the man grabbed Kasmali's hand. "What's your name, friend? You saved my life, though I can't understand how. I should know whom to thank."

"They call me Chief Kasmali," he answered.

"Well, Chief, I'll do anything you ask. My name's Peter James. Just lead the way."

Less than two hours later, when they finally reached the Indian family, the man handed Kasmali his jacket to cover himself and introduced himself. "My name's Peter," he said to the father. "I'm a nurse, and this good man told me you have someone here who needs my help."

Charles, groaning on a sleeping bag in the corner, suddenly reared up, holding his head. "Jesus, finally a White Man!" he moaned. "Get me away from these savages! I gotta get back to the ferry!" He slumped back, and Peter walked over to him and put his hand on his forehead. "I'm a nurse, son. Perhaps I can help you."

Charles again looked at him and moaned, "You a faggot? Guys aren't nurses. Jesus, my head is killing me!"

"You've got a fever, a bad one," Peter answered, ignoring his insult. "May I check to see if you have any other problems?"

"Keep your fucking hands off me, you queer," Charles said haltingly and then looked at Kasmali. "Hey, Chief, you're here too. Get this homo away from me!" He then fainted.

Kasmali watched stoically as Peter examined Charles and then looked up. "Nothing broken, just bruises," he said. "The fever may have come from exposure, and he's undoubtedly suffering from a concussion. He'll have to stay stationary for a day or so." He turned to the native. "Do you speak English?"

The man nodded. "Well, I'm sorry, sir," Peter said gently. "The boy here has probably been a burden to you, but could he and I remain with you until he can be moved?" Again the man nodded.

Kasmali then spoke. "You are a good man, Peter. I will use the time to see if there is anyone else in Valdez who survived. I have friends there.

When I return, I will somehow find a way to take you and the boy to Anchorage."

Charles suddenly awoke. "I'VE GOTTA GET OUT OF HERE!" he screamed. 'I GOTTA GET BACK TO THE FERRY!"

Kasmali and Peter looked at him, thinking he had to be delirious. "Why?" Peter asked.

"I gotta get my stuff," Charles moaned.

Peter shook his head. "You're in no condition to go anywhere, son," he answered. "Besides, the ferry was destroyed by the tidal wave."

Charles cried out in pain as he tried to get up.

Kasmali gently pushed him back and asked, "Where's your brother, Charles?"

"How should I know?" Charles moaned. "I haven't seen him."

"What stuff, as you call it, are you talking about?" Kasmali asked, suddenly curious.

Charles turned his head without answering. Kasmali, looking at Peter, just nodded, wished him good luck, said goodbye to the native family, and left.

Again finding the grove of trees, he mutated into the eagle; and knowing now that Charles would be safe, he became curious about the toppled train. He flew back toward Whittier.

Chapter Fifteen: The Train

Earlier that day, before the earthquake and subsequent tidal wave hit, Rodrigo, convinced by the recent tremors that a catastrophe was imminent, had hobbled on his crutches around town attempting to warn people. And this time, perhaps because of his intensity, some listened and began making plans to leave the coast. However, most just laughed and went about their business.

Later, when the captain of the *Merry Gale* called him telling him they'd arrived, Rodrigo told him of his foreboding and agreed to come aboard, bringing with him Dr. Watson, his receptionist, and the few who'd heeded his warning. The remaining townspeople stood by the pier and scoffed as they watched them board the launch and head out to the ship.

After he'd met with the captain to tell him of the details of the catastrophe at Prudhoe Bay, the cruiser was well on its way out into the Sound when Rodrigo, standing alone outside his cabin, heard a tremendous roar to the northeast. Shouting, "THIS IS IT!" he cringed and braced himself against the railing, expecting an inevitable repercussion; but all he could feel was a subtle shift of the ship's direction. Curious, he looked out to sea and gasped as he saw a gigantic wave not more than a few hundred yards away coming right at them.

Fortunately, the captain must have seen it too and thus pointed the bow toward it just before it hit. Rodrigo was washed against a far railing. Holding on and wrapping his legs around it, he closed his eyes as the cruiser, soon almost vertical, struggled to churn to the crest of the mammoth wave. To Rodrigo, it seemed like hours until it finally made it and crashed down with a violent thud.

The captain immediately grabbed the intercom to check the damage.

Struggling because of his leg in a cast and the rocking of the ship, Rodrigo crawled into a cabin and then made his way down to the crews' quarters. Bodies were strewn all around him. He hobbled to a phone to call the captain who immediately asked if he and the others were okay. Rodrigo said he was and that he'd check. When he returned, he informed the captain that one man was dead, but the others were alive though in bad shape. The ship was now rocking gently.

After seeing to the men and the townspeople, he hobbled out to the side of the ship, grabbed his binoculars, and looked north toward Valdez. Stunned, he saw nothing but carnage. "Those poor people," he groaned.

Full of grief, he crawled up to the bridge and was relieved to find the captain and his officers unharmed and busy seeing to the ship. Noticing him, the captain shocked him by smiling. "Lose your crutches, sailor?" he asked calmly.

"The least of our problems, Captain," Rodrigo answered, gasping. "The coast's a mess."

The captain nodded. "Thank God you and your friends were onboard. The medic's checking them and the crew now. It's a miracle we only lost that one man."

"Is the helicopter still functional?" Rodrigo asked. "I'd like to fly over there with the medics to check for survivors."

"You have to be kidding," the captain answered. "With your leg? Even if we can even get the chopper up, why don't we just leave it to the medics? You'd probably just be in the way."

"I have to try," Rodrigo answered pleadingly.

The captain called the deck officer. After a brief conversation, he smiled at Rodrigo and said, "I'll get it up and running as soon as the crew and passengers are seen to, but I think you'll be wasting your time." He pointed to what used to be the town. "Nothing could have survived that tidal wave."

As it turned out, caring for the battered crew and the passengers from Valdez took the rest of the day, so Rodrigo and two medics weren't able to fly off the ship until late the next morning. Rodrigo made sure he had the bloody shirt in his backpack.

Skimming along what used to be the coast, he gazed in horror at what once was Valdez. "Jesus!" he cried. "Look! It's like a bomb hit! Fly south, would you, Lieutenant? Let's see how bad it hit the other towns."

The pilot nodded and checked his instruments. "Southeast, Sir?" he asked. "Without landmarks, it'll be hit and miss."

As they flew over the now ebbing flood, the pilot called out where he thought the towns once were. "Sitka," he said, pointing down. "Nothing but sea and wreckage." Later, they hovered 0ver what he thought were Ketchikan then Juneau then Cordova. They saw nothing but parts of buildings strewn for miles in heaps, the water now muddy with acres and acres of silt that had once been the coast.

"Let's try for Anchorage. I have to get there anyway," Rodrigo ordered. "If it was hit by the earthquake, there'll be hundreds, maybe thousands, of casualties."

The pilot veered west. After less than an hour, again he pointed down. "People are down there, Sir. Natives, I think. What do you want me to do?"

"Land, damn it!" Rodrigo snapped. "They probably need help!"

The pilot looked at him for a moment. "Are you sure? The ground's still shaking, It won't be easy."

Rodrigo reached over, kneading his shoulder. "You can do it, Lieutenant," he said.

It took the pilot two tries, but finally he landed about fifty yards away from a native family waving beside an ice hut. As soon as the rotor blades slowed, the medics jumped out, Rodrigo following them slowly, using his crutches as best as he could.

"Hello," he said as they approached the eldest man standing with a woman and three young children. "Do you speak English?"

"Of course," the man said indignantly.

"Is your family all right?" Rodrigo asked after introducing himself.

"Nice to meet you too. We're fine," the man answered sarcastically,

Peter came out of the igloo. "You must be Navy," he said, holding out his hand. "Thank God you're here. My name's Peter. I'm a nurse. A heroic Inupiaq brought me and an injured boy here a few hours ago. He then left, and now the bastard's run away taking my parka and boots!"

"The boy? Was he Inupiaq, too? Who was he?"

"I don't think so. He was white and the nastiest kid I've ever met."

Rodrigo immediately thought that maybe Kasmali was the Inupiaq. Who else could make it in the middle of an earthquake? "The Inupiaq? Did he give his name?" he asked.

"Yeah, Kasbali, or something like that. He said he'd be back for the boy."

Rodrigo looked at Crash. "You want to try to find the kid?" he asked.

Crash nodded. "I guess we should, Sir, but I don't have a lot of fuel. We'll have to get lucky."

Rodrigo turned to the Indian. "You sure you're all right?"

Surprisingly, the man scowled. "Why do people keep asking that? Listen, White Man, we've survived worse than this without your help!" He turned and waved the family back into the hut.

Peter, Rodrigo, and the two medics boarded the helicopter. The pilot then began heading south, skimming the still shuddering earth, both men and the medics searching for any sign of the missing boy. Suddenly, just as the pilot was about to demand that they return to the ship to refuel, Rodrigo managed to see a body below next to a pile of rubble. "THAT COULD BE HIM!" he yelled. "SET IT DOWN!"

The pilot skillfully landed on a patch of level ground; and, following the medics, Rodrigo struggled out and hobbled over to the body. He yelled, "IT'S HIM! HE'S NOT MOVING!"

When one of the medics turned the boy over to check his pulse, Rodrigo reared back when he saw it was Charles Murray. "He's alive," the medic said. "Let's get him in the chopper and find some blankets for him. He's bound to have frostbite."

Suddenly Charles jerked up, slashed at the medic with a knife, and then fell back in a swoon. "CRAP!" the medic screamed. "HE TRIED TO STAB ME!"

Rodrigo shook his head. "At least we know his right hand isn't frozen. Come on, let's carry him."

Once they reached the chopper, the pilot stopped them, saying, "We've got a problem, Sir. The bird can only carry four people. Either we leave the kid or somebody's going to have to be left behind."

Before Rodrigo could answer, Peter said calmly, "I'll do it. The boy's now safe, and I'm just in the way. I'll find my way back to the natives."

Rodrigo knew he was right, so after wishing him good luck, they were on their way to the ship. Suddenly, Rodrigo thought of the pipeline, its oil spurting out, covering acres of the permafrost and tundra. "My God!" he gasped. "I hope they got my report!"

"Report?" the pilot asked.

Rodrigo didn't seem to hear him.

"What report?" the pilot repeated.

"What?" Rodrigo answered, a stricken look on his face.

"You mentioned a report. What report?"

Rodrigo shook his head. "I'm sorry," he answered. "I was just thinking of Valdez and the pipeline. I have some friends there who I think were on their way to Anchorage when the earthquake hit. I'm worried about them. The report? A while back, an Inupiaq and I were up at ANWR when the permafrost cracked apart and swallowed men and trucks off the edge of the platform. I sent a report about it and other signs we saw to people who know about such things."

"My God!" the pilot cried. "Was there anything left?"

Rodrigo looked at him sadly. "Yeah," he answered, "but at that point we were concerned about our own survival so we didn't notice. It was during our trip back that I broke my leg." The pilot nodded.

For the next hour or so, they flew east until they reached the cruiser and landed softly on the heliport.

"Take the boy to sick bay," Rodrigo said to the medics as they got out. Then, turning to the pilot, he added, "After you gas up, are you game for another jaunt? We have to get Peter."

"It's been a long day, Sir, and what about your leg?" the pilot answered, smiling. "What the hell, if you're game, so am I; but I'll need about an hour. Then I guess you'll also want to check out that train, right?"

A few hours later, he and the pilot were off. They found Peter with the natives. With him now aboard, they began to search for the train.

"You know, sir," the pilot said. "The odds are against us finding it in all the wreckage."

"Yeah," Rodrigo answered. "But we have to try."

Even though the pilot was highly skilled, they were only able to see rapidly receding floodwater. Finally, feeling heartsick, Rodrigo ordered him to continue flying east. Mile after mile, however, all they saw was mud and the remnants of houses, trees, and huge slabs of ice.

Then suddenly they saw it, halfway up a mountain, its engine completely covered by mud with two passenger cars on their sides behind it. "TAKE US DOWN, LIEUTENANT. PEOPLE ARE PROBABLY HURT!" Rodrigo shouted. The pilot had already begun his descent. After only a moment they floated gently to a landing a few yards away.

When Rodrigo and Peter struggled out, the only sounds they heard were the hissing of the engine and the distant roar of the receding waters. While Peter began checking the wreckage, Rodrigo hesitated and then somehow managed to hobble over to the nearest toppled passenger car. Throwing his crutches aside, he grabbed some rungs and struggled up to the shattered windows. Looking in, he saw luggage, broken glass, and ripped apart seats everywhere, but no people. He jumped down, intending to check the second car, when Peter, above him on a slope, pointed down, and yelled, "OVER HERE! THEY'RE OVER HERE!"

Hopping furiously on his crutches, Rodrigo made it to the top of the slope and saw at least fifteen people huddled together under a shelter made of tree limbs. He and Peter stumbled down the slope, Rodrigo scanning the crowd for Janie. A man met him with a wide grin and open arms. "IT'S ABOUT TIME! CHRIST, I'M GLAD TO SEE YOU!" he shouted.

"How bad was it?" Rodrigo asked. "Do you know a woman named Janie Cramer? Is she here with you?"

The man grabbed his shoulders. "How bad?" he said. "Bad, real bad, hit like a bomb. Only one dead, but the rest are in bad shape. Yeah, Mrs. Cramer's still on the train, but she's not doing very well."

"What happened to her?" Rodrigo asked anxiously.

"Best as I could tell, she's got a broken collarbone and some facial wounds. We stopped the blood and tried to get her out, but we were worried we'd make her worse, so we left her where she was after making her as comfortable as we could on a couple of seats we made into a bed. She's not complaining, but she's gotta be freezing and in terrible pain." He pointed to the second car further up the hill.

Rodrigo asked Peter to see to the people and then hobbled to the car, clawed his way onto its side of the car, and lowering himself through a shattered window. Gaining his balance, he quickly scanned the rubble and saw the back of Ricky's head. "RICKY!" he yelled and began climbing back to him. The boy, his face bloody and swollen, looked up, smiled, and waved.

Janie was lying on her side, several articles of clothing packed over her, her face turned away from Ricky who was holding her left hand. He was crying as Rodrigo climbed over the rubble to reach him, trying hard not to believe Janie was dead.

"I knew somebody would come," Ricky whimpered. "Now Mrs. Cramer'll be okay. I know it. She just fainted."

Relieved, Rodrigo patted him on the shoulder. "Do you remember me, Ricky? I'm Rodrigo. I came in a helicopter with some people that'll help. If we can get her out of here without doing her more damage, I'll get the pilot to get her taken care of on our Navy ship. They've got a hospital there."

Ricky nodded and stood up. "She's freezing, Mr. Rodrigo. We have to hurry."

"Climb out and get a couple of strong men, will you, Son? I'll keep an eye on her."

Like a mountain goat, Ricky scrambled noisily over the rubble and was out of the window before Rodrigo could say another word. Janie then turned her head and looked at him. Her face, once smooth and pink, was now scraped and bloody. "Rodrigo," she whispered, shivering. "How'd you find us?"

"That doesn't matter, Janie. Right now we have to get you out of here and to the sick bay on the ship," he whispered back.

She tried to sit up. "No," she said quickly, wincing with pain. "I have to get to Anchorage to see if Jack's all right. Besides, the other people need more help than me. They must be frozen by now."

Rodrigo thought for a minute. "I'll tell you what, Janie. I've got a helicopter. A trip to the ship and back will only take less than an hour. What about flying you there first so the medics can check you out? Then I'll have the pilot fly back here with food and blankets for the others. While the medics are making sure you're all right, we can fly them in shifts to the ship. Maybe then we can fly to Anchorage. What do you say?"

She'd fainted. Rodrigo turned as he heard the men climbing through the rubble.

After they wrapped her in whatever additional coverings they could find, they carefully began carrying her through the rubble. The job of getting her through the window was difficult and took more time than Rodrigo wished, but they finally got her outside. Rodrigo ran to find the pilot as Ricky lay on top of her, trying to keep her warm. Finally finding the pilot tending to the people huddled under the shelter, he pulled him aside. "There's a woman down there who needs to get to the sick bay right now. I told her you'd fly her there and bring back food and blankets for these people." He pointed to the people who seemed to be comatose.

"I'm way ahead of you, sir. I was just waiting for you; but as I told you, four passengers is my limit. You pick the remaining two." He nodded and ran to the chopper.

Rodrigo looked at the people and shook his head. Then, hearing yelling, he turned to see the man he'd been talking to arguing with another man. "What's the problem?" he asked as he came up to them.

"I HAVE TO GET TO ANCHORAGE!" a filthy, malodorous man was screaming. Rodrigo pulled them apart.

"He's Slim Carter, Valdez's town drunk," the other man muttered as he fell to the ground. "He's saying his poor mother's in Anchorage and he's got to get to her. It's a crock, of course. I know the guy. I'm Joe Ballard, and more than once I've had to kick him out of my liquor store!"

Rodrigo's mouth flew open. "CHRIST," he yelled. "HE'S CLIMBING ON THE CHOPPER!" Sure enough, while they weren't looking, Slim Carter must have heard the sound of the helicopter's rotors and had run to the open hatch. They ran to catch him; but by the time they reached it, Slim was in a seat with his arms wrapped around it.

"WHAT THE HELL DO YOU THINK YOU'RE DOING?" Rodrigo shouted as he struggled onboard and grabbed his shoulders. 'THERE ARE WOMEN AND CHILDREN OUT THERE! THEY GO FIRST, YOU SON-OF-A-BITCH!"

Slim, his teeth clinched, his hands firmly on the bottom of the seat, closed his eyes tight and didn't answer. "Listen, you bastard!" Rodrigo snarled. "I don't know if you told Joe here the truth about your mother, but you're gonna have to wait to see her until we get all the sick people taken care of! Now be a man and get off this ship!"

Slim didn't move. Disgusted, Rodrigo jumped off on his good leg and walked up to the men who'd helped get Janie out of the train. "I need you guys for a minute," he said, pointing to them. "We gotta get some guy out of the chopper."

"You mean Slim?" one of them asked. "Be my pleasure." He and the other two men, along with Joe Ballard, jumped in the hatch, grabbed Slim roughly, pulled him out, and dragged him under the lean-to. "We'll watch him," Joe said.

In the meantime, the pilot and Ricky had managed to lift Janie aboard. Rodrigo then hobbled back to find Peter who could help him to determine which of the injured most needed help. Peter made it easy by pointing to a man hugging a pregnant woman. Trying to be nonchalant, using his crutches for balance, he struggled down to them, pulled the man aside, and whispered. The man nodded and then spoke to his wife who shook her head. Rodrigo hobbled back up the slope to Peter. After a few minutes, the man led the woman up to them and said, "My wife's ready." She was weeping as Rodrigo, Peter, and the man led her to the helicopter.

Once Janie and the other three were strapped in, Rodrigo hobbled forward to the pilot. "I DON'T KNOW YOUR NAME, LIEUTENANT," he yelled over the noise of the rotors.

"CRASH," the pilot yelled back. "MY FRIENDS CALL ME CRASH!"

Rodrigo, laughing, moved next to him and said, "Damn! I'm glad I didn't know that before we flew off the ship!"

The pilot grinned. "Jealousy, that's all," he answered. "Never crashed in my life, thank God."

"Well, Crash, hurry back," Rodrigo said as he turned away and jumped out the hatch. The pilot waved as the helicopter rose, hovered, and then slowly flew away.

Peter went back to the passengers. Rodrigo looked around and thought of Joe who was guarding Slim. Thinking the guy'd probably had enough, he walked over, told him to try to get warm, and stood over Slim, suddenly feeling compassionate as Slim sat morosely muttering to himself. Rodrigo sat down beside him, leaned against a tree, and decided to talk to him. He pointed down at the first train car. "Look, an eagle," he said amiably. "Friendly bird, being so close to people." Slim just kept looking at the ground.

"I've seen you at Gus'," Rodrigo then said, trying again.

"I gotta get to Anchorage," Slim suddenly whined. "You'll be sorry if you don't let me get there before Cramer's trial ends. You're his friend, aren't you?"

Surprised by his mention of the trial, Rodrigo sat up. "What do you care about his trial?" he asked angrily. "Did he do something to you? Do you just want to see him convicted?"

Slim cackled. "You got it all wrong, Mister. I can prove he didn't do it."

Rodrigo looked at him skeptically. "And how in God's name can you do that?" he asked, smiling at his obvious phony attempt to find another way to get on the helicopter.

Slim smiled enigmatically. "I saw what happened," he said smugly. "I was on the pier that night, and I was the one who found the body. I saw the whole thing."

"Sure you did," Rodrigo said sarcastically. "I heard about your drinking problem and your lying. You can stop now."

Seemingly affronted, Slim sat up. "I can prove it," he said stiffly. "I can tell exactly what happened and how it wasn't Cramer."

Still skeptical, Rodrigo continued his sarcasm. "You can prove it? Right. How are you going to do that?"

"I had a lady friend with me. We were up on the pier having a good time when we heard the fight. Anyway, we rolled over to the edge of the pier and saw the whole thing. Then, when the kid left, I saw the guy lying there and went down to see if he was all right. He wasn't. He was dead. My lady friend and I then decided to keep our mouths shut, That is, until we heard about the reward."

"What kid? What reward?" Rodrigo yelped.

"One of those kids who wander around the town all the time. I don't know his name. The reward? You haven't heard? Mrs. Cramer is offering ten thousand dollars to anyone who knows anything."

"What?" Rodrigo snapped. "Why didn't you tell somebody about this before?"

"Are you kidding? They'd probably take the reward away from me. No way. I just want to get to Anchorage so I can tell my story to Cramer's lawyer, if he has one. So if you're really Cramer's friend, you'll get me on the next chopper."

Joe walked up. "What's the old sot telling you?" he asked.

"Tell him!" Rodrigo demanded. Slim turned his head. "Tell Joe here what you told me or we'll just leave you here to die!"

Shrugging, Slim told his tale. When he was finished, Joe just laughed. "A woman was with you, you say?" he asked sarcastically. "And I'm sure we can find her to verify your story?"

Slim smiled. "Yup," he answered. "She runs the shop right next to your office."

"She did, you mean," Joe said. "She and most of them who stayed in Valdez are long gone. Now where's your proof?"

Slim wilted. "I hadn't thought of that," he said, almost weeping, but then added angrily, "There's me, anyway! I know what I saw!"

Rodrigo, disappointed and worried about how the bloody shirt bundled in the chopper would be used against Jack, just shrugged.

However, when the helicopter returned a few hours later, Slim was among the four selected to fly to the ship. Rodrigo stayed with the remaining passengers.

Chapter Sixteen: Kasmali Finds Rodrigo

The earthquake having subsided, it only took Kasmali a few hours to fly south to where he remembered Whittier had been; but once there he saw nothing but wreckage and receding flood water. And, while soaring over the desolation, he became confused by a feeling of what he imagined the humans called sadness.

I'm getting worse, he mused and then thought of Rodrigo who'd been in Valdez the last time he'd seen him. Now the town was gone. He knew Jack was in Anchorage and may have avoided the worst of the catastrophe; but he had no idea if Rodrigo was alive or whether Janie and the little boy she was so fond of had made it to the city.

Struggling to control his feeling, he began flying northwest, knowing that Peter and the teenager were waiting for him. Suddenly, however, he decided first to veer west to see if the train had made it to Anchorage.

He saw it below him, just as he was about to give up, its engine covered by snow, its passenger cars scattered and on their sides, and a helicopter nearby with a number of humans around it. He was tempted to land in a secluded spot and mutate back into Kasmali to join them, but he knew it would be difficult to explain how he got there, so he landed instead on the top of the passenger car closest to the helicopter. Amazed and again experiencing the strange sensation, he watched as the men began to board the helicopter.

One of the men pointed at him; and Kasmali, not wanting to be a distraction, rose from the car, soared above them, and lit in a tree on a hill. He then noticed Rodrigo. Now satisfied that he was alive, he rose from the tree, soared back into the sky, and headed northwest to return to Peter and Charles.

Eventually he landed behind a stack of uprooted trees, mutated back into the Inupiaq, and trotted toward the hut. The elderly native came out. "The boy's been taken in a helicopter to a Navy ship," he said calmly. "They told me d they'd be back soon."

"Who? Sailors?" Kasmali asked.

The man shrugged. "Yeah, and a young man named Rodrigo. He seemed to be in charge. Maybe they'll give you a ride."

Kasmali smiled, thinking it would be a lot easier flying in one of the humans' machines than on his own as an eagle. Though he was tempted to tell the man he'd just seen Rodrigo, he simply nodded and went into the ice hut to check his family.

It was late afternoon when they heard the helicopter return. The native family ran outside; but, because he wanted to surprise Rodrigo, Kasmali stayed in the hut. Finally, after he heard the greetings, he calmly walked out and approached the group.

Rodrigo saw him, ran over, and grasped his hand. Kasmali smiled. "I heard you were out here somewhere, Chief," Rodrigo said. "You get around!"

Kasmali simply nodded. "You humans finally did it, didn't you?" he asked. "You finally destroyed this beautiful country."

Rodrigo stepped back. "I'm glad to see you too, Chief," he said sarcastically. He turned to the pilot. "This is Lieutenant Crash. He's our pilot. What do you think, Crash?" he asked. "You willing to take a surly Inupiaq on board?"

Crash nodded, looking cautiously at Kasmali.

Rodrigo looked back at Kasmali who was now smiling. "You've missed a lot, Chief. Jack's in jail up in Anchorage, Janie's on our ship with Ricky being tended to for her broken collarbone, and we've also got Charles on the ship. He's got frostbite, and we've got an eye witness who'll testify that he, not Jack, is the killer."

Noticing that Crash had walked away, Kasmali calmly answered, "You're right. He admitted it to me."

Rodrigo was stunned. "He did? How? When? Where?"

Kasmali grinned. "He thought I was Ricky. We were on the ferry when the earthquake hit."

"You mutated? Jesus, Charles? It all makes sense, but how'd you get him off the ferry and to the Inuit camp?"

Kasmali shrugged. "Flew, of course. I mutated into an eagle."

Rodrigo started to laugh. "Damn, that means you can't tell the court about it!" He suddenly turned serious. "Crap," he muttered. "What'll you tell them? That you changed into Ricky and then into a bird? They'll think you're crazy!"

Kasmali nodded toward Crash who was now waiting by the helicopter. "You're right, of course, but there may be another way I can get to him." He pointed toward the pilot. "Shouldn't you get to Anchorage?"

Rodrigo hesitated, remembering the shirt. "I told the constable about that bloody, ripped shirt," he said. "I only hope Jack's lawyer can prove Jack wouldn't have put it in the storeroom. You're right, though, about Anchorage." He turned and yelled to the pilot, "Okay, Crash. Let's get this miserable Inupiaq aboard."

Soon they were ready, Rodrigo the last to jump on; but Kasmali remained standing outside. "Come on, Chief. It'll be a new experience for you," he said.

Kasmali shook his head. "You go on," he answered. "I still have things I have to see." He watched the strange flying machine flutter out of sight and then walked Into the fallen trees. Once there, he lifted his arms and slowly mutated back into the eagle. He then flew north.

Chapter Seventeen: Onboard the Cruiser

Lying in a bed in the sick bay, her shoulder wrapped and her facial wounds bandaged, Janie was frantic. "Doesn't anyone know anything, sailor? For God's sake, my husband's in Anchorage! He could be hurt!" she snapped at the medic who was trying to check her blood pressure.

Trying to be patient, the medic stepped back. "You know what the doctor said, Mrs. Cramer," he said calmly. "You have to stay here for at least a few more days. Your blood pressure is still too high, and the slightest bump could dislocate your shoulder again."

She tried her best smile. "Oh, come on, sailor," she murmured coquettishly "You know I'd be careful. The blood pressure? It's just high because I was angry. Really, I'm fine, and my friend Rodrigo can take me. He'll take care of me."

"Nice try," the medic answered as he wrapped up the blood pressure cord. "Professor De La Cruz isn't here. He's already flown to Anchorage. The captain said he's gonna find out about your husband, so try to relax."

She lay back weeping, her face away from him, and muttered, "Please, Lord, make him all right."

Embarrassed, the medic backed away. "Maybe we should just wait for the captain, Mrs. Cramer," he said. "Who knows? He might have good news."

Janie wasn't listening. Unwilling to let the young man see her crying, she'd buried her head in her pillow.

Just then the captain walked in and saw Janie in distress. "What's going on, sailor?" he growled to the medic.

"She's worried about her husband," the medic quickly answered, moving toward the door.

Brushing past him, the captain strode to the bed, looked down at Janie's back, and said brusquely, "Your husband's fine, Mrs. Cramer."

Awkwardly because of her shoulder, Janie whipped her head around. "He's alive?" she managed to ask.

The captain smiled. "Alive and a little busy right now."

"TELL ME!" Janie demanded.

The captain chuckled and turned to the medic. "She's a spitfire, isn't she, son?"

"Tell me about it," the medic answered as he went out the door.

The captain sat in a chair beside Janie's bed. "Relax, Mrs. Cramer. As it turns out, your husband's more than just fine. The team I sent out with Professor De La Cruz just sent back word that Anchorage was only partially damaged. But when the county jail collapsed …"

"MY GOD, JACK'S THERE!" Janie screeched.

The captain reared back. "I told you he was all right, Mrs. Cramer. Relax. As a matter of fact, according to the professor, he's become quite a hero. The word is that he saved quite a few of the guards and calmed down the other prisoners. It seems that when the earthquake hit, for some reason the cell doors opened but the prisoners were too frightened to escape. Here's where it gets good. Somehow your husband convinced them that the best place for them to be was to stay in their cells. Then, believe it or not, he ran up to the floor above the jail and began dragging the injured people out. And I guess it wasn't easy because the building was crumbling all around him. Anyway, the guards now want to help your husband escape."

"You're not serious," Janie asked, incredulous.

"Your husband won't do it, of course. He's convinced that if the trial ever takes place, he'll be exonerated."

"*If* the trial takes place? What do you mean?"

The captain frowned. "You're probably not aware of how bad the earthquake and ensuing tidal wave were, especially on the coast, Mrs. Cramer. Luckily, though, for the most part Anchorage was spared. The information I received from the seismologists at the northern weather station was that it measured at least 8.4 on the Richter scale, almost as big as the Good Friday Earthquake of 1964. Its epicenter, they said, was in the Pacific off the Aleutian Islands, and it and the tidal wave destroyed Kodiak and the other coastal towns all the way to Juneau. There were also peripheral effects all over Alaska, huge calfings of the glaciers in Glacier Bay but also as far north as the Polar Ice Cap. Preliminary findings have indicated that most if not all of the oil drilling and the refineries have been overwhelmed by the subsequent breaking up of the ice. As I said, Anchorage wasn't hit as badly, but the city's a mess. Their main concern, I was told, was searching for the injured and getting the city cleaned up. It should be a while before they're ready for the judicial system to begin operating again."

"So where's Jack now?"

He chuckled. "The last I heard, he was helping out cleaning up the mess. Oh, by the way, the first thing he did when we contacted him was demand to know if you made it to Anchorage. I guess he heard about the train you were on. I'm sorry, I should have mentioned that before."

Janie nodded. "What did you tell him?"

"Just that you'd been injured slightly and that you were now safe on our ship. Obviously he was relieved. He said to tell you to stay here and that he'd get hold of you as soon as he could."

"When'll that be?" she asked anxiously.

"Perhaps tonight, we'll see," he answered as he got up. "Now be a good girl and stop giving my medic so much trouble." He chuckled as he started for the door.

"Wait, Captain!" she yelled. "What about the little boy I was with? He's all right, isn't he?"

He smiled. "I should say," he answered. "The crew's adopted him. They even cut down a uniform for him to wear. Now just get some sleep." He left, and Janie lay back, winced, shut her eyes, and began thinking of all she'd lost. Soon she was asleep.

The next thing she knew, the medic was standing beside her bed. "Dinner?" he asked warily. "Do you want your dinner now, Mrs. Cramer?"

She nodded sleepily. The medic pulled a table over her bed and placed a plate on it which held a filet mignon, a baked potato, and a heap of corn. Beside it, he put a glass filled it with wine and handed it to her, now smiling. "The captain must like you, Ma'am," he said.

"Goodness," she said, looking at all the food. "I can't eat all this!"

"He might be insulted if you don't, Ma'am," he answered as he put a huge piece of cherry pie next to the plate.

Janie pushed the plate aside and began picking at the pie. "It's going to go to waste," she said, trying to atone for her previous outburst. "Why don't you help me?"

The medic shook his head. "Thank you, Ma'am, I'm tempted but it's against regulations. Why don't you just eat what you can?"

She nodded, began picking at the corn, and asked, "Tell me, sailor, do you know anything about the little boy who came with me?"

The medic chuckled. "Sure do, Ma'am. Ricky's become one of the crew and the friendliest of the lot. He says he's gonna join the Navy as soon as he's old enough. He's been asking about you."

"He's a fine boy," Janie said. "I wonder why he hasn't come to see me."

"Doctor says you need rest, Ma'am, and the captain said he wanted him out of sight."

"Why?"

"I shouldn't tell you, I guess, but from what I heard, it's mainly his brother. The medics treating him tell me he's a mean son-of-a … gun. For some reason, the captain doesn't want Ricky to know his brother's on the ship."

Janie sat up quickly, knocking the tray aside. "Charles is here? Treating him for what?" she cried.

The medic frowned. "Yeah, but he's on the ship and in pretty bad shape. The professor flew him in, and they put him in the trauma unit. Suffers from frostbite and exposure. I heard if he survives, he'll probably lose at least one of his legs and maybe some fingers on his left hand."

She couldn't help feeling glad, but instead she just nodded. The medic began cleaning up as the captain came back, this time with Ricky beside him in an abbreviated sailor's white uniform and cap. As soon as Ricky saw her, he broke free from the captain, who'd been holding his hand, and ran up to her. "Mrs. Cramer," he whispered. "Are you okay?"

Janie took his hand. "I'm fine, Ricky, just a little problem with my collarbone. I see you're in the Navy now."

He took off his cap. "I just wanted to help, Mrs. Cramer," he answered. "They gave me these new clothes." He laid his head on the bed. "The earthquake scared me, Mrs. Cramer."

"It scared all of us, Ricky," Janie answered. "It was like an explosion, wasn't it? But here we are now, safe and sound. That's good, isn't it?"

He nodded and looked up sadly. "I heard the men talking, Mrs. Cramer. They said Valdez's gone."

The captain knelt down next to him. "That's true, sailor," he said gently. "We had a bad, bad earthquake. and then a huge wave flooded the coast. But fortunately for you, that wave didn't make it to the train you and Mrs. Cramer were on."

"But the earthquake did," Ricky muttered. Janie squeezed his hand. "It probably killed lots of people." He began to cry. "My brother… I think my brother is one of them, Sir. Can you find out?"

The captain looked at Janie who shook her head. "We don't have to, young man," the captain answered. "I've was told he survived and is in a hospital. You don't have to worry about him."

Ricky nodded, grinning. "I'm glad, Captain, but he's made a lot of trouble for Mr. and Mrs. Cramer."

Janie squeezed his hand again. "But that's all over now, isn't it, Ricky? Now because of you we know the truth; and soon Jack and you and I will be together again."

Where? the captain wondered; but he said nothing as he watched the boy holding Mrs. Cramer's hand. Then, deciding three was a crowd, he silently left the room and headed for the other end of the sick bay to check on Charles.

However, hearing screaming in the trauma unit, he hesitated, but then reluctantly opened the door. "IT HURTS! IT HURTS! DO SOMETHING, ASSHOLE! GIVE ME SOMETHING!" Charles was yelling as he writhed in his bed, a doctor and a medic standing beside him looking disgusted.

"I told you, Son, we've given you as much pain medication as your system can handle." He saw the captain, raised his eyebrows, and walked over. "Not the gutsiest patient I've ever had," he whispered, "but he *is* in pain. His nerves are just regaining sensation. If we can just keep him still, he should recover so we can amputate. I understand his little brother's also aboard. It might calm him down if he saw him."

The captain shook his head. "I doubt it," he answered. "Bad blood between them. Has he said anything about him?"

The medic shrugged. "Maybe. The other medics tell me that sometimes he mumbles about somebody, but he's pretty incoherent and everything's laced with cursing. The pain perhaps."

The captain nodded. "Well, let's keep him from hearing about his brother for the time being. Just keep me informed," he said as he turned and quickly left.

Chapter Eighteen: Anchorage

Flying northwest over the coast, Rodrigo was aghast at the devastation and dreaded what he'd see in Anchorage once he and Crash and the medics reached the city. He'd heard reports, of course, but his job was to see it himself.

A while later, Crash suddenly pointed down and cried over the noise of the rotors, "THERE IT IS!" Rodrigo leaned forward, scanned the horizon, and saw miles and miles of desolation.

"TAKE IT LOWER, CRASH!" he shouted back.

Crash nodded, pushed the stick forward, and flew a few hundred feet off the ground. "THE SUBURBS, THE OUTSKIRTS!" he yelled as the scene below them became clearer.

"THANK GOD, IT DOESN'T LOOK TOO BAD!" Rodrigo shouted.

"LOOK CLOSER!" Crash yelled back and pointed to an area at the right.

Rodrigo gasped. House after house had been ripped from their foundations, and a crowd of people were scurrying around a mountain of rubble at the end of a street. "WHAT ARE THEY DOING?" Rodrigo yelled.

"ALASKANS ARE TOUGH, AND THEY'VE BEEN THROUGH THIS BEFORE," Crash yelled back. "THEY'RE PROBABLY SEARCHING FOR SURVIVORS!"

Rodrigo nodded as they flew past. Soon they could see the skyline of Anchorage. This time, Rodrigo didn't comment; but the closer they got, the more hopeful he became. Most of the buildings were at least partially intact, or at least as many as he could see. But rubble edged the streets, and huge bulldozers and backhoes were moving it into flatbeds. People were digging and hauling everywhere. Crash set the helicopter down in a field a few yards away from the main street; and Rodrigo hobbled out and immediately went to find a person in charge, Crash following with the medics. He saw a man giving orders and walked over to him. "Hello," he said. "We've been sent as an advance team from the *Merry Gale*, a Navy ship moored outside of what used to be Valdez. More men will be coming soon from Thule. What's the situation?"

"Look around," the man smirked. "Advance team, huh? We need strong backs, not sightseers."

Crash stepped forward. "Just tell us what you want us to do," he said. "My team's ready to help."

The man laughed. "I should have known," he said. "Navy, huh? Find a group and grab a shovel." Immediately, Crash and his team walked over to a few men shoveling debris. The man then turned to Rodrigo. "What about you? You their officer?"

"Nope, just a scientist here to check out how bad the city was hit," he answered. "And to find a friend of mine."

Again the man smirked. "Are you crazy? You expect to find someone in all this chaos?" he said sarcastically. "Good luck! What's his name? I might have come across him."

"Actually there's two. The first is named Jack Cramer. The other is…"

"JACK?" the man yelled. "JACK CRAMER? JESUS, WHY DIDN'T YOU SAY SO?" He turned and shouted to the group Crash and his men were helping. "HENRY!" he yelled. "THIS GUY KNOWS JACK!"

An older man covered with dust ran over and grabbed Rodrigo's hand. "Any friend of Jack Cramer's a friend of mine," he said passionately. "I'm Henry Fontaine. He saved my son."

Rodrigo shook his hand. "Sounds like him. I'm Rodrigo. Do you know where I can find him?"

"Rodrigo De La Cruz?" the man said, stepping back. "Jesus, Cramer's told me all about you! Welcome to what's left of our city. Jack's just on the next street." He pointed north. "He's helping Mike and his crew."

Rodrigo thanked the two men and hobbled carefully around a corner through the rubble. He saw Jack immediately, his shirt off, sweat covering his face and torso. "JACK!" he shouted as he ran toward him. Jack smiled and poked a man lying amid a mass of cement blocks. Ralph Eston, dust covering his body, wriggled out, looked up, and saw where Jack was pointing.

The three men collided. Jack was the first to react. "Crap, Rodrigo!" he said. "You almost killed me!" They broke free. "How's Janie? I heard she was in a train wreck and she's on the *Merry Gale* now. How is she?"

"She's fine, Jack," Rodrigo said quickly. "The train was ruined, but she and Ricky came through it all right. She's got a separated shoulder and some scratches and bruises, but the doctor said she'll soon be good as new. Ricky's okay too. He's become an honorary sailor."

"Thank God," Jack muttered as he sank on his knees to the ground.

Ralph pulled Rodrigo aside. "Hi, Professor," he said. "You bring the Navy with you?"

"They'll be here, Constable," Rodrigo answered, wondering with Jack right there if he should tell him about the shirt in his backpack. Instead, he answered, "We're only the first wave."

Jack got up and wiped his eyes. "Sorry about that, guys," he said. "One less thing to worry about now."

Rodrigo grinned and asked, trying to lighten the mood, "Are you really a hero, Jack? I heard you rescued some of your own guards."

Jack just shrugged. "I only wanted to get out of that damned cell, Rod. Besides, they weren't bad guys. Ralph here somehow got an okay for me to help out with the cleanup. But tell me more about Janie and the others."

For the next few minutes, Rodrigo brought them up to date, including Kasmali's claim that Charles had confessed to him. When he'd concluded, Ralph looked at him and said, "I told Jack about the shirt."

Rodrigo swung his head to see Jack's reaction. He was furious. "The little shit put it there!" he snarled. "But why the hell does he want to frame me? And he's just a kid. You really think he had something to do with Cole's murder?"

"I've seen kids younger than him in L.A. slaughtering people," Ralph answered. "His motive could as simple as you hitting him. Who knows what goes on in the head of a kid like him."

"How bad is it?" Rodrigo asked. "The shirt, I mean. Maybe the jury will know Jack wouldn't be stupid enough to leave it where anyone could find it."

Ralph shrugged. "Depends, I guess, but you know we have to hand it over. You have it with you?"

Rodrigo pointed to his back, "In there, in my backpack."

Suddenly Ralph heard a noise, looked up, and gasped, "THE WALL'S CRACKING!" he yelled, pulling Jack out of the way. "LOOK OUT!"

The wall fell just right where they'd been standing. "WHERE'S RODRIGO?" Jack screamed, looking around. Then they saw it, a huge girder on the ground where they'd just been standing. "I DON'T SEE HIM!" Jack screamed again. They began to run to it.

They saw Rodrigo's legs protruding from under the girder. "Oh, Jesus! Oh, Jesus!" Jack moaned. "RODRIGO, CAN YOU HEAR ME?" he yelled and heard an answering moan.

"HE'S ALIVE!" he cried to Ralph. "Thank God, but we've gotta get him out of there! Try to keep him conscious while I get help." He turned to run, but Ralph grabbed him again. "We've got no time," he said. "We have to do it!"

Kasmali, having just arrived on the scene after searching for Jack, heard the crash and came running. When he saw Jack and Ralph struggling with the beam, he ducked into the building and in the darkness quickly mutated into a huge brown bear. He then loped toward them, causing them to scatter. He, or it, then lumbered over to the exposed end of the girder, lowered itself on its haunches, put its paws under it, and slowly lifted it from Rodrigo's torso.

Coming out of their shock, Jack and Ralph quickly grabbed Rodrigo's legs and pulled him free. The bear, hearing shouts, turned, saw the crowd of men coming around the corner, looked briefly at Jack, and then down at Rodrigo, and lumbered back into the building.

Jack sank to his knees beside Rodrigo. "Talk to me, my friend," he pleaded just as the men came up.

Rodrigo opened his eyes. "I … can't move," he moaned.

"Just lie still," Jack answered, trying to smile. "We'll get you help."

"Jesus, is he all right?" the first man asked as he came running up. "What did that bear do to him? And how the hell was a bear in the middle of the city anyway?"

Jack looked up and scowled. "It wasn't the bear, you damn fool! A girder from the building fell on him! Help me get him to the first aid station!"

Three of the men moved forward, constantly looking at the building, half-expecting the bear to reappear. Suddenly Kasmali reappeared, dragging a litter. "HERE!" he yelled as he reached them. "USE THIS!"

Surprised, Jack yipped, "Kasmali! Where'd you come from?"

"I heard the crash," Kasmali answered quickly. "Forget about that. I'll help carry him!"

As they lifted Rodrigo on to the stretcher and began carrying him away, Jack nudged Kasmali and said, "Thank God you were around. A girder fell right on him. Jesus, you'd think the poor guy had had enough bad luck. First a broken leg and now this! Where you been?" He leaned closer. "The bear. That was you, right?"

"It was the only way I could think of to get Rodrigo out," Kasmali whispered back.

Long since accustomed to Kasmali's mutations, Jack just nodded. When they reached the first aid station, a doctor was waiting. They laid Rodrigo on a gurney, and the doctor immediately told the crowd to wait outside. He then began to check Rodrigo who was now unconscious.

Ralph came up to Kasmali. "You see the bear?" he asked. "Christ, if it hadn't been for it, we never would have gotten Rodrigo out. Weird! Why the hell would a bear do that? And where'd it come from?"

Kasmali shrugged. "In my time as an Inupiaq I've seen animals do kind things," he answered. "Who knows?"

Ralph nodded. "Anyway, let's hope Rodrigo's all right," he said and then peaked into the first aid station.

Jack walked over to Kasmali. "You know things, my friend," he said. "Is Rod hurt bad?"

Kasmali just looked at him. "You're confused, Jack. I told you before that I can't tell the future. Now tell me about this thing you call a trial. I understand that someone thinks you killed a man."

Jack just nodded. "Yeah," he said. "I didn't, but there's so much evidence against me, Ralph, the constable, had to bring me here to await my trial. Have you heard? Janie was in a train wreck, but she's okay, thank God."

"Yes, I heard, but tell me about this trial," Kasmali asked. "I gather that you people are often confused when it comes to the truth, any truth, and that you have to have a meeting to discuss it. But why do you call it a trial? That's a strange word for such a meeting."

Jack thought for a moment. "Damn if I know," he finally said. "But it's going to be more like a war than a meeting, especially after Ralph told me Rodrigo found a ripped, bloody shirt in the café. I've no idea how it got there."

"Yes, I know about the shirt," Kasmali was saying. "I wouldn't worry about it."

"Easy for you to say," Jack answered bitterly. "One guy, the district attorney, is going to do his best to say I'm a killer; another guy, my lawyer, is then going to try to prove he's wrong; and it's gonna get nasty." He stared at Kasmali. "I get it, again you're ignorant about us humans. They do such things differently where you come from, right? You and your species just know the truth somehow, right?"

"Something like that," Kasmali answered and grabbed his hand. "Relax," he said calmly. "Charles admitted to me that he was the killer." He laughed. "Besides, everybody knows you're a hero."

"Yeah, but that's not going to help much. Rodrigo told me about Charles confessing, but when? And how the hell did you get him to do it?" Jack sputtered.

Kasmali smiled. "I was as surprised as are. I decided to follow him and eventually mutated into Ricky. I'll tell you all about it later, but now you should see how Rodrigo is doing."

Jack took a step but then hesitated, frowning. "I will, but you obviously can't testify; and I'm no hero, believe me."

Kasmali shook his head. "This trial thing seems to me like an awful waste of time," he said. "Surely the truth will come out. Even you humans can sometimes see what is right in front of you. But I'm curious to see how you go about it so I'll be there."

Three men came around the corner. "I've got to go," Kasmali said quickly. "I want to see Rodrigo."

Jack nodded and answered, "I'll be there in a minute." Kasmali smiled at the men as he passed them.

"Where's the Indian going?" one of the men asked as he came up.

Jack shrugged. "He's a friend of Rodrigo," he answered. "How is he?"

"Don't know," the man answered. "But the doctor's looking over him now. We came back as fast as we could because of the bear. Where'd it come from, by the way? You must've freaked out when it started going at your friend!"

"Yeah, at first," Jack prevaricated. "But then I saw it was just curious. When you guys ran up, it just took off. I've no idea why it was in the city. I'd better go check on Rodrigo." He began walking to the aid station, the three men following him, occasionally looking cautiously back at the crumpled building.

As he entered the tent, the doctor looked up and shook his head. Rodrigo was lying motionless on an examination table. Jack went up to him. "How ya doin', Buddy?" he asked apprehensively.

Rodrigo tried to smile, looking at the men behind Jack. "Thanks to you guys, at least I'm alive," he muttered. "The strangest thing, though. For some reason I vaguely remember a huge bear hovering over me. Was that just a hallucination?"

Jack looked around at the doctor and the men. "No," he answered. "There was a brown bear that just showed up, but it took off. Rest, I wanna check with the doc here about when you and I can get back to work." Rodrigo nodded and laid his head back.

Jack motioned for the doctor to follow him out of the tent, hesitated, then asked, "He's gonna be all right, isn't he, Doc?"

The doctor just looked at him. "Are you a friend of his?" he asked. "Being as he's Hispanic, you couldn't be a relative, so I'm reluctant to discuss his situation."

Frustrated, Jack was ready to plead. "Oh, come on, Doc. I've known Rodrigo ever since he was a kid living on a Chumash reservation down south. You can give me some idea how long he'll be laid up, can't you?"

The doctor continued to look at him. Finally, he spoke. "Laid up? He'll need many more tests, of course; but from my initial examination, I'd guess he'll be laid up, as you say, for a long time, if not permanently. I don't have specialized equipment, but I think his spine is shattered. I could be wrong, of course, but he still can't move his lower extremities."

Jack was stunned. "Does he know?" he asked.

The doctor again shook his head. "I haven't said anything about it to him, of course, since there has to be more tests; but he must suspect since he can't move his lower torso. If I were you, I wouldn't confront him about it. It could result in depression, which would be very harmful to him."

Jack braced his back. "We've got to get him back to the ship. They have the medical equipment in the sick bay there that may prove you wrong. When can he be moved?"

The doctor shrugged. "Depends on how carefully you treat him. I imagine you're talking about a helicopter. That could be a problem."

Jack nodded and went back into the tent. "Hey, Buddy," he whispered to Rodrigo who seemed to be sleeping. Rodrigo opened his eyes.

"What … what did the doctor say," he muttered.

"Just that you need more tests," Jack lied. "We're going to take you back to the sick bay on the ship, but the doc said you riding on a helicopter might not be a good idea."

Rodrigo attempted a weak smile. "The shirt? Did you find it? It must be under the rubble."

"We'll get it," Jack answered. "Don't worry about it. Right now, we've get to get you to the cruiser."

"Get Crash," he said. "He'll take care of me."

Chapter Nineteen: Charles Confronts Ricky

A month went by. Charles, still in the sick bay now recovering from the amputation of his lower right leg and two of the fingers on his left hand, looked around and finally saw his chance. He was alone. "The stupid sailors must be feeding their faces," he whispered. He pulled out his IV, grabbed his stump with his right hand, and lifted it on the side of the bed. Groaning, he then maneuvered his left leg to the floor and pulled himself up.

Stifling a scream, he snarled, "I'll get that little shit." He groaned as he slowly stood upright. The pain was bearable, but the itching from his missing leg was driving him crazy. He began blubbering as he fell back on the bed, his stump and his good leg dangling over the side.

Sitting in a cabin on the other side of the ship, Janie was tired of her confinement. Her shoulder had mended well, though she still had to wear a sling and the scratches on her face and arms were now barely noticeable. She'd read all the newspapers and magazines, and even finished two novels the medics had given her; but she was constantly distracted by wondering about Jack.

She decided to walk out to the deck. Once there, she stood against the railing looking west. "Roberto's Mexican Café," she muttered into the wind. "It was a good idea at the time, but it's just as well."

She smiled as Ricky came up and stood next to her. "What'll we do now, Mrs. Cramer?" he asked, also looking at what was left of the coast.

She looked down at him. "Depends, Ricky," she answered. "Once the sea recedes, maybe the town will be rebuilt. It's been done before. When the last big earthquake hit

Alaska, some brave people just rebuilt Valdez up on higher land. I don't think Mr. Cramer will want to do that, though."

"Why not?" Ricky asked.

"Well," she answered, shifting her position so she could put her left arm around his shoulder, "It seems Mr. Cramer's lost interest in the café. Besides, when his problems are over in Anchorage, he might want to leave Alaska."

"Would you go, too?" Ricky asked, frightened he would be alone again.

Janie laughed. "Of course, sweetheart, he's my husband." Suddenly she understood. "Besides, wherever we go, we'll be fine because we three will be together."

"WE?" Ricky yelled, unable to hold back his excitement.

"Of course 'we,'" Janie said, smiling broadly. "You're one of us now: you, Mr. Cramer, and I. Did you think we'd leave you?"

Overwhelmed, Ricky couldn't answer. He grabbed her around the waist and cried.

"All right, Ricky," she finally said. "Anyway, in a while they'll let us leave this ship; and I'm hoping then we can rejoin Mr. Cramer in Anchorage. Then when he's exonerated, we'll figure out what to do next. How does that sound?"

Ricky grinned but then looked up, frowning. "But what about Charles? The doctor said he was in a hospital. What's going to happen to him?"

Janie winced, unwilling to tell him that Charles was on the ship. "That's up to the doctors, Ricky," she answered slowly. "I know you're worried about him, but I have a worry, too. My husband is about to be tried for murder, so we have to be by his side."

Not far away, Charles lay back in his bed constantly pushing the button for more morphine, unaware that the doctor convinced he wasn't in as much pain as he claimed, had now injected the IV with a very mild glucose solution. However, whatever the case, Charles didn't want to give the doctor any satisfaction so he continued to moan and pretend to sleep which gave him the chance to overhear the interns and sailors talking. It helped pass the time.

He'd heard all about how the earthquake had destroyed the coast, how Jack Cramer had become a hero, how Cramer's wife had broken her shoulder that was being mended right here on the ship, and how everyone loved Ricky. One night, however, he stiffened when he overheard them whispering about Ricky and the trial.

"Yeah, he's a great kid," one of them was saying. "He's probably in the mess hall right now swabbing the floor or shining the silverware, but I wonder how he's going to hold up at the trial."

"Cramer's trial?" another guy asked. "What's he got to do with it?"

"You haven't heard?" the first guy whispered. "No, I guess you wouldn't have. I overheard him when I was in the mess hall. He was crying to Mrs. Cramer about it." He pointed to Charles seemingly still asleep. "I heard he can tell how this son-of-a-bitch lied about some knife. The thing is, they're brothers, and the kid's feeling guilty telling on him."

Fuming, Charles concentrated as the two men continued to praise Ricky. Finally one said, "I'm going to get some shuteye. You okay here?" Then there was silence.

Charles slowly raised his head, looked around, and saw the intern who'd stayed in the sickbay climbing up on a cot near the far wall. He waited until he heard the man snoring; and then, filled with hate, he managed to ignore the itching in his stump and this time make it out of bed. "Mess hall," he muttered quietly.

Using his good leg to steady himself, he stood up, searched in the darkness for something to use as a crutch, and saw a broom against the side of the door. Gathering his strength, he started to hop toward it but quickly collapsed. He cursed to himself as he waited for the intern to wake up and tell him to get back in bed, but the guy just continued to snore.

The itching was getting worse, but he somehow crawled slowly over to the broom, grabbed it with his right hand, pulled himself up, and began using it to help him stagger through the door.

Having left Janie, Ricky was in the mess hall humming 'Danny Boy,' a song Mrs. Cramer had often sung to him, as he polished the silverware. He knew he should be in bed in the crews' quarters, but he was determined that the knives and forks and spoons would be sparkling clean.

He jumped when he heard the door slam open and gasped when he saw Charles standing there in his hospital gown holding a broom. "Hi, Kid," Charles croaked. "I heard you were in here." Grimacing, he hobbled closer. Totally confused, Ricky dropped the silverware that clattered on the floor and echoed around the mess hall.

"What's the matter, Kid?" Charles whispered as he came up to him. "Shocked to see your brother" I'm the guy who took care of you most of your life."

"How come you're here, Charles?" he answered hesitantly. "They told me you were in a hospital. What's the matter with your leg?" He'd noticed his flapping pant leg.

Charles managed a grin. "What leg?" he answered. "The bastards sawed it off. Wasn't easy getting here, you know, Kid, not with this stump. But I had to see how my little brother was doing, you know. Just like in the old days. Give me a hand, will you? I haven't been out of the sack for a month. Let's go out on the deck to get some air."

Ricky looked down at Charles' leg. "Does it hurt?" he mumbled.

"It hurts like hell, but you can't keep this fucker down," Charles answered, still grinning. "I missed you."

Ricky knew he had to say something, so he mumbled, "I told you. They never told me you were on the ship, and they put me to work... just like at the café. They made me one of the crew."

Charles laughed, causing him to stumble. "Cabin boy, more likely. No problem," he said. "You can tell me all about it out on the deck. Come on, give me your shoulder." He grabbed him and, using the broom with his damaged hand, he began pushing them out the door.

As they made their way down the forecastle to the hatch, Ricky couldn't decide whether to break free and run or help his brother; but he didn't seem to have a choice because Charles' grip was so tight.

Heaving it against the wind, he opened the hatch for them and helped Charles out on the deck and up to the railing. He felt the cold immediately and wondered how Charles could stand it, dressed only in his hospital gown. But Charles just kept grinning.

"I HEARD YOU TOLD THE CRAMER BITCH ABOUT THE BUTCHER KNIFE. DID YOU TELL HER ABOUT WHAT I SAID ON THE FERRY?" Charles shouted into the wind.

Ricky was confused. "WHAT FERRY?" he shouted back.

Charles, no longer smiling, grabbed him and pulled him nose-to-nose. "Don't lie to me, you little shit," he growled. "Did you tell her what I told you?"

Ricky was terrified. "I did tell her about seeing you with the knife, that's all," he managed to answer. "I don't know anything about being on a ferry with you!"

Charles gripped him so hard, he was bruising his shoulder. "I'd like to believe you," he said calmly. "You wouldn't like getting your big brother in trouble, would you?"

Ricky shook his head and tried to break his grip, "You know me, don't you, Kid?" Charles continued. "You know how I can get back at people, don't you? Even my own little brother or maybe the bitch he's so fond of?"

Shocked, Ricky jumped back, but Charles' grip was too tight. He growled, "Where ya goin', Kid? It's a nice night. Let's look out at the moon." He put his arm around Ricky's shoulders and, using him for balance, pulled him until he was hanging his shoulders over the railing.

"Water looks cold," he growled. "I wonder how long a person could swim in it."

"I won't tell anything, Charles!" Ricky shrieked and broke free. "You're my brother!"

Charles tried to push him up on the railing but lost his balance and fell on the deck. "That I am, you shit," he growled as he struggled to get up.

Seeing his chance, Ricky ran back to the hatch. "YOU KEEP YOUR MOUTH SHUT, RICKY!" Charles shouted. "I CAN GET TO THE BITCH, YOU KNOW!"

Part Three
The Trial

Chapter Twenty: Day One

Years later, many people who were there at the time maintained that Jack Cramer's trial was really what brought Anchorage back to life since it took their minds off their worries about how to rebuild their lives as well as their homes.

Whether that was true or not, on the first day of the trial so many people gathered at the repaired courthouse a lottery had to be held to select those who would be allowed into the courtroom; and eventually bleachers even had to be constructed outside for the remaining crowd. Inside, the media sat in the first row of the balcony – a few reporters at first, but then more and more as the trial developed.

Jack Cramer was the main draw, of course, for over the last few months his reputation as a hero was debated in the media, initiated by the prosecution that had clandestinely leaked the evidence against Jack.

Stephen Aiken, the longtime district attorney, believed he had an open-and-shut case, for he was convinced that all the evidence and his eye-witness would overcome any sympathy the jury might still have for Cramer. However, he wasn't about to be over-confident because he was up for re-election, and the polls were close.

Miles Holcomb, Jack's defense attorney, new to the bar, was cautiously optimistic mainly because he considered the evidence against Jack circumstantial; but he was concerned about the bloody shirt which the constable had given it to him. At the time, he had wanted to curse the man; but his conscience forced him to send it to the district attorney as the law proscribed. Among his other problems was that his main witness was Valdez' town drunk and could easily be discredited on the witness stand. What kept him going was his belief in Jack's innocence and his knowledge that Charles Murray, the real killer, had for some reason framed Jack. Holcomb knew he had to show that Charles was lying when he took the stand as the prosecution's main witness.

Circuit Court Judge Margaret Stein was an elderly, crotchety woman with a wry sense of humor who had sat on the bench for over thirty years. Aiken was pleased because he was used to her peccadilloes, but Holcomb was scared to death.

Because of the circumstantial nature of the evidence, Holcomb had hoped the case would be dismissed at the arraignment; but Judge Stein had summarily rejected his motion, adding to his anxiety. So for the next two months Jack sat in the rebuilt jail waiting anxiously for his trial to begin.

Toward the end of these two months, Janie was getting desperate. Her money was running out. The cost of Jack's defense, as well as the expense of two rooms at the hotel and the money it took for food, decimated their savings, so she was forced to give up Ricky's room and have him stay with her. They also began to eat at the relief stations where they often met people who had lost everything. Misery loves company, she began to think.

One of these people was Bess, a woman who'd lost her husband and her home in the earthquake; and during the long days as Janie awaited the trial, they talked. Bess, a woman at least sixty, had, like Janie, been brought to Alaska by her husband and had lived near Anchorage for over thirty years. However, unlike Janie, Bess never once complained. Instead, after listening to Janie's whining about Jack being in jail and the loss of the café, she just commented about the wonderful times her husband and she had had over their forty-year marriage. And as Bess talked, Janie began to realize that she had been less than empathetic about Jack.

She began leaving Ricky with Bess and visiting Jack as often as the RMP's would allow, which surprised him, for he knew how much she disliked the despair permeating the cellblock. Gradually, though, she learned compassion for the inmates and even occasionally smuggled in doughnuts to them and Jack.

When the day of the trial finally arrived, Holcomb made sure Jack had rid himself of his rustic outfit and scruffy beard and was clean shaven and dressed in suit and tie. When Jack was led by guards into the courtroom, half the crowd cheered while the other half booed.

He and Holcomb sat quietly at the defense table. Janie, Ricky, Slim Carter, and the constable were behind them. At a table to their right were Aiken and his assistant D.A. Charles was sitting a few rows behind them, his new leg sticking out the aisle. The room was buzzing.

Rodrigo was not there, Neither was Chief Kasmali, After Rodrigo had been air-lifted to the ship where the doctor discovered he needed more specialized care, he was flown to the Naval Hospital in Bethesda, Maryland, for further treatment. Kasmali was in an asuskwa he'd created outside of town.

Suddenly the bailiff rose and shouted, "OYEZ, OYEZ, PLEASE RISE FOR HONORABLE JUDGE MARGARET STEIN!" Immediately there was silence. Measuring her steps, she slowly mounted the bench, stood, looked out at the crowd, and frowned.

Today, Judge Stein, having just lost her home in the earthquake, was in no mood for drollery. Still standing, she banged her gavel, stared at the audience, and said loudly, "OKAY, PEOPLE, RIGHT FROM THE START I WANT YOU TO KNOW THAT IN MY COURT THERE'LL BE NO SHENANIGANS! WITH THAT IN MIND, I'VE ORDERED THE BAILIFF TO THROW OUT ANYBODY WHO INTERRUPTS!"

She then sat down, brusquely motioned to the crowd to do the same, and nodded toward Aiken. "You'd better be ready, Counselor."

Aiken rose and answered, "Yes, Judge," walked in front of the jury, and swept his gaze to each one of the twelve. Finally, as if he were talking to neighbors, which some of them probably were, he began: "Okay, Folks, let me put my cards on the table. I know some of you have heard the stories about how Jack Cramer was supposedly heroic during the recent earthquake, how he saved people. You probably even like him. After all, he's a good-looking guy with a pretty wife." He stepped back and grinned.

"However, all that has no bearing on this case. None in the slightest. The evidence will show that hero or not, Jack Cramer killed a man named Billy Cole, a man he hated; and the oath you took demands that you must put your feelings for him aside. I know it might be hard; but I also know you're Alaskans who won't let emotions get in the way of common sense!" He sat down, feeling good about cutting his remarks short.

Judge Stein nodded brusquely to Holcomb, who rose, stepped behind a lectern between the tables, and set down his notes. "Ladies and gentlemen," he began. "First of all, I want you to know there's no reason for us being here. All the evidence the prosecutor will present is entirely circumstantial, as I will prove. Not only that, but I will show that Jack Cramer is a victim of a scurrilous attempt by someone who is the real killer, a person who hates him!

"In one respect, however, I agree with the prosecution. You must put aside whatever admiration you have for Jack simply because if you do, you'll then be able to feel justified in your exoneration of him. Now relax. Once you hear what a weak case the prosecution has, we should be out of here in one or two days." He sat back down.

The crowd began murmuring, causing Judge Stein to bang her gavel and shout, "I WARNED YOU PEOPLE! ONE MORE OUTBURST AND I'LL CLEAR THE COURT!" She then turned to Aiken. "Let's get going, Counselor. Let's hear your case."

Aiken once again moved in front of the jury, this time holding a book. "This, my friends, is just about all the proof I need, though I have much more. I call it Exhibit A." He handed it to the bailiff who marked it and handed it back. Grinning, he then showed it to Holcomb, who started to rise, and then held it high for the audience and the jury to see. "In this book is an account of how Jack Cramer once before tried to kill the victim, Billy Cole."

Holcomb jumped up. "I OBJECT, YOUR HONOR!" he shouted. "FOR GOD'S SAKE, HAT BOOK'S FICTION. IT'S A NOVEL!"

"Sit down, Counselor," Judge Stein snapped. "We went over this in the arraignment. As I told you then, I read the book; and, while the whole thing may indeed be fiction, the section that deals with your client's confrontation with the victim seems real. Why haven't your presented the writer, as I suggested?"

Holcomb gulped. "He's unavailable, Judge. Besides, whatever he says would only be hear-say."

Judge Stein nodded. Aiken smiled and asked, "May I continue, Judge?" She nodded, and Holcomb sat back down trying not to show his concern. "Well, my friends," Aiken continued. "The defense attorney is right. It is a novel because it primarily deals with the life of an alien from another world. Ridiculous, huh? However, interspersed in this alien's story are the recollections of a man named Luke Scribner, who's now dead but was Cramer's best friend. It's those recollections that concern us here. First, though, with the permission of Judge Stein and the defense, I'd like to fill you in on those recollections so we won't waste time."

The judge again nodded. "Go ahead, Counselor, but keep it brief. Mr. Holcomb can object at any time if he hears any inaccuracies."

Aiken turned to the jury. "Okay, friends, this book is called *Metamorphoses,* and here's what happened. The accused, it seems, had been in love with a woman named Cleo Marston who allegedly was shot by Billy Cole. There seems to have been some great amount of money involved. Anyway, later in the account, the accused encountered Cole in an ancient village down south in California. Now, without stopping, I'll read to you the pertinent passage." He waited for suspense to build and then, standing in front of the jury, began to read a passage aloud.

"Jack didn't seem to hear her. He grabbed Cole by the neck and pulled him so they were nose-to-nose. 'Good to see you again, Cole,' he sneered. 'Maybe now you can tell me what happened in Elk!'

"You could tell Cole was scared to death. He began whining that he had nothing to do with anything that happened there, but Jack wasn't convinced. Incidentally, this was a long time before we got him to tell the whole story. Anyway, Jack was about to beat him when Janie grabbed his arm and looked at him. 'No, Jack, not again,' she said anxiously.

"Unbelievably, he shook her off while continuing to hold Cole. 'You still trying to get the money, Cole?' he asked. Confused, Janie took a few steps backward, her hands covering her mouth. But Cole, shaking his hands, just sneered.

"I figured then I should do something, so I got behind Cole so Jack could see me and asked him to calm down. Janie then came back to life. 'Good Lord!' she cried. 'What's going on?'

'I think he responded more to her cry than to me. Anyway, he said, 'We've got to tie him up,' and started for the car. 'He'll talk to me if you two want to take a walk for a few minutes.'

"I watched as Cole's sneer disappeared and decided I'd play along, figuring Jack was just posturing. 'Sure, Jack,' I said as I turned and winked at Janie. 'Just remember what you did to those guys at the diner. Right, Janie?'

"She was so confused by then that she just meekly answered, 'All right,' and we began walking toward the ruins of the chapel without looking back. We got back just in time. Jack was standing over the cringing Cole holding a log he'd lit from the fire, just about ready to smash it into him, screaming, 'You god-damned son-of-a-bitch! You bastard!'

"I ran up and grabbed him, but he looked at me as if I were a stranger. 'Jack!' I screamed. 'It's okay!'

"He leapt back, looking confused. By that time Janie had run up. 'Jack,' she said gently. 'What happened?'

"He stared at her, tears flowing down his cheeks. 'He killed her, Janie. He said he shot her.'"

Aiken closed the book. "That's it, friends. The rest doesn't matter too much, but I guess I should explain a couple of things. First, the reference to what Cramer did at the fore-mentioned diner. It seems he beat up a couple of gallant firefighters and was subsequently jailed for also possessing drugs. Secondly, the narrator was Luke Scribner, who as I said was Cramer's best friend; and the Janie he refers to is, as you probably know, Cramer's wife. Anyway, as you've heard, Cramer here has quite a temper. And, I might add, a motive for killing Billy Cole much later."

"I OBJECT, YOUR HONOR," Holcomb shouted. "WHAT HE READ IS COMPLETELY OUT OF CONTEXT! YOU HAVE TO READ THE WHOLE BOOK!"

"Sit down, Counselor," the judge said calmly. "Your objection is denied. You'll have your chance."

Suddenly the lights flickered and the building began to shake, causing the windows to rattle and the court reporter's recording machine to crash on the floor. The American and Alaskan flags were waving.

Most of the crowd sat frozen in their seats, but a few panicky souls charged the doors and ran out.

However, as quickly as it had begun, the shaking stopped. The judge, who'd remained at the bench, rapped her gavel and said loudly, "Well. Folks, I think someone's telling us we should take a break. Let's recess until tomorrow, assuming this building will still be here."

Before she left for her chambers, however, she motioned to the court reporter, who unsteadily came to the bench, and said, "Make sure your recorder is okay. We don't want any appeals." The man nodded, turned, picked up the recorder, and then followed the crowd out.

Aiken, sitting smiling at his table, leaned over to his assistant and whispered, "God seems to be on our side, Justin. Now the jury has a full day to think about what I just read. They'll understand how much Cramer hated the Cole fella."

On the other side of the aisle, Holcomb sat staring at the judge's bench. Jack leaned over. "Come on, Miles, it's not that bad. For one thing, you can read how later I fell in love with Janie."

Incredulous, Holcomb stared at him. "Jesus, Jack," he whispered. "I knew, of course, that Aiken was going to bring the book in, but I forgot how crafty he can be. I completely overlooked the fact that he'd read that passage aloud! Besides, don't you see what's going to happen? Sure, I can read them about you and Janie, but what's to keep Aiken from then describing you as some kind of womanizer? Add to that, he can probably establish that Cole came to Valdez to make up to you, and that you ignored his pleas and killed him anyway! If the jury hears that, they'll probably change their minds about you being a hero!"

Jack was stunned. "That's why he was in Valdez?" he asked.

Holcomb nodded. "So the constable told me. You didn't know?"

Jack shook his head. "No, when I heard it was Cole who was murdered, I just thought he'd come here to get revenge." He put his hand on Holcomb's shoulder. "But about the book, Miles, what Aiken read is true. I probably would have killed Cole then, but I sure as hell didn't kill him in Valdez! I didn't even know he was there until Ralph told me about him!"

Holcomb nodded, gathered together his papers, and began to get up. "I believe you, Jack, and we're not finished yet, though we've probably lost this round. We've got the constable who's willing to testify about how he's convinced someone else was the killer. And the eye-witness, the Slim guy, though it hurts that the woman he was with died in the flood. Our whole case may rest on discrediting the testimony of Charles Murray who said he saw a guy looking just like you running from the scene."

"He's lying, Miles. You know that. Ralph told you he thinks he made it up just to get back at me for hitting him! And Slim can tell how it was a kid like him who really killed Cole, and little Ricky who'll say he saw him with the knife, and Chief Kasmali who told me Charles confessed to him! He's the killer, not me!"

Holcomb nodded. "Probably," he said as the guards came to get Jack. "But it won't be easy convincing the jury that a kid like him could do it."

Jack shrugged and then followed the guards as they led him back to his cell.

Chapter Twenty-One: Day Two

After being told by Aiken that the next day he'd probably testify, Charles hobbled out of the courthouse and then, looking around, strolled jauntily down 5th Street to the Voyager Hotel where he'd been sequestered since the arraignment. He relished the way things were working out for him -- not the least of which was the plush room -- and he was eager to phone room service so he could load up from their menu. "I'll be a star!" he began giggling, thinking of how everyone, even Cramer, would soon be focused on him.

Once he got to his room, he went to the phone, called room service, and ordered a cheeseburger, fries, a chocolate malt, and a slice of lemon meringue pie. He then flopped on the bed, laughed, and stared at the ceiling. "Beats lying on a lousy mattress in a beat-up house," he giggled. He took the cross out of his pocket, began fondling it, and tried to figure out how he could make it last for more than one day.

"Maybe if I play sick, or even blame my leg," he mumbled, He shook his head. "Nah, that's not enough, after that I'd just be old news." Suddenly he sat up and muttered, "The newspaper guys up in the balcony! Maybe I could make some cash from them!" He got up and began pacing, dangling the cross in his hand. "They're always looking for an angle."

He lay back down on the bed, dejected, and said, "Nah, I'm not important enough. Just a kid who saw a guy with his dog," Suddenly he thought of something. "What if I tell them it was Cramer I saw!" he yelled. "That'd do it!" He danced around the room until his order from room service arrived.

The waiter, a boy his own age, handed him the tray and then put his hand out. Charles ignored him, slammed the door, and went to work on the cheeseburger. .

Early the next day, he eagerly but clumsily rose from his assigned seat on the aisle as the bailiff announced the entrance of Judge Stein who curtly told them all to sit and then motioned for the district attorney to continue his case. Charles tried to suppress a smile as he noticed the grim look on Jack Cramer's face.

Aiken got up and again stood in front of the jury. "My friends," he began, "let me summarize. Yesterday, I gave you evidence that proves beyond a shadow of a doubt that Mr. Cramer did indeed hate the victim, Billy Cole. I also demonstrated his motive – that he believed Cole had killed his lover -- but let's get to some other key issues – his opportunity and means to finally get even."

For the next few minutes, Aiken detailed his case and then went to his table and picked up a plastic bag. "In this bag, ladies and gentlemen, is a torn piece of shirt the victim had in his hand when his body was discovered." He handed the bag to the bailiff who unzipped it and, using gloves, took out the contents.

"Show it to the jury," Judge Stein ordered. He did. Aiken continued. "Though sadly many of the good people of Valdez are gone, my friends," he said somberly, "I can call survivors who'll testify that this torn off fabric is identical to a shirt the accused was fond of wearing. I offer it as Exhibit B."

Holcomb was getting panicky. "OBJECTION!" he shouted.

Judge Stein leaned forward and asked, "On what grounds, Mr. Holcomb?"

"It's obvious, your honor. That piece of shirt could've come from anyone. It's a common work shirt."

The judge sat back. "True, Counselor, but you'll have your chance to discredit it when you present your defense. Now, let's let Mr. Aiken continue."

Grinning, Aiken walked back to his table and just stood there. Finally, trying to control his satisfaction, he said, "Thank you, your honor, but Mr. Holcomb is right. That scrap could be from any shirt, so it's fortunate that I have the shirt it came from."

Dramatically, he reached behind him and picked up another plastic bag. "What I have here," he almost yelled, "is a bloody shirt with a sleeve missing. It was found in Cramer's own storage room in his café!"

Every member of the jury stared at Jack as the courtroom buzzed, causing the judge again to bang her gavel. "QUIET!" she shouted and, when the buzzing died, she said calmly, "Open the bag, counselor. Let's see it."

Not wanting to overdo it, Aiken again handed the bag to the bailiff who unzipped it, took out the shirt, and held it by its shoulders for everyone to see. Aiken, sensing the importance of the moment, pointed to the shirt. "You'll notice the clotted stains on the bottom, friends," he said confidently. "My experts have identified it as the victim's blood."

Holcomb rose, thinking he had to do something. "May I have a recess to consult with my client, Judge?" he asked.

"Sit down, counselor," the judge barked. "If I'm not mistaken, Mr. Aiken is just beginning!"

Holcomb fell into his seat, trying not to look at Jack. Aiken smiled and walked back to his table where he picked up another plastic bag and held it in front of him. "In this bag, ladies and gentlemen, is the butcher knife used by the killer. Again he handed the bag to the bailiff who unzipped it, pulled out the knife, and held it by the handle for everyone to see. "The judge is right, my friends. There's more. In a moment, I'll call the coroner who'll testify to that fact that indeed it is the murder weapon. Now, some of you may know that Cramer ran a café in Valdez where he undoubtedly had such a knife. Also, it's very interesting that, though the local constable had asked Mr. Cramer to come up with his butcher knife, he never did!"

Holcomb was again about to object; but, seeing the judge glare at him, he shrugged and sat back.

Aiken called the coroner to the stand who testified that he was able to determine that the stab wounds were indeed caused by the knife based on the nature of the wound and the fact that the victim's blood was found on it. Aiken announced he had no more questions for the coroner, and Holcomb jumped up. "Just a clarification, Doctor," he said, trying to be calm. "Did you find any fingerprints on the knife?"

The coroner seemed angry. "That's not my department, young man," he answered. "You'll have to ask the constable or the lab people."

Holcomb smiled. "I will, Doctor. I certainly will." He glanced at the jury. "There weren't," he whispered.

"THAT'S ENOUGH OF THAT!" Judge Stein yelled. "ONE MORE OF THAT AND I'LL CITE YOU FOR CONTEMPT!"

Holcomb nodded and sat down. "That's all, Doctor," the judge said. "You may take your seat."

Aiken retook his post in front of the jury and chuckled. "He's clever, isn't he, folks? No fingerprints, right? I guess he thinks his client was dumb enough not to wipe them off. Besides, isn't it strange that, as I told you, Mr. Cramer never came up with the butcher knife from his own kitchen or his shirt just like the one I showed you?" Two of the jurors snickered.

"Now, let's review," Aiken continued. "The accused had motive, revenge, and the means, the missing butcher knife, not to mention that a shirt with Cole's blood on it was found in his storeroom. What's left is opportunity. Did he have the opportunity to kill the victim? I'm gonna call a couple of witnesses now who'll tell you about that. The first is Ralph Eston, the constable from Valdez at the time of the murder."

Ralph was in a ticklish position, being both a witness for the prosecution as well as the defense; but he knew the only thing he could testify to was hear-say so he wasn't that concerned, He took the stand.

Aiken dropped his folksy demeanor. "Constable," he began. "In your investigation following the murder, did you interrogate the owner of the bar in Valdez?"

Ralph didn't hesitate. "Yes," he answered. "Gus Boston, God rest his soul."

"Amen to that," Aiken said. "He died in the flood, I take it."

"So it seems," Ralph answered. "As part of my job, the day after Cole's death I talked to him and also many of the other people in Valdez."

"Let's stick to Gus Boston, Constable. Did he tell you anything about Mr. Cramer on the night of the murder?"

"He told me a lot of things, Mr. Aiken, among which was the fact that Jack had come in for a drink that night, which was not unusual for him because he and Gus were friends."

"Yes, we know how the accused can be friendly when he wants to be..."

"OBJECTION, YOUR HONOR!" Holcomb yelled.

"Keep to the facts, Counselor," the judge snarled at Aiken.

"Sure, Judge," Aiken said, smirking. "But I was only trying to get to how the accused, like most of us, has mood changes." He turned back to Ralph. "On that subject, Constable, what did this Gus Boston say was Jack Cramer's mood that night?"

"FOR GOD'S SAKE, YOUR HONOR! HOW COULD HE KNOW WHAT WAS IN MY CLIENT'S MIND?" Holcomb shouted.

Judge Stein banged her gavel. "Keep it down, Mr. Holcomb. I can hear you. He's right, though, Mr. Aiken. The constable is no psychiatrist."

Aiken was ready for this. "That's true, Judge," he answered. "But this is an unusual and, I might say, a tragic situation. In any other circumstance, I'd have the bartender tell us about how Mr. Cramer acted that night; but as we heard, he drowned in the tidal wave. My only other recourse is to call upon an officer of the law to recreate the scene. Surely a constable can be trusted to tell the truth?"

The judge hesitated and then said, "All right, I'll allow it."

"JUDGE!" Holcomb yelled again.

"I told you to keep it down, Mr. Holcomb," Judge Stein said angrily. "Get on with it, Mr. Aiken."

Aiken suppressed a smile as he continued. "Now, Constable, what did this Gus Boston tell you about the accused that night?"

Ralph shrugged. "He just said Jack seemed angry."

"Okay, so Cramer was angry. Did he say about what time that was?"

"Late," Ralph answered. "Close to his closing time."

"After the murder then?"

"That I don't know," Ralph answered. "We never determined the exact time of Cole's death."

"That's all, Constable," Aiken said quickly.

The judge motioned to Holcomb. "Do you have any questions for this witness, Counselor?" she asked.

"Just one, Judge," Miles answered as he stood at his desk. "Constable Eston, did Gus Boston happen to say why Jack was angry?"

Ralph perked up. "Yes, he did, Counselor. He said Jack told him he'd had a fight with his wife."

"Convenient," Aiken muttered loudly enough for the jury to hear.

The judge again banged her gavel. "I warned you, Mr. Aiken. Another remark like that and I'll cite you for contempt! Now, Mr. Holcomb, get on with it!"

"That's all, Judge," Miles answered. Aiken got back up and announced his next witness. "I call Charles Murray to the stand."

This is it, Holcomb thought as he watched Charles, sitting on the aisle, get up awkwardly and grimace as he braced himself on his right leg, dramatically swing the prosthesis on his left out to the aisle, stagger, and then regain his balance and hobble slowly up to the witness stand where he lowered himself to the chair and looked soulfully at the jury.

The bailiff then walked up and administered the oath. Charles groaned, "You bet." The bailiff then asked him his name, which he pronounced meekly, "Charles Murray."

Aiken approached him and said, "I'm sorry to put you through this, Mr. Murray. It's clear you're in great pain so I'll try to be brief. How old are you, Son?"

Charles was having a good time. Finally the center of attention, he savored the fact that he was about to get even with Cramer. "Almost eighteen," he answered.

"Okay, Mr. Murray, let's get this out of the way right off the bat," Aiken said, turning to the jury. "You don't like Mr. Cramer, do you?"

Charles shrugged. "Not much," he answered. "He beat me up, you know."

Aiken feigned surprise. "He did? Well, that's interesting. Why don't you tell us about it?"

Charles sat up and looked sadly at the jury. "It was probably my fault, you know," he began. "It was while I was working for him at his café. I guess I wasn't going fast enough, and he scolded me. Anyway, I said something back to him and then he walloped me."

"He lost his temper, huh?" Aiken asked, again looking at the jury.

"Yeah, but I should've known. He did it all the time."

"There were other times?"

"Yeah, lots of them. That's why I should've kept my mouth shut."

Ricky jerked forward in his chair, leaned forward to Holcomb, and whispered, "That's a lie, Mr. Holcomb. Mr. Cramer never lost his temper. Only that once."

"That's all right, Ricky," Holcomb whispered back. "We'll have our chance. Sit back."

As Charles made up stories about how Jack had treated him badly, Ricky was getting more and more upset.

"All right, Mr. Murray," Aiken continued. "I think we get the picture. Now, you may have heard me tell the jury that Mr. Cramer often wore a shirt like the one I showed them. Did you ever see him wearing one like that?"

Charles hung his head. Shyly, he finally said, "Yeah, I guess so, but lots of guys wear shirts like that."

"But you did see Mr. Cramer in one, isn't that right?" Aiken said quickly. Charles nodded.

"You have to say it aloud for the stenographer, Mr. Murray!" the judge said.

"Sure," Charles answered, this time clearly.

Aiken smiled. "All right, Mr. Murray. I just had to make that clear. Now tell us about the night of the murder."

Charles snuck a glance at Cramer and inwardly giggled when he saw how he was staring hatefully at him. "Well, as I told the constable, that night I was too tired from work to go back to my foster home, so I decided to sleep between a couple of buildings just off the street."

"Did you often do that, Mr. Murray?" Aiken interrupted.

Charles was also ready for this. "Nah, I like my foster parents, so I usually went back to their house; but as I said, that night I was really tired. Besides, I like sleeping in the open and it was a warm night."

From his seat in the second row, Ricky leaned forward and looked questioningly at his brother.

"Okay, Mr. Murray," Aiken continued. "Now tell us what you saw that night."

Charles didn't hesitate. "Well, as I said, I was trying to get some sleep when all of a sudden I heard somebody come stomping down the boardwalk right in front of me. I was scared, you know, because I'm just a kid and it could've been somebody who'd hurt me. If you ever lived there in Valdez, you'd know what I'm talking about. Anyway, I looked up and was surprised to see Mr. Cramer and his dog. They were running as if somebody was following them or something."

Jack couldn't believe what he'd heard. "HE'S LYING!" he shouted.

Judge Stein banged her gavel. "Control your client, Mr. Holcomb. One more outburst like that and I'll remove him from the court!"

"My apologies, your honor," Holcomb answered as he helped Jack back into his seat and whispered, "Relax, Jack, our turn is coming." He then glanced at Ralph Eston who was slowly shaking his head.

Aiken hesitated, surprised by Charles' new claim. He moved closer to Charles. "You're sure it was Mr. Cramer?" he asked. "It must have been dark."

"Yeah, I'm sure," Charles answered, thinking quickly. "I worked for him, you know; and besides, there was a light coming from the building next to me."

Holcomb leaned back and looked at Ralph who was leafing through a notepad.

Though he tried not to show it, Aiken was furious. He'd spent hours prepping Charles for his testimony, and now by adding Cramer's name and the new thing about the light, the little shit was ad-libbing. He decided to cut his losses. "You're a brave young man," he said, attempting a smile and patting him on the arm. "This couldn't have been easy for you."

Charles fondled the cross in his pocket and tried not to laugh as Aiken walked away. He started to get up, but stopped, confused, when the judge said, "One second, Mr. Murray. I imagine Mr. Holcomb has a few questions for you."

Delighted his moment in the sun would continue, Charles sat back down and attempted to regain his boyish demeanor. Holcomb didn't even look at him. Instead, he stood and addressed the judge. "I do indeed, Judge; but may I first recall Constable Eston?"

Aiken, fully aware of what was coming, stood up and said calmly, "Judge, the defense is only dragging this out. We've already heard everything important from Constable Eston."

"Oh, sit down, Mr. Aiken," the judge answered impatiently. "You know Mr. Holcomb has the right to recall witnesses." She turned to Charles and said, "You may sit at Mr. Aiken's table, Mr. Murray.

That way, when you're recalled, you won't have to struggle with your prosthesis."

Charles, of course, had no idea what was going on. He stood up, looked painfully at the jury, shrugged, and slowly hobbled to the table. Holcomb recalled the constable. The bailiff reminded him of his oath to tell the truth and nothing but the truth. Eston nodded.

Realizing this was a key moment, Holcomb tried to stay calm. "According to your testimony at the arraignment, Constable, Mr. Murray came to see you twice. Is that correct?" he asked.

"That's right," Eston answered.

"Being that you're a professional law enforcement officer, did you take notes during or after those meetings?"

Eston exhibited his notepad. "After each of them," he answered.

"I want you now to check those notes and tell us if at any time Mr. Murray told you it was Mr. Cramer he saw or if there was any light that helped him."

Eston dramatically leafed through the notepad. Finally, he looked up at Holcomb and said, "No, there's no mention of Mr. Cramer or any light. All I have Mr. Murray saying is first, that he saw a man, and then when we met the second time, that he noticed a dog."

Holcomb waited for Aiken to react, but surprisingly he just shrugged.

"Any objection, Mr. Aiken?" Judge Stein asked.

"Nope, Judge," Aiken answered. "Doesn't mean a thing. I imagine over time, Mr. Murray just remembered it was Mr. Cramer and that he saw him because of a light."

Holcomb smiled. "About that light, Mr. Eston. You were the constable in Valdez for how long?"

"Almost six years."

Knowing the prosecution would now try to discredit Eston, Holcomb decided to preempt them. "Before coming to Valdez, you were a Los Angeles detective, right?"

"For over thirty years," Eston answered.

"So what prompted you to come to Alaska?"

"After I retired, I wanted to get away from all the violence down there. As it turned out, I guess I was wrong."

Holcomb moved closer. "But there was a controversy about a shooting, wasn't there?"

Eston shrugged. "Yeah, my partner and I were out on a call about a hit and run. During that episode, I accidentally shot a man and department policy was that after such an event, there's an investigation. I was subsequently cleared of any wrongdoing and put on desk duty."

"But why, if you were cleared?"

Again, Eston shrugged. "They said I was getting too old for the streets."

"Okay, so then you were given the job at Valdez. Tell us about it."

Eston smiled. "It was like dying and going to heaven. Few crimes, some drunkenness and theft, and a couple of open-and-shut killings, that's all. For the most part, my routine was simple, paperwork, getting to know the people, and at night checking all the businesses to make sure the doors and windows were secure."

Holcomb wasn't surprised that he and Ralph were on the same page. "Okay, let's get to that last part. You say you routinely checked all the businesses. Tell us which ones usually left on their lights."

"Well, as I said, I made sure everything was secure, but the shop owners were pretty good about conserving electricity, so they just left on a single light inside their shops, that's all. Kind of like a night light."

Holcomb feigned surprise. "That's strange, Constable. Mr. Murray testified that he saw Jack Cramer because of a light. Could one of these night lights have lit the street?"

"No, Sir, no way," Eston answered.

"Thank you, Constable. That's all," Holcomb said as he went back to his seat.

Even before the judge was able to ask if he wanted to redirect, Aiken jumped up. "No way, you say?" he asked immediately. "You're able to remember every single night?"

Ralph sat up straight. "No, Sir, I don't," he answered. "But I remember the night of the murder all right. The previous night there'd been a break-in at one of the shops so I spent longer than usual patrolling the town. I remember especially because it was so dark I twisted my ankle."

Aiken smiled. "That's interesting, Constable," he said, looking at the jury. "You say you spent a long time patrolling Valdez. Earlier you testified that Mr. Cramer was at the local bar that night. Why is it that you didn't see him when he allegedly walked from the bar to his house behind his café?"

Eston sat up. "A lot of reasons, I guess," he answered. "For one, it was dark, as I said. For another, I was away from the street a lot, checking the rear of the shops."

Knowing he was getting nowhere with Eston, Aiken tried a new approach. "You like Mr. Cramer, don't you, Mr. Eston? One might even call you friends?"

"OBJECTION!" Holcomb yelled, coming out of his seat.

"To what?" Judge Stein asked, obviously irritated.

"To what?" Holcomb angrily answered. "The prosecutor is trying to impugn the integrity of the constable! He's suggesting Mr. Eston is lying because he, like many of us, likes my client! Besides, everything the constable has said can be verified! The break-in, for example."

Judge Stein shrugged. "I don't see the problem, Mr. Holcomb, Objection denied, but I'm glad you interrupted. I need to go to the bathroom. Besides, I think it's time for lunch. Court is adjourned until … let's say two."

Chapter Twenty-Two: Kasmali Intervenes

The crowd having dispersed for the recess, Kasmali sat alone in the bleachers outside the courthouse trying to come to grips with the sensations inside him. It just wasn't in the nature of his species to experience such things, but for some reason he found himself sad, especially when he overheard the passersby comment about how Jack was obviously guilty.

He thought back and remembered when he'd seen Rodrigo being carried away from the rubble of the collapsed building, how a sensation of loss had suddenly overcome him. He'd been surprised then, but he'd just attributed it to being away from his origin. Now, however, he was beginning to understand that something strange had come over him.

He also remembered back to the trek with Rodrigo up to Prudhoe Bay. They'd spent many weeks together then, and he recalled how he felt when Rodrigo had stubbornly plodded along. "I was proud of him," he murmured. "Then at the clinic and finally when the building collapsed, I had similar feelings."

He thought of Jack and cringed. "All the voice asked was that I keep him safe," he muttered. "Now he's in a cage, and I don't know what to do."

Throughout his mission, he'd often been confused by the behavior of humans--- their pettiness, their propensity for violence, their ignorance -- but he was beginning to understand that he'd becoming like them, at least in his self-pity.

He also didn't understand what was going on in the courtroom. In his world, if there was a rare transgression – which was always due to an aberration in the offender – the matter was dealt with expeditiously and without discussion of any sort. But here on this chaotic planet, when a transgression occurred – which often was a result of their propensity for violence -- they debated the issue endlessly.

Their ignorance of the truth was most troubling to him, though again he had witnessed it often in these humans. But now, their prevarications had a chance of wronging an innocent man, and he couldn't let that happen. He knew Charles Murray had killed the man – the boy had confessed it to him when he'd adopted the form of Ricky on the ferry – but he didn't know what to do about it. He couldn't harm Charles. That wasn't in his nature. Finally he decided the only way was to get to him somehow to convince him to admit what he'd done.

He knew from overhearing the deputies that Charles would probably be in what they called the Voyager Hotel during the lunch recess, but he had only two hours or less. Deciding it was probably now or never, he rushed to the abandoned building in which he and Astay inhabited during the trial, greeted the dog, and together they exited the building and headed east past the courthouse, scattering people. Luckily he found the hotel just down the street.

When he and Astay came to a deserted alley, he went into the shadows and slowly mutated into Ricky. Astay, by now used to its master's strange changes in appearance, shook its huge body and followed Kasmali as they entered the hotel, the people leaping back when they saw the huge Husky. But no one stopped them as he maneuvered up the stairs. When he reached Charles's door, Kasmali whispered, "Growl, my friend. Show your teeth." He then knocked.

When Charles opened the door a slit and saw his little brother smiling at him with the mammoth dog growling at his shoulder, he stepped back terrified. "What do you want, you little shit?" he snarled. "And keep that monster away from me!" Continuing to hold the door almost closed, he then said, "You told on me, didn't you?"

"Astay's my friend," Kasmali answered, adopting Ricky's voice. "Can I come in? I'm worried about you 'cause you seemed to be in awful pain."

Charles, remembering his act, moaned, shifted his weight, causing him to lose his balance and release his hold on the door. Kasmali, Ricky, seeing his chance, stepped around him into the room. Frightened into immobility, Charles stood with his back to the door, anxiously watching the dog a few feet, continuing to growl at him.

Ricky smiled, sat on a chair, and patted Astay. "I won't let him hurt you, Charles. As I said, I just came to see if you're okay."

Somewhat mollified, Charles sneered. "You're worried about me, you little shit? You should be worrying more about yourself or maybe that bitch, Cramer's wife, your new mama. Pretty soon she's gonna be all alone!" Then, figuring Ricky didn't deserve a performance and that the dog was harmless, he muttered, "What the shit!" and walked effortlessly to the bed.

Ricky clapped his hands, saying, "You're better!"

Charles had had enough. "Okay, Kid, whadaya really want? You know what I told you I'd do if you didn't keep your mouth shut!"

Kasmali knew exactly what he wanted. He imitated Ricky's childlike smile. "I 'member, Spike. See? I 'member the butcher knife, and I 'member how you told me it was you who killed that man."

Charles exploded. "YEAH, AND I HOPE YOU REMEMBER WHAT I ELSE I SAID!"

Ignoring the outburst, Ricky kept smiling. "You've gotta tell the truth, Charles. You gotta."

Charles leapt off the bed toward him, but Astay was quicker. Just as Charles was about to reach Ricky, the dog charged, pinned him to the floor, and growled down at him, saliva dripping on his face.

"GET HIM OFF OF ME! GET HIM OFF!" Charles yelled, trying to untangle himself.

Ricky nodded to the dog that then slowly got off Charles and returned to its position. Charles crawled back to the bed. "Shit, that crazy dog almost killed me," he muttered. "Keep him away from me."

Kasmali continued to smile Ricky's smile. "Sure, Charles," he said. "What 'bout telling the truth?"

Looking fearfully at the dog and pulling the cross from his pocket, Charles snapped, "Are you crazy? Why the fuck would I do that?"

Ricky slowly rose, raised his arms to the ceiling, and began to melt. Charles screamed as almost immediately Kasmali appeared before him. He then fainted, which surprised Kasmali, for he didn't have a lot of time before the lunch recess was over. Not knowing what else to do, he grabbed a large cup of Coca-Cola from the table and threw it in Charles' face.

"WHAT THE FUCK ARE YOU DOING?" Charles yelled. Then noticing Kasmali again, he muttered, shaking his head, "How'd you get in here? Where's Ricky?"

Kasmali stood for a moment, and then, certain Charles was alert, he began to speak. "I was your brother, Charles. Now I am one who knows how evil you are, and I must do all I can to make certain you do not hurt innocent people as you hurt the man under the pier. Astay and I are here to convince you to tell the truth. If you do not, Astay will follow you wherever you go. You will never know when he strikes. However, If you do tell the truth, who knows? You might even be called a hero like Jack Cramer."

Charles continued to look around the room for Ricky. Finally he clutched the cross and whimpered, "A hero? They'll put me in jail!"

Kasmali raised himself to his full height. "Wouldn't that be better than being mauled by my friend?" Astay growled and gnashed its teeth.

Buoyed by the security of the cross, Charles sneered, "I'll tell them you forced me to lie."

Kasmali shrugged. "Who did? Ricky, your little brother? I think all those people who saw Ricky come in will wonder how a tall Inupiaq got into your room. All they saw was a little boy with his big dog."

The color drained from Charles' face. "What … are … you?" he stammered. Kasmali started for the door, Astay following. "Something who has a dog you should fear, Charles," he answered. "We will be in the courtroom this afternoon watching and listening to you up there beside that judge." Smiling, he and Astay then turned and left.

Charles crumpled to the floor and began sobbing. Kasmali quickly found an open vacant room, mutated again into Ricky, walked down to the lobby, and began skipping out the door, making as much of a scene as he could. Once outside, he and Astay found the alley where he mutated again into Chief Kasmali.

Chapter Twenty-Three: Charles Back on the Stand

Returning to the courtroom, Judge Stein exploded when Aiken informed her that his witness, Charles Murray, was not yet in the court. "FOR THE LOVE OF GOD, COUNSELOR, I TOLD YOU I WANTED A QUICK TRIAL! CAN'T YOU EVEN KEEP AN EYE ON YOUR OWN WITNESS? WHAT KIND OF LAWYER ARE YOU?"

Aiken began to see his case in jeopardy. "I'm sure the boy'll be here in a minute, Judge. I've got men out looking for him right now."

"WHAT?" she shrieked. "HE'S MISSING?"

Noticing the people in the court snickering, Aiken whined, "No, nothing like that, Judge. He probably just lost track of time. He'll be here soon."

With that, the people began openly laughing.

Judge Stein was beside herself. "I TOLD YOU PEOPLE TO BEHAVE!" she yelled. "BAILIFF, IF THEY DON'T SHUT UP, GET READY TO CLEAR THE COURT!"

Holcomb couldn't believe his luck – and Jack's. Calmly, he rose and said, "With all due respect, your honor, if the boy doesn't return, we've got a real problem. As you know, I haven't finished my cross examination."

Aiken started to object, but the judge cut him short, speaking through her teeth. "He's right, Mr. Aiken, and I'd only be too glad to end this fiasco. I'll tell you what. I'll give you and your witness another half an hour. We'll have another short recess until then. However, if he isn't then in this courtroom, I may have to call a mistrial!"

Judge Stein was out of the room before Aiken could answer. He then rushed out of the court.

Jack was confused. "What just happened, Miles?" he asked Holcomb who was smiling broadly.

"Rules, Jack, that's all," Holcomb answered. "I have to be given the chance to cross-examine Charles; and since he's not here, the judge said she may call a mistrial. If that happens, you'll be a free man," He was amazed when he saw Jack frown.

"Free, maybe, but not innocent," Jack answered. Just then two policemen led a staggering Charles through the door and helped him into the witness box where he slumped and grinned insipidly at the people rushing to re-enter the court.

Holcomb leaned over to Jack and whispered, "Damn, he's back, but he looks like he's drunk!" Some of the people began snickering, knowing the judge was gone. However, Ricky, sitting behind Jack and Holcomb, was cringing.

At that moment, Kasmali, wearing sun glasses, tapping a cane and leading Astay, entered the court, the crowd around them giving way. He gazed down at a woman who was in a seat near the front, and quickly she jumped up and ran to the rear. He took her seat. Astay crouched in the aisle.

"Isn't that your Inupiaq friend?" Holcomb asked Jack who shrugged, still looking at Charles. "Since when is he blind?"

Jack turned around and grinned. "He's up to something, if I know him. They gonna let the dog stay there?"

"I don't know," Holcomb answered. "But I can't wait to hear how Judge Stein'll react."

The bailiff called the court to order, and the audience rose, all except Charles who still seemed to be in a stupor. Judge Stein then entered, her eyes down, took her seat at the bench, looked out, and jumped up when she saw Astay taking up most of the aisle. "WHO THE HELL LET THAT BEAST IN HERE?" she shouted. "BAILIFF, GET THAT ANIMAL OUT OF HERE!"

The scream seemed to awaken Charles who looked out dazedly. Then, seeing Kasmali and Astay, he leapt to his feet, scattering his chair, fell out of the witness stand, and landed heavily on the floor in front of Aiken who'd just come in followed by a white-haired man. "Shit, what's next," Aiken muttered as he tried to help Charles to his feet. The bailiff came over to help; and then, after they sat Charles, now seemingly petrified, back in his seat in the witness box, Aiken turned to the judge about to try to explain.

The bailiff interrupted. "About the dog, Judge, It's a seeing-eye dog for the blind native there." He pointed to Kasmali. "He told me earlier that he's an Inupiaq chief who's come to represent the Native Tribe Council. I didn't see how I could avoid letting him and his dog in."

Judge Stein, known for being politically sensitive, smiled. "Is that true, Sir?" she called out to Kasmali, who seemed to be staring at Charles who was now pale and sitting like a statue clutching the cross with both hands.

"Yes, Judge," Kasmali answered loudly, looking at the back wall. "I am here because my people, the indigenous natives of the Yukon, have too often witnessed injustices to us in your courts. I have therefore come to hear for myself how your judicial system does or doesn't work. However, if it upsets your witness I will leave."

Judge Stein nodded. "I share your frustration, Chief. I've seen how your people have been ignored and even abused. However, feel assured that in my court, justice and truth will prevail." She smiled again. "However, might I ask you to wait outside the courtroom with your dog until the lawyers are through with this witness? He seems frightened by your beautiful animal."

Kasmali nodded, reached down, grabbed Astay's mane, and followed it out. Judge Stein then turned to Charles, leaned forward, and then turned to Aiken. "What's the matter with him, Counselor? Is he drunk?"

The bailiff again stepped forward. "I think I can answer that, Judge. The officers told me that when they came to his room in the hotel to escort him to court, they saw he was asleep so they tried to get him up, but he wouldn't budge. They said he just curled up and began screaming and crying. They knew they had to get him here, but he was acting so weird they didn't know what to do. Finally, they decided he was probably just drunk or on something, so they – you gotta understand they didn't have a choice – anyway, they threw water in his face, and that seemed to do the trick. After that, they brought him – carried him really – to the court."

Judge Stein nodded, her brow furrowed, and leaned over to Charles. "Are you all right, Mr. Murray?"

Charles, his eyes riveted on Kasmali walking out of the court, didn't reply.

The judge tried again. "Can you hear me, Mr. Murray?"

Without changing his focus, Charles mumbled, "Ricky."

Ricky, sitting nervously behind Holcomb, suddenly jumped up and ran past Kasmali and Astay from the court room, causing murmurs from the rest of the gallery.

The judge banged her gavel. "ORDER!" she yelled and then pointed to a guard in the rear. "OFFICER, GO SEE WHAT'S WRONG WITH THE BOY!"

When the people calmed down, she redirected her attention to Charles. "What about your brother, Mr. Murray?" she asked.

Charles again didn't seem to hear. The judge slowly shook her head. Suddenly, Charles stuttered, "He … melted."

Judge Stein had had enough. She banged her gavel softly, sighed, and said, "He's in no condition to…" when suddenly interrupted, shouting, 'I'LL NEVER TELL! NEVER!" The court erupted.

The judge leapt up and screamed, "ORDER! I SAID ORDER!" but this time it had no effect. The media and the audience continued to buzz, and Holcomb and Jack sat stunned as Janie crawled over them after Ricky. Charles slumped back into his seat.

Judge Stein plopped back down and waited for the clamor to subside. It took a while, but when it did she banged her gavel again and snarled, "I'll see both counselors in my chambers." She then addressed the officers in the back of the room. "Gentlemen, escort Mr. Murray into an anti-room and make certain he stays there. And see if you can find Mrs. Cramer and that boy." She then rose sluggishly and walked into a room to the right of the bench.

As Holcomb got up to follow her, Ralph grabbed his sleeve and whispered, "That cross, Miles. Did you notice Charles holding it?"

"Yeah, so what?" Holcomb answered brusquely. He was eager to get into the judge so he could hear how she intended to proceed.

"The cross. Miles. It might be enough to connect him to the murder."

Holcomb broke free. "Maybe, but explain it to me after I see what the judge wants." He rushed away, entered the chambers, and saw the judge scowling at her desk tapping her fingers. Unable to control himself, he spoke first. "Well, Judge, thank God it's over. I can tell Mr. Cramer we've now got a mistrial, right?"

Judge Stein looked at him in disbelief. Aiken laughed. "You're kidding, aren't you, Counselor? On what grounds?"

Deflated, Holcomb stammered, "But, Judge … Charles is crazy as a hoot owl. You heard him!"

Judge Stein continued to tap her fingers. "I don't know anything of the kind, Mr. Holcomb. All I saw was a kid who's probably drunk. Why he said, 'I won't tell' could mean anything."

Aiken was relieved and yet worried. That the judge discounted Charles' words was hopeful, but the fact that she thought he was drunk would probably delay the trial – which he certainly didn't want – or even toss the case out on the grounds that the defense was unable to conclude its cross-examination. "I ask for a recess, your honor," he said quickly.

"Or for God's sake," Judge Stein muttered. "I assume it's so you can sober up the boy?"

Holcomb exploded. "Judge, you can't let him get away with that!" he said loudly.

Judge Stein sighed, obviously frustrated. "Don't worry, Mr. Holcomb," she said. "I'll make sure the officers get him sober enough to continue. But in the meantime I'll call a recess. I need a break. We'll convene again early tomorrow. That should give them enough time and maybe give me a chance to get drunk too." She waved them out of her chambers.

When she was sure they were gone, she shook her head and stared at the ceiling.

Jack had been led away when Holcomb returned to the courtroom. He found Ralph alone. "Where's Mrs. Cramer?" he asked as he sat down beside him.

"Still trying to find Ricky," the constable answered. "What did the judge want?"

"I hope the boy's all right," Holcomb said disconsolately. "The judge wouldn't go along with me. She said Murray could've been talking about anything."

Ralph interrupted. "The cross, Miles," he said. "I've gotta tell you what the warden at Folsom told me about Cole and the cross."

Still upset by the judge's decision, Holcomb barely looked at him. "What about it?" he asked indifferently. "Anyway, how do you know it was a cross? As far as I could tell, he was just holding a piece of metal."

"No, Miles, it was a small cross," Ralph objected. "I could see it clearly from where I was sitting, a small, crudely made cross on what looked like a piece of string. The thing is, after the murder I called the warden at Folsom, and he told me that Cole had turned religious in his last year or so. Anyway, he said that when Cole was released he was clutching a Bible and had a beat-up cross around his neck!"

Holcomb was stunned. "So you think Charles took it off Cole?"

"Yeah, probably after he stabbed him," Ralph said, getting excited.

Holcomb sat up a little straighter. "Why?"

"Who knows?" Ralph said. "The kid's loony."

Holcomb sat back and began to think. Finally, he leaned forward and said, "Well, it's something, but I don't see how we can use it. For one thing, Charles could just say he found it."

"Found it?" Ralph cried. "Where?"

Holcomb shrugged. "We'll see what happens if and when Charles retakes the stand. I'll ask him about it. Right now I wanna find out what Kasmali's up to."

Ralph got up, saying, "Okay, but what about Slim Carter? Maybe he saw Cole take the cross."

"The town drunk?" Holcomb snorted. "Forget him. If I put him on the stand, Aiken'll have a field day with him!"

Ralph nodded and left. Holcomb followed him until he reached Chief Kasmali sitting at the back of the courtroom with sunglasses on, Astay beside him. He sat next to him and asked, "What's going on, Chief? You're not blind."

Not bothering to remove his sunglasses, Kasmali smiled. "I wanted Astay with me," he answered. "This was the only way."

Holcomb nodded. "Anything to do with Charles?" he asked. "I noticed him staring at you."

"That cross, he rubs it when he's nervous. Did you notice?" Kasmali answered, ignoring his question.

Startled that the cross had come up again, Holcomb nodded and said, "Yeah, Ralph mentioned it. He said Cole had it on when he got out, but I don't see how I can use it. Aiken'll just claim he picked it up somewhere."

"The truth will come out, Mr. Holcomb," Kasmali said as he got up and let Astay lead him out of the courtroom.

Janie had found Ricky sitting and crying on the steps of the courthouse. "What's wrong, Ricky?" she asked as she sat down beside him. Ricky looked up her, his eyes wide and filled with tears. "I'm scared, Mrs. Cramer," he muttered. "If I tell what I know, he's gonna get back at me or maybe even you."

"Who, Ricky?" she asked. "Charles?"

He nodded. "When he's drunk like that, he gets mean, really mean. He could hurt me and you!"

Janie was getting frightened. "What, Ricky? What did Charles say he'd do? Did he threaten us?"

"He knows, he knows, Mrs. Cramer!" Ricky said, sobbing. "He knows I told you about him having the butcher knife, and he thinks I heard him say he killed the guy! He said if I said anything, he'd get us!"

Horrified, Janie got up and said, "I'll go make sure the guards watch him. I won't let him do anything to you."

In the meantime, as the guards were driving Charles back to his hotel, he was slowly coming out of his shock and trying to remember what he'd said. Then he heard the cops in the front seat.

"Bonkers," one of them said disgustedly. "How the hell are we gonna bring him out of it?"

"Maybe he *is* just drunk," the other said. "Let's just get him up to his room and hope he sleeps it off."

"Jesus, that could take all day, maybe longer," was the reply. "You mean we have to spend the whole day babysitting the kid? Shit, I've got better things to do!"

"You heard what the kid said," the first man answered. "We gotta keep an eye on the little shit."

The other man laughed. "Christ, Jake, you're letting the time you spent with Cramer get to you. All the kid said was, 'I won't tell.' We don't know what he was talking about. It could be anything!"

"Like what, Hank?"

"Jesus! Well, for one thing, he might have been scared and said the first thing that came into his head."

The car stopped and the two men lugged Charles out and helped him to his room where they plopped him on the bed. "Take a snooze," the taller of the two said. Charles lay back and pretended to sleep.

"What do we do, just sit here?" he heard the other man say.

"Nah, one of us is enough," the other answered. "Why don't you get us something to eat? I'll grab a chair and sit outside the door."

Charles waited until heard the door close, then sat up and began thinking about what had happened. After a few minutes, he shrugged and muttered, "Just a dream, a nightmare. I must've been sleeping when I was here before."

Somewhat satisfied, he began pacing, clutching the cross, trying to think of a way he could explain what he'd said. The guy's right, he finally decided. I could just say I was scared. He lay back down on the bed but suddenly jumped up, muttering, "Ricky! He'll tell! I've gotta stop him!"

He knew Ricky was frightened by him but also realized that Cramer's wife seemed to have a hold on him. "Maybe I'll get her too," he muttered, smiling. "But how the hell do I get out of here?"

Hearing voices at the door, he crept over and listened. One of the guards was talking to a woman, though he couldn't make out what they were saying. He waited and then chuckled as he heard footsteps down the hall. Luckily, the door was unlocked, so he peaked out and saw the guard and the woman into a room. The people at the trial would have been amazed as he ran so effortlessly down the hall to the staircase.

Half an hour later, Ralph was relieved as he came down the hallway and saw the guard sitting in front of Charles' room. "Just came to check," he said as he came up. "Everything quiet?"

"Yeah," the man answered. "He's sleeping it off."

"Where's the other guard?" Ralph asked, looking around.

The man smiled. "Sent him to get us something to eat. He'll be back in a minute. You're the Valdez constable, right? Sorry about your town."

"And the people," Ralph answered. "Mind if I go in?"

"Be my guest," the man said, "but try to be quiet. We figured he'd sober up by sleeping it off."

Ralph nodded, slowly opened the door, and saw the bedroom was empty. He checked the bathroom and the closets, and then, furious, walked back to the guard, who was now eating a hotdog with his partner. "YOU STUPID HACKS! YOU LET HIM GET AWAY!"

The two men crammed their hotdogs in their mouths and rushed into the room. "Fuck," the taller man cried as he came back out. "We'll find him. He can't be far!"

"How the hell did he get past you?" Ralph asked, furious.

"I was only gone for a minute," the man he'd spoken to first said. "I had to take a pee."

Ralph sensed he was lying. "Where?" he asked. "Why didn't you do it in the bathroom in the room?"

"I didn't want to wake him," the man lied.

Knowing he was just wasting time, Ralph turned to the second man and told him to go down to the lobby to see if he could catch Charles trying to leave. Then he told the other man to go with him to check the other rooms and the exits.

The people in the court, who had previously seen Charles so painfully struggle to the witness box, would have been amazed to see him, prosthesis and all, so agilely rush down the staircase and into the lobby. Once he was outside, he hesitated, trying to think of what to do; and then, knowing he couldn't just stand there, he snuck into an alley, sunk to the ground, took out the cross, stroked it, and waited for an idea to come.

After searching for more than an hour, Ralph became panicky, so he told one of the guards to remain at the exit and then forced the other guard to go with him to tell the judge what had happened. When they got to her chambers, the bailiff stopped them. "She's sleeping," the bailiff said. "I'm not about to wake her."

Knowing Judge Stein's normal contentiousness would be aggravated if he interrupted her beauty sleep, Ralph asked the bailiff to inform her that Charles had run. Leaving the guard to face her rancor, he then decided Holcomb had to know.

He found him in a side office with Janie and Ricky. He burst in and told them Charles had skipped. Backing toward the far wall, Ricky's face went white. "He'll get us now, Mrs. Cramer. I know him!" he cried.

Janie looked at Ralph and asked anxiously, "You don't know where he is? For God's sake, Ralph!"

"He'll show up, Mrs. Cramer," Ralph answered, trying to be calm. "He's too crafty not to think up something to explain what he said. Besides, he wants to see Jack locked up. He'll show up."

Holcomb looked puzzled. "I don't know about that, Ralph. I think the kid got himself into such a mess, he'll just take off."

Hearing a knock on the door, Holcomb opened it. The bailiff wasted no time telling them the judge wanted to see him in her chambers. Holcomb nodded and told Janie and Ralph he'd be right back. Terrified, Ricky was still standing against the wall.

Judge Stein was right in the middle of berating Aiken when he came in. "You idiot! What kind of guards did you send with him? How could've he got past two grown men?" she snarled.

Aiken was shaken. "I don't know, Judge," he answered, flustered. "But no one expected him to run away. Why would he?"

"ARE YOU KIDDING!" Judge Stein bellowed. "YOU HEARD HIM! YOU SAW HIM!"

Aiken bristled. "Oh, come on, Judge. He was probably hysterical because of his leg, that's all."

Holcomb decided it was time to interrupt. "Well, Judge, what happens now? If I can't finish my cross, the truth may never come out. I think it's now obvious what we have to do."

"WAIT JUST A MINUTE!" Aiken bellowed. "HAVE YOU FORGOTTEN ALL THE REST OF THE EVIDENCE?"

"What evidence?" Holcomb asked calmly, turning to him. "It seems to me all you have is a shirt, a butcher knife that could've belonged to anyone, and a highly irrelevant excerpt from a piece of fiction: all very circumstantial, by the way. Without Charles Murray, it seems to me you don't have much of a case."

Aiken looked at him suspiciously. "I get it now, Judge. Holcomb here hid the kid away!"

"That's ridiculous, Aiken," Holcomb sneered. "How the devil did I do that? You were in charge of Charles, and I was in the lawyers' room with Jack's wife and Charles' brother during the recess. Even the bailiff can tell you that!"

Judge Aiken waved her hands in frustration. "ENOUGH!" she shouted and turned toward Aiken. "I'll give you one more hour to produce Charles Murray. If you don't, I'll be forced to call a mistrial. Now get out of here, both of you!"

Aiken and Holcomb rushed out of her chambers, Aiken immediately going to the elevators, Holcomb returning to Janie and Ralph and Ricky in the private room. When he told Janie what was happening, she didn't react as he thought she would. "But doesn't that mean he won't be declared innocent, Miles?" she asked.

Holcomb was aware of that, but he also knew when he had a good deal. "Not really," he answered, "though there may not be a verdict, everybody knows he didn't do it. Besides, he'll be free; and I don't think there ever will be any retrial."

Janie frowned. "I hope Charles comes back," she said. Ricky, sitting nervously, couldn't believe what she said. Holcomb excused himself, saying, "I have to make a call."

Ralph also got up from his chair and said, "I'm going out to see if I can help to find him." Before Holcomb could stop him, he was out the door.

Charles knew what he had to do. Now convinced that seeing the Indian melt was just a dream and that he was just staring at him because he didn't like him, he figured he'd go back to the court and explain that his leg was killing him and make up something that happened when they sawed it off.

"That'll get 'em," he chuckled as he walked to the courthouse. Suddenly he muttered, "What'll I say about running out of the hotel room?" He smiled. "Easy. I was hungry and went to get something to eat." He laughed. "And the guards weren't there! Great! Wait 'til I tell them one of them was in a room with the cleaning lady!"

As he approached the courthouse, he began hobbling, feigning trouble with his prosthesis. Though some people looked at him pityingly, no one accosted him as he went through the lobby and up the elevator.

Holcomb, the first to see he'd returned, muttered, "Shit!" as he and Janie and Ralph and Ricky came out of the lawyers' room. Janie smiled, but Ricky tried to hide behind her.

Charles was delighted. "Hiya, Kid," he yelled to Ricky. "Your brother's back. You and your mommy glad?" He then laughed as he went into the courtroom where Aiken was talking animatingly to the bailiff. When Aiken saw him, he rushed up to him and blustered, "Where have you been, Murray? We've been looking all over for you!"

Charles shrugged. "Just went out to get a burger," he answered as he took a seat. "What's the big deal?"

The bailiff, having alerted Judge Stein that Charles was back, announced that she would soon return to the bench. The crowd entered noisily, followed by Holcomb, Janie, Ricky, and Ralph.

Charles hobbled over behind Holcomb, sneered at Ricky, and whispered, "I'm glad my little brother's here, Counselor. I want him to see me destroy Cramer. Incidentally, I hope you're not expecting him to say anything that might help you." He hobbled back to his seat, trying not to laugh.

Startled, Holcomb just turned and looked at him until Judge Stein entered. He stumbled to his feet, joining the others as she banged her gavel. "Have a seat, people. Let's get this damn trial over with! Bailiff, call Mr. Murray back to the stand."

Chapter Twenty-Four: Charles Panics

Holcomb now sensed this wasn't going to be easy, despite the kid's age and especially when he saw Charles trying not to smirk. "The little bastard's way ahead of us," he muttered to Jack who'd been brought in from his cell and was sitting beside him.

"You can get to him," Jack answered, unaware of all that happened.

Holcomb shrugged, got up, stood in front of Charles, and said calmly, "I don't know if it means anything to you, Mr. Murray, but as the bailiff told you, you're under oath and can be prosecuted for perjury if you lie."

Charles again adopted his guise as an injured victim. "Gee, Mr. Holcomb, I know that. I only want to tell the truth, that's all." He winced with imaginary pain.

"Well then, let's get to it, the truth I mean," Holcomb said as he moved closer to him. First, we'd all like to hear what you meant earlier by saying 'I won't tell.' Won't tell what?"

Charles struggled to bring tears in his eyes. "Gee, Mr. Holcomb, I guess I was so messed up with the pain from my leg, I must've been remembering that the doctor said he'd screwed up when he chopped it off. It hurts bad."

Holcomb knew the battle was on. "The doctor said he made a mistake? Are you sure?"

"Nah," Charles answered, looking down. "They put me under, you know. But that must've been what I was imagining when I shouted that out."

Jesus, the kid is crafty, Holcomb thought. Getting desperate, he decided to try a new tact. "It's interesting, Mr. Murray, what you say about your prosthesis causing you so much pain, especially when I remember you in the hallway walking quite well."

"It comes and goes," Charles winced and answered quickly, looking first at the jury and then at the crowd that by this time had filled the room. He fingered the cross he'd put around his neck.

Holcomb noticed. "I see, Mr. Murray. By the way, that's an interesting cross you're wearing. Unusual. Would you mind telling us where you got it?"

Unnerved, Charles put it back under his shirt. "Found it," he answered.

"Oh, do you remember where?" Holcomb said quickly, hoping he'd caught the boy.

Charles again was way ahead of him. "Yeah, I do," he answered meekly. "It was when I was looking for my little brother that time. I was worried about him, you know, because I hadn't seen him for a while. Anyway, I went to the bus station, thinking he might be there, and on my way back I saw it on the ground. I thought it was kind of cool so I took it."

He tried not to grin as he watched Holcomb walk back to his table. Confidently, he surveyed the crowd, all looking at him, and then stared at Ricky sitting in the first row with his head down. He then noticed the door open at the rear of the courtroom, the two guards oblivious because they'd moved up behind the crowd for a better view. Deciding it probably was another reporter, he straightened up but then leaned forward and saw Ricky standing there smiling at him!

He swiveled his head and looked back to the first row and saw another Ricky. He gasped, suddenly remembering what had happened in his room at the hotel, and leapt up, his face white. Holcomb stepped back thinking the boy was having some kind of seizure. Charles then crumpled back into his chair and covered his eyes. The crowd began to murmur.

Judge Stein, also stunned by his behavior, looked down, muttered, "Not again," and then asked, "Mr. Murray, are you all right? Can you hear me?"

Charles peaked through his fingers, looked at the back door, and saw no one except the two guards. Shaking his head, he straightened up, looked at the judge, and mumbled, "What?"

"I asked you if you were all right, young man," Judge Stein said. The room was as quiet as a library as the people sat anxiously, wondering what was going on.

Coming around, Charles looked at her and suddenly realized where he was. He shook his head, trying to think how he could explain, and remembered the prosthesis. Groaning, he said, "My leg! It's killing me. I'm sorry, Judge. I didn't mean to scare anybody. It's fine now."

Aiken was staring at him, knowing he was in a pickle. On the one hand, he didn't want a mistrial; but on the other, he didn't like the way Charles was acting at all. And he was becoming more and more convinced his main witness was crazy. But by this time he knew he was in it too deep, that if his case blew up, it would give his rival for his job all the ammunition he needed. So he just sat and waited anxiously to see what the boy would do next.

Holcomb, in the meantime, was confused. When he looked at the back of the courtroom, he noticed nothing to warrant Charles' reaction. However, when he saw the confusion on the faces of the twelve jurors, he sensed an opening. Charles was looking at him defiantly as he approached him. "Are you feeling better, Mr. Murray?" he asked solicitously.

Charles smiled. "As I told you, Sir, it comes and goes," he answered, adopting again his boyishness.

"Comes and goes, huh?" Holcomb asked sarcastically. "I noticed you looking at the back of the room. Why was that?"

Charles shrugged, took out the cross, and began fondling it. "I wasn't looking at anything, Sir. I guess it was a charley horse."

Holcomb knew he was getting nowhere, so he again decided to try a new strategy. "Getting back to the cross, Mr. Murray. That's a unique cross. You say you found it?"

Disgusted, Aiken shouted, "Objection, your honor. Mr. Holcomb is just wasting our time!"

Judge Stein hesitated. "Where are you going with this, Counselor?" she asked.

"If you give me a moment, Judge, I'll show you and the jury." Holcomb answered, hoping she'd go along with him.

"Get on with it," she barked.

Holcomb moved closer to Charles, checking his notes. "Well, Mr. Murray, about that cross. Perhaps I should mention that the warden at the prison from where the victim was released told the constable that he was wearing exactly the same cross the last time he saw him."

Charles wasn't fazed. Again shrugging, he said, "I don't know anything about that, Sir. I just found it one day on the boardwalk."

Holcomb was beginning to feel this kid could come up with an answer for everything. "So you say, Mr. Murray. I think we all find it very interesting though."

Judge Stein frowned. "For the love of God, Counselor, would you just get on with it?" she snarled.

Holcomb nodded. "Well, Mr. Murray, let's again get to you saying, 'I won't tell.' If I recall, you answered that you remembered that the doctor on the ship said he'd done something wrong when he was amputating your leg. Is that right?"

Charles pretended to be confused. "Yeah ... I think so. It's just that I was hurting so much, you know."

Holcomb pointed to a distinguished man in a Navy uniform in the audience. "What if I were to tell you the same doctor is here today and that he'll testify?"

Charles just shrugged. "Could've been my imagination, I guess," he said nonchalantly. "I could've said anything the pain I was in."

Holcomb wasn't finished. "Let's talk about that pain, okay? The doctor told me that when you were released from the sickbay on the Navy ship, you'd adapted very well to the prosthesis and was walking without pain. Shall I call him up here to explain this to the jury?"

Aiken was on his feet to object, but Charles was ahead of them both. "The doctor saved me, Mr. Holcomb. I can't thank him enough for that; but he hasn't walked in my fake legs. Golly, I don't want to get him in trouble because he's such a nice man. I'm sure sorry you had to bring him all this way and take him away from people who need him."

Holcomb knew his cross-examination was dissolving. He changed the subject. "You're such a nice guy, Mr. Murray," he said sarcastically; and before the judge could censure him, he continued. "All right, let's talk about the night of the murder. You heard the constable testify there were no lights…" He stopped, noticing Charles was again staring at the back of the room, his eyes wide. He stepped back. "What's wrong, Mr. Murray?" he asked.

Charles pointed to the door, his finger shaking. "It's the Indian," he mumbled. "He's going to melt again!"

Holcomb looked up and saw Kasmali, again wearing the sunglasses, standing by the back door. "Are you pointing at Chief Kasmali?" he asked. "You know him. He was at Valdez."

"DON'T!" Charles yelled, jumping up.

"Sit down, Mr. Murray," Judge Aiken said calmly. "There's no one here who'll hurt you."

Charles looked at her pleadingly but remained standing. "You'll see, Judge. You'll see," he whined. "Watch, he'll change into Ricky again. I just know it!"

Though Holcomb had no idea what Charles was talking about, he was wary. The kid seemed to be ready for anything, but this time it didn't seem like an act. "He's gone bonkers again," he warned the judge.

Charles tried desperately to control himself, but he couldn't stop staring at Kasmali who continued to smile at him.

Judge Stein sighed and said, "I'll see Mr. Murray and the counselors in my chambers." She rose from her seat as the guards gathered Charles from the witness stand and followed her with both Holcomb and Aiken behind.

She sat heavily in the chair behind her desk and then motioned for the guards to sit Charles in a chair in front of her and then leave. Aiken stood next to him. Holcomb sat, fully expecting Charles to come up with a reason why he was acting so strangely, but hoping that this time he'd blown it.

For a moment Judge Stein just looked at Charles, but finally, she asked if he was all right. Charles, now out of the view of Kasmali, was slowly regaining his poise. "I'm fine, Judge," he answered.

She nodded, leaned forward, and said, "Well, you must know you've been acting rather oddly. What's going on?"

Charles shrugged. "He's out to get me, that's all," he answered calmly.

"Who, Mr. Murray?"

"The weird Indian," Charles answered, sitting up. "He threatened me. Him and his dog."

"You mean Chief Kasmali? What's the dog have to do with it? And why would they threaten you?"

"He said he'd sic the dog on me. I don't know why!"

"I don't understand," Judge Stein said, now convinced the boy was unbalanced.

Charles leaned toward her, deciding she might be one of those motherly types he could manipulate. Maybe she'd soften up if she knew what he'd gone through, he thought. "I know now I must have been dreaming, Judge," he began, "but I thought I saw Ricky come to see me in my room at the hotel. At least I thought it was Ricky. Anyway, right in the middle of us talking, I imagined Ricky suddenly melting and change into that Indian!"

Holcomb was delighted. The judge was stunned. "You mean you thought he turned into Chief Kasmali?"

"Yeah, and then he threatened me, but like I said, I must've been dreaming."

She sat back, trying not to show her shock. "Then what happened? In your dream, I mean?"

Ignoring Holcomb and Aiken, and thinking she was beginning to believe him, Charles decided to tell the whole story. "Well, Judge, you remember when I ran? I know I said I had a charley horse, but the real reason was because when I looked out at the door, I thought I saw Ricky. When I looked down and saw another Ricky behind Cramer's lawyer, I remembered the dream and thought the Indian was using him to get to me, so I freaked."

Now wondering if he was deranged, she decided to go along with him. "So, you thought he was now Chief Kasmali. Why would he want to get to you, as you said?"

Charles, realizing he'd slipped up, had had enough. "Fuck!" he snarled. "How the hell do I know? I guess he's one of those crazy Indians who hates Whites!"

"Watch your language, Mr. Murray," Stein said calmly. "But why you in particular?"

Frustrated, Charles jumped out of his chair, Yelled, "SHIT! I DON'T KNOW! I'M OUTA HERE!" and burst out of the room. Panicking, Aiken ran after him.

Holcomb turned to Stein, trying not to grin, and said, "Well, Judge, what do we do now?"

Stein, looking furious, just stared at him. After a moment, she said, "Don't look so pleased, Counselor. This thing isn't over yet. Tell the guards to come in, will you?"

When he came in with them, Stein told them to find Charles and put him in a secure room and have someone guard him. Then she ordered them to get the bailiff.

The bailiff came in. "Get Mr. Aiken in here!" she barked and added, "And ask the Inupiaq chief if he'll come in, too."

Drumming her fingers on her desk again, she glared at Holcomb. "The boy may be crazy as a loon, Counselor," she said abruptly. "Before I do anything, though, I want him examined."

The bailiff returned, followed by Aiken and a guard leading Kasmali by his arm. She ignored Aiken and directed her attention to Kasmali. "I apologize for this, Chief," she said calmly. "Thank you for coming in. Something has come up that I feel I must ask you about." She then turned to Aiken and asked, "Do you have a psychiatrist on call?"

Aiken, hoping she was overreacting, answered, "You sure it's necessary, Judge. You saw how the boy's in awful pain from his leg. He might say anything."

Judge Stein bristled. "That may or may not be, Aiken; but what I asked was if you could get a psychiatrist!"

Aiken thought for a moment. "Yes, Judge. I'll get one if you think it's necessary,"

"Do so," Stein barked. "I want to know if the boy's in his right mind! For God's sake, he said his brother melted and changed into the chief here!"

Stein waited until Aiken scurried out and then addressed Kasmali who was standing, his eyes hidden by the sunglasses. "I'm sorry to ask this, Chief," she said diplomatically, "but Mr. Murray said he had a dream where you changed into his little brother. He also claimed you threatened him." She smiled. "It's ridiculous, of course, but I just wanted to clear it up."

Kasmali remained passive. "I am a chief of the Inupiaq, Judge Stein. That is all. The young man you speak of may be frightened by Native Alaskans. Many of your people are."

Again she nodded, thinking of her ticklish political situation. "As I said, Chief, I'm sorry to waste your time; but I hope you understand I had to inquire about the boy's comments."

"Of course," Kasmali answered brusquely. "May I go now?"

Stein rose. "Yes, of course," she answered as graciously as her nature would allow. "And once again, thank you."

When he was led out, she looked sternly at both lawyers, shrugged, and said, "The boy may have just dreamed it, I guess."

Chapter Twenty-Five: The Prosecution Rests

Sitting in the quiet room, Charles was getting nervous. He'd thought the stupid judge believed him, but he wasn't sure; and he had no idea why the two guards were standing against the wall just looking at him.

When a gray-haired, paunchy man walked in and smiled, however, he began to relax. "You can leave now, officers," the man said to the two men and then sat down opposite him. "I'm Doctor Friedman," he then said calmly to Charles. "Mr. Aiken said we might have a chat, Mr. Murray. Is that all right?" The men left.

Charles shrugged, figuring he knew why the old man was here. "You're a shrink, right? They think I'm crazy, but I know what I saw."

Doctor Friedman continued to smile. "Well, let's talk about it, all right? If it's all right with you, let's talk about with your comment to Judge Stein that your brother turned into a native. I believe you said he, your brother, just melted, and the next thing you knew he was an Indian. Is that right?"

Charles again shrugged, suddenly realizing how weird that sounded.

Friedman maintained his smile. "I'll take that for a yes, Charles. May I call you Charles?" Again Charles shrugged.

"And then in the courtroom, you told the judge you saw your brother in the balcony and behind Mr. Holcomb at the same time. True?"

Charles decided it was a good idea to get this guy on his side, though it was obvious he was just like the others, just another guy out to get him. "That's not the whole story, sir," he answered politely. "After my brother turned into the Indian, I figured it was just a dream, that I'd been sleeping. Then at the trial, I was out of my head my leg hurt so much, and I lost it. I don't know what happened then."

Friedman nodded. "Sounds reasonable," he said. "Maybe I can help. May I examine your prosthesis? It's the prosthesis that's causing the pain, right?"

Charles, way ahead of him, winced and adjusted his seat. "Not just that, sir. It's both legs, my back, and even my butt; but for some reason the pain comes and goes. Right now, it's just my butt." He hoped the old fart got his joke.

But Friedman again just nodded and said, "Well, I don't think we'll be here long. Let's talk just for a moment about you crying out, 'I won't tell.' The judge also told me about that. She said you were thinkin about the doctor, right?"

Charles was way ahead of him. "Yeah," he answered. "It was just that I hurt do much I started thinking about him hacking my leg off back on that ship. Somehow I thought I heard him saying he screwed up. Anyway, I didn't want him to get in trouble so I guess that's why I might have said I wouldn't tell. On him, you know."

"The doctor said he made a mistake? Is that what you're saying?"

Charles shrugged again. "I guess so, sir, but I could have just imagined it. I was really out of my head with the pain."

"Yet when I talked to the doctor -- yes, I had a chance to chat with him --he told me the operation went fine."

Again Charles shrugged. "Golly, sir, I guess I did imagine it. They put me under, you know."

Once again, Friedman nodded. "All right, can we talk for a minute about you saying the Inupiaq threatened you."

Remembering his comment, Charles thought quickly. "Oh, that, Doc. I told you he changed into Ricky but I could've been dreaming, I guess."

Friedman nodded. "All right, can we now talk about your childhood? I'm aware you and your little brother were abandoned by your parents and are now living with foster people, though your brother seems to have found a new situation with Mr. and Mrs. Cramer. How do you feel about that?"

"Good for him," Charles answered calmly.

"Very mature, Charles," the doctor said. "Most of others faced with that would probably feel a little resentment, perhaps even jealousy. And from what I've been told, you don't like Mr. Cramer very much. Mr. Aiken said he hit you. Is that right?"

Charles was getting into this. "Yeah," he answered. "He lost his temper a lot."

"Did he ever hit your brother?"

Again, Charles shrugged. "Gee, Doc," he answered coyly. "You'd have to ask him."

Friedman smiled. "I did. Before I came to talk to you, I took a few minutes with him, and he said Mr. Cramer never hit him."

Charles jerked up and barked, "You talked to Ricky? What lies did he tell you?"

Friedman was stunned. "Lies?" he asked. "Well, perhaps. Among other things, he told me Mr. Cramer was very kind to him."

"Sure he was. The kid's a real kiss-up, and he lies all the time about me."

"You're confusing me, Charles," Friedman answered. "What lies would your brother tell about you?"

Charles, suddenly remembering that he'd heard somewhere that a shrink couldn't repeat what he was told, decided he was tired of acting like a helpless kid. "I know what you're doing, old man," he sneered. "He told you what I said to him, didn't he?"

Friedman, previously convinced Charles had been a victim of a lousy childhood, began to wonder. He sat forward and nodded. "Your brother seems to me to be a good boy," he said obliquely.

"THAT'S WHAT YOU THINK!" Charles yelled, taking out the cross. "HE'S GOT EVERYONE FOOLED!" He controlled himself. "Anyway, I told you he was a liar, so if he said I had anything to do with killing that guy at Valdez, he's lying again, just like he's always done!"

Amazed at the change in Charles, Friedman sat back, no longer smiling. Charles continued to sneer. "Well," Friedman said, "that's interesting. Why do you think that is?"

Once again, Charles shrugged. "I don't know," he scoffed. "You tell me."

"I have no idea," Friedman answered. "But perhaps together we can find out. For a long time, there was really only you and your little brother. True?"

Charles nodded. "Yeah, just him and me and those fake families."

Friedman nodded. "There were a lot of them?"

Charles laughed. "A shitload," he sneered. "We'd just get settled and bam, out we went. Then we ended up with the family we're with now."

"But before that, why'd the others ask you to leave? What happened?"

Charles slumped in his chair. "I don't know, man!" he mumbled. "They were all idiots." He now was stroking the cross nervously.

"You lose your temper with them? Maybe you thought they weren't giving you enough attention. Or did your little brother do something?"

"Ricky? You gotta be kidding! They all loved him."

Friedman smiled. "So, again, how'd you feel about that?"

"About them liking Ricky? What do you think? I didn't care! I told you, they were all idiots."

"Idiots for liking Ricky?"

Charles bristled. "No, you asshole! I didn't say that!"

Friedman sat back. "Okay, Mr. Murray, just relax. I didn't mean anything by that, but I get the idea those people didn't like you that much. Did they?"

Charles shrugged. "Nah, I'm not a kiss-ass like Ricky."

"Okay, as I understand it, then Mrs. Cramer came along and gave you and Ricky jobs at her cafe. From what I understand, she saved you from going to juvenile hall. Do I have it right?"

"Typical do-gooder," Charles snorted. "Ricky and me saw a lot of them."

The doctor, sensing he was on to something, said, "She seems to have taken to him, from what I saw at the trial. How does that make you feel, considering that you're testifying against her husband? It might seem as if he's betraying you. By the way, you seem to be fond of that cross. It's important to you, right? Why is that?"

Charles laughed sarcastically. "Forget the fucking cross and my brother. He'll never rat on me. He knows better."

"What do you mean?"

Charles jumped up. "Listen, old man, I've had it!" He burst out of the room, slamming the door behind him. Friedman rose, shook his head, and left the room on his way to give his report to Judge Stein.

She was waiting in her chambers with Holcomb and Aiken. Seeing him come through the door, she asked abruptly, "Well, Doctor, is the boy crazy or not?"

Friedman stopped short. "Crazy's not the word I'd use, Judge. It's not a clinical diagnosis," he answered, somewhat insulted.

"Oh, get off your high horse, Doctor," Stein retorted. "Just tell us what you found out about the kid."

Friedman took a seat in front of her desk. Holcomb and Aiken stood against separate walls. "Well," he began, "I only had a few minutes with him, so anything I say is purely conjecture, and most of it is covered by patient-doctor confidentiality. But I can tell you the boy is very intelligent with a highly developed defense mechanism. Also, he has a precocious way of adapting to different situations. For one thing, I suspect he's using his prosthesis to elicit sympathy. For another, when I mentioned his brother, he changed right in front of me. I'd been convinced before that that he was just another thrown away child; but after seeing his reaction, I suspect he's paranoid-schizophrenic. But, remember, I only saw him for a few minutes, so that diagnosis is pure speculation based on his defensiveness and his violent change of moods. If I had more time with him, perhaps I could be more specific. One other thing I'm curious about is his reliance on a metal cross when he gets agitated."

Judge Stein turned to Aiken. "Well, Mr. Aiken," she asked. "What do you want to do? You want to put Mr. Murray back on the stand?"

Holcomb interrupted. "If he does, Judge, I think I have the right to call the doctor. When they hear what he has to say, they won't believe any of Charles' testimony."

Friedman reacted quickly. "If you put me on the stand, Counselor, I'll only be able to speak in the most general terms. Besides, as I said, what he said to me I can't repeat."

Anxiously, Aiken stepped forward. "Let the boy back on the stand, Judge. He may be whacko, but he's capable of telling what he saw."

Judge Stein rose. "It's your funeral, Mr. Aiken. You heard the doctor. The boy is troubled, to say the least. Go ahead. On the way out, tell the bailiff we're about to continue this mess."

Charles, confident that once again he'd fooled them all, rose for the judge and then was led by the bailiff back to the witness box.

Rapping her gavel, Stein motioned to Holcomb. He smiled as he approached Charles. "Let's get back to that night, Mr. Murray," he began. "So far you've testified that you recognized Jack Cramer the night of the murder because of a light coming from a store, despite the fact that Constable Eston has told us there were no lights."

"He wasn't there," Charles interrupted.

"Actually he was, but let's ignore that for a moment. Instead, let's go into when you were working for Mr. Cramer and his wife. According to your testimony, he hit you, correct?"

"That's right, Sir," Charles replied politely.

"And you reacted how?"

"I got mad, that's all."

"All right, you got mad; but didn't you call him a … excuse me, your honor. Didn't you call him a 'fucker'? And after that, didn't you say you'd get even with him?"

Stein glowered but said nothing. Charles shrugged and answered calmly, "I told you I was mad. When I get that way, sometimes I use bad language."

Holcomb knew Charles was slipping away. "But what about you threatening him?" he asked.

Again Charles shrugged. "Golly, Sir," he answered. "I was just mad. What could I do to a big guy like Mr. Cramer?"

He did it again, Holcomb thought as he stepped back to consider where to go next. Finally he turned to Judge Stein. "I'm through with this witness for the moment, Judge; but I'd like the option of calling him back."

Judge Stein nodded and said, "You're dismissed for now, Mr. Murray." Charles, wincing with imaginary pain, struggled out of the witness box.

"Back to you, Mr. Aiken," she said. "Do you have any additional witnesses?"

Aiken stiffened. “No, your honor, the prosecution rests. The jury’s heard all it needs. Perhaps now the poor young man can rest.” He turned to Charles hobbling back to his seat. “Thank you, Mr. Murray,” he said and sat down.

Judge Stein stood up and stretched her back. “Thank goodness. There is a God. We’ll adjourn until three this afternoon. Then we’ll hear from the defense.”

Chapter Twenty-Six: The Defense

Sitting in a folding chair behind a long table that displayed plates of sandwiches, bowls of chips, and even hotdogs recently cooked by the lunch wagon down from him, E. Frances Chadwell was smiling, his lumberjack outfit perfect, his black hair unkempt as if he'd just come from helping clean up the city. A Diet Pepsi and a hotdog were in front of him. "The yokels'll love it," he whispered.

He'd figured his presence in the courtroom would be impolitic, so his lackeys had been informing him of the progress of the trial; and, from what they told him, Aiken was making a fool of himself and making it easy for him to take his job. He couldn't care less about Jack Cramer; but if he was found innocent despite all the evidence against him, it'd be obvious to everyone that Aiken had been district attorney too long. He laughed. "What a jerk," he muttered.

Smiling, he watched as the crowd streamed from the courthouse, many wearing T-shirts Chadwell had told his lackeys to distribute: "SAVE THE HERO," some read. Others, "GET RID OF AIKEN:" Most headed right for the free food. When enough people gathered around him, he rose and stood on his chair.

"MY FRIENDS!" he hollered. "WELCOME! YOU ALL KNOW ME, AN ALASKAN JUST LIKE YOU! I HEARD HOW SO MANY OF YOU HAVE BEEN ALL DAY AT THIS … TRIAL. I FIGURED YOU HAD TO BE HUNGRY SO I DECIDED TO HELP OUT!"

Many cheered, most with their mouths filled. "HOW'S THE TRIAL GOING?" he asked.

One man closest to him, a plant previously arranged by Chadwell, suddenly yelled back, "THAT JACKASS AIKEN NEVER SHOULD'VE TRIED THE CASE! HE'S TOO DAMN OLD!"

Chadwell waved his arms defensively. "Now, come on, people," he said more calmly. "Mr. Aiken is trying his best."

Another plant laughed loudly and yelled, 'THAT'S THE PROBLEM! HIS BEST IS LOUSY!"

Chadwell shrugged, again waved his arms, and sat back satisfied as he watched many in the crowd nodding in agreement.

At the same time, lying on the bed in his hotel room, Charles was worried that maybe he'd gone too far with the shrink; but even more, he was upset that his moment in the spotlight might be over. The cushy hotel room, the room service, the people in the courtroom looking at him, even the battles with that stupid defense guy: after all of that, he wasn't ready to go back to living in some abandoned shack.

He got up and paced around the room, trying to think of something he could do to prolong his moment. He thought of the piece of shirt and the butcher knife and figured he couldn't do anything more with the shirt, but the knife he really hadn't considered before. During the few days he'd worked for the Cramers, he'd heard them talking about losing it and buying a new one. Then he remembered how after he'd swiped it, he'd made a nick in the handle when he was throwing it against a tree. "That's it!" he yelped and ran to the door. Suddenly he stopped. "Ricky!" he muttered. "The little shit told them I took it!"

Discouraged, he sat back on the bed. Suddenly he smiled. "If they use him as a witness, I can get around it. He's just a kid," he whispered. "Kids lie. Besides, he knows what'll happen if he says anything." Chuckling, he walked back to the door to tell the guards he had to talk to Mr. Aiken. Reluctantly, they called Aiken and were told to bring Charles to him.

Charles found him in a room looking out the window. "Damn!" Aiken snarled without looking around. "Look at Chadwell! What a phony!"

"Sir?" Charles said meekly. "Sir? I have to tell you something."

Looking depressed, Aiken turned and asked curtly, "What is it, Mr. Murray? Not another comment that can't be proved?"

Charles feigned embarrassment. "Gee, sir," he answered. "I only told what I saw. You asked me to do that, didn't you?"

Aiken looked closely at him. "The doctor you met with said you've got … some problems," he said hesitantly. "What'd you say to him?"

Charles wasn't surprised at this. "Gee, I don't know, sir. I tried to be nice to him, tell the truth, you know; but he kept confusing me. I didn't know what he wanted so I guess I got a little mad. For some reason, he didn't seem to like me, you know."

I believe it, Aiken thought, but he just shrugged and sat at a table. "Well, he may not be much of a problem if you continue to tell the truth. You are, aren't you?"

Charles tried to squeeze out some tears; but, failing that, he just moaned. "I just want to go home, back to my foster home," he whined. "I tried to do the right thing, and now even you won't believe me."

Aiken jumped up from his chair. "Jeez," he said, coming over to Charles. "I'm sorry, Mr. Murray. It's just that I'm getting worried. You and I both know Cramer did it, and now he may get away with it."

His head down, Charles muttered, "I've been thinking about that, sir. Would it help if I told you something I just remembered about the knife?"

Aiken sat up. "The butcher knife?" he asked. "What about it?"

Charles shrugged. "Gee, sir," he answered. "I don't know if this'll help, but I remembered that one day he cut himself with the knife and then threw it against the wall. Then, when I went to pick it up for him, I noticed he cracked the handle. I was just wondering if you noticed if the knife you have had a crack in it."

"CRAP!" Aiken bellowed. "STICK AROUND, KID!" he cried as he rushed from the room.

When the trial resumed, Aiken immediately jumped to his feet and said, perhaps a bit too loudly, "Your honor, new evidence has come to light. May I reopen my case before the defense begins?"

Judge Stein frowned. "Oh, for the love of God," she muttered. "What now?"

Aiken seized the moment. "It won't take long, your honor. If I could just recall Constable Eston?"

Surprised, Holcomb jumped up. "Objection, Judge. The prosecution already rested its case!"

Stein frowned. "Overruled, Mr. Holcomb. Let's hear what Mr. Aiken has to say." The bailiff then instructed Eston to come to the stand where he was reminded about his oath. Aiken, looking quite serious, approached, holding the butcher knife between two fingers, and said. "I apologize for recalling you, Constable, but something has come to light I feel I must ask you about."

"No problem," Eston answered.

"May I, your honor?" he asked. She signaled her okay, and he handed Eston the knife. "Would you examine this butcher knife, Constable, and tell us if it is the murder weapon?" he asked.

Eston took it and turned it over and over. ""Yes," he finally said, "it appears to be the one I found at the murder scene."

"Indulge me, sir," Aiken asked. "Would you look it over more carefully and tell the jury if you notice any cracks or nicks in the handle?"

Holcomb sat up and whispered, "What's going on, Jack?"

"I haven't the slightest idea," Jack whispered back as they watched the constable check the knife.

Eston gave the knife back and said, "There does seem to be a small crack there," he answered.

Aiken smiled. "Thank you, Constable. No further questions, your honor."

Obviously curious, Judge Stein released Eston and asked, "Is that it, Counselor?"

"Almost, your honor," Aiken answered. "I'd just like to recall Mr. Charles Murray for a quick question."

"Not again," the judge muttered and then nodded. The bailiff called Charles back to the stand. Limping badly and frowning, Charles started up the aisle from his seat in the gallery and suddenly stumbled near his brother who'd been watching him warily. Making sure no one else noticed, Charles then looked at Ricky, waved his finger across his neck and then pretended to struggle to get up. As he took his seat in the witness box, he continued to look at Ricky.

Still holding the butcher knife, Aiken approached him and said, "I'm sorry to make you go through this again, Mr. Murray. We can all see what pain you're in. However, would you examine this knife? Is it all right, Judge?"

As Judge Stein nodded, Holcomb sat up concerned. Aiken handed the knife to Charles, who pretended to shudder and then laid it on the ledge in front of him. "Is ... that the knife ...the killer used?" he stammered.

"Yes, I'm afraid it is," Aiken answered, looking at the jury, many of whom were leaning forward. Holcomb looked questioningly at Jack who merely shrugged.

"I'm sorry to do this, Mr. Murray," Aiken said, "but would you look at the crack in the handle of the knife and tell us if you've ever seen such a knife with such a crack before?"

Charles tentatively turned the knife over. "Yeah, that's Mr. Cramer's knife," he said. "I saw him break it one day."

"THAT'S A LIE!" Jack yelled, jumping up. Ricky went white.

Judge Stein banged her gavel over and over as the crowd reacted. "WE WILL HAVE ORDER!" she shouted. The crowd went silent.

She glared at Holcomb. "If you can't control your client, Mr. Holcomb," she snarled. "I'll remove him from the court."

Holcomb placed his hand on Jack's shoulder, pushing him back in his chair. "Yes, your honor," he answered. "He'll be fine. I just hope now that the prosecutor is finally finished."

"Are you, Mr. Aiken?" the judge asked calmly.

Aiken smiled. "You bet, your honor." He sat down, looking very confident. Charles was still in the witness box.

"Your honor," Holcomb, realizing he had to have time to talk to Jack, said, "before I call my witnesses, would you allow a brief recess? This young man's in obvious pain, and it just so happens his doctor's in the courtroom. Perhaps the Navy doctor could examine him in your chambers to see if there's a problem with his prosthesis."

"I'm all right," Charles said quickly.

"No, you're not," Judge Stein retorted. "Good idea, Counselor. We all could use a break."

His limp noticeably better, Charles was led into her chambers, the doctor following. The judge remained on the bench. Only the two of them, together with a male guard were in the room when the doctor politely asked Charles to remove his pants. Noting the guard, Charles, obeyed, though with feigned difficulty, for it should have been easy due to the special zipper down the length of his pants covering the prosthesis.

Without a word, the doctor began testing the prosthesis by moving it up and down and twisting it from one side to the other, Charles moaning constantly. The doctor looked curiously at him and asked, "Where does it hurt?"

Worried, Charles answered, "At the stump, Doc."

The doctor then examined the stump and said, "That's odd, Mr. Murray. There's no sign of inflammation. Are you sure it's not the other leg?"

"Yeah, that's it," Charles quickly answered. "Or maybe what you told me about phantom pain. Remember?"

The doctor began checking his other leg, flexing it up and down and twisting it. "Seems fine," he said. "And any imaginary pain should be long gone." He got up. "Well, son," he said, "I've gotta be frank with you. When you were in the sick bay on the ship, we noticed you had a low tolerance to pain. As far as I can tell, your prosthesis is fine and your other leg seems strong. You're just going to have to be a man about it and quit whining."

Charles was shocked. The doctor continued, "I was told you accused me of saying I did something wrong during your operation. Of course, I said no such thing, and besides, you were unconscious. Why would you say such a thing?"

Seemingly unaware now that the guard was listening, Charles sneered and said calmly, "You took off my leg, you quack! I told you not to, but you did it anyway!"

"I had to, son," the doctor answered as he motioned for Charles to be led by the guard back into court.

"Good," Judge Stein said as she put away the magazine she'd been reading. "Now can we get back to it? Mr. Holcomb, are you now ready?"

"Sure, your honor," Holcomb replied. "And since he's right here – he pointed to the doctor who was just coming out of her chambers – we can start with Dr. Sandeen."

Judge Stein nodded submissively, and the doctor took a seat in the witness box and was read the oath.

Holcomb didn't waste any time. "You are the primary doctor on the Navy ship where Mr. Murray was treated, is that true?" he asked.

"Yes," Dr. Sandeen answered. "I've been leading the medical corps on the ship for almost four years now."

"Let's talk about Charles Murray. First of all, he's testified that you said he did something wrong when he amputated your leg. To your best recollection, did you say anything like that?"

Dr. Sandeen sat up, bracing his hands on the wooden partition. "No, I did not!" he answered brusquely. "The amputation was uneventful. Moreover, I have a team of medics who can verify that! By the way, you might want to call the guard who was with the boy and me in the room. He might be able to give some insight about Mr. Murray."

Charles, back in his seat in the gallery furiously stroking the cross, looked around as the crowd murmured.

Holcomb ignored the murmuring. "Let's forget that for a moment, Doctor. We might want to hear from the guard later; but as long as you're up here, why don't you tell us about all the pain Mr. Murray seems to be suffering. I'm sure we'd all to glad to hear if you were able to help him."

Sensing where Holcomb was going, Aiken jumped up and yelled, "OBJECTION, YOUR HONOR! HAVEN'T WE WASTED ENOUGH TIME ALREADY? DOES IT REALLY MATTER HOW MUCH PAIN MR. MURRAY IS IN?"

Amused, the judge looked down at him. "I'm surprised by your lack of compassion, Mr. Aiken. Aren't you interested to hear if your witness is better? Objection denied."

Holcomb tried not to chuckle as he asked the doctor to continue. Dr. Sandeen sat back, saying, "As far as I could tell, the boy is fine. The prosthesis is working well, and there is no inflammation on either leg."

"That's wonderful, Doctor," Holcomb said sarcastically. "I'm sure we're all happy to hear that. Thank you." He turned to the judge. "I'm finished with this witness, Judge," he said as he went back to the defense table.

Judge Stein looked at him questioningly and then turned to the district attorney. "Do you have any questions for this witness, Mr. Aiken?" she asked.

Aiken shook his head. "No, your honor. As Mr. Murray said, his pain comes and goes."

Judge Stein nodded and turned to Holcomb. "Do you want the guard to take the stand now, Counselor" she asked.

"It can wait, your honor," Holcomb answered. "I'd like to begin the defense now."

The judge shrugged. "Thank you Doctor. You're dismissed. Now, Mr. Holcomb," she almost yelled. "For God's sake, will you get on with it!"

Holcomb walked slowly up to the jury. "Ladies and gentlemen," he began calmly, "the case against my client totally rests on circumstantial evidence – a bloody piece of shirt, an alleged motive, an everyday butcher knife, and the testimony of one confused young man. I won't waste your time talking about the shirt, for it could've belonged to anybody. The alleged motive – that, despite the fact that my client now is happily married, he wanted revenge for an evil done some ten years before, is hard to believe. However, in a moment I will call a witness who might be able to shed some light on that. But first, let's talk about the butcher knife that Mr. Murray claims to have belonged to Mr. Cramer. That and the fact that Mr. Murray has testified that he saw my client running from the murder scene seems to be the prosecutor's whole case. Let's go into all of that now. I suspect it won't take long.

"Oh, on second thought, I'll bet we're all curious about the guard Dr. Sandeen mentioned. Why don't we begin by hearing from him?" He turned to Judge Stein. "May we now call him to the stand, Judge?" he asked politely.

The judge motioned to the guard who was standing by the American flag at her right. "Officer," she said, "let's get this over with."

The guard stiffly walked to the witness box and sat down. Aiken, showing his disgust, muttered, "For Christ's sake;" but he made no objection.

After the guard was read the oath and gave his name, Holcomb asked, "As you may have heard, Officer, we're all curious about what Dr. Sandeen was referring to when you three were in the judge's chambers. Can you help us out about that?"

The guard looked at the judge and then hesitantly said, "I guess the doctor was talking about what happened just before I took Mr. Murray back. The doc had told him he'd never said he'd done anything wrong during the operation; and then Mr. Murray, in kind of a sneer, said he told the doc not to do it. He was angry."

"OBJECTION, YOUR HONOR!" Aiken roared.

Judge Stein nodded. "Just keep to the facts, Officer. Your opinions are irrelevant." She looked at the jury. "Ladies and gentlemen, you must disregard the officer's comments about Mr. Murray's tone and also his opinions." She turned to Holcomb and, looking bemused, asked, "Just where are you going with all this, Counselor?"

Holcomb turned and pointed at Charles sitting two rows deep in the gallery. "I beg your indulgence, your honor," he answered, "but considering the flimsiness of the prosecution's case, it seems it really comes down to the testimony of one person, Charles Murray." He turned to the jury. "Over and over, he's lied, ladies and gentlemen; and you must be wondering why. I will now call someone to the stand who will be able to tell us."

Over the murmurs of the crowd, Judge Aiken banged her gavel and shouted, "ENOUGH!" She then turned to Holcomb, "All right, get on with it! Are you finished with the officer, Counselor?"

"Yes, your honor," Holcomb replied and waited patiently for the man to regain his post by the flagpole. Sensing the right moment, he then turned to the jury and announced, "I call Ricky Murray to the stand."

Shaking, Ricky grabbed Janie's hand and whispered, "I can't, Mrs. Cramer. I can't. Charles'll hurt me."

The court waited and watched as Janie hugged him. "He can't hurt you any longer, Sweetheart. Just tell the truth," she whispered back.

"You don't know him, Mrs. Cramer," Ricky answered, looking down. "He'll find a way. He always has."

She picked up his head. "Not this time, darling. If you just tell what you know about the butcher knife, the judge will get him help. Go on, now. You can do it."

Releasing her hand, Ricky slowly rose and, with his head still down, stepped out to the aisle.

Charles, sitting to his right, was getting even more worried as the people around him seemed to shift away. However, as he watched Ricky walk so reluctantly to the witness box, he was fairly confident the little shit would remember his warning. His face in a sneer, he looked menacingly at his brother as Holcomb approached him holding the butcher knife by his side. Ricky was looking down at his feet.

Charles continued to glare, his anger at Ricky growing. Holcomb, however, was smiling as he watched the bailiff give Ricky the oath. "Thanks for being so brave, Ricky," he began when the bailiff finished. "I know how tough this is for you. Let's introduce you first. Your name is Ricky Murray, right? And you are Charles' brother?"

Ricky nodded, causing the judge to ask him to say his answers. "Yes," Ricky then said, his voice quavering.

Holcomb realized he had to be gentle, for the boy was obviously very fragile. "Don't be nervous, Ricky," Holcomb said softly. "I won't let anyone harm you, nor will the judge or even Mr. Aiken over there." He pointed at Aiken. "Besides, if you look to your left and right and at the back of the court, you'll see big, strong guards."

Ricky looked up and saw Charles staring at him. He forced his head back down and mumbled something incoherently.

"What, Ricky?" Holcomb asked as he and Judge Stein leaned toward him. "I couldn't hear you."

"He's looking mean at me," Ricky whispered.

"Who, Ricky?" Judge Stein asked.

Ricky looked up at her, tears in his eyes, and muttered, "My brother, lady. He said he'd hurt me."

Stein took over. "Charles?" she asked. "Why would he want to hurt you? He's your brother."

"He said he would if I told," Ricky muttered and glanced at Charles who sat up, again wiped his finger across his neck, and nodded toward Janie sitting a few rows in front of him. The crowd began murmuring. Holcomb, seeing Ricky looking at Charles, quickly blocked his vision.

"QUIET!" Judge Stein shouted and then turned again to Ricky. "Told what, son?" she asked gently.

Looking now into Holcomb's chest, Ricky opened his mouth to answer but could only groan.

A woman sitting across from Charles suddenly jumped up and pointed at him. "HE WAS LOOKING AT THE BOY AND PRETENDING TO CUT MRS. CRAMERS' THROAT!" she yelled. "I SAW HIM!" The murmurs were now becoming ominous.

"SIT DOWN, WOMAN!" Judge Stein roared. "I'VE HAD ENOUGH! BAILIFF, CLEAR THE COURTROOM EXCEPT FOR MR. MURRAY AND THAT WOMAN!"

The bailiff signaled to the guards who began to usher the people out. Charles, growing panicky, saw the judge was pointing at him. He shrugged and smiled innocently.

Ricky had collapsed. The crowd started yelling. Judge Stein leapt up, roaring, "ALL RIGHT, THAT'S IT! OFFICERS, CLEAR THE COURT AND BRING CHARLES MURRAY INTO MY CHAMBERS!"

"What now?" Charles said immediately as he was thrust into a chair in front of her as she sat glaring at him.

She spoke through her teeth. "You heard the woman. She said you were threatening Mrs. Cramer! Why her?"

"That's crazy," Charles said, chuckling. "That thing about wiping my finger across my neck? I was only scratching myself. I had an itch, that's all. I have nothing against Cramer's wife."

Judge Stein thought for a moment. Finally she asked, "Why'd your brother say you'd hurt him if he told? Told what?"

Charles laughed. "You gotta know Ricky, Judge. He's shy, really shy. Sitting up in front of all those people with that lawyer harping away at him! Hell, I know him. He just couldn't take it so he made up something about me."

Stein frowned, looked at him, and began to wonder if he was really as crazy as she thought. "Perhaps," she said, "but I'll tell you it's all very suspicious." She sat back, concerned at what she had to do. "Well. Mr. Murray, I realize you're a key witness for the prosecution, so l have to permit you back in the courtroom; but I'll be watching you. One more interruption from you and I'll have the bailiff throw you out!" She waved him toward the door.

And he left, feeling proud that he'd got away with it again. But as he feigned hobbling into the empty courtroom, he stumbled when he saw noticed Kasmali standing at the back of the courtroom. Forgetting his pretence of not being able to walk well, he shrieked and ran out a side door.

Chapter Twenty-Seven: Kasmali's Plan

That evening, Ricky, lying on his bed in his hotel room, felt better. The constable had just left him saying he'd done fine and that they'd celebrate by having dinner with Mrs. Cramer in the restaurant. However, he couldn't stop from shivering as he remembered he'd have to go back in front of all those people the next day. He knew he should do it for her and Mr. Cramer, but he shuddered at the idea of all those eyes looking at him, even though Charles wouldn't be one of them now that the judge had forbidden him to be there.

Hearing a knock on his door, he jumped up, expecting to see the constable. But just to make sure, he asked, "Who is it?"

"It's me, Ricky, Chief Kasmali," said a deep voice behind the door. "May I come in?"

He opened the door and looked around. "The constable is coming to take me down to the restaurant," he answered politely. "He'll be here soon."

Kasmali smiled. "I saw him down there, Ricky. I told him I'd walk you down. I won't take long," he said gently. "May I come in? I just want to talk to you about a fun game you and I maybe can play on the Cramers. They could use a little fun, can't they?"

Ricky smiled as he saw the tall Indian grinning at him. "I like games," he said as he let Kasmali in.

Kasmali hugged him. They sat together on the bed. "Here's my finny idea," Kasmali said as he put his arm on Ricky's shoulder.

The next day was found Charles in his hotel room by Aiken who asked him what had made him run out. Charles, having come to the conclusion that he'd just imagined the Indian, answered quickly that he had had another charley horse.

Aiken sighed and told him the judge wanted to see him and then walked him to the courthouse and into the judge's chambers. Charles wasn't worried, though he remembered the judge's warning. The trial hadn't started again, after all, so he hadn't interrupted anything. When the judge finally came in, he began groaning.

Frowning, Stein looked at him. "What now, Mr. Murray?" she asked.

"The leg, Judge," he answered, kneading his prosthesis. "When I came out of the room here, my leg cramped up, I didn't want to do anything to make you mad, so that's why I ran out the side door."

Stein nodded. ""You want me to get the doctor to look at it?" she asked with feigned compassion, now wary of Charles' machinations.

"Nah, it wouldn't do any good," Charles answered, still kneading his knee. "I guess I'll just have to live with it. Can I go back to my seat?"

Stein had a problem. In her heart she knew Charles had tried to intimidate his little brother, but she also knew if she didn't allow him back in the courtroom it would suggest to the jury that he was absent because she believed the woman. She continued to stare at him. "How do I know you won't try something again?" she asked.

Charles sat up straight. "Gee, Judge," he answered politely, "I promise I'll just try to handle the pain. I can do that."

Stein nodded, knowing she had no choice. "All right, Mr. Murray. Get back in the courtroom, but at the first sign of any problem, I'll have the bailiff escort you out."

Charles was delighted as he took his seat on the aisle, confident when Ricky saw him, he'd be too scared to say anything. The bailiff called the court to order and Judge Stein took her place on the bench. Aiken immediately stood up and said, "Your honor, if I might. I think we've all deeply troubled by Mr. Holcomb forcing Ricky Murray to take the stand. Obviously the boy is not up to it. Perhaps the defense can proceed without him."

Ricky, sitting next to Mrs. Cramer and the constable, surprised them by suddenly standing up and announcing, “I’m fine, Ma’am.”

The judge nodded and looked at Holcomb. “Is he really able to testify, Counselor?”

This is it, Holcomb thought. He rose and answered, “Yes, Judge. As you can see, he’s fine.” He turned and smiled at Ricky. “Are you, son? You want to go back to the witness stand?”

Ricky nodded, maneuvered his way around the others in his row, and walked up to the witness box, his head held high. The bailiff administered the oath, and Ricky clearly answered, “Yes.”

Holcomb approached him cautiously, remembering how fragile he’d been. “We’re sorry to put you through this again, Ricky, but the jury has to be shown that Mr. Cramer isn’t the killer.” Aiken was tempted to object but decided it was imprudent.

Ricky nodded, looking him in the eyes. “I’m ready, Mr. Holcomb,” he said.

Holcomb hesitated, sensing the change in him. Jack and Janie and the constable sat up, looking confused. Finally, Holcomb asked, “How are you feeling, Ricky?”

Ricky seemed to wilt. Lowering his eyes, he answered, “I’m okay, sir. I’m trying.”

Hearing the sighs from some of the jurors, the judge glowered at them. Holcomb continued to hesitate, looking at Ricky. Finally, he said, “We can see you are, Ricky. Can I ask you some questions?”

Ricky nodded, causing the judge to lean toward him. “You must say the words, Mr. Murray, so that lady with the typewriter thing can record them,” she said gently.

Ricky looked at her, smiled, and said “Yes, Ma’am.” The judge smiled and nodded to Holcomb.

Holcomb knew he had to be careful, for if he came on too strongly, Ricky could become erratic again. He also knew how frightened the boy was of his brother, so he stood in front of him hiding his view of Charles. “This shouldn’t take long,” he said. “You just have to tell the truth. You know that, don’t you?”

Ricky started to nod again but then muttered, “Yes, sir.”

"All right then, Ricky, let's talk first about the butcher knife, the one that is said to have come from the café. Do you know anything about it?"

"I saw my brother with it," Ricky muttered under his breath.

The judge again leaned toward him. "You'll have to speak up, Mr. Murray. Remember that lady with the machine."

Ricky again smiled at her. "I said I saw Charles with it," he answered, this time more clearly.

Hearing the commotion, Judge Stein immediately looked at Charles, but he seemed to be looking elsewhere. She then banged her gavel over and over. "SILENCE!" she yelled. When quiet was restored, she asked, "Are you certain, Mr. Murray?"

Before Ricky could answer, Aiken was on his feet objecting. "Are you taking over for the defense, your honor? There seems to be a bias here!"

"Oh, sit down, you idiot!" Judge Stein retorted. Steaming, Aiken sat back down.

Holcomb took the hint. "The judge asked a good question, Ricky. Are you sure you saw your brother with the butcher knife?"

"Lots of times," Ricky answered clearly. Judge Stein stared again at Charles but still she saw no reaction.

"Can you tell us when, Ricky?" Holcomb asked, holding his breath.

Ricky straightened up. "A long time before Mr. Cramer got in trouble," he answered. "He took it from the café and showed it to me lots of times."

Shielded by Holcomb from seeing Ricky, Charles sat up, moving from side to side, trying to catch Ricky's eyes as the judge banged her gavel when the murmurs once again erupted. The tension was palpable as she waited for silence.

Realizing Aiken would jump on the issue of what knife it was, as soon as Holcomb had a chance, he asked, "Ricky, is the knife you saw with your brother the same one you saw Mr. Aiken –that man over there -- hold up for the jury to see?" He pointed to Aiken who sat stone-faced.

Ricky nodded. "I wasn't sure until he mentioned the nick in the handle, Sir," he answered. "I remember when it was broken."

This was news to Holcomb. He hesitated, remembering the old lawyer's adage never to ask a question without knowing its answer. Finally, however, he decided to risk it and asked, "When was that, Ricky?"

Smiling as if he and Holcomb were just talking, Ricky answered, "Out back of the café, Mr. Holcomb. Charles was trying to throw it into the side of the house and broke a piece off."

Holcomb stood back smiling and waited for Judge Stein to react as the crowd around Charles looked at him and began to whisper. Stein, however, did nothing. Holcomb turned around to try to see what she was looking at and saw the people next to Charles edging away from him. Charles, however, seemed to be in a stupor as he just stared ahead.

"Enough!" Stein finally yelled. "Let's get on with it! Any objections, Mr. Aiken?"

Aiken didn't know what to say. Charles' little brother was obviously too sympathetic to be challenged. "A recess?" he finally asked. "This information is completely new to me. May I have time to consult with my staff?"

Stein bristled. "Don't be ridiculous, Counselor. This mess has gone on too long already. Besides, you'll have your chance to cross exam the boy! Get on with it, Mr.Holcomb!"

Holcomb couldn't wait. Moving closer to Ricky, he asked, "Do you know what happened to the knife after that, Ricky?"

Calmly, Ricky continued. "I told you, Sir. I saw him with it lots of times after that."

Aiken jumped and shouted, "OBJECTION, YOUR HONOR. THERE'S NO EVIDENCE OF THAT!" Aiken yelled.

Judge Stein nodded, "It's about time, Mr. Aiken. He's right, Mr. Holcomb. Unless the boy can prove it, it's inadmissible."

Holcomb nodded, satisfied that the jury couldn't help but believe Ricky. "I guess we'll all have to trust you, Ricky," he said. "There's no way you can prove you saw your brother with the knife before the murder, right?"

Ricky seemed to be confused. "The man saw him with it, too," he muttered.

"What man?" Holcomb asked quickly before the crowd could react.

"The man at the foster home," Ricky answered. "He told Charles to get rid of it, and that was when Charles just left."

"When was that, Ricky?" Holcomb again asked quickly.

Ricky hesitated and then said, "It was in the afternoon the day before the man was killed. I remember because the next day everyone was talking about it."

Again Aiken jumped up. "HEARSAY, YOU HONOR!" he yelled. "CAN THE DEFENSE PRODUCE THIS ALLEGED MAN?"

Holcomb knew what Aiken was doing. He turned to the jury and said calmly, "Mr. Aiken knows most of the people of Valdez were drowned in the tidal wave, friends. I guess once again we just have to trust Ricky's recollections. Besides, why would the boy lie?"

"He has a point, Mr. Aiken," the judge said. "Objection denied. Get this over with, would you, Mr. Holcomb?"

Holcomb waited for the murmurs to die down. "You're doing fine, Ricky, but let's move on. Let's talk about the shirt, the one with the blood on it that Mr. Aiken showed us. Did you ever see Mr. Cramer wearing such a shirt?"

Ricky nodded again. "Yes, Sir," he answered, "many times, but one time he told Mrs. Cramer he couldn't find it. I was there. I worked for them, you know."

Aiken, hearing commotion behind him, turned around and saw Charles staring malevolently at Janie. Jesus, he thought, what's he thinking about?

Holcomb, standing in front of Ricky, didn't notice, of course. Neither did Ricky. He continued. "That's interesting, Ricky, but let me ask you this. Did you ever see your brother wearing such a shirt?"

Everyone in the courtroom, including Aiken, the judge, Jack, Janie, and Ralph Eston, but not Charles who continued to stare at Janie, seemed to be on the edge of their seats as they waited for Ricky to answer. "Yes," he finally said. "He wore it all the time until just before the man got killed."

When the people in the court erupted again, Judge Stein had had enough. "THAT'S IT!" she shouted. "WE'LL RECESS UNTIL TOMORROW. THEN THE PROSECUTOR CAN BEGIN HIS CROSS!"

Charles shifted his stare from Jack to Janie to Ricky, who was being helped from the stand by Holcomb. Frowning, he then returned to see Janie getting up.

While this was going on, the real Ricky Murray was laughing in his hotel room as he watched cartoons on the television. He couldn't have been more delighted because the big Indian had said it would be funny if he pretended to be him at the trial. He'd agreed, of course, because going back on that witness stand scared him half to death, and the Indian seemed to know about Charles.

The thing was, though, the Indian had made him promise not to ever tell anyone about their trick, no one, even Mr. or Mrs. Cramer, saying that it would ruin the fun. He also had to pretend he was there, which struck him as being even better.

That evening, when Mrs. Cramer and Chief Kasmali came into his room, she rushed over, hugged him, and asked, "Where'd you go, Ricky? We were worried about you. Everybody wanted to thank you, Sweetheart, but we couldn't find you!"

He looked over her shoulder at the Indian who winked. "I'll bet he was just too shy to be any part of that. Right, Ricky?" Kasmali asked.

Ricky, remembering his promise, got the hint. "I just told the truth," he muttered.

"Yes, you did," Janie answered, releasing him and looking into his eyes. "Now all we have to do is hope Mr. Holcomb can convince the jury that Jack's not a killer."

"It's not over?" Ricky asked, surprised.

Kasmali took his hand and led him to the bed where he sat beside him. "You and I," he began, "we're new to all this. I guess now the other lawyer will ask you some questions. Don't worry, though. Mr. Cramer's lawyer, that nice Mr. Holcomb, said you just have to keep telling the truth."

Ricky looked at Janie. "Is that right, Mrs. Cramer?" he asked.

"Yes," Janie answered as she came over and sat beside them. "And because of you, Jack may soon be back with us. Ricky noticed Kasmali winking at him again.

That same evening, Aiken was pacing in his office. "God damn!" he cursed. "I swear that was a different kid up there! What the hell am

I going to do now, Justin? The only thing left is my cross, and I don't have a clue what to ask!"

"Well," Justin answered calmly, "There's the obvious. You've gotta demolish the kid."

Aiken looked at him. "How the hell do I do that? Besides, even if I do, they'll think I'm a bastard for picking on him!"

"You've got no choice, Steve," Justin said, remaining calm. "If they believe Ricky, you're dead, though you may be dead anyway after the Charles debacle. We'll have to dig up some dirt on him, maybe make him out to be so jealous of Charles he lied today."

Aiken perked up, "You know, I was wondering why we weren't told about his story about the knife and the shirt before today?"

"Maybe they knew and covered it up," Justin answered, grinning. "That's downright unethical, you know."

"It sure as hell is!" Aiken answered. "That could be it!"

The next day, Kasmali found it impossible to get Ricky alone. Janie and the constable constantly hovered over him. So, when they made it to the court, he could only hope Ricky would remember his promise not to say anything about their joke and withstand the prosecutor's questions. They sat, Janie on one side of Ricky and the constable on the other.

Seeing their attention riveted on the door leading into the judge's chambers, he quietly excused himself and walked up the balcony where he forced himself into a seat in the front row in clear view of Charles below him. He could see that the tension was making Ricky nervous. For a long time, Ricky fidgeted, but eventually he sat up as the bailiff got out of his chair and shouted, "OYES! OYES! RISE FOR THE HONORABLE JUDGE MARGARET STEIN!"

She wasted no time. Banging her gavel, she said, "Thank God we're almost finished. I assume the prosecutor is ready?"

"Yes, your honor," Aiken answered."May I recall Ricky Murray?"

"All right," she said. "The floor is yours, Mr. Aiken. Mr. Murray, would you please take the stand again?"

As he got up, Janie hugging his hand, he tried not to giggle. He remembered the game he and Chief Kasmali were playing on them, and he was determined not to say anything about it. Charles leaned forward in his seat.

When Ricky was settled in the witness box, Aiken approached him and said calmly, "Mr. Murray, you've made some remarkable accusations against your brother. Charles is your brother, isn't he?"

Ricky smiled, unaware of what Kasmali might have said, but he smiled and answered, "Yes, sir. Charles is my big brother."

Aiken walked closer. "Well, I'm confused. From what I've read in the reports and heard from others, until very recently he took care of you. It's strange that now you've turned on him. Betrayed him, really. That doesn't seem to me that you're very grateful." He paused. "Perhaps we can try to see why." Again he paused. "Maybe it has something to do with the Cramers. You like them, don't you?"

Charles began to relax. Ricky didn't hesitate. "They're nice," he answered.

"How nice?" Aiken asked quickly. "After your brother was asked to leave them, you stayed, didn't you? And Mrs. Cramer even brought you with her here and gave you a room at the hotel. Isn't that right?"

Ricky had no idea what this man was driving at. "Mrs. Cramer's my friend. She bought me clothes and we even went to places to eat. And when we could, we'd work together on a story I'm writing."

"Let's talk about stories, Ricky," Aiken said soothingly, figuring he had the angle he'd been searching for. "I'll bet she even suggested one or two, right?"

"Yes, sir," Ricky answered. "Things the little boy in my story might do."

"You love her, don't you?"

Ricky realized it was true. "Yes, sir," he answered, tears beginning to come.

"And you'd do anything for her. Isn't that true?"

"Yes, sir," Ricky answered, looking through him at Mrs. Cramer.

Aiken came closer. "Even lie for her?" he asked quickly.

Ricky wiped away a tear. "No, sir," he said. "She never asked me to lie. She always told me to tell the truth."

Aiken saw he was getting nowhere, though he was satisfied that the seed had been planted in the jury's minds. He decided to try a new tactic. "Ever since you were kids, Ricky," he began, "Charles has always been the one who got all the attention. That is, until the Cramers came into your life. Then Mr. Cramer was arrested. You must be feeling bad about that, at least because he might go to jail – as I suspect he will. When that happens, your cozy little life will be over, won't it?"

Charles stifled a laugh.

Stunned, Ricky looked at Janie who furiously was shaking his head. "She likes me," he answered.

"I'm sure she does," Aiken said. "But with her husband gone, will she really want to be bothered with you?"

Holcomb shot out of his seat. "COME ON, JUDGE! HE'S BADGERING THE POOR KID!"

Judge Stein nodded. "He's right, Counselor. Tone it down."

"Sure, Judge," Aiken answered, smiling. "I was just trying to get to why Mr. Murray turned on his brother."

"Get on with it," she snorted.

He turned back to Ricky. "Why don't we just get to the crux of it, Mr. Murray? You want your old life back with the Cramers so you came up with those ridiculous accusations against your own brother! Isn't that right? You promised Mrs. Cramer you'd tell the truth, so do it!"

Ricky began to cry. Through his tears, he said, "I did."

"So you say, Mr. Murray," Aiken said, turning his back on him and looking at the jury. "We'll just let these fine people decide."

He returned to his seat, confident he'd established doubt. The judge sat up and motioned to Holcomb. "Redirect, Counselor?"

"No, your honor," he answered. "I think the boy has been through quite enough."

Judge Stein nodded. "I agree, Counselor. I assume you and the district attorney are prepared to present your summations?"

Holcomb reared back, his brow knitted. Aiken, on the other hand, grinned, and said loudly, "Yes, your honor, the prosecution's ready." Seeing Holcomb scrambling to get his material together, he turned to Justin and whispered, "Perfect, the idea the boy lied will be fresh in the minds of the jury!"

Looking down at Ricky, Judge Stein smiled, told him he could go back to his seat in the gallery, and then nodded to Aiken. "Good," she said, "let's get started. The floor is yours, Mr. Aiken."

The son-of-a-bitch is really pretty good, Charles thought as he relaxed back in his seat.

Chapter Twenty-Eight: Summations

Aiken rose, walked slowly over to the jury, and stood smiling in front of them. He looked at each of them, sighed, and began to speak. "I know this whole trial has been an emotional time for all of us, ladies and gentlemen, certainly the most emotional of all my years as a lawyer. Any murder trial is, of course, but this one has amazed me. For that reason, if I seem upset perhaps you will forgive me. My colleague, Mr. Holcomb, was correct in suggesting to you at the beginning that you wouldn't be here long; and you shouldn't have been. With all the evidence against the accused, you should have been home now; and he should have been incarcerated. So what happened? I'll tell you. Part of it was my fault. As I said yesterday, I should have checked out Charles Murray's background more thoroughly, especially his tendency for violence. I know now he never should have taken the stand."

Charles grimaced.

"However," Aiken continued, "let's consider the testimony given by Charles Murray. Why would he lie, as I'm sure Mr. Holcomb will claim? Oh, sure, he was angry about Mr. Cramer hitting him, but can we really believe he go to all the trouble to frame him? For the love of God, he's only eighteen years old!" He paused. "I know what you might be thinking – that this eighteen year old kid may have stabbed the victim and then had to find someone to blame it on. Think about that for a minute."

Again he paused. "What was his motive? Robbery? Self-defense? You might also begin to wonder how he could possibly overcome a man who'd just got out of prison – yes, Billy Cole had been released from Folsom Prison down in California just a few weeks before he was killed. You and I both know what it must take to survive prison. It's survival of the fittest, and Billy Cole was a survivor. Is it credible that an eighteen- year- old could overcome a veteran of years in prison? Forget about Charles Murray being the killer." He took a breath.

"If indeed a motive is needed for the killing of Billy Cole, only one person had one – Jack Cramer – and though there might be some doubts about the testimony by Charles Murray because of his erratic behavior and the claims by Ricky, his cute little brother, you can't discount all the evidence. Let's consider the shirt for a moment. We've heard that perhaps almost everyone in Valdez wore such a shirt, but how many had one hidden with blood on it!" Again he paused.

"Let's get back to the matter of a motive. I read it to you, remember? What other evidence do we need that Mr. Cramer killed Billy Cole? He almost did it before! Let's talk about the victim. We've heard that he came to Valdez to seek forgiveness from Cramer, but did Cramer know that? Isn't it more likely that he thought Cole had come to seek vengeance? And if that's so, isn't it likely that Cramer got to him first? Finally, there's Ricky Murray who just testified for Mr. Cramer against his own brother! You saw him. He didn't hesitate to betray him! Why?"

Charles grinned as Ricky buried his head in Janie's shoulder.

Aiken continued. "I love kids. I've told you that. But in the interest of justice, you and I have to wonder if his affection for Mrs. Cramer had something to do with it. Look at him, the poor kid, cradled in her arms. I'm not suggesting that he's bad. Hardly. But is it too hard to believe that he'd do anything for her?"

Janie was seething. Ricky had his hands over his ears.

"Believe me, it's tough to call a sweet kid like Ricky Murray a liar, but that seems to be my only choice if we are to get justice for the victim. Moreover, I can't help wondering why he only chose yesterday to tell his story. Certainly he had many other chances. However, you, ladies and gentlemen, don't have to decide just on the basis of which of the two boys was lying. Remember the book, the one I read a passage out of for you? Motive is key here. In a rage, the accused once before attempted to kill the victim!" He paused.

"Though it's ridiculous, friends, in his desperation I'm sure my opponent will attempt to confuse you by suggesting someone else, say Charles Murray, is the killer. Let's think about Mr. Murray. For God's sake, why would he do it? What motive did he have? The fact that Mr. Cramer hit him and so he decided to frame him? That's a little far-fetched even for a crusty old lawyer like me. My friends, ignore Mr. Holcomb's feeble subterfuge and remember that only Jack Cramer had the motive, the means, and the opportunity to kill Billy Cole!" He nodded and walked slowly back to his table.

Holcomb leapt up. "Only Jack Cramer?" he asked even before he made it to the jury. "Only Jack Cramer? Let's think about that! Motive? If we believe the incident Mr. Aiken read to us, Jack had a fight with Billy Cole years ago because Cole confessed to murdering a woman Jack knew. Years ago, ladies and gentlemen. Why in God's name would he kill him now, now that he was happily married? Means? The butcher knife? His fingerprints weren't on it; and according to his brother Ricky, Charles had stolen it from the café. Even if you don't want to believe Ricky, you have to consider that anyone else could have stolen it. The shirt? Come on, ladies and gentlemen, do you really think Mr. Cramer would be so stupid to throw it in plain view if he was wearing it when he killed Cole?" He waited.

"Let's consider the victim, Billy Cole, who had just been released from prison. According to the coroner with whom I spoke, he was in terrible condition. Anyone who saw him under the pier could have overwhelmed him!" He paused and then said, "Even a kid!"

"OBJECTION, YOUR HONOR!" Aiken yelled. "THERE'S NO FOUNDATION FOR THIS; AND EVEN WORSE, MR. HOLCOMB'S ALLUDING TO CHARLES MURRAY WHO'S NOT ON TRIAL HERE!"

Though the jury seemed impassive, the rest of the people, including Jack, Janie, Kasmali, Ralph, and Ricky, sat up on the edge of their seats as Stein warned Holcomb. Charles, however, sat placidly, glaring at Holcomb.

"All right, ladies and gentlemen, let's talk about both the Murray brothers for a moment since the district attorney mentioned one of them," Holcomb continued. "First, however, think about Ricky. Ladies and gentlemen, I could call witness after witness, his current foster parents, his previous foster parents, his teachers, even my own wife – though that would just show you how loving she is. I could call all these people, and they'd tell you Ricky Murray doesn't have a spiteful bone in his whole body! But they, except for Constable Eston and my wife, are gone, drowned in the tidal wave that swept Valdez away. So why didn't Ricky tell about the knife and the shirt earlier? I'll tell you why! He loved his brother so much he couldn't believe Charles could do anything really bad! Believe me, he went though torture until he heard his brother's lies. It was only then that he decided to come forward!" Now some of the jury were glancing at Charles who was trying not to show his anger.

Holcomb continued. "Okay, now about his brother Charles. Let me tell you about him. If the prosecutor had bothered to look into Charles Murray's background, he would have discovered a kid who'd been thrown out of one foster home and another because of his incorrigibility. But Ricky loved him so much he tagged along behind him, even when Charles vandalized houses and they had to be arrested. The second time was when Mrs. Cramer intervened and gave them jobs. How long did Charles last? We could ask Mr. or Mrs. Cramer or even Ricky, who was also there, but I'll tell you. No more than two days! Then, as Ricky told you, Mr. Cramer simply asked Charles to do some chore, and Charles told him to … screw himself! That's when Jack hit him, not because of Charles being lazy, but because he'd used the F-word in front of his wife!

"That's Charles Murray! Why am I telling you this? Simple. It goes to whom you should believe; and that's the key to this trial. Let's get back to motive. I was curious about kids and their potential for violence, so I talked with the psychiatrist about it. You know what he said? Mere supposition, you understand. Anyway, he told me that after being repeatedly beaten and controlled, even such a child could want revenge!" Again he paused.

"OBJECTION, YOUR HONOR!" Aiken again yelled. 'HE'S DOING IT AGAIN!"

"Hold your horses, Counselor," Stein answered. "It seems to me that Mr. Holcomb was only talking about kids. What's your objection?"

Seeing his case against Jack falling apart, Aiken was desperate. "He's wasting our time, Judge!" he answered. "He's just clouding the issue by implying Charles Murray's the killer!"

Stein laughed. "Oh, sit down, you damned … Counselor," she said. "The defense has the right to suggest alternative scenarios!"

Noticing the giggles behind him, Aiken quickly sat back down,

Charles, suddenly aware of what was happening, swiveled his head to look at the people next to him who were edging away.

Holcomb wasn't finished. "Finally, ladies and gentlemen, there's the eye-witness who allegedly saw my client running down the boardwalk that night. According to this witness's testimony, he was able to see him because of a light coming from a shop he'd been sleeping beside. However, you also heard Ralph Eston, the constable at Valdez, testify that the shops in Valdez had no such lights. So whom do you believe? An officer of the law or a young man whose veracity has been questioned before?

"Please keep all this in mind when you retire to the jury room, Jack Cramer may or may not be a hero, but he's no killer." He turned toward the audience, stared at Charles, and said quietly, "Once you find my client innocent, the district attorney can then try the real killer."

Having learned their lesson, the courtroom was silent when he returned to his table. Charles glared at Holcomb. Judge Aiken nodded and then said to the jury, "All right, people, it's now in your hands. Just keep in mind there's only one charge you will decide: first-degree murder."

As the jury walked slowly into the jury room, Jack turned to Holcomb and whispered, "What do you think, Miles?"

"I have no idea," Holcomb answered.

Chapter Twenty-Nine: The Verdicts

Two months later, at the trial of Charles Murray, which again kept the people of Anchorage distracted from their own troubles, two different attorneys argued over why Charles had done what he did, the defense claiming he was legally insane, the prosecutor, F Francis Chadwell, charging manslaughter and attempted murder. However, neither was able to make his case; and Judge Stein, again presiding, was sick of the whole mess.

Throughout the proceedings, Charles, whether by design or by the fact he'd really become manic, interrupted repeatedly by screaming that they all were out to get him until the psychiatrist allowed him to be medicated. With that, lying in his cell, especially at night, he agonized over why he hadn't been able to get away with it.

Chadwell had no trouble laying out the facts. His first witness was the woman, a Mrs. Stevenson, a well-respected member of an ecology group, who claimed she saw Charles making threatening motions toward Mrs. Cramer while Ricky was testifying, Then, after releasing her, he described what happened next. He turned to the gallery.

"Many of you were there," he began. "But for the jury, I'll recount what the accused did. After the judge called a recess and during the people's exit, the accused jumped up and attempted, it seems, to get to his brother, Ricky, but the boy was surrounded. He then ran out and disappeared until he later showed up at the front of the courthouse. Then, before Mr. Cramer's trial could resume, he snuck up behind Mrs. Cramer and stabbed her!

"You may ask why. Why would he want to kill Mrs. Cramer? Could it be for the same reason he blamed the killing of Billy Cole on her husband? He hated them, her husband for hitting him that time, and her for taking his place with Ricky! I could call Ricky or Mrs. Cramer to testify that he'd threatened them both, but neither of them is in any condition to be here, but it doesn't matter anyway. The accused has confessed to the killing of Billy Cole, and his stabbing of Mrs. Cramer is fact. As far as he being mentally incompetent, consider that fact that he was sane enough to run away! No, he knew exactly what he was doing!" He walked back to his table and sat down.

Charles sat quietly, his mind now clear because of the medication the psychiatrist had forced upon him; and he knew what he had to do. When his defense attorney called his first witness, the psychiatrist, he began mumbling loudly, so loudly that Judge Stein had to admonish him. With that, he leapt up on the table in front of him and began stomping his feet and screaming incoherently. The courtroom erupted.

Sitting beside Janie's hospital bed, Jack Cramer couldn't have cared less whether Charles was crazy or not. All he cared about was his wife who was lying in a coma. But he couldn't get that day out of his head. The guards had been leading him in the side door when he heard the crash, the roar, and the screams. He'd turned and saw Janie lying on the floor with people all around her. Shocked, the guards had loosened their grip on him, and he roared and ran to her. Then he saw the blood. "HELP! SOMEONE GET HELP!!" he'd screeched as he picked up her head and looked in her lifeless eyes. Then suddenly Chief Kasmali was on his knees beside him.

"Let me help," the Inupiaq had said calmly as he began to lift Janie from his grasp. He then carried her out the side door. When he got her inside an anteroom, he'd said, "See to your wife! I'll get Ricky!"

One of the guards then came up and told them Charles was missing. In a daze, he'd fallen on his knees beside her. Later he heard that Kasmali had found Ricky still in the witness box sobbing.

Kasmali came up and sat beside him. "Remember Bobby?" he said. "It be okay."

Jack smiled and answered hoarsely, "I hope so. What about Ricky?"

"He wants to be with her, Jack," Kasmali answered. "Could he join you?"

Jack nodded and Kamali left. A few minutes later, he and Ricky came in the room. Without a word, Ricky walked slowly to the bed. "He hurt Mrs. Cramer," he said and then collapsed into Jack's arms. "Is she gonna be all right?"

"We'll see," Jack answered, hugging him tightly.

Kasmali sat in a chair and watched. Tears were forming in his eyes. Still holding Ricky, Jack looked at him and said, "You did something, didn't you?"

Kasmali wiped his eyes, smiled, and nodded toward Ricky.

"You were up to your old tricks, weren't you?" He pulled Ricky loose, looked into his eyes, and said, "You're one of us now, son. You have a right to know about our friend Chief Kasmali." He turned back to Kasmali. "Tell us," he said.

Kasmali smiled. "Might as well," he answered. "After Charles stabbed your wife and ran out, the troopers began looking all over the city for him, I knew, though, that I had a better chance of finding him." He motioned to Ricky.

"Go ahead," Jack said quickly. "He'll understand."

Kasmali shrugged and continued. "Anyway, for a while now, I knew I was becoming more and more human and that my powers weakening, but I had no other choice." He hesitated and then blurted out, "I used the last of them to mutate into a giant eagle."

Ricky whipped his head around, his mouth open. Jack grabbed his face with both hands. "It's all right, Ricky," he said gently. "Chief Kasmali is our friend." He motioned to Kasmali. "Go ahead. What happened next?"

"It took a while," Kasmali answered quickly, "but eventually as I flew above the city, I saw him in an open yard filled with trucks. He was running toward one that had its back open. I then swooped down, grabbed him with my talons, and carried him screaming back to the courthouse. By the time I got there, he was unconscious, so I just lowered him to the pavement in front of two officers."

Jack laughed, seeing Ricky with his mouth open, his eyes wide. "That must have caused quite a scene," he chuckled.

Also chuckling, Kasmali said, "I don't know. I was long gone by then."

Chapter Thirty: Post-Trial Comments

A day later, Judge Stein sat wearily in her chair staring at Aiken and Holcomb. "How's Mrs. Cramer?" she finally asked.

Holcomb sat up. "She's lost a lot of blood, Judge, but the doctors say she'll recover. She's come out of the coma."

Stein nodded. "And the boy, Ricky?" she asked.

"Under sedation, but the doctors said it would help him if he were allowed to be with Mrs. Cramer in her room. Despite her own condition, she's trying to soothe him."

"And Charles? One thing I don't understand, How the hell did he end up in front of the courthouse?"

Aiken shook his head, "Nobody knows, Judge; but some crazy witnesses say a huge eagle dropped him there."

"An eagle, huh," Judge Stein smirked. "Well, it doesn't matter now." She sighed and leaned forward. "I just thought the three of us could chat about the last few weeks. That's why I asked you in. You have any second thoughts, Mr. Aiken?"

Aiken smiled wryly. "Yeah, but what's the point now? I lost the election. I'll say this, though. I wasn't the only one that little bastard fooled!"

Holcomb grinned. "Charles?" he asked. "You're right there. He had me going, too."

"You think he got justice?" Stein asked abruptly.

Surprisingly perhaps, both men shook their heads. Holcomb was the first to answer. "Right up to the end he was conning people, Judge.

He may be seriously troubled, but he knew exactly what he was doing during Jack's trial and then when he seemed to go crazy at his!"

Aiken nodded. "I wouldn't put anything passed that little shit," he added.

Stein nodded and asked, "So you think putting him in a psych hospital was wrong?"

"They should've put him in prison and thrown away the key!" Aiken snarled.

"How do you feel now about Cramer being found innocent?" Stein asked Aiken.

Aiken shrugged. "I did the best I could with what I had, Judge, though I know now I should've looked better into Charles. Justice was served I guess, at least to Cramer. To me, I don't know now that I'm out of a job."

Back in Janie's hospital room, Kasmali was struggling with his new sensations. Stroking Ricky's head as he slept, he now understood that his melancholy was a result of his evolution into becoming human. He had witnessed such behavior in humans before – in the grief of the survivors of the earthquake and ensuing tidal wave, in the anguish of Janie throughout Jack's ordeal, in the heartbreak of Jack and Ralph at the news of Rodrigo's paralysis, and even in the despair of Ricky when he'd seen Janie covered with blood. But through it all until now, he'd dismissed it as the result of human frailty.

But now that he was becoming one of them, and he didn't know how to respond. His home was beckoning, his origin, though it was gradually fading, replaced by images of earthly chaos and violence.

When the boy looked up at him and smiled, he smiled back and felt a warmth inside. He spoke softly. "I've heard of a boy like you, down south in a little village, who had a way of throwing off sadness. Would you like to hear what he said, Ricky?" Ricky nodded.

"It's simple," Kasmali answered. "He just said, 'It be okay,' and it usually was. Why don't we say it?"

Ricky nodded again, and Kasmali hugged him tighter as they said the magical words together. The constable came in and laughed. "It will be," he said. "The doctor just told me Mrs. Cramer is doing fine."

Ricky looked up at him. "Charles cut her with a knife," he said, tears again beginning to form. "What's gonna happen to him?"

Ralph patted his head. "He'll get good treatment at a hospital, Ricky. He needs help, and he's in good hands."

"I knew something bad was gonna happen," Ricky said, wiping his eyes. "He'd changed, you know, after that man was killed. Before, he took care of me. Are they sure he did it?"

Ralph nodded. "Yes," he answered. "Though it now seems like it was more or less an accident, at least from what he told the men who questioned him and from what Slim Carter said he saw. The bad thing was that he tried to blame it on Mr. Cramer and then hurt Mrs. Cramer."

Ricky gulped. "They'll take care of him at that hospital?" he asked. "Will they make it so he won't hurt people anymore?"

Kasmali answered first. "We all hope so, Ricky, and now you can feel safe. Didn't I hear that the Cramers are taking you to California?"

Ricky nodded. "We're going on a vacation," he giggled.

Having left Ricky and the constable in Janie's room, Kasmali hurried to the abandoned building where he'd left Astay and found him lying like a huge bundle of fur in the shadows. Sitting down beside him, he reached over to him, but the mammoth dog gently laid his huge head on his lap, his whiskers ticking Kasmali's chin.

Kasmali smiled and peered through an opening in the roof into the sky. "You know, don't you, my friend. Somehow you sense I'm different." He patted the dog's head."I don't really understand how this happened," he whispered. "But it is good. Though we humans can be ignorant and cruel, we also can feel things for each other."

He didn't expect a response, nor did he get one, so he leaned against the wall and began to consider how strangely his mission had changed. It had been a long day, and soon he fell asleep and began to dream of a small, shimmering whirlwind speaking to him.

"Though only I understand why you have evolved, your present state has caused consternation," it was saying, "when I was on my mission, some selfless humans called me Sam, and I too became affected by them. However, unlike me, you allowed yourself to be lost in your immersion into a Homo Sapiens. For this reason, the Mentor has determined that you are to remain human, never again to experience the wonders of our home."

Though seemingly asleep, Kasmali smiled and answered, "I understand and accept the judgment of the Mentor. However, I understand now that you were the voice that asked me to protect the human, Jack Cramer. Why?"

The whirlwind suddenly started to solidify. Within a moment, Kasmali saw a small terrier sitting on its haunches. It spoke: "During my mission, I witnessed the human's violence and cruelty. However, I also experienced the kindness and goodness of some. One of these was Jack Cramer, a foolish human who, without some guidance, was fated to be harmed. When I left Earth to return to our home, I promised another human that I would protect him and certain other humans. You have done that, and I am satisfied. What you do now is up to you."

Kasmali awoke with a start, causing Astay's huge head to fall from his lap. "Come, my friend," he said. "We have to begin a new life."

A few days later, Janie sat with Jack on the bed in her hotel room and murmured, "Jack, I want to leave Alaska, at least for a while, and Ricky needs to get away."

Jack put his arm around her, pulled her close, and nodded. "As soon as he's better, Sweetheart, I know just the place we can go."

She looked up at him. "You're okay with the adoption, then?"

He nodded again and whispered, "He's a great kid, Janie, and we'll make a great team. How about being warm for a change?"

"You're thinking of Nuevo Inocentes," she muttered, snuggling up to him. "That'd be great. It would be nice to see Bobby again."

Jack laughed. "As usual, you surprise me; but if I know Bobby Scribner, he and Ricky'll quickly become good buddies."

Judge Stein was very pleased, not just because the trials were over but also because Aiken had lost the election. "Jackass," she murmured.

Her husband walked in. "You thinking of me again?" he chuckled.

She got up and gave him a peck. "No, that idiot Aiken. After Cramer was freed and Charles Murray was convicted, he's blamed everyone but himself. The idiot never should have even tried to convict Cramer, and he sure as hell should have put Charles Murray on the stand."

"Well, he's gone now," her husband answered. "Now you've got a new idiot to deal with, that Chadwell fellow. I heard the people are calling for a new election. They're touting Miles Holcomb."

She shrugged. "Not a bad choice. He's young, but he seems to have a good head on his shoulders."

"Do you think Charles was putting on an act during his trial?"

"I wouldn't out anything past him, but it's still hard to believe he went through all those machinations just because Cramer hit him."

Her husband shrugged and sat beside her. "Maybe he *is* crazy," he said as he took her hand. "But he certainly got off easy."

She looked at him. "I don't know about that, Henry. For God's sake, I saw him! He has hallucinations! He's obviously deeply troubled, which makes sense considering all the trauma he's gone through – no father, his mother killed right in front of him – and then there's Ricky who was everyone's favorite."

"How do you explain Ricky then? He went through the same trauma."

She shook her head and said, "Christ, Henry, I'm no psychiatrist. Maybe he was too young to understand how bad he had it. Maybe, just maybe, in his older brother he had the father Charles never had."

"You may be right, but like you I wonder why Charles hated Cramer so much. Heck, other people must've hit him."

Again, the judge shook her head. "I told you what Holcomb said," she answered. "He may be right."

"Whatever," Henry answered. "What do you make of that tiny metal cross? Why, of all things, did he take that from the guy he murdered?"

"For goodness sake, Henry, first you think I'm a psychiatrist and now I'm clairvoyant? Maybe something in his past, maybe a little guilt. I don't know!"

"Well, Margaret, if you're right about him, perhaps the psych hospital can help him, and then he'll probably get out in a few years free as a bird. I guess we'll see."

"The law's the law, Henry," she retorted, getting up.

He stayed sitting. "That Inupiaq's an interesting fellow," he said. "Did he go back to the Yukon?"

"I think so," she answered, suddenly feeling very tired. "The last time I talked to Cramer, he told me the chief was thinking of getting more involved with the native movement."

"Good for him," Henry said as he too got up from the couch. "Hey," he turned and asked, "What about the constable? He seemed like a good man. What's he going to do now that Valdez's destroyed?"

"Now that's interesting," she answered. "You know the office of the chief of police is open, right?" Henry nodded. "Well, I suggested he try for it."

"What'd he say?"

"He said he'd think about it, but Cramer said he was considering working with Kasmali on the Tribal Council. Isn't that a hoot?"

Near the top of Thompson Pass, Chief Kasmali looked behind him and yelled, "Speed it up, old man! At this pace, we'll never get there!"

Ralph Eston, though exhausted, was more enraptured by the beauty around him. "Stop for just a minute, will you?" he shouted back.

"Whoa!" Kasmali yelled to Astay, who stopped in his tracks, causing the other dogs to bunch together. He walked back to Eston. "Too much for you, city-man?" he asked, grinning.

"You got that right," Eston answered as he sat in the snow. "This is gorgeous!" he said as he waved his arms around. "I've never seen anything this beautiful!"

Kasmali shrugged. "As long as it lasts," he answered ruefully. "Unless you White Men do something, it won't be long before it's long gone."

"There's signs," Eston said. "The drilling's stopped, and the mining, and then there's Rodrigo. I heard he's back as one of the leaders of the global warming crusade."

"Doesn't surprise me, Ralph," Kasmali answered. "But he and the others have the entire economy against them. Besides, it can't be easy for him being stuck in a wheelchair. I only wish there was some way I could help."

Ralph laughed. "Don't be coy, Chief," he chuckled. "If I know you, you'll find a way."

"I wonder how much good I'd be," Kasmali answered, groaning. "I'm not the man I used to be." Shrugging, he stretched his shoulders and said, "But I'm still strong enough to beat you to the top of the pass!"

Patting Astay on the head, he yelled, "MUSH!" and was off before Eston could take a step.

In the meantime, Charles was contented as he tried to get used to the routine of the psych hospital. He still maintained his erratic behavior, but now less violently, for he knew that once he showed enough improvement, he'd be free. His only regrets were that he hadn't killed Mrs. Cramer and that Ricky was now happy while he was stuck with a bunch of loonies. His consolation, though, was that once he was released he would find them, even if it took years.

Chapter Thirty-One: Nuevo Inocentes

Situated in the center of the Santa Ynez Valley northwest of Santa Barbara, California, surrounded by ranches and sun-drenched hills but off the beaten path, lies Rivotorto, a Capuchin retreat house. Below it on its eastern boundary is a valley with a stream flowing past a farm, complete with gardens and a barn, and a complex of one-storey buildings that lead down a well-kept avenue to a larger two storey building. In front of this building is a large statue. This is Nuevo Inocentes, created some years before by the Capuchins and others for the housing of disadvantaged men and boys.

Friar Gerald, the prior of Rivotorto and the overseer of this impressive village, sat on a bench on the edge of the bluff looking down at the village. Hearing a noise behind him, he turned, saw Jack and Janie Cramer and a young boy walking toward him, jumped up, and yelled, "IT'S ABOUT TIME! WE'VE BEEN WAITING FOR A MONTH!"

He grabbed Janie and Jack in a group hug, looked at the boy, and reached out to take his hand. "I'm very happy to meet you, Son," he said warmly. "I've heard a lot about you."

The boy smiled and said, "I'm Ricky." He held out his hand, which Gerald grasped. "Mr. and Mrs. Cramer told me about you, too, and about this place."

Janie grinned. "Ricky's our adopted son, Father. If it weren't for him, Jack may have been convicted of murder. You heard about his trial?"

"Yes, we were worried sick," Gerald answered, putting his hand on Ricky's shoulder. "Thank God the truth came out. And so this is your son. How wonderful that you've brought him here. My name's Gerald, Ricky. Welcome to Rivotorto." He pointed below. "And Nuevo Inocentes."

Ricky looked down at the village. "Thanks," He said shyly. "Is that it? Mr. and Mrs. Cramer told me it has magical powers."

Gerald chuckled. "Well, I wouldn't say that, Ricky," he answered. "But it does have a way of comforting people."

"It does that, Father," Jack said, giving Ricky a hug. "That's why we're here as I wrote you. We can use some comforting after the tidal wave took out Valdez and our café and home. It didn't take us long to think of Nuevo Inocentes."

"Of course, of course," Gerald answered quickly. "I hoped Rodrigo'd be with you, but I imagine he's still recovering."

"He's doing as well as could be expected," Jack answered. "The Navy is taking great care of him. At first, they thought he'd never walk again – the crushed spine, you know – but they didn't count on his stubbornness."

Janie interrupted him. "He's determined, Father, to get out of his wheelchair; and if I know him, he will – and soon."

"What about you two?" Gerald asked. "How long do you want to stay? I'll bet after you've been here a while, you won't miss Alaska."

Janie squeezed Jack's hand. "It's our home, Father," she answered, "though most of the coast is gone now. Perhaps someday the three of us will go back to help rebuild Valdez; but for now we're hoping we can earn our keep by somehow helping out. I hope Maureen and … Rebecca are still here, plugging away."

Gerald grinned. "Don't be coy, Jack," he answered. "You should know we make no distinctions here, The love Maureen and Rebecca have for each other is an inspiration to all of us. They're fine, though they're getting older. Maureen is probably in the main hallway working on a fresco of Luke." He pointed down at the farm. "If you look closely, you might be able to see Rebecca in the corn rows with some of the Radiants."

Jack turned to Janie. "That's what they call the residents, Sweetheart. You remember.

Look, there she is!" Janie looked down to where he was pointing and saw an elderly woman sitting on a folding chair in a clearing, men all around her.

Jack turned back to Gerald. "There's another reason we're here, Father," he said, grinning.

Gerald laughed and then said, "Bobby! Well, why are we just standing here?" He leapt from his chair. "Let's go see what he and Rebecca are up to! That's him, right beside Rebecca."

"I can't wait," Janie said, standing up and straightening her dress.

Bobby was the first to see them as they walked down the hill. Throwing down the corn he was holding and burrowed through the stocks, he shouted, "CAMER, YOU BACK!" He and Jack collided, causing Jack to lose his breath.

Finally, he extracted himself and said breathlessly. "I am, Bobby, and I brought my wife Janie and my son to see you." He pointed to them.

Bobby didn't hesitate. He leapt forward and enveloped both of them in a hug. Janie, having remembered Bobby Scribner from their trips, was prepared; but Ricky wasn't. He pulled himself loose and ran to Janie who quickly said, "It's all right, Ricky. Bobby just loves everyone."

Rebecca grabbed a cane hooked on her chair, got up, and walked awkwardly up to Jack. "It's been a long time, Stranger, ever since Luke died." She reached out her hand. "It's good to see you, Janie. Who's this young man?"

Janie took her hand and waved Ricky forward. "My son," he answered proudly. .

Bobby, looking sadly at Ricky who was obviously uncomfortable, slowly walked over, stood in front of him, and said gently, "It be okay, Ricky. It be okay."

Suddenly remembering how Kasmali had once said the same thing, Ricky smiled. However, this time it wasn't okay. Perhaps because of the earthquake, perhaps because of Jack's trial and his own brother's attack on him, or more likely because he was frightened by the actions of a fifty-year-old retarded man, Ricky turned and ran into the barn.

Momentarily shocked, Janie hesitated but then ran after him. Jack started after her, but was stopped by Friar Gerald. Bobby, confused, reached down, picked up a cat that was at his feet, and began stroking it. "Let them be, Jack," Gerald said. "Your boy just needs time."

Jack, putting his arm around Bobby, said, "Ricky is sad, Bobby. He's seen some bad things. He needs a friend, but it may be a while before he's ready." Bobby nodded, still stroking the cat.

Rebecca grabbed his hand and said, "I'll tell you what, Bobby. Let's wash up and then go see your mom."

Bobby grinned and answered, "I make pictures with Mom." Gerald turned to Jack, said, "It be okay," and led Bobby down the street toward the classrooms.

Eventually Janie returned leading Ricky by the hand. "I told Ricky we'd take a walk, Jack," she said as she came up. "He's fine. Maybe you could introduce us to some of your friends here and show us around." Ricky swiveled his head, looking all around him.

"Ricky and I talked, didn't we, Ricky?" she said to the boy. "We talked about how people who seem different can sometimes be special."

"We're on our way to see Maureen," Jack said, "But first, let's check out the statue. One of the figures is Soulful Sam, Ricky. You remember him from the fables, right?"

Ricky nodded, and they walked down the lane toward the two-storey building at the end of the village. When they reached the statue, Ricky grinned. "It's just like him from the pictures in the books," he muttered. "See, at the top!"

"Look below him," Jack said. "Who's that guy?" Ricky looked up and shrugged. "That's Bobby, Ricky, just a younger version of him. The man who made this statue put him in it because he loved him and wanted people to know it was people like him who make this village special. Cool, huh?"

Ricky's step became livelier as they walked into the building and up the stairway. Suddenly they saw Maureen balanced on a ladder, her back toward them, paint speckled on her hair and smock. Gerald turned toward them, put his fingers on his lips, and then walked up and stood beneath her.

"Hi, Padre," Maureen said, her eyes remaining on her fresco. "You worried that I'm messing up your wall?"

Jack, unable to contain himself, yelled, "Holy Toledo, Maureen, it looks just like him!"

Maureen jerked around, causing the ladder to tilt; but Gerald was able to steady it. "Jack! Janie!" she cried while holding on. Rebecca helped her down, and she hobbled to them, laughing, and then hugged them both. "Thank God you're all right. We heard about the earthquake and the trial. We were told you were coming!"

Jack held her out and said, "Where else would we go?" he answered.

She broke loose, hugged Janie again, laughed, and looked at the boy standing behind her. "And who's this?"

As Jack introduced Ricky to her and they chattered about their troubles in Alaska, Bobby walked over to a desk and began painting on a drawing pad.

Later, after Maureen said she'd get cleaned up, Gerald and Rebecca took the group on a tour of the village. When they finished and were walking back to the retreat house, Janie asked, "Do you like it, Ricky?"

Nodding, Ricky pointed back to the largest building. "Can I go see the art room again?" he asked.

Jack glanced at Janie and said, "Sure, Ricky."

Ricky looked up and grinned. "It be okay, Dad," he answered.

As they watched him walk away, Janie had tears in her eyes. "I'll bet he wants to work on some illustrations for his fable," she said.

They sat on a bench in front of the residents' huts. "This place *is* special," she whispered. "So is Bobby."

"Yes, he is," Jack answered. "Yes, he is. I was just thinking about Kasmali. I wonder if he's adapted yet? By now he's probably seen it's not so wonderful being human."

"He didn't have a choice, it seems," Janie answered. "You told me that once he decided to find Charles, he lost all his powers."

"I just hope he's all right," Jack said.

"He'll be fine, but what about Ricky?" Janie answered. "How long do you think we should let him stay here?"

"As long as it takes," Jack said. "It's up to Bobby and Nuevo Inocentes and us to help him forget."

Chapter Thirty-Two: Kasmali Finds Love

Dressed in only his ceremonial cape and leggings, a woolen snow cap on his head and leather-lined moccasins on his feet, now alone but for Astay, Chief Kasmali stood shivering on the shore of the Arctic Ocean. "There was a time I could have mutated into a huge eagle, grabbed you in my talons, and flown us around," he said to the Husky. He moved closer. "There was also a time, being an Inupiaq, that I could bear the cold. Perhaps I've lost more than I thought. You're fortunate having fur, my friend. May I share your warmth?"

The dog nodded, allowing him to huddle between its legs and under its massive body. "That's better," he said, gradually feeling warmer. "Let's stay here for a while to enjoy the beauty." He enjoyed talking to the dog who seemed to listen, unlike so many of the humans. Leaning to avoid the dog's head, he gazed into the white sky, smiled, and shouted, "BECAUSE I'M NOW A HUMAN, I REALIZE YOU WON'T HEAR ME, BUT I AM CONTENT!"

Reaching up, he stroked the dog's mane. "It is better," he said. "I'll miss Jack Cramer and his woman and Ricky and Rodrigo, but you and I have no place in their world, you who frightens them, and I who cannot adapt to their ways."

He rose and began to jump around to warm himself. The Husky shook its head. "Well, my friend, where shall we go?" he asked. "Now that I'm truly human, I need shelter and food. Shall we try for Prudhoe Bay?"

After traveling for weeks and by occasionally finding warmth by burrowing in the snow and food from the rodents he and Astay were able to catch, he eventually made it to the mountain overlooking Prudhoe Bay and was not surprised to see nothing but permafrost. Dejected, he sat on an exposed rock and said to the dog, "I was hoping there would be something left, my friend, some kind of shelter Rodrigo and I didn't see before, but it seems it all has sunk into the bay."

After a few moments, he got up. "Let us go down, Astay," he sighed. "Perhaps we can find something beyond where Rodrigo and I were before."

Holding on to strands from Astay's tail, he struggled down the mountain, falling repeatedly; but eventually they reached the base where he fell on his knees, gasping for air. Astay ambled over and stood covering him. He grinned, got up, patted the dog's rump, and began walking down the shore.

When they came to the pass where he'd become an eagle and lifted Rodrigo and the dogs out of the oil spill, he laughed, causing Astay to look at him. They traveled for hours until suddenly he yelled, "LOOK, ASTAY! AHEAD! CAN YOU SEE IT? I THINK IT'S A STRUCTURE!"

Slipping, sliding, and falling, he followed Astay down the shore and then began running toward a shack half-covered with snow and ice. Struggling up to it, he began walking slowly around its outer walls. "There must be a door here somewhere," he muttered to the dog.

Using his gloved hands, he began scraping the ice and snow away from the front, thinking the door had to face the bay. Astay, seeing his intention, used its claws to work beside him. Finally, when they had a door cleared, Kasmali grabbed the latch and pulled, but the door was frozen shut. Looking at Astay, he untied his belt and smiled. "Are you feeling strong?" he asked.

He attached one end of the belt to the door latch and held the other end to Astay. "Bite it, my friend." Immediately sensing Kasmali's intention, Astay grabbed the belt in his huge teeth and began pulling. The door came open with a loud crack. Kasmali laughed and entered the shack.

The steel walls had withstood the earthquake and subsequent avalanche, and the ice-coated concrete floor was littered with trash:

electronic equipment, including two computers; paper, cans and broken bottles and a pot and pan; overturned desk chairs; and blankets and cold-weather clothing were scattered around the freezing room. Steel cabinets, some with their doors open, were on the south wall.

First, he grabbed one of the snow pants and a parka, put them on, and was pleased that they fit adequately. Then he searched through the cans to see if they contained anything still edible. Those that looked safe he placed on a table that had been bolted down. Next he picked up the blankets and set them on a cot that was fastened to the floor. He didn't concern himself with the computers or other electronic equipment, other than kicking them aside. He saw the air vents on the ceiling.

Astay was still standing in the doorway. "Come in, Dog," he said, chuckling. "This hut will do for us, at least for a while. "See the vents? I'll make a small fire with the broken chairs. The vents will let the smoke out." Astay trotted in but remained by the still open door.

Chuckling, Kasmali stepped around him and went outside. Eventually he came back carrying a load of rocks he set in a center of the room. He left the door open and then began gathering loose paper that he squeezed into the rocks to use as kindling. He then went lit the paper with matches he'd found in one of the cabinets, and stoked the fire with wood he broke off and whittled from a chair. Once the fire was going, Astay moved in front of it.

He looked more closely at the cans. "You're in luck, my friend," he said as he held up two cans. "Tuna."

He pried open the cans, emptied the contents into a plate he found on the floor, and placed it in front of the dog, who sniffed it briefly and then wolfed it down. He then took the largest pot and again went outside. Soon he returned with the pot filled with snow that he placed beside the fire. Within minutes he had water, which he also placed beside Astay, who lapped it up.

The fire warmed the room, causing the snow covering the windows to begin to melt, making it possible for him to see the room more clearly. He then closed the door and noticed how small the hut was. He smiled as Astay. "Finding wood and kindling will be a problem if we stay here long, Astay," he said. "We had better see what we can discover outside. There must be wreckage from the oil field. Perhaps you can also find game."

With the aurora borealis flashing around them, Kasmali soon found small pieces of wood that he stacked beside the front door while Astay wandered along the coastline. After having piled enough for their immediate purposes, he then looked for Astay who was nowhere in sight. However, just as he was about to search for him, the dog trotted in with two snow bunnies in his jaws.

"GOOD DOG! NOW WE HAVE WARMTH, WATER, *AND* FOOD!" he yelled and opened the door. The dog trotted in and set the rabbits by the fire.

Despite his past life as a changeling and as an Inupiaq, Kasmali had changed. No longer was he adventurous, nor did he have any plans beyond an existence away from the human world. Therefore, he was content remaining in the hut as long as he and Astay could.

And they did, for many months until their food ran out. "It's time to try to find a new shelter," he said to the dog as he tore down a piece of paneling that was on the left wall. "We'll use this as a sled," he said. "I'll help you pull it."

Taking the piece of paneling outside, he gathered together the blankets, the extra clothing, the remaining food, and a load of wood, and loaded it on it and then tied one end of the rope to Astay's shoulders and another to the paneling. "We'll take turns," he said as they trudged away from the hut.

After weeks of struggling, as they came to the top of a mountain, Astay, whose turn it was to pull the sled, suddenly barked and began trotting away. "WHERE ARE YOU GOING?" he shouted as the dog disappeared. Running as fast as he could in the snow, he came to the crest, looked down and stopped, dumb-founded. Below him, Astay was sitting on the edge of a verdant meadow in a valley hidden on three sides by mountains. "Impossible," he said, wiping his eyes. "But perhaps it was caused by the global warming."

However impossible it may have been, though, it was real, as he discovered as he ran down the mountain into the grasslands.

Within a few days, they'd made a new home in this valley. He built a log cabin beside a stream and discovered enough wood in a forest that would last them years. When he and Astay hunted, they found the valley full of game. To Kasmali, this was a paradise where he thought he and Astay could spend the rest of their days.

The months and years passed comfortably for the two friends, but eventually Kasmali, now totally human, began to miss human companionship. Ironically, just as he decided to leave the valley, he saw a White Man approaching with what seemed to be a young native girl stumbling behind him. His first thought was to run to them, but there was something about the pair that made him wary.

The man was looking down, staggering and measuring his steps. Suddenly he saw Kasmali standing beside what he thought was a small bear. He hesitated but then began stumbling toward them. "HELP ME!" he shouted. "HELP ME!" He then fell, dragging the native girl down with him.

Kasmali ran to them though Astay remained growling where he was. When Kasmali came within sight of the man and the woman, he saw the man, covered in rags only partially covering a bloody gash on his left shoulder. A thong connected him to the girl, who was now sitting up looking pleadingly at him.

"I'm dying," the man groaned as he staggered closer. Kasmali answered, "It's from a bear. I'll help you to my shelter."

The man shuddered and fell. "That beast," he muttered, pointing with difficulty at Astay. "It'll attack me like the other bear did."

"The beast, as you call him, is my friend and is no bear," Kasmali answered as he helped the man to his feet. "Why do you have the woman tethered?"

The man, frozen with fear, didn't answer. Kasmali cut the tether that bound the woman and then grabbed the man by the shoulders and pulled him up to Astay, but neither the dog nor the man cooperated as he tried to lay him on the dog's back. He then said, "The man will not harm us, Astay. Help me by carrying him to the hut." Astay continued to show his teeth, but did as he was told, the man holding on to its mane with both hands, his teeth chattering more with fear that the cold.

The woman, whom Kasmali was surprised to see was an Indian like him, got to her feet, hesitated, looked around, but then stumbled after them. When they reached the hut, Kasmali lifted the man from Astay's back, carried him inside, and laid him on the cot. He then went into a cabinet and took out a first aid kit, found some grain alcohol and some bandages, and began tending to the wound, the man crying out. The woman remained in the doorway. The man eventually fainted, and

Kasmali covered him with blankets and turned to the woman. "What happened to this man? Was it a bear?" he asked.

Surprising him, she began weeping. Kasmali waited, but finally she whispered, "He is evil. I was glad when the bear mauled him." She then collapsed in the doorway. Kasmali picked her up, stunned at how light she was, and laid her next to the fire. After covering her too with a blanket, he looked at Astay and shrugged. "It seems we have two guests," he said. "It is good."

While he stoked the fire, the man became delirious, shouting about Indians and a huge bear. The woman remained unconscious for a while but then slowly awoke. "Who are you?" she said to his back. "Will your beast eat me?"

For the first time, he noticed that though she was small, she was an adult and very beautiful. "I am Chief Kasmali of the Inupiaq," he answered. "The Husky called Astay is my friend. He will not hurt you or the man unless you mean me harm. Tell me, why are you with a White Man you hate?"

The woman turned her head to the wall. "I had no choice," she muttered. "My father gave me to him."

"Are you now his mate?" Kasmali asked. She didn't answer.

Sensing he could do nothing more for her, he went back to the man and, taking a rag from a cabinet, wet it in a bucket of snow-water, and placed it on the man's forehead. He then bandaged the wound as best he could. The man didn't wake. He then again stoked the fire and went to the table and began cutting up some fish he'd caught. Astay walked slowly over to the fire and lay down, his eyes on the man in the cot.

Kasmali cooked enough fish for the four of them, gave Astay his portion and one to himself, and set the rest aside for the two sleeping figures. Eventually, he lay beside the dog and fell asleep. Astay remained awake.

A few hours later, he awoke with a start and saw Astay standing beside the cot. He ran over and saw the man was staring terrified at the huge beast hovering over him. "Save me," the man groaned.

For some reason, Kasmali started to laugh, which awoke the woman. "Let the beast eat him," she muttered from across the room. Kasmali pulled Astay away. The man lay back, turned his head, and scowled at the woman. "Shut your mouth!" he snarled.

The woman rose from the cot, staggered, and slowly walked over to Astay, who, on four legs, was almost as tall as she. Somehow sensing the Husky was no threat to her, she rested her hand on his shoulder and said defiantly, "I no longer am frightened of you, White Man. The beast will protect me. I hope you die!"

Astay growled. The woman patted him, walked away, and stood by the fire. Kasmali watched, wondering what he should do. Finally, seeing she needed no help from him, he went to one of the cabinets and pulled out a can of peaches, opened it with his knife, and handed it and the fish to her.

She sniffed the peaches, looked at him, and asked, "Are they all right?"

"Try them," he answered. "They're sweet."

She tilted the can to her mouth, drank some of the juice, and smiled. "It is good," she said. She then gulped down the entire can and started on the fish. When she was satisfied, she said, "I am Awahay, Moon-on-Water. I am Chumash from the island called Anyapakh. Who are you?"

"Kasmali of the Inupiaq," he muttered. "I know not of an island called Anyapakh. Is it in the ocean in the north?"

She smiled. "No, foolish man, it is an island far away in what the Whites call California. I have not seen it now for many years."

Kasmali was startled. "I have friends who are now in this place you call California. How is it you are so far north?"

She shrugged and then told him her sad story: how the man had come to the island to poach goats and had convinced her father that she should be his mate, how he then had stolen their boat and sailed north, ravaging her repeatedly until they finally settled on an island in a place called Puget Sound. "I fought him," she said, "but he was too strong. He had found what he thought was an abandoned cabin, and he kept me bound there for a long time. But one day the man who owned the cabin showed up, and he – she pointed at the sleeping figure – he killed him." She stopped and began weeping.

He wanted to put his arms around her, but didn't for fear she would think he was like the man on the cot. Finally, when she seemed calmer, he asked, "But how did you find this valley?"

"I tried to escape many times when we traveled north," she began, ignoring his question. "But he always found me. Soon I gave up, but that was when he tied me to him. We continued to go north, him stealing automobiles and money from strangers. He said if we came up to Alaska, no one would ever find us. When we finally came to the big city called Anchorage, we found it in ruins, so we continued north by getting rides from men in trucks and walking. Often he stole blankets and jackets from the men. One he killed by hitting him with a tire iron as the man was checking his truck. He then drove the truck to Nome, another city on the sea. We stayed there for months in an abandoned warehouse until a man saw the truck that he knew belonged to his company. That's when we left and began traveling along the coastline until we reached the place he called Prudhoe Bay. It took us a long time; and if I didn't keep up with him, he beat me. He was getting weaker, though, so his blows became harmless slaps. Then, on the pass above this valley, he was attacked by the white bear. You know the rest. Are you or the beast going to kill me?"

Kasmali stepped back, shocked. "No, Moon-on-Water," he said. "I do not kill humans. And you no longer have to fear the man. He may die of his wounds."

She shrugged. "Well, if you or the beast do not kill him, I will," she said as she ate the rest of the fish. "I must regain my honor."

Stunned, he left her and went outside to walk and think. Suddenly a shimmering mass appeared before him that he immediately recognized as a being from his planet. Surprised, he stepped back and saw it mutate into a mirror image of himself. "You've found me," Kasmali said calmly.

His twin looked at him questioningly. "You are CVDIILL" it said.

"I am now Kasmali," he answered, "but you know that. I no longer know the name CVDIILL. Why have you now appeared?"

His twin studied him. "The Mentor instructed me to make contact with you. You are CVDIILL," he said sternly. "You have rejected us. Nonetheless, you must give your final report. I will then leave."

Kasmali chuckled. "I think you know all I can tell you," he answered. "My report? Neither you nor the Mentor will understand. As you undoubtedly know, the prediction of a natural disaster proved true:

earthquakes, flooding, deaths. However, the Mentors underestimate humans. Already they have begun to rebuild their cities. They also have begun to change their ways by ceasing their drillings in the north."

His twin remained stoic. "One other thing, you are the only one of us who did not return," he said. "It isn't logical."

"Again, you wouldn't understand," Kasmali answered, again chuckling. "You are right, it isn't logical; but that's the point! The more human I became, logic started to become irrelevant. The feelings I now have inside me are beyond your comprehension. You see, we humans have conflicting emotions inside us. In my years on Earth, I've seen things that have made me wonder how humans have survived – cruelty, beastliness, violence – but I've also seen kindness, valor, and gentleness. Why have I rejected you? You cannot understand."

Unchanged, his twin asked, "So you have nothing more to add to your report?"

"Just one question. My transformation into a human may have begun with a voice I heard in my subconscious, not the Mentor's, but one that seemed human. Do you know of any of our – your – species that has the ability to use the subconscious to communicate with those of us on Earth other than the Mentor? Anyone who is called Sam?"

"Again, illogical," answered the twin. "You obviously have lost your ability to be rational. Since you have no information worth repeating, I will go now and leave you to final days on Earth."

Before Kasmali could respond, the changeling was gone in a silvery mist. He then shook his head and went back into the hut.

Kasmali soon learned from the woman that the man lying on the cot was named Patrick Murphy; and primarily because of Kasmali's care, he didn't die of his wound. And, as he grew in strength, he demanded that Moon-on-Water continue to serve him. When she ignored him, he flew into rages. "YOU ARE MY WOMAN!" he would scream. 'YOU MUST DO AS I SAY!"

One day, when she laughed at his outbursts, he became so furious he came at her with a knife. But Astay, who appeared to be sleeping by the fire, leapt up and barreled into him, knocking him against the far wall. Unfortunately, however, he had managed to hold on to the knife and began trying to slash the dog. Kasmali ran up and kicked the knife out of his hand. The man began weeping like a girl.

"You have shown you now are strong enough to leave us," Kasmali said calmly. "I will give you food and clothing, and you may take your knife; but no longer will you be welcome in my home."

Murphy whined and pleaded, but Kasmali was adamant. In the meantime, the woman cowered on the cot. "Must I leave too," she asked.

Kasmali smiled. "Only if you want to, Moon-on-Water," he answered. "You may rest with Astay and me as long as you wish."

Within a few minutes, the man was sent on his way without Moon-on-Water.

For the next year or so, Kasmali experienced the totality of being human as he grew fond of Moon-on-Water. He understood that she still suffered from the man's cruelty, and kept a respectful distance, but he was beginning to developed strange urges toward her.

For months, the valley continued to be their haven, with its verdant vegetation and plentiful game; and perhaps inevitably they became sexually intimate, which amazed and delighted him. One day, as they sat on a log looking out at the vista, he nodded and said, "I have been thinking of what we should name our valley, Moon-on-Water. What is Chumash for 'White Innocence'"?

"'O'wow Inocentes,'" she answered.

"Good," he said. "We will call it that in honor of the snow around us and a village I have heard about near where you were born."

She nodded and nestled in his arms. "Innocence," she murmured. "The word reminds me of the innocence of infants."

He nodded and continued to look out at the valley. She sat up. "You are stupid, my love," she said brusquely. "Look at me! Have you not noticed I am growing fatter?"

He shrugged. "It is of no matter. We are fortunate to live well in 'O'wow Inocentes."

Smiling, she gazed at him and said. "It is not food that makes my stomach grow, my love."

Suddenly he understood. "You are with child?" he asked.

She nestled again in his arms. "Yes," she murmured. "Your child."

He gently raised her face, confused. "I gave you a child? Me, Kasmali?"

She laughed. "Who else, my Inupiaq chief? Have I not been alone with you these last few years?"

He rose, began to pace, and then turned back to her. "I am new to this, Moon-on-Water," he said anxiously. "What do I do?"

Again she laughed. "Nothing, my Inupiaq chief," she chuckled. "I understand. You have never been present at a birthing. Am I right?"

He gazed at her, trying to decide if he should now tell her of his origin. Finally he sighed and said, "It is time you knew, Moon-on-Water. I have but recently evolved into being human. I came to this planet from another."

She sat up, beginning to laugh, but the serious look on his face made her hesitate. "I have not known you to make jokes, my love. Are you serious?"

Looking away, he nodded. "I like many others from my planet was sent to Earth to investigate recent changes. To do this, we were given certain abilities, such being able to mutate into your indigenous creatures. Eventually I became as you see me now, Chief Kasmali of a tribe of Inupiaq."

She drew back. "You do not lie, whoever you are. I know this having lived with you." She began to cry, causing Kasmali to reach for her, but she moved away.

"Do not be frightened, my love," he said soothingly. "I am now as human as you and the others. Before Astay and I came to this frozen environment, I rejected my origin. I have told you this because of the child you are carrying. I am concerned that it will not be born totally human."

She rushed into his arms, saying, "Do not worry, Chief Kasmali of the Inupiaq. Whatever our child turns out to be, we will cherish it."

If he hadn't known before, at this moment Kasmali knew he'd become completely human as love filled his heart. He held her out to look into her eyes and said, "For the rest of my life, Moon-on-Water, I will cherish you. But the child. I do not know how to help you birth it."

Smiling, she took his hand. "You can help me, my love, by agreeing to two things. The first is that we rear our child in this valley. The second is that when the time comes you take me to a tribe the man and I saw in our travels, The women there can help me when the birthing begins. You will need do nothing."

Kasmali embraced her but then drew back. "I will do as you ask, Moon-on-Water, but they then will know of our valley."

She looked up to him and smiled. "You and I and Astay have been happy in O'Wow Inocentes. Is it not time for us to share it? What do you fear?"

Kasmali embraced her more tightly. "Yes, Moon-On-Water, we have been happy, me for the first time; but you and I have witnessed the jealousies, cruelty, and violence when humans gather together. I cannot allow our paradise to be corrupted."

She buried her head in his chest. "It seems you are new to being human, my love. You have not yet felt the need for a woman to have contact with others of her sex. I have met these few gentle people. They are starving, and O'Wow Inocentes has much to offer them."

Kasmali slowly shook his head. "You who were raised on a secluded island have only experienced an innocent life until the White Man took you from it. If we allow the tribe to come to our valley, others will soon follow; and our serenity will be lost. I am sorry, my love, but I cannot allow it."

Moon-on-Water sat up; and, knowing his mind was made up, slowly nodded. Seeing this, Kasmali said, "With the child inside you, will you be well enough to travel?"

She smiled. "Yes," she answered. "Besides, the tribe is only a week or so away."

Kasmali felt like shouting to the sky, but instead he gently rose and declared, "I will build you a fur-lined sled! Astay can then pull it to the tribe! We will call our son 'Sam,' for that is the name of the one who led me to Jack Cramer and then to you!"

She laughed so hard, he was frightened she would hurt the baby. "You foolish man," she finally said. "We do not know it will be a boy; and, besides, we have many months to wait!"

He gently picked her up. "You are carrying my son, of that I am certain," he said lovingly. "And he will be human."

As Moon-On-Water had said, Patrick Murphy also knew of the village; and, after being exiled from the valley, he had forced one of the

Inupiaq families to take him in. Moreover, over the year or so he was with the tribe, he used his size and aggression to dominate the tribe of peaceful men and their mates and nine children. He ate their food, of which there was little, conscripted their largest igloo, and constantly demanded reverence. Things were good for Murphy; and he was in no hurry to leave, for he'd finally found a perfect hideaway.

However, one day as he lay in his igloo, he heard the jabbering of the Inupiaq who seemed to be welcoming visitors. Anxiously he rose, looked out the flap, and saw Kasmali, the woman, and the beast surrounded by the villagers who were pointing at his igloo. Cursing, he grabbed his knife, gouged through the ice at the back to make an opening large enough for him to crawl through, and then hid behind another igloo close by.

He watched as the man left the woman and the tribe and walked into his igloo and then come out and look around. "Now's my chance," Murphy whispered. "When I see his back."

Just then, Kasmali turned to return to the tribe. Murphy jumped out of his hiding and ran at him. However, before he reached him, he found himself lying flat in the snow, the beast on top of him, slobbering in his face. Not this time, he thought, as he plunged his knife into the beast's throat.

Running up, Kasmali saw the blood, shouted, "AYEE," and pulled Astay off, falling beside him. "No, my friend," he moaned as he looked into the dog's vacant eyes.

Murphy, now free from Astay, rolled over and saw Kasmali with his back to him. He struggled to his knees, held the knife high and stabbed him. Stunned, Kasmali turned, leapt up, grabbed the knife out of Murphy's hand, and plunged it into his stomach.

"LET ME DO IT!" Moon-on-Water cried as she waddled up. "LET ME FINISH HIM!" However, she couldn't wrench the knife from Kasmali's hand as he lay in the snow, his blood dripping on the snow.

"YOU'RE HURT!" she cried.

He hadn't noticed that he was still holding the knife. Angrily, he threw it into the snow and groaned. "This must be what you humans call death," he muttered. "I must get to the sea as my tribe demands."

The villagers slowly came up. One man, presumably their leader, nodded and said, "Your dog is dead and you will be with him soon.

Have no care. We will take care of your woman and her child that is to be."

Kasmali struggled to sit up. "Help me to my feet," he asked. The man did, and Kasmali staggered a moment and then regained his balance. He looked at Moon-on-Water. "I must leave you, though I have great love for you," he managed to say. "I will end this life according to the Inupiaq custom. Be strong; and after the birth of our son, tell him of me. Now lead these good people to O'Wow Inocentes."

Caressing him, she began to weep, blood covering her chest and bulging abdomen. He wrenched himself free, smiled down at her contorted face, and began stumbling away. She stood and watched as he struggled to the top of a hillock, often stumbling. Each time he fell to the snow, she was tempted to go to him, but she remembered his final words.

Silhouetted against the silvery sky, he turned his head and, using what strength he could muster, shouted, "REMEMBER ME!"

Moon-on-Water took a few steps toward him, but the Inupiaq women held her back. "Let your man go," they sighed to her. "He must join with the spirits on the ice." She crumpled to the snow but watched him as he disappeared over the ridge.

Incredibly, he did make it to the sea, more than a mile away. Once there, he lay on the shore on his stomach and looked out at the ice floes. One was floating near him. Using his last ounce of strength, he crawled into the freezing water, often submerging, until he reached it. His hands slipping often, he finally pulled himself up and lay gasping on it, his face frozen on its surface. He groaned, ripped his face free, and turned over.

As he floated away from shore, he was able to smile as he imagined he heard a little boy's voice saying soothingly, "It be okay."

Fifteen years later, two men stood talking and smoking in a hut reserved for smokers a few yards away from the atomic reactor when one, looking out a frosted window, squinted and said to his friend, "Look, Jimmy, I may be seeing things, but there's I think there's an Eskimo out there in the snow coming toward us."

Jimmy moved over to the window. "You're right. Jesus, he's just a kid, and isn't that a wolf beside him? They must be lost."

Within minutes, they heard a knock on the door. The first man opened it and saw a young native boy dressed in ancient Inupiaq garb standing in front of him. A large grey wolf sat on its haunches next to him. "Come in," the man said. "You must be freezing, but you'll have to leave that beast outside."

Smiling, the boy said in clear English, "I'm fine. You are the first White Men I've ever met. I hope you can help me. I come from the far north in search of a man I have heard stories about ever since I was a child. He once lived in a town called Valdez, but I was told it had been destroyed."

"You'd better come in," the man asked. "That stuff you're wearing can't possibly keep you warm enough. Hell, the only time I saw an outfit like that was in the museum in Anchorage."

"I'm fine," the boy repeated. "Can you tell me anything about Valdez?"

The man shrugged and answered, "It's been rebuilt, but it's a hell of a long way from here. You and your wolf friend traveling alone? You'll never make it."

The boy continued to smile. "We will. I've been preparing for this journey ever since I was a child. Can you tell me the way we should go?"

The man turned to his friend and chuckled. "What do you say, Jimmy? Should we help this kid?"

"We've no choice," Jimmy answered and then motioned to the boy. "Come on in, kid. The wolf will be all right. We'll give you a map. What's your name?"

"Sam," the boy said amiably and then turned to the wolf. "I'll be right back, Astay. These men will help us."